THE OPERATION

DYLAN YOUNG

BLOODHOUND
— BOOKS —

Print ISBN 978-1-913419-21-9

ALSO BY DYLAN YOUNG

The Appointment

This one's for you, Eleri.

1

TUESDAY 7TH MAY 2019

TWITTER FEED #findkaty

Lea Sandler @LeaSand3 7May2019
Katy Leith missing for too many days #findkaty Someone must have seen something. Stand up and be counted. God bless you, Katy angel.

Jamila the Hunny @Jamilihun 7May2019
I hope she's safe. But all the odds are against it #findkaty Hate killers, hate murderers, hate kidnappers.

Ken the scooper @kenscoop 7May2019
Police have told young women in Oxford to be on the look out. Not to go anywhere alone. WTF is wrong with people? #Safestreets #findkaty

Tod Machine @todmychine 7May2019
When they find who took her, they need to behead the turd. Bring it on. #findkaty. #eyeforaneye

FEARS GROW OVER MISSING NURSE KATY

"We'd like to hear from anyone who knows anything. Even the slightest detail could be vital." These are the desperate words of Detective Inspector Joanna Ridley as Oxford police ramp up appeals for help in the search for Katy Leith, missing since leaving a works party four days ago.

The headline, white print on a black banner, glares up from yesterday's newspaper. A bank holiday edition lying folded on the counter of Paws for Claws that I study idly as I wait for my charge. I've seen headlines like this before. Harrowing, terrifying stories of abduction and murder. Trite phrasing that hardly touches the sleepless suffering of those closest to the victim. But when she's known to you, albeit vaguely, the words somehow take on a heightened level of vileness.

I drag my eyes away as the door opens and in bounds Sid, the Labrador Rottweiler cross I'm about to take out for a walk. He's a black and tan bruiser. A handsome showstopper. His energetic greeting drives all thoughts of Katy Leith from my head as the assistant hands over the leash. Sid neither knows nor cares about missing nurses.

He's keen to go. I'm with him there so we scramble out, Sid's claws scrabbling on the linoleum as we head off. The world is a cornucopia of smells for Sid who seems to point his snout in a hundred directions at once. I have to drag him away from a couple of gateposts but soon we're into it. We have an agreement, Sid and I; off the leash as soon as we can. But that means no stopping until we get there.

There, of course, is a park where he immediately spots a jogger on the path ahead. He stops, curiosity aroused, tail wagging. I pull him close on the lead. Not easy since he's thirty-five kilos. I don't know this jogger. She's not one I've come across on this route. She's young, lululemoned from head to toe, pony-tail swinging rhythmically as she approaches.

Sometimes, when they see Sid, they'll slow down. Occasionally, they'll veer off the path – survival instincts kicking in – to give him a wide berth. Understandable given Hollywood's predilection for Rottweilers as their attack dog of choice. But, though he's a boisterous dog, Sid's just sociable. He doesn't have a nasty bone in his body. He won't attack anyone unless attempting to lick someone to death qualifies as assault. He's five and has scars on his face and only half a left ear where other dogs have mauled him. His previous owner thought it would be fun to put him up against the odd pit bull.

People can be arseholes.

This jogger, I'm glad to see, is not. She's a good judge of dogs' characters. She doesn't veer off. Instead, she smiles at me and at Sid as she passes. A transient greeting in an angel's face. He watches her go and lifts his nose to follow her scent. I ruffle the fur on his head and tell him he's a good lad. Which he is. Two months ago he would have lunged at the jogger because he didn't know any better. But I've been teaching him manners and how to socialise on our walks, which I do three times a week for Paws for Claws.

I know, it's a cringeworthy name, but as a shelter they do a great job rescuing the Sids of this world. So they can call themselves whatever they like as far as I'm concerned. And they're happy for me to take Sid out because, to begin with, no one else would. He was just too much dog. But I know he's a pussycat, really. Not that I'd ever tell him that because it would be asking for trouble, given that they're two of his favourite trigger words.

When you walk dogs, you meet other dog walkers. Most of us have regular routes. So it's the same handful I normally see. Wednesdays it's Ella; a bubbly smiley mother of one. Saturday mornings it's Galina; young, withdrawn, Eastern European. Memorable for all the wrong reasons. But today, on a frosty Tuesday morning, it's Rob Eastman.

I haven't seen him for almost a month, neither here, on a walk, nor at the hospital where he's a surgical colleague. Mid-fifties, bespectacled, with an unfashionable bottle-brush moustache and windblown hair, Rob's a bit of an enigma. I've lost count of how many children he has, though he proudly peppers conversations with their names. Now he's striding towards Sid and me with a lurcher called Maisie.

When we get near enough, the dogs say hello in their usual unabashed nose-to-tail manner.

Rob grins. 'Jacob, good morning. Cool though for May.'

The sun is up and there's dew on the grass. 'It is. And yes, we must be mad.'

'Bit off your patch, aren't you?'

'This is Sid's neck of the woods.'

Rob nods. 'Bloody awful about that nurse, isn't it?'

'Terrible,' I agree.

'She's just a year or two older than our Harriet. Doesn't bear thinking about.'

I nod. There's suddenly an empty void in the conversation that neither of us wants to walk into. Sid ends it by barking at a terrier a hundred years away. Maisie joins in. I calm Sid down with a quiet word and a hand on his head.

Rob stares at the terrier, not seeing it, his thoughts elsewhere. He's dressed in an ancient waxed jacket with ripped pockets and paint-stained jeans. When I bump into him in the corridors at work, his suit and fat stained ties are from the same dishevelled wardrobe. 'Isn't it about time you took this feller home?' he asks with an accusing nod at Sid.

'I wish.'

'You'll just have to sit her down and have that talk.'

I smile. We both know who he's talking about. 'Her' is the reason I don't have Sid at home. But easier said than done and this is a football we've kicked about over old ground many times. Rob's diplomatic enough to change the subject.

'Were you on call over the weekend?' he asks.

'No. Bryony had that pleasure. You're just back from leave though, aren't you? Go anywhere nice?'

Rob shrugs. 'One of my unpaid months.'

'Ah. Where were you this time?'

'The Sudan. The damned fighting started up again. Fifty gunshot wounds last week.'

I shake my head. 'Christ, Rob. I take my hat off to you.'

'Once you've seen what needs to be done it's hard to say no.' He looks up at me, eyes slitting. 'You've never thought of VSO?'

'I've thought about it,' I say. And it's true. Whenever I see Rob I think about it. Only to file it away as soon as we say goodbye.

'I have all the connections you'd need in MSF if you ever decide to go. I have another mission scheduled for nine months' time. You ought to come. Be happy to show you the ropes.'

'Maybe,' I say. Because it's polite. But the truth is, any thoughts I've had about volunteering my skills abroad have been fleeting. Elbowed quickly out of the way by work and holidays and house hunting. I try to recall what MSF stands for and eventually it flashes into my head: Médecins Sans Frontières. Oui.

'Sid's looking so much better,' Rob says, patting the dog's broad rump. 'God, he was wild when I first saw him.'

'He's doing well.'

My phone rings. It's the private clinic where I also do sessions. One of the secretaries there tells me a patient wants to talk to me about her surgery and she's due in on my next list.

I ask for the patient's number, but then, while she has me, the secretary asks about further clinic dates.

I wave Rob an apology while I answer. Maisie rubs her thin body against my knee.

Rob calls her to him and mouths, 'See you later, Jake.' So as not to disturb me. I watch him go. Rob's a straight-up bloke and I admire him. He's an excellent surgeon. But I don't envy him. He and his wife Fay live in an unpretentious semi on the edge of the park. Fay works as a health visitor. He's told me more than once that the local schools are "bloody good". There's never been any suggestion of him sending his kids for private education, and he doesn't believe in private practice. When he volunteers abroad, he goes to the worst places, the ones with the least facilities, the most in need of help. Though he goes as a general surgeon, he ends up doing obstetrics, orthopaedics, plastics, you name it. The last place he went to, somewhere on the Syrian border, had "no X-ray facilities at all". I don't understand how he does it, but he has all my respect. It must rub off on his kids because I know at least one of them is following in his footsteps.

Twenty-year-old Harriet Eastman accompanied Rob on one of his Maisie walks last September wearing a T-shirt with Miseris Succerrere Disco, her med school motto, emblazoned across it. I knew what that meant because it's my, and Rob's, alma mater. "I learn to care for the unfortunate" is a laudable ethos. Needless to say, irreverent med student humour adulterated it into "miserable suckers at the disco" when I was there. Puerile, I know, but that's how I remember it.

Yet Rob, God bless him, is a believer in the system. He also believes in giving back. It's something to aspire to. But not for me. Not yet. Too many rungs of the ladder to climb.

The jogger is coming back again, looping the park. Difficult to know how old she is, but probably not much older than the missing Katy Leith. A little flicker of anxiety dances along a nerve plexus in my guts again.

I do know Katy Leith as a colleague, albeit vaguely. But there's no denying that I'm probably also one of the last people to see her before she went missing. The police know that too. And today, after I've finished with Sid, they're going to be asking me all sorts of questions.

Routine, I'm sure. I quell the flock of butterflies in my stomach that flutter up by putting in a little spurt of speed with Sid. He watches me run and bounds after me.

As she passes us, the jogger smiles again.

3

I get a text from the secretary with the patient's number, so I pull up. By the time I've read it, Rob and Maisie are a hundred yards away and Sid's onto the next set of smells, the jogger forgotten. There's no one around so I let him off. My phone rings again. It's Sarah. It's 7.10am, and she always knows where I am this time in the morning on a Tuesday. She'll be on the train, *Times* open on her iPad, FT still folded, coffee – double-shot cappuccino with oat milk – on the tray table in front of her. I left the house before she got up, and she'll be away in London until Thursday. This is how we live. Regimented, some might say. Some do say.

But it's how we like it.

At least I thought we did.

'Hi.'

'How's Sid this morning?' Newspaper rustles.

'Sid's fine. He says hello.'

Her lack of response and refusal to play my game tells me that Sarah, though expecting this affectation from me, finds it mildly irritating. Sarah doesn't like dogs. Nor cats. Nor animals in general. She's definitely allergic to cat dander, but with dogs, it's something else. Fear possibly. It doesn't matter. I respect that. We both agreed that we would not have a dog in the house. That was the second thing in the unwritten contract we drew up when we moved in together. The first was that we did not want children.

I can accept that.

But when it comes to dogs, I need my fix. Hence my thrice-weekly dates with Sid. Hence my blank stare when Rob Eastman jokingly suggests I need to sit Sarah down and have that talk.

'Beautiful morning,' I say.

'It is. Jake, I forgot to tell you last night that I said we'd have a drink with Will and Chloe on Friday night.'

Fait accompli. 'Fine.'

'Oh, and I've left more brochures for DOT. There's one... you know the cottage on the edge of that farm? It's come down by thirty. We ought to go over and look at it. I thought Saturday afternoon? And then maybe grab a late lunch at The Miller?'

'Sounds good.'

There's another rustle and Sarah says, 'The papers are still full of your missing nurse.'

'They would be. Still no sign of her?'

It's rhetorical. I listened to the early bulletin on the way to get Sid. The press have the bit between their speculative teeth.

'Not according to the *Times*,' Sarah says. There's a pause. I visualise her taking a sip of coffee, lipstick leaving a mark on the reusable bamboo mug she uses to avoid an unnecessary cardboard cup.

'When are you talking to the police?' she asks after a swallow.

'This morning, after ten.'

'Is that going to mess up your list?'

'A bit. But I'm starting early and I've got some help.'

'Good. Okay, have a good one and try not to kill too many patients, darling.'

Gallows humour. She's learned how to dish it out. You do when you live with a surgeon.

'See you Thursday,' I say, but she's already rung off.

DOT is our shorthand for Dorchester on Thames. Three pubs, Wisteria-strewn cottages and beautiful South Oxfordshire countryside. We've talked about moving for a year, and DOT is top of our list. It's eight miles from Oxford and close to Didcot station, which will cut Sarah's commute by quite a bit. It would be a great place for a dog too.

I quash that idea. Sarah Barstow, that's her name, is a bright, beautiful, career-minded woman. I'm a lucky bloke. She's fully supportive of my volunteering as a dog walker, so long as she doesn't have to go anywhere near. I keep an old jacket, jeans and sweatshirt in the garden shed, so she doesn't have to be exposed to them, and I take them to the launderette once a fortnight when they get too mud spattered and furry. Though I suspect Sid wouldn't mind if I never washed them again.

I like dogs. We always had one when I was growing up. I enjoy their company. I love the feel of their fur and their unfettered joy at the sight of a ball. University, training and career moves meant I was never in a position to own a dog. But now we're settled, I have more time. Sid is a four-legged compromise.

As I said, I generally walk him three times a week. The easiest is a Saturday morning because work doesn't impinge. When I'm on call, it might be difficult, but usually, I can easily squeeze in an hour. Wednesday afternoons are the next best. That's when I theoretically have an SPA – supporting professional activity – afternoon. Of course, that ends up being more like two hours than a whole afternoon, but it means I can leave the hospital early. So I pick Sid up at four or a little earlier in the winter, while it's still light. And finally, there are Tuesday mornings like this one, when I get to Paws for Claws for six thirty and drop Sid off an hour later.

At 7.35am, I bike back into town. On the way, I think again about Rob Eastman's approach to work, his choices. No chasing private practice. Volunteering his service abroad. It sounds like an uncomplicated life. A simpler existence.

Much like a dog's.

There's a lot to be said for that. How much fun would it be to swap lives with Sid for a day? I let my imagination ponder this imponderable for a while and then put it from my mind. Because there are other things to consider within this construct.

Much as I might enjoy chasing after a ball, Sid wouldn't thank me if he found himself being interviewed by the police about a missing girl.

4

Detective Inspector Joanna Ridley is, by my estimation, a runner. She has a lean, almost gaunt, look about her as she sits opposite, appraising me. She's milk pale, make-up free except perhaps for some eyelash thickener and a touch of shininess on her lips. Something hangs on a silver chain around her neck. Whatever it is, it's not on view under the primly done-up button of her white shirt. Her hair is dark and practically short. Her charcoal suit is creased and has a stain on the sleeve. Its ochre colour suggests ketchup or soup. I doubt it's blood. I know what blood looks like.

I'd put her at a year or two younger than me; somewhere around her late thirties. But she could be older because she looks tired. Pressures of the job have etched wavy lines in her forehead. It makes me wonder if there are children at home just to add a little grist to the daily grind of police work. She listens and watches with cold sharp oxy-acetylene eyes as her fellow officer, Detective Sergeant Ryan Oaks, asks the questions.

'Did you speak to Katy Leith at all that evening, Mr Thorn?'

I shake my head. 'No. I knew she was there. But then so were most of the nursing staff from the surgical unit. It was a good turnout.'

Oaks is younger, taller, with a footballer's build, evident even though he's sitting. Not enough upper body for a rugby player, I'd guess. Unlike his boss, there are no lines on his smooth dark skin. And not even a hint of grey in his cropped hair. His eyes narrow. 'Why do you say that?'

'You don't always get a huge turnout at leaving dos. But this was for one of the nursing sisters. They're usually well attended.'

'So you know Katy.'

I note his use of the present tense. It's reassuring. 'I do. Not well. She's only been on the unit a few months–'

'Six,' Oaks says.

'Right,' I say. 'I've come across her on ward rounds. The odd lecture I may have given.'

'But not socially?'

'No, Sister Morris's leaving do would have been the first time we'd ever been in a social gathering together.'

'What about at Christmas time? No ward party?'

I bark out a laugh. 'They usually organise something. I pitch up for half an hour to show my face and leave. They can be dangerously boozy affairs. If she was there at the last one I didn't see her.'

'She was,' Oaks says.

'What do you mean by dangerously boozy?' Ridley asks. Her voice is even and cool and precise.

'I mean people do things when they drink. Things they sometimes regret. As I'm sure you know.'

'Why would I know?' Ridley's eyes bore into me.

'Crime is like medicine. Alcohol is a major contributor to workloads in both.'

She doesn't nod or smile. Hard case, this one.

'Have you ever done anything you regret after drinking?'

Oaks slits his eyes. It makes him look much younger than he already is.

'When I was younger, undoubtedly. Same as you have, I expect.'

'What sort of–'

'Oh, come on,' I cut in, realise I'm being impatient, so qualify it by adding, 'You know what I mean. I'm in a position of responsibility. I try to remain responsible when I'm with co-workers. Nothing worse than seeing all those inhibitions evaporate around you.'

'Nothing worse?'

I don't comment.

Ridley shifts in her chair and sits forward. 'You left the Duke of Wellington at what time, Mr Thorn?'

She's not local. Her accent stretches the first vowel of the word "time" far too long.

I shrug. 'I'd guess around twenty past ten.'

'And you went directly home?' Oaks again.

'I did. I had a list the following morning.'

'List?'

'Operating list. Surgery.'

'And you parked where exactly?' Ridley asks.

'One of the streets nearby. I think it was Bacham. The pub car park was full.'

Ridley continues, 'CCTV shows Katy leaving the pub at 10.25pm. She was meant to be working the next day too. Her last sighting is her crossing the road opposite the pub. We can find no record of her calling a cab or Uber. But you did not see her leave?'

I shake my head. 'I'd have long gone by then.'

The DI has a habit of maintaining eye contact long after I have answered her question. Some people would find her intimidating. Some people say the same thing about me. Goes with the territory, I presume. Responsibility. Leading a team.

Eventually, Ridley leans back.

Oaks is reading his notes, preparing for his next question. I glance around. We're in a seminar room in the Post Grad Centre. Tiled ceiling with sunken lights, white walls, laminated floor. Someone has drawn and labelled a brain on the flipchart in the corner. It's a soulless room. One I'm very familiar with. Ridley picks up on it.

'What normally happens in here?'

'Lectures, CEPOD meetings–'

Her brows furrow. 'What's that?'

'Confidential Enquiry into Perioperative Deaths. Sounds very secretive. It isn't. It's where we come to confess our sins. Where the pathologists criticise our skills, or lack thereof, if one of our patients dies.' My attempt at lightening the mood elicits only a grimace.

Oaks has found his next question. He looks relieved. 'And what time did you get home?'

'It's twenty minutes from Jericho, where the Duke of Wellington is, to Headington. So somewhere around a quarter to eleven, I think.'

'Can someone confirm that?'

'My partner was at home, but she was in bed. I can't remember if my arriving back disturbed her. You'd have to ask her.' I should have said that I doubt I would have disturbed her since we sleep in separate rooms during the week. Sarah commutes to London. To a plush office in the city. The train takes an hour, and she's on the 7am most days, unless she stays over. And when I'm on call, I might not be home until late, or even have to go in at some silly hour. We've become adept at not disturbing one another. Weekends we shared a bed. Sarah and I are practical people.

'We may well do that, Mr Thorn.' Oaks says it primly.

'I can give you her number.'

A nod. 'That would be helpful.' He pushes a notepad towards me and I write down Sarah's number. It's an untidy scrawl. But contrary to what people think, there isn't a course on bad handwriting at medical school. It's more about impatience; the waste of time having to put pen to paper.

Oaks looks at it and offers up a grateful smile. 'I think that's about all we need for now.' He glances across at Ridley who nods. It's a small movement. Tiny.

Oaks shuts his notebook. 'Thanks for coming across so promptly, Mr Thorn. We're doing what we can to piece together Katy's movements. We appreciate your co-operation.'

'Of course. Anything I can do. You have my secretary's number, I take it?'

Oaks nods.

'Okay, so you know how to find me if there is anything else.' I get up and push back from the pale wooden table they've set up for interviews. There's been a police presence at the hospital for days. All entirely understandable under the circumstances. I stand up to take my leave but hesitate. 'And you have no idea what's happened to her?' I ask.

Ridley gives me the stock answer. From her it sounds like a challenge. 'We're pursuing several lines of enquiry.'

I shake my head. 'It's awful. You hear about this sort of thing in the news but you never think it could happen to someone you know. The whole hospital, nursing staff especially, is in shock.'

'It's a difficult time for everyone,' Oaks says.

Ridley adds, 'But someone must know something.'

Oaks glances at her before a final, 'We'll find her, don't you worry.'

5

I leave the room and head to the café in Post Grad to feed my caffeine habit. I nod to a few people, but I'm thinking of DI Ridley. The way she watched my face as I answered Oaks's questions. She was looking for something. A flaring of nostrils, a slide away of eye contact. Some bullshit pop-psych physical indicator of a lie. But two can play at that observational game. DI Ridley had a scar over a lumpy wrist bone – an enlarged distal ulnar styloid. I'd say a nasty wrist fracture that needed pins or a plate. Maybe she's a skier. Or a snowboarder; it's a typical injury.

All that from a one-inch scar.

I catch myself. Okay, so I found her a little intimidating. But that good cop, bad cop setup is designed for exactly that, I'd say. And who doesn't get a little anxious when talking to the police? Especially about a girl who's been missing for four days.

That brings my mind around to Katy Leith. I'd noticed her at Sister Morris's do. Who wouldn't have? Professionally, as a consultant on the unit, I'm not supposed to look twice. And at work, I don't. But I have blood coursing through my veins. And some of my colleagues (not all) even believe it's warm. Katy is mid-twenties, blonde, and at the Duke of Wellington was in a short dress and heels, fully made-up and delightful. Like many of the others and yet not quite. Because Katy stood out. Something about the way she held herself, or the big eyes and the full mouth and the firm limbs. She might even have been one of these kids who's had a boob job. Personally, I think it's criminal to even offer it at that age, but then I'm not raking it in as a plastic surgeon. Amazing what the filthy lucre does to ethics.

Yet, it wasn't only me who noticed. She drew admiring stares, and not just from the men.

I check myself. Opt for the "only saying" justification with my conscience. Not that I was in any way being lecherous. And least, I didn't think so. Women can dress however they like. Express their sexuality however they like. My body, my closet, my rules. I know all that. Sarah makes sure I do.

Yet, like most men, it always confuses me when women choose to show off their physical attributes and then not expect people to look. All a part of being young and feeling good about yourself is my understanding. As long as it is just looking, then there's no harm done. Katy knew what she was doing and probably felt great about herself. If you look like that, why not? She came across as very confident and aware and capable. She was all of those things as a nurse.

Besides, I'm "only saying", or rather "thinking", all of these things because I'm in a relationship with a beautiful partner, aren't I? And even more besides, who the hell am I trying to kid? Katy was way too young for... well, for anything.

But that's the thing about social gatherings linked to work: I find it weirdly disorientating to mingle with colleagues no longer camouflaged by the chrysalis of gender-neutral NHS uniforms. The vast majority scrub up really well. It's often quite a shock, though a very pleasant one, to see what butterflies they transform into. Everyone there had made an effort to say goodbye to one of their own. And that's always a cause for celebration in this business. When someone completes the obstacle course and reaches forty-plus years of service without going mad or burning out, it's definitely time to get out the bunting, or shots, as was obvious on many tables. There was even a DJ. You can always bank on NHS staff needing minimal excuse for a knees-up.

Of course, I'd never say any of this anti-woke non-PC stuff to DI Ridley. If I ever did, I imagine green lasers shooting from her eyes instantly aimed at cutting me in half. Like that scene from the Bond film with Sean Connery strapped to a table.

Ouch.

I order a cappuccino to take away and wait for it at the end of the counter. Behind me, people sit at tables, reading, talking. It's a light airy space courtesy of a two million conversion project in the first decade of the new century. A recognition of the fact that education remains a vital cog in this university city. Even in its hospitals.

To distract my mind from thoughts of poor Katy, I let my eyes drift. Inspirational quotes written in original old fonts, blown-up and framed, hang in spaces on the walls. I can see one from where I stand. It's the one that always appears in my eye-line when I wait at the counter.

The physician must... have two special objects in view with regard to disease, namely, to do good or to do no harm.

It's Hippocrates. His *Epidemics, Book 1*. I can quote the clip verbatim because I've read it so many times, which says a lot more about the amount of coffee I drink than it does about any obsession with medical morals. Okay, as a launching off point for discussions on medical ethics, it's a doozie. Euthanasia, abortion, informed consent; they all start right there with the big "H". The original Hippocratic oath specifies, "I will utterly reject harm and mischief". These days, it sounds more like a Harry Potter quote than an ancient text. It's commonly misquoted as "First, do no harm." That has a better book and film title ring to it. But the interpretation on the wall is close enough.

Still, it's all a bit too kitsch for my liking. All a bit too old hat. Just like Miseris Succerrere Disco. And as for Hippocrates; someone thinks it'll do no harm in these days of web-based learning, whistle blowing and abuse of privilege, to remind us all of ancient maxims as we snatch a fresh cup of arabica. Even if the misplaced nobility and altruistic simplicity of 2,500 years ago has little relevance in today's modern society. Now we have targets to meet. Budgets to not overspend. Drugs to invent and make profits from.

I confine DI Ridley, DS Oaks, Katy Leith, and the merits of Hippocrates to the mental drawer marked "someone else's problem". I need to compartmentalise. I have work to do and for that I need to apply myself.

I head up to the main theatres, keen to get back and find out how Melvyn Prosser is getting on. He's been asleep on the operating table for a good hour. Time I paid my respects.

I snap a lid on my coffee cup to drink as I walk. I've forgotten my bamboo cup. Sarah would be furious. On the way back to theatre, I phone my private patient. She wants to know if she has to take off all her nail varnish before she has her surgery.

I tell her no, that I'm sure that it'll be okay to leave things as they are.

6

W ith Thorn gone, Inspector Ridley let the interview percolate in her head.

She knew her silence drove Ryan Oaks mad. He wanted to pull things apart immediately, but she preferred a period of reflection before analysis. But Oaks was restless. He put a mug of tea down on the desk in front of his boss and, holding his own while stirring in two spoonfuls of sugar, walked over to the flipchart on one side of the room. Underneath the drawn brain on a separate sheet, someone had drawn an enlarged ECG trace – a weird hill-scape with one large spike. All neatly labelled with a P, Q, R, S, and T.

'He's a real charmer, isn't he?' Oaks spoke to the chart, but Joanna Ridley knew he was talking to her.

'As in snake, you mean?'

Oaks swivelled around, frowning. 'First, that doesn't work at all as an analogy. Other than you wanting to equate the bloke unflatteringly to some reptile. And second, isn't that a bit harsh? I mean, it's not like you to be judgemental.' He raised the mug to his lips to hide a smile. But it was there, visible in his eyes over the rim. The sardonic glint that let her know how much her statement epitomised the sort of response he had expected.

'Much too sure of himself if you ask me.' What she didn't add was that he'd been younger than she'd expected, and fitter, in an exercise sense. He'd worn a suit that must have been three times more expensive than the off-the-shelf-special Ryan wore every day. Thorn wore his dark hair cut short, and he'd had small, neat features and eyes that almost danced with sharpness. She hadn't liked him. But then she didn't like anyone she'd had to interview in an investigation. On principle. Sometimes, after elimination, she might consider someone as reasonably okay. But not at a first meeting. She didn't allow it.

Oaks was having none of it though. 'I'd have said more confidence than swagger. And being sure means nothing. He's a surgeon. They have to have a bit of an ego to get where they are, don't they? Goes with the label.' Oaks walked over to a table under a window where someone had laid on hot water, tea bags, and granulated coffee – the kind that hardened with exposure into a stale solid mass that has to be broken up by poking a spoon through the crust. And a plate of biscuits. He picked one up and dunked it in his mug before adding, 'The bloke that did my snip was brilliant. Hands like shovels but I didn't feel a thing. Told rude jokes all the way through. Exactly what you want with your tackle on display.'

Ridley pursed her lips. One of her default expressions. 'Spare me the banter. And the gory details.'

'What I'm saying is that surgeons are hardly ever wilting flowers. They're usually at the top of their game.'

'So you agree he's confident, but not arrogant enough to abduct a young girl, hide her away and then play poker with the police at an interview?' Ridley asked.

'Yes, I mean no. Where's his motive for starters?'

She didn't answer because, as yet, she hadn't got one for

Thorn. She looked at the file in front of her. She'd asked for brief summaries of everyone they were looking at. Just the basics. Address, background, previous convictions. Thorn's file was very sparse. He had no previous. But there was some information. 'He's good at his job. Growing private practice. Nine out of ten stars on bestdocs.com. Sits on ethics committees, lectures. In other words, a narcissist.'

The biscuit, on its way back for a second dunk, stopped three inches from the surface of the tea in Oaks's hand. 'Wow. That's pretty scathing, even for you.'

'Yes, well, he looked guilty of something.'

Oaks shook his head. 'You say that about everyone.'

'And I'm usually right. Someone will know something. They always do.'

'An unpaid parking ticket doesn't make you a sexual predator.'

'You asked me what I thought,' Ridley said. And she guessed it would be what others thought too. Gone were the days when being a doctor guaranteed probity. They were human and stuffed with all the psychological frailties that went with the label. And having a certain social standing meant power there to use or abuse. She never allowed status to affect her judgement. Especially not in cases like this. High flyer though he might be, Thorn remained very much on her radar because he was male, knew the misper, and was in the vicinity when Katy Leith was last seen. It was early days, but everyone linked to the case knew that with each hour that passed, the chance of finding Katy alive diminished. Like a candle slowly burning down until, with a sputter, it finally extinguishes. In Thorn's case, Ridley sensed this would not be the last time they'd do the Q and A paso doble together across a desk.

When she looked up, Oaks was staring at her. 'I know that look,' he said. 'Biscuit?'

'No thank you.' She would have loved one, but today was a no-carb day. She'd eaten some nuts earlier on and there'd be half an avocado for lunch. She had a half marathon looming in five weeks and was way behind schedule, thanks to this damned case. Knowing it made her cranky. 'And no more for you either.'

'It's the one perk of the job,' Oaks protested in a whine. 'I need that soggy biscuity comfort to get through this.' He waved a digestive-toting hand. 'I hate bloody hospitals.'

'I told Nola I'd watch your snacking.'

Oaks feigned offence. 'Since when are you and Nola besties?' Oaks's significant other was a sergeant in traffic. She and Ridley sweated at the same gym.

'We share mutual interests. One of which is the size of your gut. I'm not having her blaming me for your first stroke.'

'Harsh, harsh, harsh,' Oaks said. But he put down the second biscuit.

'Right.' Ridley turned back to her files. 'Who's next?'

7

I dress in scrubs in the changing room. The space smells faintly of feet and sweat. I tie on a blue scrub cap and step out into the theatre corridor. Once across this threshold it's fancy dress only. We're in Theatre 4 this morning, as usual. I nod to a couple of orthopaedic colleagues and an ENT surgeon following a trolley bearing a patient with bandages over his (or is it her?) nose. Everyone walks with purpose, like ants in a nest. Operating theatre suites are not environments where anyone dawdles.

I enter Theatre 4 through the anaesthetic room. White walls, ceiling-mounted lights, the cloying smell of blood and iodine. I'm at home here. There are seven people in the room, not including our patient, Mr Prosser, who is on the table and mercifully unaware of anything and everything that is going on around him. Everyone is in scrubs, but three of the seven are gowned up: a diminutive Filipino called Florry (short for Flordeliza) who is the scrub nurse, a third-year surgical trainee called Sonia Goyle, the scrub assistant, and my fellow, Mr Patrick Connor, who has two feet of Mr Prosser's intestine on a

wet towel outside his abdomen. Everyone, bar Patrick and Mr
Prosser, looks up as I enter.

'They didn't arrest you then?'

The voice that delivers this irreverent tasteless remark
belongs to a man sitting at the head end of the table next to an
anaesthetic machine throwing out pulses and beeps. Dr Ashish
Hegde has worked with me since I became a consultant almost
five years ago. Hegde is a Goan surname, but Ashish has a
Surrey accent as befitting someone born and bred in that county
and who follows their cricket team, and the Indian national
team, avidly. He does not have many graces, but the one he does
have that saves him is the fact that he's a bloody good anaesthetist.

'That's uncalled for,' I say, shaking my head.

Indeed, his comment has triggered a couple of raised
eyebrows from both the medical student who stands back
against the wall and a second nurse who is running for the case.

Ashish grins. 'I'm talking about previous offences, obviously.'

I ignore him and step forward. I slide up a mask to cover my
mouth and nose and peer in to the operating field over Sonia's
shoulder. Mr Prosser is a thirty-three-year-old Crohn's disease
patient with worsening symptoms. Workup showed that he had
multiple ileal skip strictures and adhesions from episodes of
recurrent inflammation. He's been heading for total bowel
obstruction for weeks. That's why we are all here. Crohn's is an
unpleasant disease.

'How are you getting on?' I ask. It's an innocent enough question, but Patrick tenses immediately and looks up. The little
pillows of fat just above the rim of his mask are flushed from
stress. Below us, pink bowel glistens.

'As you thought,' Patrick says. 'Most of the stricture was adjacent to the appendix, but all was healthy proximal to that. I've
resected almost a foot.'

'How the hell is he going to walk?' Ashish quips.

I ignore him and swing around. Florry picks up a ten-inch mass of ruffled and scarred bowel from a stainless-steel bowl. Patrick has opened the intestine for inspection. The strictures and ulcers are obvious. I look up at the med student.

'You've seen this?'

He nods.

'It's a good example,' I say. 'Very typical.' Then I turn back to the coils of bowel on the towels. Patrick has used a staple gun to cut the intestinal ends and sewn and stapled a three-inch segment together lengthwise in a side-to-side anastomosis so that a large open junction can function. The "function" of the "junction" is something the team in Theatre 4 has heard me emphasise many times. It's with significant restraint that I don't repeat it now.

'You're oversewing?' I ask.

'About to begin.'

I look at the clock. It's almost 11am. 'We should have finished this by now.'

'I had a bleeder.'

I nod. Patrick is a competent surgeon, but he's slow. Speed will come with experience. But for now, time is not his friend. There's more to get through and my interlude with the police has been an unnecessary distraction.

'Okay,' I say. 'I'll scrub and finish off. Get some coffee. Take Alex,' (the med student) 'and check in on Mrs Voden, our hepatectomy from yesterday. There's a gall bladder after this and–'

'I'd like to finish this case,' Patrick says. It comes out oddly petulant. Not everyone oversews the staple lines to the extent that I insist he does. But this isn't his decision. It's mine.

'This looks like a nice job, but I'll finish up. Go and see Mrs Voden.' I narrowly avoid adding, 'there's a good lad.' Patrick is only a few years my junior and has taken his time to climb the

ladder. He, much more so than me, is acutely aware of the lack
of difference in age.

But there is no more argument. I walk to the prep room and
begin scrubbing. By the time I get back to the table, Patrick has
gone. Florry holds up a mounted three o absorbable suture on a
needle driver. I take it and start working. There's music playing.
Nothing pretentious like jazz; the idea is to promote a relaxed
efficient atmosphere, not impinge recherché tastes onto a
captive audience. So we have Smooth Extra. Old-school hits that
Sonia has never heard of. But I know them all, thanks to my
parents' insistence on having music throughout the house when
I was growing up. While Chairmen of the Board pleads ironically for us to give them "just a little more time", I make Sonia
run through the blood supply to the mid gut. She's done her
homework and we go over what's needed for good anastomosis.
This is how teaching should be. The way I like to do it.
Hands on.

We finish up quickly and hand Mr Prosser over to Ashish
and recovery.

The laparoscopic cholecystectomy that follows goes quickly
and well. We get through the list by twelve forty. Not bad.

Afterwards, in the changing room, Ashish is a tad more concilia-
tory in his questioning about the police. He has a wrestler's
build; long body and short legs. Together with the beard he now
sports, he wouldn't look out of place in the foothills of the
Hindu Kush toting a rifle astride a horse. I've told him this
several times, and it always ends up with him striking a pose and
shouting a battle cry. Not that he's ever been to the Himalayas.
Nor ridden a horse. But today we stay away from the mild recip-
rocal racist banter (I'm just a privileged white boy – 'leave your
top hat in Eton, did you, Thorn?' Even though I've never been to

Eton except a look at the gates when I went on a school trip to Windsor on a bus) we sometimes, and ridiculously, indulge in. Never do it in front of other staff members of course, for fear of injuring PC sensibilities, though Ashish struggles with that. He's even more anti-woke than I am. Today, however, Ashish wants information.

'What did they ask you?'

'If I saw Katy at Sister Morris's leaving bash. If I saw her leave Sister Morris's leaving bash.'

Ashish nods.

'The answer was yes and no.'

'I'm glad I wasn't there.' Ashish throws his scrubs into an overflowing laundry basket and stands in his underwear. He needs to think about a 5:2 diet. 'But four days with no trace,' he shakes his head. 'I have a cousin in the Met. He says it doesn't sound good. Her being missing for that long.'

I nod and slip on my suit trousers, trying not to think of what "not sounding good" actually implies.

'Oh, and you were a bit harsh with young Patrick. He did good. Handled the bleeder very competently.'

'He is competent. But if you have five on the list and three and a half hours to finish it, you can't afford to spend half your allocated time on one case. He needs to understand that. Because that'll mean cancellations and I'm buggered if I am going to tell someone we can't do their operation because Patrick's slow in sewing up.'

Ashish shakes his head. 'But he thinks you think he's incompetent. You could tell from his eyes. That hangdog look. He was humiliated in front of Sonia.'

'He needs to toughen up a bit. And speed up even more. He'll be me in another couple of years. He needs to see the big picture.'

'So it's not because you're a control freak, then?'

Ashish is pushing my buttons, and he knows it.

'No.'

'No, you're not a control freak? Or no, the reason you're hard on Patrick has nothing to do with you being a control freak?'

'Jesus, how many coffees have you had today?'

'Just the three.' Ashish grins.

He pulls on fresh scrubs. That's one of the big plusses of being an anaesthetist, you get to play fancy dress for far longer.

I sigh. 'I'm not here to be the trainees' mother or their friend. I'm here to make sure they're safe to be let out into the world. End of.'

'I think Patrick's getting that message loud and clear, Jake.'

'Good. So he should.'

'But you *are* a control freak, you know that.' He pinches some belly fat.

'Nice,' I say.

'Hey, I'm off the cakes.'

'And not a moment too soon, may I say.'

'It's fine for you cyclists with your fancy bikes.'

'I have one you could borrow,' I offer.

'Nah, senior squash. That's my thing. Going back to it now that the kids are older.'

'I hope you have an ECG before you start. Is there a defibrillator on the court?'

'Very funny. When I come to visit you in prison, I'll be lithe and sinewy.'

I throw a bunched-up scrub shirt at him. He ducks, but his reflexes are not that good. Like I said, he should consider shedding a few pounds, or he's never going to learn how to shoot that rifle in the high passes.

8

S arah's a consultant too, only not of the medical type. Her skills were learned in the city, working her way up from sales through capital markets and regulations, even a spell in mergers and acquisitions. She's freelance now. Called in by a variety of big and not-so-big banks and institutions to troubleshoot and deliver projects. She's been in Canary Wharf for the last six months, with at least another four to go on her current little "jolly". Her term not mine, delivered with steely irony and a grimace. Something to do with outsourcing a big chunk of their business to Mumbai, from what I can recall.

I don't pretend to understand it.

Sarah has given up expecting me to.

Monday she works from home. Tuesday, she commutes. Wednesday, she stays up for two nights with her old college friend, Jessica, who has a flat in Newington Green. That way Sarah can get away lunchtime on Fridays and be back in Oxford mid-afternoon. Obviously, all of that is only possible because we have no children. Work keeps us busy.

I get home before Sarah on Tuesdays and so I prepare dinner. She's a vegetarian. I'm not. It's an easy negotiation when we eat out, but at home, I am happy to compromise. Partly because some part of me believes it may do me good not to eat too much red meat. I've read the studies. I know that the methodologies used use lab conditions and extremes of intake way beyond the normal human diet. Even so, removing tumours from people's colons is a big part of what I do. As such, I have a healthy respect for not overdoing anything even in the slightest bit risky. The haem of red meat included. I hear myself thinking these thoughts and smile. All empirical. Not a very scientific approach. But what the hell.

Tonight is one of the two on our 5:2 regimens. We don't go mad. Not like some. But we both think it has benefits. Tonight, we're having roast cod with broccoli dusted with almonds and pecans. I'm throwing together a rocket and pomegranate side salad for its polyphenols and for added pretentiousness.

When I was growing up, it would have been fish fingers and chips.

Sarah arrives home at just after six fifteen. I'm in the kitchen in an apron. She puts her briefcase down in the hall, sings out, 'Hi', and walks across the tiled floor to kiss me on the cheek. She has one eye on the food. 'Mmm,' she says, 'looks delish.'

'As do you,' I reply.

She lets out a snorted, 'Hah', but she's already walking away, keen to get out of her working clothes. I glimpse bare calves above three-inch heels with red soles. She loves her Louboutins. And with calves like she has, why not? She trots up the stairs and I can hear the squeaking boards in her bedroom. Sometimes she'll shower before we eat, 'to get the grime out'. I get on with laying the table. There's something reassuring about this little routine of ours. Something very satisfying about these few moments of domestic intercourse that flows deep into my soul. It's welcoming. As satiating as thick dark chocolate.

At least it has been.

And yes, I know it sounds smug. But then it's what people, normal people, strive for, isn't it? A relationship, enough money to eat, somewhere to live where you can pull up the drawbridge and keep the wild world away. While I put down place mats and cutlery, I ponder this self-awareness and chide myself for not being able to accept it for what it is. I look around at the kitchen. It's at odds with the rest of the house, which is all beams and stone fireplaces. Here, an existing extension has been converted into a small but usable space with lots of light coming in from the tiny back garden. The worktops are polished concrete, the cupboards elm and modern. The type that glide shut on their own when you push them with your hip. An Everhot oozes warmth and keeps the place cosy.

Upstairs there are two bedrooms and a bathroom and a study with a glass-topped table and a Mac for when Sarah works from home.

Okay, it's not big enough for what Sarah wants to do to it, but it's ours. We've even managed, between us, to pay off all but twenty per cent of the mortgage. We've been lucky. When my mind strays to Sarah upstairs, probably in her underwear by now, I know I have.

But then, everyone's luck runs out eventually.

I find the virgin olive oil and the balsamic vinegar, put them on the table. Then I cut the pomegranate in half and spoon out the lush red seeds.

Sarah and I met on top of a hill in New Zealand. I'd gone out after I qualified and got a job in Auckland for six months. Spread my wings after five years of grind to get my degrees.

Sarah was with Jessica, backpacking. We were on the North Island, Mount Maunganui. It was windy. We'd trekked up the lava dome separately, unaware of each other's existence. On top of the Mount, Jessica had something in her eye and I, the doctor, casually wandering past snapping photos of the cruise ships on one side and the beach on the other, offered to take a look. I took out her folded contact lens with a clean tissue. Jessica's short-sightedness was the start of it all. She's never let me forget it.

'You're not the first person to look into my eyes and see only Sarah, Jake.'

That self-deprecation came with the suggestion that she was the less attractive of the two of them. They were both in their early twenties, tanned from walking all over New Zealand, bare-limbed and fit. But she is right. It was only Sarah that I truly saw on that hill. What followed was a relationship tested by separation. Sarah's career was London centric, while mine, thanks to Deanery training, took me to Stoke Mandeville and Berkshire. But when the chance came for a fellowship in California, I took it. Against the odds, we had survived it all. When I got the job back in Oxford, Sarah gave up her contract with the business consultancy firm she'd worked with for three years and became freelance. We pooled our resources for a deposit on the house.

Sedgewood was – is – a tiny detached cottage with added-on reception rooms on Quarry Hollow. The previous owners spent a lot of money modernising it so there was not much to do. Nothing in fact. We bought it as an investment as much as a place to live. Sandstone walls made up the house and enclosed the garden. The windows are casements, modern but small with bars to represent the tiny squares that would have all been individual panes to begin with, and clay tiles on the roof. There is room for one car outside the garage entrance, which means I cycle a lot and Sarah takes a taxi to the station and back. But this side of Headington has a village feel to it. A couple of pubs and its proximity to local hospitals, plus parks in which to run or cycle, had all combined to sell it to us.

But we are outgrowing it. We both want to escape work and people when we can. So we're hunting. Hence, DOT.

Good old DOT.

When Sarah comes down from upstairs, she's three inches shorter in jeans, a T-shirt, and ballet pumps. She opens the fridge and pulls out a Margaret River Chardonnay. It's "barely oaked", the way she likes it.

'Want one?'

I say yes.

Over dinner, we talk. Small stuff. The usual. But it soon comes around to my interview with the police. I tell her it went well and add, 'But they may contact you. They wanted to know if anyone could confirm what time I got home.'

Sarah's carefully plucked eyebrows rise. She stops forking apart the fish. 'Last Friday?'

'Yes. I knew I'd be late, so I stayed in my room. Didn't want to disturb you. Remember?'

'Oh. Yes.' She nods. 'It worked, because I didn't hear you come in.'

'I told them that. But they insisted on having your number.'

'Really?'

'I doubt they'll contact you.'

'If they do, then I'll have to lie.' She tilts her head and smiles showing no teeth.

An opportunity opens up, like a door creaking open on oiled hinges. An invitation to step through and say something. In my head, the snarky comment that springs to mind is, why not? You're bloody good at that.

But what I say, quietly, reassuringly, is, 'There's no need. I explained you were asleep.'

Sarah shrugs and gets back to eating. She does it in a neat controlled way. As she does everything else. I watch her for a few seconds as she concentrates on getting a forkful of food. First a one-inch cube of fish, then a floret of broccoli, then three balanced pomegranate seeds.

Sarah would make a good surgeon. I say good, not great. That's because she might put off some of her patients, like very good-looking people sometimes do. Men would be self-conscious in her presence. Women – well, who knows about women. I don't.

Obviously.

Not that Sarah can help any of that. She looks taller than she is. But she's five-seven in stockinged feet. It's the heels that add height. Her hair is light, dark at the parting which is slightly off-centre – she told me once that she hates pretending to be anything that she isn't – blonde where it frames her amazing cheekbones. Her teeth are small and very white in a generous mouth. She thinks her chin is too big and her nose is too long. They aren't. But it's her eyes that slay me whenever I look into them. Pale brown and expressive. But in a certain light, the outer rims can appear hazel, or taupe. As if the colour is shifting.

She glances up, catches me looking. 'What?' Her eyes narrow.

'How's the fish?' I try deflection.

She nods and makes an approving noise in her throat.

A minute later, we're on to Jessica's latest romantic escapade; he's South African, five years older than her, and just separated. And then there's our usual debate about what there is to watch on TV at 9pm. The answer is nothing much except a Netflix box set. Series two of something we liked the first time around, but which seemed to falter after the first episode of this new production. The curse of the second series. Sarah explains that the *Sunday Times* urged people to persevere and that it improves by the end of episode two.

In the end we have another half glass of wine each and chat and watch the news. Katy Leith is still the headline. Sky spends ten minutes telling the nation that police are intensifying their efforts. But they've found nothing. I look at Katy's photograph filling the screen. They've chosen one of her in uniform. A headshot taken for inclusion on the hospital's website introducing the surgical team. Katy's smile is warm. The sort of smile you'd be delighted to see as you look up from your hospital bed in pain. A smile full of caring.

Sarah is in bed by ten fifteen. I stay up another half an hour and do some work. An audit that Sonia's preparing for a presentation next week. It's good and only needs a little tidying up. It's a departmental meeting. One that Katy would normally attend.

I'm in my bed by eleven. I can hear Sarah's steady breathing in the room next door, telling me she's asleep. I shut my eyes and wonder how Sid's getting on in his kennel. Sleep doesn't come for several hours. Not because of Sid. It's Katy Leith and Sarah who keep me awake.

9

WEDNESDAY 8TH MAY 2019

Paula king @plaking44 8May2019
So worried for Katy #findkaty I'm praying every day.

Angrybastaard @sicknesst5 8May2019
Chances are she's toast #findkaty Bring back hanging.

Lola limon @lolimon123 8May2019
I don't feel safe anymore. I have a pepper spray. Everyone should
have one. #rapesafe #findkaty

Tod Machine @todmychine 8May2019
Like I say. Beheading should be on the list. #findkaty #eyeforaneye

10

I get up to say goodbye to Sarah. I won't see her now until Friday. I'm in a T-shirt and boxers, in need of a shower, my hair pillow-sculpted. She's in a dark suit and heels, scrubbed up and smelling wonderful. There's a Mulberry handbag over one shoulder and she clutches the pull handle of an overnight bag in her hand. It's the kind that's small enough to fit in an overhead locker on a plane or a train. She kisses my stubbled cheek as she leaves.

'Don't forget we're meeting Wil and Chloe on Friday. Around eight. We'll eat before we go out, okay?'

I nod. I had forgotten. Things not work related tend to get pushed out of my memory banks. Sarah knows this. Knows it's best to reinforce. I watch her enter the taxi and then I head for the bathroom. If she's seen anything in my expression, she hasn't let on. But then, there's no reason for her to be suspicious. It's only me who knows this might be the last ever Wednesday we go through this little charade. But that's my decision to make and I realise I'm too conflicted to make the leap. I only know it'll be soon.

. . .

The midweek ward round starts at eight thirty. Mr Prosser is doing well. He's comfortable and cheerful. By contrast, my hepatectomy is not. She isn't young and the underlying pathology that necessitated the surgery – cirrhosis – means that the liver we left behind is not in the best nick.

Sonia's already been to see her and we review the chart. Patrick's happy to take a back seat. His patient is doing fine. I greet Mrs Voden. She looks ill. Her temperature's up, fluid intake down.

Her, 'Good morning, Mr Thorn' is delivered in a tobacco-ravaged voice. I smile and reciprocate. Mrs Voden's face has skin like a Martian desert; the dry red look that comes with years of an excess of nicotine and alcohol. We both know that vodka is the primary cause of the situation she finds herself in. I look, gently palpate and make some reassuring noises. When we get out of the room, out of earshot, I wait for Sonia's verdict.

'The abdomen's more swollen,' she says. 'So definitely ascites.'

'Should we do something about that?' I probe.

'Surgically?'

I wait.

She contemplates and says, 'No. Diuretics and albumin and then watch and wait.'

I nod. 'Correct. There's been enough trauma already. That last thing we need to do is stick a bloody great cannula into her abdomen to drain fluid we know will re-form. But what about the elevated temperature?'

'I've asked for a chest X-ray,' Sonia says. 'She has some crackles at both bases.'

I smile. Sonia's on the case. Post-incisional pain means that patients like Mrs Voden are afraid to cough and breathe normally. The prolonged bed rest just adds to the risk of pneumonia. 'Okay. Get some sputum and start antibiotics.'

And onto the next.

11

A t ten, I spend an hour signing letters and answering queries. At eleven, I wander along to the admin block for a meeting with the management team. As always, it's all about money.

Efficiency drives them.

Making sure that the people we cut open survive and live normal lives – as much as possible – is what motivates me.

Sometimes, it's an oil and water mix. More often than not, we muddle along side by side, each aware of the other's brief. But occasionally, panic sets in and someone on the board of the Foundation Trust running the hospital will have the bright idea that in order to manifest change, you need fresh blood. This was the thinking behind appointing Frank Kierney as Director of Change. He's brought a "facilitating team" with him to see what savings we might make.

For facilitating team, read hatchet men, or rather, women.

Kierney's latest idea is to cull the secretarial support staff across the board, reduce numbers and change the way we work by trialling voice recognition software in clinics. He wants dictated letters to go straight into the computer's electronic patient record with no secretarial input. I can't think of a better way to undermine morale in the secretarial staff, send my colleagues' blood pressure soaring, and waste time on digital cock-ups; the software froze at least half a dozen times in the first two weeks.

But, Kierney and team want feedback from the surgical team leader.

That's me.

Okay. Then feedback it is.

We meet in a pokey room with refreshments provided. Oxymoron alert; the stale instant coffee and flasks of tepid water are anything but refreshing. Olivia Ibbotson, a capable woman who's worked in Urology for fifteen years, represents the secretaries. She's already there, sitting with a notepad open on her knees, on one side of an oval desk opposite Kierney and his team. She smiles as I enter. She looks glad to see me.

Kierney is balding, has his jacket off and tie loose. He stands as I enter. The bottom button of his too-tight shirt is undone, gaping just before it tucks in to his trousers. A roll of pale flesh is visible. The management equivalent of a builder's bum. He's worked on teams that have been called in to run failing hospitals, those in special measures, prior to his appointment with us. He may be good at his job, but I find his approach abrasive and unpleasant.

'Ah,' Kierney says, 'Jake, thanks for coming. You know Alma Bilton and Janet Catterick.'

I nod. Bilton is a black woman with large expressive eyes. She's stick thin and wears lipstick the colour Mrs Voden's cirrhotic liver appeared in the bowl after I'd cut it out. Catterick is as pale as flour and has fluffy blonde hair that contrasts with her dark eyebrows and blue highlights. Her glasses look thick and are dark-rimmed. They both wear dark suits over white shirts. Business-like. A la DI Ridley.

Kierney sits. 'So, Jake, the dictation software.' Kierney has a Midlands accent and a greying stubble that he thinks makes him attractive. But to me, it just makes him look like someone too lazy to shave. 'How did it go?'

'Too many bugs,' I say.

'I heard about the glitches, but overall, how did it go?'

It's the same question. I suspect he's fishing for a different answer. I say, 'If we're looking to save time, it'll never fly. The software needs to be trained. It needs to get used to your voice and to the vocabulary. I can see that with several hours of use, maybe hundreds of hours, it might become useful. But we will never get a bunch of surgeons to buy into that.'

Bilton speaks. 'You say that, but–'

I don't let her interrupt. 'Assume a three and a half-hour clinic. Ten new patients. If we dictate a letter on each one at the end of the consultation, three minutes each, that's half an hour. Using this software, I took six minutes because of having to go back and correct the errors. It took me an hour.'

Bilton and Catterick exchange a glance. It's unreadable. But I have a feeling that this might be their baby. They don't enjoy having it smacked.

'This is also what we've been finding on checking the dictation,' Olivia says. 'It's full of errors.'

'But it's possible the error rate might reduce with time, yes?' Bilton asks. It sounds a little desperate.

'True, but you'll have an uphill battle convincing my surgical colleagues of that.'

'Everyone has to adapt,' Catterick says.

I smile and sit back. So this is how it will be. I don't think they really want to hear what I have to say. This is all a sham. I think they've made up their minds already.

'You asked for my feedback,' I say. 'But typing up letters is only a small part of what medical secretaries do, you are aware of that?' I turn to Olivia for confirmation.

She bobs her head. 'As I've already explained, most of us are more like personal assistants. Arranging tests, chasing up results, liaising with other departments. And more often than not, we're the first point of contact for patients–'

Catterick seizes on this. 'That's something else we'd like to revisit. In Scotland they've had a great deal of success with centralising patient queries.'

I suck my teeth. 'Centralising queries? You mean a call centre?'

The smile Catterick sends me is one hundred per cent fake. 'We prefer client liaison operations.'

'You would,' I say with a straight face.

Kierney sits back. He snorts and then smiles. 'I don't think either of you quite understand what's going on here. I've been tasked with restructuring administrative services and I always deliver. Change is often difficult to handle, but do I need to remind you that you are both employees of this trust?'

Olivia shuffles in her seat uncomfortably.

I say, 'But change for change's sake isn't always the best option.'

'It's not a discussion,' Bilton says. She is Kierney's attack apparatchik for policy. 'This Trust is riven with outdated thinking and poor performance. You only have to look at equality standard measurements.'

I wait. This is a switching up of gears. One I've already experienced several times. I decide to stoke the fire. 'Are you saying we don't treat people equally?'

'I'm saying that entrenched roles need to be challenged.'

'So using speech recognition software to dictate patient letters is nothing to do with saving money; it's a tool for secretarial liberation?'

Kierney tries for oil on troubled waters. 'It's a multipurpose tool.'

'Maybe you ought to ask the secretaries how oppressed they feel?' I look at him. He smiles.

'Many of them are anxious about their jobs–' Olivia says.

Catterick shakes her head and interjects. 'This is not only about secretaries' roles. It's part of a wider brief.'

'What brief?' Olivia asks.

I pity her naivety. 'Equality and diversity,' I say. I don't add the word agenda, though I am sorely tempted. I try not to sound tired or sceptical, because I am neither when it comes to this. But I am irritated because I know what comes next. I have a lanyard with an ID card that spells out my name and what I do. But I have another label that defines me in this little trio's eyes. I'm white, male, and a surgeon.

'This year's workforce equality standard report shows no improvement in BAME representation in many areas,' Bilton says.

'BAME?' asks Olivia.

I let Kierney explain. 'Black and Asian minority ethnicity.'

The irony of this statement doesn't escape either of us given that Olivia has a Somalian mother, who left Africa as a refugee and married an Anglo-Saxon bus driver from Kent. She throws me a glance and I respond with an insipid smile. Olivia thought she was here to discuss dictation. 'But...' her sentence falters.

Catterick jumps in. 'And my background has been centred on research at the Inequalities Hub. I'm here to advise Human Resources of their responsibilities.'

'We're lucky to have Janet,' Kierney says. 'Her work on sexual orientation monitoring and the gender pay gap has been vital in our understanding of what we need to do to bring this Trust up to standard.'

Olivia looks bemused. 'I still don't understand what that has to do with dictation.'

I nod. 'Oh, I do. Apart from the huge saving using this stuff will not achieve, it means the secretaries will no longer be shackled to the computer screen typing up letters because that's some kind of male plot to keep them subservient. A woman's place is at the PC, as we all know.' I smile apologetically to emphasise the irony. 'If you'll excuse the pun.'

They all look at me. Their expressions are a stark reminder of why I should never try stand-up.

'I'm glad you find this funny, Mr Thorn,' Catterick says. We're back to the more formal Mr Thorn. Jake, I notice, has now left the building. But Catterick has the social justice bit between her teeth. Her cheeks are flushed. 'Tell me, what percentage of surgeons in your department are female?'

I know the answer. We both do. But I reply anyway. 'Fifteen per cent. A little above the national average.'

'Fifteen per cent,' Catterick repeats. 'And doesn't that bother you?'

'Yes, it does, especially since fifty-five per cent of medical students are now female. I worry about who is going to be me in thirty years' time.'

'Would you care to explain the discrepancy?'

'Can we put the dictation software to bed then?'

Stony silence.

I sigh. 'It's multifactorial. Mostly it's because surgery poses a big conflict between personal and career decisions. Young women are under pressure to fulfil career and family ambitions with the clock ticking. The hours are terrible. Just at the time when training is at its most intense and demanding, women know they're going to have to have children, if they want them too. But that is their choice.'

Bilton shakes her head.

I ignore her. 'And undoubtedly, there is also external discrimination. Patients will often assume a female colleague is a nurse as opposed to a surgeon. Is there an easy answer? Not that I know of. We need more female role models. More male surgeons willing to mentor female colleagues. We need more women in high-profile leadership positions. Tell me when you'd like me to stop.'

Catterick's glare would melt aluminium.

But I'm quoting from the literature. Better people than me have looked at this. It's a harsh reality with a societal origin. But a denial of the facts – that it comes down to individual choice more than anything else – would be to perpetuate a myth. As an individual I do what I can. But we're talking about a tough profession. And I embody all that is wrong with it in these ideologues' eyes by dint of simply existing. I consider myself gender and race blind, but not blinkered to the realpolitik of the NHS. Kierney and co don't like me, and that's the ultimate irony. They know nothing about me personally, but they have an unconscious bias because of my gender, status and ethnicity, the very things they are railing against. But I doubt they have any insight. I look at my watch. 'I ought to get going. I'll put my feedback on auto dictation in writing.'

'You think you're untouchable, don't you?' Bilton says. It looks like she doesn't appreciate my brand of sarcasm. But today there's an added barb. 'You're not.'

Kierney sends her a savage look. Threats are never pleasant or constructive. Especially when there is someone else in the room to witness them.

'Charming.' I beam at her. But the cudgel has been offered and so I take it. This is a debate Sarah and I have had many times. And it's always Sarah, the hard-nosed businessperson, who's been the one to shoot down the canard that years of misinformed zealots have been peddling, while I play the establishment viewpoint's devil's advocate.

Oh, yes. I've been schooled by one of the best.

I turn to Catterick. 'You're an expert in the gender pay gap, right? I thought it was illegal to pay an equally qualified and experience female employee less than an equivalent male.' I light the blue touch paper and sit back.

'It is–' Catterick begins.

'Then, why isn't the Trust in court if there's a pay gap?'

No one answers. Until I do. 'Is it because perhaps we're mistaking a pay gap with a gender differential?'

'We need more women consultants,' Bilton says. Again.

'I agree,' I say. 'But you're talking about a gender differential, not a pay gap.'

'You would say that.' Bilton almost spits out the words.

I shake my head. 'Medicine is an open field, based on meritocracy. But we all know that there's a huge gender bias in the health service with women doing many more of the lower-paid jobs. So if you take an average, which is what the gender pay gap calculation does, it's bound to show a big difference. But that doesn't constitute illegality.'

'Women and girls have been conditioned and suppressed. There are invisible barriers–'

'There are more females than males in medical school now,' I interrupt, 'but once they qualify, many make a choice not to take part in the brutal, socially crippling, sleep-depriving, exam-cramming, uphill slog that is a consultant's training. Many take time out to have children and, as a consequence, work fewer hours, which brings their average earnings down compared to male colleagues. Nothing illegal in taking home more pay for longer hours worked. You're confusing workplace economics with illegal practice.'

Carrick joins in with a snort. 'You're pandering to the social conditioning that steers women towards stereotypical career paths and family roles.'

'Or, maybe some women want to enjoy the reward of having kids and a family. Some might feel that's more fulfilling than sitting in a clinic all day.'

'Do you have any idea how patronising you sound?' Catterick says.

I nod. 'To you, maybe. But do you have any idea how brain-washed with propaganda you sound? You're not from Venus, and I'm not from Mars. Time we exploded the myths, isn't it?'

Kierney interrupts. 'I'm sure that I can arrange a boxing ring for you two if you like.' He keeps it light, but I can see he's getting irked.

Catterick has flushed pink. Bilton just seethes.

'And there's me thinking this was mere banter.' I stand. 'If you like, I'll do my report on the dictation software at home so as not to involve my secretary. She has enough on her plate, what with making tea for me and arranging for my car to be cleaned. Can we do this again sometime? It's been fun.' Olivia realises I'm about to leave and looks terrified. I won't leave her alone with the wolves. 'Coming, Olivia? I think we're done here.'

She gets up and we leave together. No one thanks us or says goodbye. Needless to say, there is no standing ovation.

'They give me the creeps,' Olivia says when we're outside the door. Her large expressive eyes look troubled. 'All these agendas. Why can't they let us get on with our jobs?'

'Couldn't have put it better myself.'

As we walk back towards the surgical unit, I see DI Ridley and DS Oaks waking towards Post Grad. Another grilling for someone, no doubt. I think about asking Olivia if she was at Sister Morris's leaving do but decide against it. I don't want to spoil her lunch.

12

I pick Sid up at 3pm. First, he's bouncing, then he's wriggling, twisting his body up against mine as I try to get his lead attached. He's glad to see me. Paws for Claws like us to walk the dogs out of the compound and along the road to one of the parks. Florence Park is the closest. It's where I usually bump into Rob on a Tuesday morning. But on Wednesdays and Saturdays, I drive, and Sid and I take a trip across to Shotover Park. I'm not sure if Paws for Claws would approve, but what you don't know doesn't harm you. And Sid doesn't mind. Shotover isn't that far from Headington and the cottage Sarah and I share, ironically. A 2,000-acre estate just off the ring road managed by the city council. But it's somewhere I can let Sid off the lead to chase squirrels.

That's a good enough excuse for the twenty-minute trip.

But the other reason for going to Shotover, by far the better one in my book, is who else will be there.

I take the Old Road east from Headington over the bypass to where the tarmac peters out into the car park. Five minutes later, we're on a path in the woods, and Sid is haring around like a shiny black and tan squirrel-seeking missile.

A quarter of a mile in, Sid sees a caramel-coloured labradoodle called Lulu and takes off towards her. Lulu does the same in the other direction. Just when it looks like a collision is inevitable, both dogs adopt evasive manoeuvres and end up chasing one another into the woods, emerging periodically to cross the path at breakneck speed.

Lulu's owner watches with a smile of indulgence as I approach.

'Do you think they like one another?' I ask.

Ella Danes nods and smiles. It's a great, beaming, welcoming smile. 'I think all we need to do is stand here and let them get on with it.'

'Wouldn't that look a bit suspicious?'

'Probably.'

'Whereas if we walked, we're just two dog lovers sharing an afternoon stroll.'

'Devious,' she says.

'My middle name.'

'Ella Devious Danes,' I say. 'Has a certain ring to it.'

We turn and head off along the track. As we have done several times over the last two months. Every Wednesday without fail. Ella has Wednesdays off because she works the unpopular Saturday pm shift in her four-day week as an ITU nurse. Work is where we met and got chatting about dogs. Standing over the bed of a moribund octogenarian with sepsis we were trying to save. His daughter had wondered aloud during visiting about who would look after the dog. It all stemmed from that. And then we bumped into each other in the park. Ella isn't here for Paws for Claws; lucky Lulu is hers as a permanent fixture.

We usually walk for an hour, rain or shine. Today it's shine and warm with it, but Ella still has a jacket over her jeans and walking shoes. Unglamorous practical clothes that don't detract from her looks, which are olive-skinned with blue-grey eyes that suggest a little Irish blood.

When you spend an hour talking to someone every week, you learn a lot. And besides dogs, we've had a lot to talk about. Ella is open and friendly and I still can't understand how anyone in a relationship with her would ever do anything to jeopardise it. But Kyle Danes, the entrepreneur and ex-husband, did so spectacularly well thanks to a drug and gambling habit that bankrupted his business and almost destroyed his family. But Ella is a remarkable person. I'm in awe of her ability to be so positive having lived with a partner so full of lies, secrets and false remorse. Since he came out of prison, he's made no attempt to see her, nor their little boy, Ben, a six-year-old having tea with his grandmother as we speak.

Ella wants it to stay like that.

There are other walkers on the path, but only a few. Our Wednesday afternoons with the dogs is something I look forward to a lot. And I like to believe Ella does too.

'Did the police talk to you?' she asks.

'Yes.'

'It's so awful about Katy.'

I nod.

It's peaceful on the path. Hardly anyone sees us, and we're away from the gaze of hospital staff who would undoubtedly end up putting two and two together and coming up with much more. It's a terrible place for gossip.

'They asked me about what I did after I left Sister Morris's leaving do.'

Ella nods. 'What did you say?'

'I told them the truth. I went home. That Sarah was asleep when I got there. And she was. She doesn't remember me coming home. Just that I was there in the morning.'

'If they ask me, I'd have no alibi. Ben was at my mum's.'

But we both know that's not strictly true. She has an alibi for the time between leaving the pub and midnight at least. Because it's the same one as mine, if I cared to tell the police the absolute truth. Midnight was the time I got out of her car, got into mine, and drove home from the same car park we've used this afternoon. I drove there to meet Ella after leaving the pub. We'd sat and listened to music, chatting and canoodling like teenagers. There was no sex. Not then. There are other places for that. But it was too good an opportunity not to spend some time together.

The walker ahead of us disappears around a bend. We're alone on the path. Ella stops, looks back and sees no one behind us either. She turns to me, grabs my coat and pulls me to her. She's shorter than I am. Shorter than Sarah. I feel Ella's lips on mine. They taste of cinnamon gum.

Later, we get back to the car park, get into our separate cars, and drive to our separate homes in different directions. Sarah is in London, we both know that, but I haven't taken Ella to Sedgewood. Not yet. It still feels like too much of a betrayal. I'm old-fashioned like that.

By the time I get Sid back to Paws for Claws, it's after five. They don't mind. They know me well enough by now. I kneel and ruffle the big dog's head. He tries to lick my face and I pull back just in time. He's a good lad.

I call in to the hospital on my way home. Check through the admissions for tomorrow's list and say hello to the patients I will be cutting open. They're always glad to see me. I ease their anxieties. It's part of the job. An important part.

. . .

By eight I'm at home and wondering what Sarah is up to. I toy with ringing her, telling her everything. But I don't.

Not yet.

I go to my desktop, wiggle the mouse. The screen lights up and my wallpaper image appears. Sarah and me in ski gear with Mont Blanc as a backdrop. I check the news. It's depressing. I click Facebook. See if anyone on my small – I like to think select – contact list has posted anything of note.

Ads for things I had no idea I was interested in, but which Facebook's algorithms do, litter the thread. But there's nothing of interest.

I hardly ever post anything, preferring to keep what's on my mind private. But it's fascinating to see so many people willing to brag, share, or irritate. I don't tweet. And Sarah's the one who instagrams. I have an account but with only half a dozen followers and followings. I opened it mainly because she goaded me into it.

I turn to my phone and message Sarah via WhatsApp.

Me: Hi. All good?

She's online. I can see she's typing.

Sarah: I'm fine. Bit tired.

Me: Not out clubbing with Jess?

Sarah: Avocado on toast and a Riesling for the TV later. You?

Me: Walked Sid. About to have an omelette.

Sarah: We know how to live, right?

Me: We do. Enjoy.

I realise I'm hungry but know that I won't be able to eat until I do this one last thing. I click on the 'find my phone app'. Sarah and I have a downloading music account that I set up. With it comes family sharing and that, unless you disable it in settings, allows you to share your location. Very useful if you lose your phone. Not so useful if you want to stay off the radar. I select Sarah's iPhone from the list. A map appears. A phone icon pulses away. Jessica's address, where Sarah has just told me she is, is in Islington.

I zoom in on the map. Names appear. It's a restaurant in Marylebone. I could look it up, but I don't. It doesn't matter. All that does is that it's unlikely to be serving only avocado on toast.

Nor is it anywhere near Islington.

13

THURSDAY 9TH MAY 2019

Sammy Samunwise @samunwise 9May2019
OMFG have you seen this? #findkaty https://vimeart.3489.com Who
is this guy? #isthishim

Denise Lockhart @Denisethenurse 9May2019
I work at the same hospital as Katy #findkaty I see this bloke every
day. Thought he was straight as an arrow #isthishim IMHO

Larry Zoltan @Lzoltan4 9May2019
Cops need to jump on this bloke sharpish #findkaty Cuff him and
rough him up. Waterboard him until he confesses #isthishim

14

I'm tying the scrub trousers drawstring around my waist the next morning when there's a knock on the changing room door.

Ashish is with me. He's in his underwear, being rude about my bike helmet, so I shout, 'Come in!'

'Mr Thorn, it's Sonia.' Her voice comes through the door but she doesn't open it.

'Don't come in!' Ashish rushes to pull on some trousers of his own.

'Mr Thorn, can I have a word?'

Sonia sounds anxious. I slide my feet into clogs and step outside without my nifty scrub hat. Urgent discussions before the commencement of a list are not good news. It usually means one of the patients has forgotten to stop their anticoagulants or hotel services has slipped someone a breakfast by mistake. Cock-ups happen. But Sonia looks anxious. More worried than I think I've ever seen her.

'Is it that bad?' I ask.

Patrick appears from the corridor behind us. 'Want me to kick off?'

The first case is a splenectomy. 'By all means,' I say. I'm feeling charitable this morning.

'I'll be there in a minute,' Sonia says.

Patrick offers a half smile, but it's tinged with suspicion. He thinks she's my favourite. He's right in a sense. Sonia is much more personable, and she has a beautiful pair of hands. Not that Patrick isn't competent, but he gets nervous and that shows itself in a certain irascibility. It manifests under stress and especially when he operates. I've warned him about it. It'll win him no friends during his career. I've seen it in many colleagues and it's a shame. The tyrant surgeon is a cliché of old. But these days, if you're not careful, it can end up in bullying complaints. Patrick needs to work on all of that as much as his speed.

'Can we go to the coffee room?' Sonia asks.

I follow her along the corridor. It's early and the coffee room is empty. We find some battered seats in the corner, throw off yesterday's scattered newspapers and sit.

'What's happened, Sonia?' I ask. I have a hunch that this isn't work related. She's keeping her eyes down. This is something personal.

'I...' Sonia hesitates. I'm disturbed to see this lack of confidence in her. She's a tall girl, pale from the hours indoors the job brings. The slender fingers of her right hand worry at a hangnail on her left. There are no rings, but I know she's in a relationship with another medic. When she looks up, there are dark circles under her bright eyes. She sighs. 'This may be none of my business, but I wanted to tell you because I think you deserve to know.'

Something cold rolls over inside me. My first thought is Ella. Someone has seen us. It's a fear that's stoked by Sonia reaching in to her pocket and taking out a phone. With enviable dexterity, her thumbs fly over the screen and she brings up a video. I stare at the tiny screen. There's no audio. At first, I feel nothing but relief. This isn't Shotover Woods. It's a hospital ward. A side room with the door open. There's no wobble. I register the fact that it looks like the camera is fixed. I'm inside the room with another person and we're having a discussion. The body language tells a story. I'm standing, arms folded, the other person is animated, hands moving expressively, demandingly. The other person looks upset. And then she's crying, dabbing her eyes. On screen, I reach out and touch her arm reassuringly.

She's wearing nursing scrubs. But it isn't Ella.

The tear-streaked face that turns away to leave the room belongs unmistakably to Katy Leith.

I look up into Sonia's eyes with my mouth open. I'm a blinking goldfish. Sonia looks upset. Almost as upset as Katy Leith does in the video. I shut my mouth and swallow. 'What is this, Sonia?'

She shakes her head. 'Someone sent it to me. Another trainee. Someone's posted it on Facebook.'

I feel my pulse thudding in my throat.

'It's going viral,' adds Sonia.

My pulse accelerates.

Going viral.

'I don't even remember–' I splutter.

Sonia looks at me. I notice her eyelashes. The dark line at their base. I wonder if she's had an eyeliner tattoo. But then I do remember and I frown, desperately trying to drag up the details. Before I can, someone appears at the door of the coffee room. He looks out of place with plastic overshoes on his feet and a loose gown over his cheap suit.

'Ah, there you are, Mr Thorn. We were hoping to catch you before you began. Hoping to have a quick word.' He's polite, but we both know this isn't a request, not really. I get up and follow Detective Sergeant Oaks out of the surgical unit without looking back at Sonia.

15

Ridley is waiting for us in the seminar room. She doesn't smile as I enter ahead of Oaks.

'Have a seat,' she says. She's almost cheerful. As if me turning up again has won her a bet.

I sit. Oaks sits opposite.

'You'll be aware of why we've asked you to come at this short notice?' Oaks asks.

'I presume it's because of the video.'

Oaks nods. 'You told us you didn't know Katy.'

'That's not true. Of course I know her.'

'But you gave us the impression she was just another member of staff. Someone you nodded at in the corridor.'

I feel the heat rising in my neck. 'She is. But of course I'd spoken to Katy at some time in the last few months or weeks. She's a staff nurse on the surgical unit.'

'Tell us about the video,' Ridley says.

'Firstly, I had no idea there was a video until five minutes ago. My trainee has just shown it to me. She said it had gone viral.'

Oaks checks his phone. 'Twenty-three thousand views so far.'

'But who posted it? Who the hell shot it?' I hear my voice rise.

'We're trying to find out,' Ridley says. 'However, for the moment, I think it would help if you explained the circumstances.'

'The circumstances were that I'd gone to the room to see a patient but he or she had gone for an MRI. I was checking the chart when Staff Nurse Leith came in. We'd lost a patient that morning. A male who'd suffered a massive PE – a pulmonary embolism. He'd come through surgery and was doing well. It happens when a massive blood clot lodges in a vessel in the lung. It's a known surgical risk from a deep vein thrombosis in the leg. These things happen. She was upset because she'd checked in on him just half an hour before. She felt she'd missed something. She hadn't. I took time to explain that to her, but, like all of us, she is human. The deceased patient was the same age as her father had been when he passed away. It was a big emotional trigger. I did my best to comfort her.'

Ridley watches and listens impassively.

'And there was nothing else?' Oaks asks.

'Like what?'

'Like some sort of relationship between the two of you?'

'For God's sake. She was almost half my age.'

'Was?' Oaks says.

'Is almost half my age.'

Oaks nods. 'And you still claim to have no idea where she is?'

'Claim? What does that mean?'

Ridley answers. Slowly, deliberately. 'It means, Mr Thorn, that we're worried about other things hiding in the shadows.' I see she's put fresh shiny stuff on her lips. The room has no window open, and it's as dry as parchment. A little rivulet of sweat runs down inside my scrubs from my armpit. I tell myself it's because it's stuffy.

'I'm not hiding anything,' I say. But of course, I am. My eyes want to slide away, but I stop them from doing so. I get the impression Ridley sees that. She studies me, looking for signs. It's bloody hard not to shift in my chair.

'We rang your partner, Ms Barstow,' Ridley says. 'She confirms that you came home the night that Katy went missing. But she can't confirm the time.'

'I told you, she was asleep.'

'You did,' Ridley says. 'That's... unfortunate.'

She's baiting me, but I opt for repeating what I've already said. 'I have no idea where Katy Leith is, or where she went after she left the pub that night. And now I have an operating list with patients already on the table.'

'We know,' Ridley says. 'It's the one reason we're not taking you somewhere else for questioning. But we will if we have to.'

It's a vague threat. Almost a test. The kind that demands a response. I say, 'Of course. Anything I can do. But I'd prefer to do it after I've finished my list.'

My answer seems to satisfy Ridley.

'You on social media much, Mr Thorn?' Oaks asks.

'No. I dip my toe into Facebook now and again. Instagram occasionally. For the photos.'

Oaks nods. 'You need to be prepared for what's coming. People get very angry when young girls go missing.'

'What's that supposed to mean?'

'It means that the days of keeping information out of the public domain, information like this video, have long gone. As I say, be prepared.'

'Like the scouts.' Once again, my pathetic stab at humour gets no reward. I get up. 'Right. You know where to find me if you need anything else.'

'Oh, we do,' Ridley says. Unnecessarily, I think.

When I get outside, I find I'm shaking. Halfway back to the surgical unit, my phone rings. It's Sarah.

16

I accept the call and say, 'Hi.' I'm hoping this is to do with the logistics of our Friday night arrangements. Maybe she's going to catch a later train. God knows there's enough Network Rail disruption, but when she speaks my name, I know there's more to it than leaves on a line.

'Jake?' Sarah's voice is tense and urgent.

'Yes?'

'What's going on?'

'What do you–?'

'There's a video of you and the nurse arguing. Simon showed it to me. It's everywhere.'

Simon Harding is Sarah's co-worker. He's something in mergers and acquisitions. I've met him once or twice. I somehow know it would be Simon who let the genie out of the bottle.

'I know.'

'So you've seen it?'

'Yes. I've seen it. And it wasn't an argument. She was upset about a patient–'

'It looks like an argument. It looks like you knew each other very well.' It's accusatory. Difficult to ignore.

'Well, we didn't.' The past tense again. I hear Oaks's reprimand in my head and automatically correct it. 'We don't.'

'But that's what it looks like.' I hear a deflated sigh. 'And now the press have it too. I've seen comments and headlines. It's bad.'

'Why is it bad?' I ask.

'Are you serious?' Sarah throws that out in soprano.

I counter with, 'Who shot the video, that's what I'd like to know.'

'What?'

'Someone must have shot it.'

Sarah dismisses my question. 'What does it matter? The fact is, it's out there for everyone to see.'

'So what?'

'So what?' This time Sarah hurls the words back in a hissed whisper. It sounds like she wants to shout but can't in case someone else overhears. 'It's all over Twitter, is what. Hashtag findKaty. Hashtag isthishim? My God, Jake, they think it's you.'

'It isn't me, Sarah.'

Silence.

'For Christ's sake.' My turn to shout. People turn to stare. I drop my voice. 'Is this why you're phoning? To make sure I didn't do it?'

'I phoned to find out what the hell it all means.'

'For who? Me, us or you?'

She ignores that. 'What do the police say?'

'The same thing you just have.'

'Oh my God.'

'Sarah, I've got nothing to hide. This is someone trying to make trouble.'

'Succeeding.'

'Maybe.'

'I'm scared to look at my Twitter feed.' A whine now.

'Then don't. Look, I, we, can't let something like this paralyse us. You've got work to do and so do I. People are depending on us.'

'It's just so horrible.'

'If it's too much for you, come home.'

'No, I can't. We're in the middle of something huge and it has to be signed off tomorrow.'

I sigh. 'Then I don't know what else to say.'

'Okay. I'll try to get away early tomorrow, but no promises.' There's a pause before she finally asks, 'And are you... all right?'

I want to say, took you long enough to sodding ask, but I don't. Instead, I reassure her. 'I'm fine. Why wouldn't I be? I've done nothing.'

'I know, I'm sorry. It was such a shock to see that video.'

'I'll see you tomorrow.' I kill the call. I'm in Post Grad so I head to the café and buy a coffee. I'm a creature of habit. Sarah would say "boring old fart", though she shortens it to "bof". I order a flat white. It's probably exactly the wrong thing to do to settle the nerves. Coffee does nothing to help the adrenaline shakes and I have them now. If this was a Victorian novel, and I'd been to see Holmes and Watson, I'd be drinking a brandy.

Holmes and Watson. Don't know what makes me think of Oaks and Ridley that way. But if they were, Ridley would definitely be Holmes, Oaks, her trusty Watson. Ridley's definitely thin enough to have a coke habit. Can't quite see her playing the violin though.

I shrug off these distracting thoughts reluctantly, because they're not unwelcome. I walk back to the unit, unable to shake the feeling people are looking at me. But when I return their gaze, their eyes slide away. It's probably nothing, but I'm relieved when I get back to the familiar territory of the operating theatres. I finish my coffee in the changing room, don a cap, and a minute later, I'm pushing open the doors of Theatre 4.

I'm not sure what I'm expecting, but no one stops what

they're doing. All is calm and business-like. If everyone here does know about the video, they are all professional enough to not say anything.

Well, almost all.

'They didn't arrest you this time either, then?' Ashish pipes up from his seat next to the anaesthetic machine. He's grinning under his mask. I can tell from his eyes.

'Not quite,' I say.

I look into the operating field. The spleen is out. It's much larger than normal. The patient has polycythaemia and her spleen was becoming hard and painful. Normally, splenectomies can be done through a laparoscopic approach. But not this one. This one is a whopper.

'Okay?' I ask Patrick.

'Two point seven five kilos. It's a boy,' he says, nodding at the purple mass in a bowl next to the scrub nurse.

Sonia says, 'I think it's a girl. I've named it Mylene.'

'Mylene the spleen. Very original.' I smile.

Ashish says, 'So come on. I've seen the video. What did you say to that poor nurse to make her cry?'

I shake my head and turn to him. There's no getting away from it and I realise that I can either get angry and tell him to shut up or accept his leg-pulling and respond. I know which the healthier option is. 'I had to break the news to her that she was going to have to rotate to theatre and work with you.'

'Now that's uncalled for,' Ashish says, feigning offence.

'If you must know, I was trying to be kind. She was upset because we lost a patient.'

'Wow. You must be consoling nurses every day then,' Ashish says.

'So very droll,' I reply. 'But who shot the video, that's what I'd like to know?'

Sonia looks up from where she's using suction to dry the field for Patrick. 'One of the other nurses?'

Ashish weighs in. 'Or one of the junior doctors? Or maybe a patient?'

I ponder who else was on the ward at that time but it's a hopeless task. It's a busy place. Quite apart from the doctors, patients and nurses, there are clerks, indexers going through notes, phlebotomists, physiotherapists, X-ray technicians. The list is endless. But why take a video of Katy talking to me?

'Suction, please,' Patrick drags everyone back into the room.

Sonia returns to the task in hand.

Ashish asks, 'Should we send for the next?'

The suction cannula gurgles and hisses as it vacuums the field. Patrick nods. 'Ten minutes to close, so yeah, I think so.'

The next case is a partial gastrectomy. A big case for a big tumour and this one not laparoscopic. Definitely one for me.

For the next two hours, I bury myself in the job, confine the video to the back of my brain where it festers. But Ashish's irreverent humour has diluted my anxieties enough to let me function. And we all know there's a job to do.

For now, it's time to forget about Katy Leith and get on with it.

17

Oaks ran the video for the umpteenth time. This time on his laptop so they could both watch it.

'It's difficult to say what's going on,' he commented. 'It would fit with what Thorn has told us. He could be consoling her.'

'Or, she could be asking him why he didn't turn up for their date the night before and that he promised to leave his partner and that she was fed up of waiting,' Ridley said.

Oaks turned his head slowly. His eyebrows were sceptical arches. 'Really?'

'Of course, really. Without audio, or Katy to ask, we'll never know, will we.'

'We can ask her when we find her,' Oaks said.

Ridley wanted to squeeze her eyes shut at that. Tell him not to be so bloody naïve. That Katy Leith was more than likely dead, if not in several pieces in plastic bags by now and that the chances of them ever asking her anything again were pretty minimal. But she didn't. Oaks, annoyingly upbeat though he was, didn't deserve any of Ridley's pragmatic despondency poured over him. He was still young, still not mired in cynicism and relatively unscathed by the depths to which their fellow humans could sink. It would come. Another few years of investigating disappearances and murders would bring that on. Like creeping lichen on a rock, or rust on a hinge. No, better she played the hand they now had. The cards in front of her. For his sake.

'You're enjoying this, aren't you?' Oaks turned back to the screen.

'I told you I thought he was cocky.' Ridley forced a smile. 'Come on, you know I'm right.'

'This could mean everything, and it could mean nothing. It doesn't actually help.'

Ridley kept smiling. 'But I did tell you that your Mr Thorn has things to hide.'

'Yes, you did. Your sixth sense. Just tell me when you start seeing dead people.' Oaks punched keys, and the video froze. 'What do you want to do with this? Should we take him to the station and caution him?'

'Why not? Let's get him out of his comfort zone.'

'You don't seem too enthusiastic.'

Ridley tilted her chin up in thought and then said, 'I firmly believe Mr Thorn does not know what's in store for him. Yes, let's have him in, but we'll keep the station's thumbscrews in the drawer for now. Facebook and Twitter are going to do that job for us.'

'You think so?'

Ridley nods. 'You're on both, aren't you?'

Oaks's turn to nod. 'And they're hotting up nicely.'

'Then you can do the monitoring. Meanwhile, let's give Mr Thorn a ride on the bumper cars, see how he stands up to a little jostling.'

18

The morning goes well though a dull anxiety beats behind my eyes. The operating theatre is a universe all of its own. A universe made up of a few square inches of blood and tissue that I navigate slowly and delicately. It's always a high-stakes journey that demands all of my concentration. There's music, and the odd joke, and banter between Ash and me, but it's all background noise to the main event of being inside someone else's body with very sharp instruments. I have no idea what's been going on in the outside world. But a lot has.

Oaks is waiting for me as I leave the changing room. He stands in the corridor, expectantly. His smile is not deferential, more apologetic. I like him.

'Mr Thorn. You've had a busy morning.'

'Always something to do, sergeant.'

Oaks nods. 'Inspector Ridley wonders if you can spare us an hour to come down to the station in Kidlington.'

'I'm supposed to be at a meeting,' I say.

Oaks tilts his head as if to say, "So what?"

'Why not here?' I ask when he doesn't capitulate.

'Not ideal,' he says.

I shrug. 'Do I cancel my afternoon clinic?'

Oaks shakes his head. 'You're not under arrest, sir. Just a few more questions. I can drive you there and bring you back by 2pm.' He waits and then adds, 'Hopefully.'

Kidlington station is a modern building built with lots of black steel and glass. For some reason, the bottom floor is an incongruous red brick while the upper floors are a stark white. I follow Oaks along corridors and into a lift. We emerge and walk through a door that says "Major Crimes". He puts me in an airy room, and someone gets me a cup of tea.

Ten minutes later, he comes back with Inspector Ridley.

'Nice,' I say looking around. 'But not a hundred miles from the seminar room in Post Grad. I still don't know why we couldn't talk there.'

'This is why.' Ridley opens a laptop on her desk. A screen on the wall lights up to mirror her computer. I watch as the usual icons appear and then disappear as an image comes into focus. A man, grinning, with two women either side of him. It's a close-up, faces only. The women are young, made-up and attractive, wearing festive Christmas earrings. One has a tinsel crown perched on her head. The woman on the right of the photograph is giving the man an exaggerated puckered-lips kiss on the cheek, under a sprig of held up mistletoe. On the left, the other woman is grinning, her cheeks resting against the man's.

I know all the people in the image. The woman on the right is a sister in theatre, on the left a scrub staff nurse – not Florry. The man in the middle is me.

When I look back at the two police officers, they're staring at me.

'What?' I say. 'It's the unit Christmas party. The girls were tipsy. I was not.'

Neither Oaks nor Ridley comment.

I sigh. 'Look, it's easier just to agree to whatever they suggest in these situations than be a Grinch. They wanted a photo with the boss. Don't tell me things like this don't happen at your Christmas bash.'

Oaks's mouth turns down at the corners and his eyebrows dip. It's a maybe. But Ridley gives nothing away and I suspect that no one has kissed her under the mistletoe in this station.

She presses another key on the laptop. Another image appears. I'm in it. And so is another female. This time on the ward. My hand is on her elbow. I don't know her name, but she's wearing a student's uniform and is smiling as she looks up into my face. I frown but Ridley doesn't respond. I can't remember the student's name, nor the circumstances. But then there's another image, and then another. Different situations, different female in each, same broad scenario. There's even a couple of me and Sonia at a post grad meeting, standing close together, munching vol-au-vents.

I'm in all the photographs and it doesn't take a genius to work out that there's a common theme. In every one of them, I am either talking to, close to, or touching a woman.

'What the hell is this?' I ask, more irked than I should be.

Oaks answers. 'This, Mr Thorn, is social media. Someone has posted these images.'

'Who?'

'Various sources. Someone asked on Twitter if you were a lech. This,' he waves a hand at the screen, 'is what happened.'

My flesh creeps. I sit back and shake my head. The room seems to move in and out of focus for a second. 'But these are just images of me at work,' I say. 'Day to day. Interacting with people.'

'You at work with lots of young women,' Ridley says.

'Yes,' I drag the word out over a couple of syllables. I feel a spurt of anger. Reach for it and hold it. It's the easy response, but it helps me focus. 'Like it or not, my work environment involves interacting with lots of women. For crying out loud, ninety per cent of nurses are women.'

'And you seem to enjoy their company,' Ridley says.

'I like my job, inspector. A big part of that job is working as and in a team. My approach is to make it as pleasant an experience as possible. For that, read politeness, respect, and openness.'

'Don't you enjoy the power thing even a tiny bit?' Ridley asks. 'Aren't some of these young girls in awe of the clever consultant?'

More bait. But I'm not hungry. 'I try very hard to bridge that gap. Whether it works or not, I wouldn't know.'

'Was Katy Leith in awe of you, Mr Thorn?' Ridley asks. The toxic masculinity trope flashes up in neon in my head. Has she been talking to Catterick?

'You'll have to ask her.'

'I would, if you tell us where she is.'

I look away and expel air before looking back. 'As I have already explained, I have no idea where Katy is.'

'Did you meet her after leaving the pub that night?' Oaks asks.

'No.'

'Did you drive her somewhere in your car?'

'No.'

'Is there anything you'd like to share with us?'

Doubt pops up in my mind. I should tell them about Ella but I don't. I want her kept out of this. She doesn't deserve to be tarnished by all this mud-slinging. Something tells me I might be making a big mistake, but as internal discussions go, this one is very short. I'm definite about what I'm going to do.

'No.'

'You're absolutely sure about that?'

'I am.'

Ridley gets up and closes the laptop.

'Do I need to contact my solicitor?' I ask.

Ridley shrugs. 'Not unless you've done something wrong.'

'I haven't,' I say.

'Then I wouldn't waste your money.'

'But you keep questioning me.'

Ridley nods. 'And Katy Leith is still missing. We may well be questioning you again. Someone will drive you back to the hospital. We appreciate your co-operation.' Ridley gives me a smile that could freeze metal.

19

It isn't Oaks who drives me back to the infirmary, but a detective constable named MacMillan. He doesn't talk much. That suits me fine.

The clinic goes well, but I keep finding myself thinking about all those images of me that someone's posted. Where are they all from? I don't remember seeing anyone with a camera, but then, of course, those days are long gone. Now, everyone has a camera and who can tell at first glance if someone is texting or taking a surreptitious photo?

I finish the clinic at just after five. Sonia and Patrick have gone and though I have a mound of paperwork, I decide instead to go home.

There's no rain in the forecast and so I bike back to Headington, enjoying the freedom cycling offers, dodging the traffic queues, choosing backstreets where I can. I get back to Sedgewood and let myself in but note that the kitchen light is on. To my surprise, Sarah's sitting at the table, laptop open, a glass of wine at her elbow.

'Hi,' I say. It emerges with a hint of perplexity and surprise. 'I wasn't expecting you back.'

She doesn't smile. 'I had to. I couldn't stand being in London. I had to come back and find out...' She lets the sentence peter out, loaded with words unsaid.

'Find out?' I realise I'm still wearing my helmet. I remove it and flatten my hair with my hand.

'Yes. Find out what the hell's going on.'

'Nothing,' I say. 'Nothing's going on.'

Sarah's expression is incredulous. 'Are you serious?'

'I spoke to the police again today. Apparently, there's been some stuff posted on social media–'

'Some *stuff*? Jesus, Jake. Wake up. It's not stuff, you're being monstered.'

It's not a term I'm familiar with. Maybe it shows in my face. She swivels the laptop around for me to see. I join her at the table. Sarah's on Twitter. She follows all sorts: social commentators, fashionistas, TV critics, food writers. But what she shows me is not from any of those. There's a photograph; a still taken from the video of Katy and me on the ward. The accompanying tweets say it all.

#findKaty
Ziter Mano @reaperzit67 10May2019
#isthishim Castrate the bastard. Make him eat his own testicles.

Lenne Stagg @lemsterstag99 10May2019
#isthishim He's a lech. Smug doctor. Guilty as hell.

Kylethejeremiah @Jezkyle555 10May2019
#isthishim Why haven't they arrested his ass? Is he a mason? In bed
with the cops.

I scan the vitriol contained in tens, or hundreds, or possibly even thousands of messages as they scroll in front of my eyes.

Sarah says, 'It's the same on Facebook and Instagram. All being retweeted and posted. Rage and bile.'

'This isn't right. They have no right.'

Sarah lets out a mirthless laugh. 'Oh, Jake. No one can do anything about this. It's freedom of speech.' She makes quotation marks in the air with her fingers. 'Anyone can say whatever the hell they like and it's mob rule. Welcome to Troll City.'

'But–'

'The world is screaming obscenities at you; can't you hear them?'

'The police won't take any notice.'

She throws up her hands and looks at the ceiling. 'The police? No, maybe they won't. But everyone else will. Why do you think social media is so empowering? Tweets are more visceral than talk. They're written down for all to see and reread. Hashtag me too has liberated thousands of women.'

I feel the anger building. Some if it stems from Sarah's belligerence, most of it is aimed at the world in general. 'What the hell has that got to do with me? I haven't done anything,' I repeat.

A pitying laugh wheezes out of Sarah's throat. 'Since when did that matter? It's out there. And your reputation is already Swiss cheese.'

'I don't care about my reputation.' That's not strictly true, but it isn't my primary concern here.

'You should because I do. You're a great doctor. And this... this is trashing all of that.' Sarah runs a hand through her hair. It's a little tic of frustration and anxiety I know well.

I also know she's right. That knowledge triggers another spurt of ire. 'You're saying all this as if it's my fault.'

Sarah picks up her glass and slurps a mouthful of wine. 'I hope to God it isn't.'

'What the hell's that supposed to mean?'

She keeps her eyes on the wine glass's contents, as if she's searching for answers in the liquid. 'It means that I know things have not been brilliant between us for a few months and–'

'And what?' I step away, air hissing from my throat in derision. 'Because we only sleep together at weekends, my unrequited lust has driven me to abduct a young girl? Really, Sarah?'

I notice the Chardonnay bottle on the countertop. It's half empty already.

'It's what people will say, isn't it?'

'Is it?' I try challenging her, but then remember the tweets she's shown me. 'Okay, they probably will. But it won't be true, will it?'

'No, but guess what? I'm the partner who... ' She doesn't finish.

'Who what? For crying out loud?'

'Who let all this happen.' Sarah squeezes her eyes shut and realisation crashes down on me. I suddenly know what this is. This is about us. The point at which we finally open up Pandora's box and let chaos bubble out. Suddenly I have no choice.

'Oh, I see,' I say. 'You think you're going to be blamed. Collateral damage, is that it? All right, let me make it easy for you. I have not abducted Katy. This has nothing to do with us. Though, you are right, things are not good between us. But we both know whose fault that is.'

'What's that supposed to mean?' Her eyes flash.

So here we are at last. We've arrived at the crash test dummy advert where the car smashes head on into a wall in slow motion, catapulting the occupant head first through the windscreen. Horrifying and fascinating at the same time – though horrifying trumps fascination by a big margin. No matter how much you prepare yourself, when you see it – the crushed and buckling metal, the mannequin convulsing against the forces – you can't help wondering, "How the fuck does anyone survive?"

My heart is banging on the back of my sternum when I finally breathe out the words.

'I know all about you and Simon.'

Sarah trills out a laugh. It sounds forced. Like it sometimes does when I trot out one of my unfunny jokes. 'Me and Simon?'

'Please, Sarah. Do us both the favour of not pretending. I know, okay?'

Her expression hardens. Denial morphs into first doubt, and then suspicion. Words form on her lips but then disappear without being spoken. It's remarkable to watch. If there's any remorse, it appears and then disappears like some awful subliminal image in a horror film. Finally, she finds her voice and manages just the one word.

'How?'

20

Seven weeks before – March 2019

It was the crab's fault.

I wondered, more than once, if it really was an accident. Once it had happened, that is.

In a way, I hoped so. Because if it wasn't, it would have been a very devious move.

But then, Sarah is a very devious person.

I remember it was a Wednesday because I was walking Sid back to Paws for Claws. Before Wednesdays were spent in Shotover Park. Before Ella.

Sarah and I had our usual after-work chat and I'd already hung up when I realised I'd forgotten to ask her if we needed any crab for the weekend. I'd fancied a zesty seafood linguine for Sunday and I needed to check if we had any in the freezer. Simple question.

From her train, she replied:

. . .

No, we need some. Get some halibut too, if they have any.

I whatsapped back a thumbs up. I used a fish market off the Botley Road; a little out of the way but worth it. When my phone buzzed five minutes later, and Sarah's name popped up, I wondered if she'd remembered something else for me to get. The message, as it turned out, was not about crab. But it turned out to be definitely fishy.

Can't wait to see you. Weekend has been endless. Lollipop?

I read it as Sid and I reached the point where we had to cross the road. Traffic buzzed past. When a gap appeared, I put the phone in my pocket and hurried across.

Once we were safely back on the pavement, I looked at the message again. An odd one for several reasons. Sarah was not a needy person. She rarely texted me to say she missed me. Besides, she'd been with me all weekend. We'd got up late on Saturday and pottered around, meandered into town and grabbed a bite to eat. Sunday was similarly unadventurous. She'd gone to the gym, I'd gone out on the bike. Later, I'd cooked, and we ate and zoned out in front of *Chernobyl*. Less entertainment perhaps than an uncomfortable must see. We'd had each other for company. Hardly scintillating admittedly, but endless?

And as for Lollipop... that was anyone's guess.

I took Sid back to the shelter and said my goodbyes. Then I took the phone out to reread the message. To my annoyance, it had disappeared. I checked my email and other message apps, but I could find no sign of it. Yet, I knew what I'd seen. Sarah must have deleted it. I sent her a quick message.

.   .   .

Got your text. Lollipop?

She came back immediately.

Sorry. Girlfriend sharing her sexts. Incorrigible. Sent to you by mistake. Have deleted ;/

I nodded. An easy mistake to make. We'd all misdirected texts. I had once sent an old boss a profane rant about a refereeing decision in the Euros. He understood. In fact, he agreed with me. But for some reason, the Lollipop message preyed on my mind.

What if it had been a mistake, but not in the way Sarah had so cleverly explained it away?

What if that sext had come from Sarah but was meant for someone else?

I didn't like that thought. I hated the ease with which I believed it possible. But then the circumstances of our partnership were ideal for an affair. Being way from home for two nights a week provided one hell of a temptation.

Not for me.

But maybe for Sarah.

I tried for days, if not weeks, to forget it. Getting angry with myself for the mistrust. And there was nothing palpable that I could put my finger on. Not a jot of difference in the way she behaved when she was at home. We slept together on the weekends. Hardly spontaneous, but we were pragmatists. We knew what we liked. And Sarah's recurrent cystitis had become an issue... That stopped my train of thought like a landslide on the tracks. Sarah had been prone to urinary tract problems for almost a year. I'd never questioned it. I thought she coped well with what could be a miserable condition. But now, when I came to think about it, she had complained a bit more of late. And that meant we'd abstain.

God, I hated those thoughts. But I couldn't stop them. They ate into me, like a wasp on a sweet apple. I knew the answer lay on her phone. Sarah's precious, not shared, password-protected phone. Her reasoning was the confidential nature of her work and that all kinds of security issues bound her, and she couldn't take the risk of anything happening accidentally. That meant changing her password every week. So even though I could physically access her phone a dozen times a day at home where it was left charging, I couldn't get into her apps. But the phone, eventually, is what gave me the idea of how I might find out how much Sarah was lying.

Apple Music. We shared the account because it was more economical to do so. I'd set it up on her phone when she'd first had it. And when I did, I also switched on location sharing. Ostensibly so that if she ever lost it, or had it stolen, we could use the locator app. I'd forgotten all about that nifty little tool. Until, one night about a month after that text, home alone and fretting about it all, I remembered.

That night, I scrolled to my settings and looked up the location of Sarah's phone. As simple as that. She'd sent me a text to say that she and Jess had popped out to the pub for a quick supper. I knew the place. I'd been there with the two of them more than once.

But the pub's address didn't match where Sarah's phone was located. The phone was somewhere else altogether. And, I had to assume, so was Sarah.

The pattern was repeated for several weeks. Occasionally, she'd stay at Jess's with the phone clearly located in Islington.

More often than not, the location was somewhere else. But when I rang her or texted, always she would pretend to be with Jess. It became obvious too that Jess was an accessory after the fact. She had no qualms about not telling me. But then, she was Sarah's BFF.

Not mine.

Two weeks after I remembered the locator app, I took the train up to London on a Wednesday evening in March after I'd walked Sid. I knew London a bit. Knew the small patch where I'd once lived reasonably well, but the posh west, where Sarah's phone so often ended up, remained unknown territory. I gave myself ample time. On the way, I turned off my shared location, just in case. That meant Sarah could not track me, but I could still track Sarah.

The tech equivalent of a marauder's map.

London was dark and cold and damp. I monitored her as she left work, travelled by tube in the opposite direction to where Jess lived, slowly, inexorably, towards where I sat in a Starbucks – for the wifi and the warmth – some three hundred yards from the Kensington address I'd seen on the app. Later, as Sarah neared, I waited outside the tube station in a doorway, hidden behind the commuter crowd rushing out into the winter night. The street was lit up. Sarah was easy to spot.

I didn't confront her, nor the man she emerged arm in arm with. I just wanted to see and have my worst fears confirmed.

Sarah and Simon. Nice alliteration. Sounded like a child's book. The kind that helps toddlers grow up and understand the world. But there was nothing childish about the way she laughed and squeezed his arm as they crossed Kensington High Street. I didn't need any help in understanding either as I watched them walk purposefully down Campden Grove. I was thirty yards behind when they entered a building together. I stood in the shadow of a skip for ten minutes, checked the phone one final time, and then walked back to the tube station and caught first the tube and then the train back to Oxford, sickeningly elated.

Sarah's phone didn't stray from the location in Kensington until 8am the following morning.

Since that time, I'd waited for her to come clean. Braced myself for the inevitable. For her to tell me at some opportune moment; from the train perhaps, or over the aubergine and cumin labneh at the restaurant we defaulted to on Friday nights.

Perhaps I should have said something. Was it cowardly of me not to? Did I wonder if she'd wake up next to Simon and come to her senses and rush back to me to confess and ask for forgiveness? Maybe. A little. To start with at least. A bigger part of me knew that something had gone out of our relationship. A spark. Whether in shock or denial, I couldn't bear weighing up the awful consequences. Instead, I buried my head in work so I didn't have to face them.

I played her little game. Waited. And it was difficult to start with. Luckily, Sarah's recurrent infection became chronic. That put the physical side of our relationship on hold. Made it a little easier to pretend. Though I couldn't help wondering if the infection abated once Sarah emerged from the tube station on Kensington High Street. Perhaps she took a super antibiotic miraculous cure on the 7.10 to Paddington every Wednesday?

Several times I teetered on the verge of challenging her. But I didn't. I was being pathetic, I knew. Fear of what it all meant to me, to us, made me cling to the hope that Sarah might drop some explanation into the conversation that would explain it all. Prove to me how much I'd overreacted.

But nothing happened. I wasn't sleeping well. I found it hard to concentrate at work. And then, on a walk with Sid one

Saturday morning, I met Ella. I knew her from ITU. Always found her a delight to work with. Shotover was her usual venue, she admitted. But that morning was fine and bright and so she'd brought her son, Ben, and Lulu the labradoodle to the Thames towpath. And all of a sudden, my little charade with Sarah became much easier. Not that I wanted to use Ella as any sort of ammunition. But her friendliness was something I couldn't resist; a balm for my conflicted state. And that friendliness blossomed into something else altogether. Normally, I would not have even considered it. But since Sarah and Simon had entered my sphere of knowledge, all bets were off.

I told Ella right from the outset.

She understood. She sympathised. She let me take her out for a drink. To talk. Eventually, after several talks, to bed.

So I bided my time with Sarah. Waited for her to tell me. Wondering every night what it was she was waiting for. What kind of opportunity might present itself as the perceived "right" moment? Perverse? Yes. But emotion is a funny thing. In a way, by not confronting her, it felt that I might prolong her discomfort. Of having to come home and pretend.

What an idiot I was.

21

Sarah finally puts down her glass on the kitchen worktop. It clatters. Not much, but enough for her to have to steady it. Enough to tell me she's lost a little of her iron control. But it's me who speaks. 'What does it matter? You've been lying to me and shacking up with Simon for what, two months or more?'

Sarah flushes darkly. She keeps blinking as if she can't believe what I'm saying. What she's hearing. I half expect her to tap her ears to clear it of murky water. But when she finally answers, it's not to explain. Instead, in typical Sarah fashion, she returns my accusatory ace with a volley of her own. 'Have you been spying on me?'

I laugh out the next word. 'Whoa, wait a minute. You don't have the right to be the aggrieved party here. You're the one that's been playing away.'

It takes a minute for Sarah to realise that, though it is her default response to any criticism, going on the attack might not be the right thing to do now that the box is open and we can both see what's squirming inside. Her hand goes to her throat. Another tic. God, I know her so well. She does that when we watch something tense on TV or in the cinema. Protection against a threat. 'How long have you known?'

'A few weeks.'

She frowns. 'And you said nothing?'

'No. And before you ask, I don't know why. Maybe I was hoping you'd do the decent thing and say something.'

Sarah squeezes her eyes shut. 'I was... I am... confused by it all.'

'I don't see what's confusing. It looks to me like you've made your choice.'

'I know, but... I haven't.'

I blink. My surprise is genuine. 'So what? You thought you'd try a bit of both of us? Sweet and sour? Chocolate and cheese? Come on, admit it. All this talk about a cottage in DOT is just bullshit, isn't it?'

'No, I...' She drops her head.

'How long were you going to play this game, Sarah? Until we got the new property? Until I'd ploughed in a bit more money?'

Her head snaps up. 'It's not like that.'

'Isn't it? So tell me what it is like, because I really would like to know.'

Sarah says nothing.

'And now this lands in your lap,' I nod at the laptop. 'Me being publicly hung in a gibbet for something I didn't do. Still, it'll make the decision easier, won't it? I mean, who the hell in their right minds would want to get tarred with this muck, right?'

'Is that what you think of me?' Sarah looks genuinely hurt.

My turn to glare in disbelief. 'You've been sleeping with another bloke for weeks and not told me anything. What am I supposed to think?'

'Jake, I'll stay. If you want me to, I'll stay.'

'And what? We play happy families? Go to bed together and

cuddle up and pretend Simon Harding and his little love nest in Kensington doesn't exist?'

'I know you're upset–'

'You're damned right I'm upset.'

She says nothing in return, but her face registers a whole range of emotions. I see shock there and genuine pain. But mostly, it's still anger. That she's been caught out, I wonder?

'Perhaps it's best that I don't stay.'

'Perhaps it is.' I look at my watch. 'You can get a train back to London within the hour.'

We stand and stare at each other. It's Sarah who looks away first because she's on the verge of tears. Which is very not Sarah. The doorbell breaks the impasse. I answer it. I don't know the woman who stands there in jeans and a puffer jacket. Nor the man standing next to her in a peacoat holding a camera. A big one.

'Mr Thorn, are the rumours about your involvement with Katy Leith true?'

'Pardon?' I say.

I look at the man and then at the camera. For a moment I'm totally lost, but there's a red light blinking on the camera body. It's the signal for me to wake up.

'Do you know where she is, Mr Thorn?' Another question. Oh Christ. No introduction. Straight for the jugular. Ms puffer jacket is a journalistic assassin.

I have the wherewithal to turn away and slam the door shut. Behind me, Sarah is in the hall, her hand to her mouth.

'Pack a bag and go,' I say but with no venom. It's way too late for that. 'Leave by the back door through the garden so no one will see you. Go on. Do it now. You don't want any of this crap.'

She walks towards me and hugs me. Again, not Sarah's style. At least not the unfussy businesswoman I know as Sarah. 'I'm sorry,' she whispers.

I feel her tears on my neck. This truly is a night for revelations. But my hands stay paralysed at my side. Sarah goes upstairs while I move about the house, closing blinds and drawing curtains. The bottle of wine is still half full. I pour myself a glass and wait while Sarah pads about upstairs.

She comes down twenty minutes later in jeans and a coat. She has a much bigger bag with her than normal.

'I know you won't believe me, but I really hate to leave you like this.' She's on the verge of tears again, but I don't feel like making this all right for her.

'What is there to say?'

'I know you. I know how stubborn you are. I'm sorry this has happened now.'

'So am I.'

I turn away, but Sarah hasn't finished.

'But I'm scared for you because I'm not sure you're aware of how serious this is. How much it can affect people's lives and careers to be trashed on social media.'

'So my private practice is buggered. I'll survive.'

'Will you?' She stands there in her coat.

'Are you forgetting something? I. Haven't. Done. Anything.'

Sarah shakes her head. 'Oh, Jake. Sometimes that's an inconvenient little truth when it comes to being pilloried.'

'It's still the truth.'

Sarah nods. But her thin mouth and pained expression tell me she's unconvinced. 'You know where I am.'

I snort. 'Indeed I do.'

'I didn't mean that.'

'I've got your number.'

'Be careful, Jake.' With that, Sarah turns and leaves by the back door.

. . .

I finish the bottle of wine in half an hour and open another one and drink two-thirds of it, wondering how it's all come to this. How all our plans are now so much smoke blowing away in the wind. Wondering why I don't care quite as much as I should.

The doorbell rings twice more, but I don't answer it. I talk through the door instead. The first time it's the woman journalist again. Same questions. The second time someone claims to have a delivery for me from Amazon. I know I've ordered nothing from the Zon, so I ignore that too. Instead, I tell them, impolitely, with words that mainly comprise four letters, to go away.

Later, with Sarah long gone, I make the mistake of powering up the desktop and scouring the newsfeeds. She's right; it is uncomfortable reading. Apart from the obvious, several news blogs have taken up the cudgel. Monsterfeed weighs in with:

Surgeon remains person of interest in Katy Leith abduction.

'All he ever thinks about is cutting people open,' says hospital source. 'He's very focused.'

Then there's the Hugetown Post:

Police confirm questioning a hospital consultant over missing nurse after video shows them arguing.

There are photos of me. I have no idea where they've got them from. All of them show me in either sombre or almost manic attitudes. The juxtaposition is not accidental, I suspect.

All of what I read is true. But the phrasing and context does the clickbaiting damage. I succumb for almost an hour but then force myself to shut it down and go to bed.

Some time after midnight, I get up and walk to Sarah's bedroom. Seeing the bed empty gives me a sudden pang of regret, but it is fleeting. I walk to the window and peek through a chink in the curtains. The puffer jacket woman and cameraman have finally gone, though they were there an hour ago, when I last looked. I toy with the idea of firing up the desktop and looking again at what is being said about my involvement, but I know that if I do, I can say goodbye to any chance of sleep.

I go back to bed, set my alarm for 5am and lie down. Thoughts explode in my head like fireworks: the police, Sarah, Ella, those poisonous tweets and inflammatory posts.

Finally, at around one thirty, I drift off.

22

Slicer sindicate456 @SSdicate456 10May2019
Just one look at the smarmy bastard #JThorn tells you he's guilty.
#isthishim String him up by the balls. #findkaty

Edward Dandelion @edandelion 10May2019
Privileged WM of the first water #isthishim Looks like a schemer. Do
not touch with a BARGE POLE #findkaty

Too many metoo @Metwootwenty55 10May2019
#isthishim Where was he the night Katy went missing? #JThorn Must
be a person of interest #findkaty

23

I'm awake again before five with no need for the alarm. I slide out of bed, shower and dress and, illuminated only by a nightlight, let myself out and cycle to the hospital.

Mercifully, there is no press presence outside at this hour. Unless they're hiding in a parked car. But no one follows me.

Traffic is light and I make it to the hospital in half an hour. I lock the bike and pick up a coffee from a machine in the Welcome Centre and head for my office. All the paperwork from the day before is waiting. I get stuck in: look at reports, dictate letters, answer emails and try not to think about Sarah or the Net. That way I lose myself for a couple of hours.

By the time my secretary, Meera, arrives at eight thirty, I've broken the back of it and even begun to look through the "file and forget" pile on the top shelf – some of which has been pending for over a year.

When she sees the result of my labour spread out on the desk, Meera can't hide her surprise. 'What's brought all this on?' she asks, shrugging off her coat. 'Have you been diagnosed with a terminal illness and made a bucket list?'

I don't know how I attract these irreverent people into my

life. Some say it's a skill. Others that you reap what you sow. Meera is mid-thirties, married to a software developer called Sashin and has two children who are frighteningly bright. She's astonishingly capable, has wicked brown eyes, and quite often seems to know what I'm thinking before I can trot out the words. I think back to my meeting with the suits about auto dictation and downgrading the secretaries' roles. They don't have a clue.

'Couldn't sleep,' I say.

Meera frowns. 'You're not letting Twitter get to you, are you?'

I smile. Several times during the long morning, I've wondered if I should broach the subject of my social media woes with Meera. I was kidding myself if I thought she wouldn't know.

'Trying not to. Oh, and you should probably be the first to know that Sarah and I have split up.'

Meera doesn't bat a thick eyelash but her face adopts a rictus grimace. 'Oh no,' she sings. 'What a time for that to happen. Want some tea? I'm having one.'

'Love one.'

I smile. Meera doesn't want details. She isn't the type. But neither is she an ice-queen.

When she comes back with steaming mugs, she sits at her desk and asks, 'You and Sarah, is it because of the Katy Leith thing?'

'No. Nothing to do with it.' The tea is hot and sweet.

'These Internet trolls are bad enough, but it's worse that there are even more awful people out there who believe what the sods say. Sash thinks they should pass an Internet defamation law.'

I nod and hear my stomach rumble. I'm not a big breakfast fan. I'd rather not give my body a bowlful of sugar and carbs first thing in the morning, so I generally wait until lunchtime. But today I'm hungry because, I realise, I didn't eat anything the evening before.

'I'm going to get a bite before clinic,' I say.

She nods. I'm halfway to the door when someone knocks. I open it to find Kierney and Bilton standing there. Kierney is wearing a tie. I wonder if this is the admin equivalent of a judge's black cap. Bilton, slightly behind him, wears a thin-lipped smile. I want to believe it isn't a smirk.

Kierney is all business. 'Mr Thorn. Glad we caught you before you start your day. Can we have a word?'

I note the officiousness of the title. 'By all means. Come in.'

'It would be better if you came to the admin block.'

'No, this will do,' I say.

Bilton looks like she might object, but Kierney says, 'Fine, this will indeed do.' He turns to Meera. 'Could you give us a moment, umm...' He leans forward and stares at her ID. 'Mrs Gupta.'

'Meera stays,' I say. 'She's my right-hand person.'

'I think it would be better if–'

'She stays.'

'As you wish.'

We find two more chairs and we sit in the small room. Meera is uncomfortable. I can sense that, but something, some inner instinct, tells me it's better that I'm not alone with these two. In case I do something rash.

Kierney smiles. It's the kind of smile you practice for when you tell someone bad news, or when you sense something bleeding in the water. 'Jake, the switchboard has taken lots of calls last night and this morning.'

'About?'

'About you, mainly. One or two cranks, but mostly from patients who are worried about being under your care.'

I wait and say nothing. Silence is an art.

Bilton steps into the breech. 'They feel uncomfortable at the thought of having you operate on them.'

'Why? In case I abduct them?' I say.

'That's in very bad taste,' Bilton says.

'So is suggesting that I would harm a patient.'

'We're not suggesting anything. It's the patients who are.'

'And I hope you are disabusing them of those thoughts and ideas.'

Kierney sighs. 'If only it were that easy. I've had a word with the medical director and the Chairman of the Trust. The fact is that at least half a dozen people have cancelled their admissions for next week on your list.'

'Then bump someone up.'

'We suspect that things are only going to get worse,' Bilton says. 'Our media officer is having to field calls from the established press and TV. There's a Sky News van outside the front entrance, and they're probably going to do a piece from there today. Patient relations say that already our ratings have fallen.'

'Ratings? Since when were we on Trip Advisor?'

'You know how this works, Jake,' Kierney says.

Familiarity now. The cliché is right. It does breed contempt.

'No, I don't. Is this a hospital or a hotel?'

'We are always trying to improve the patients' experience,' Bilton says. It sounds trite. I hold back from saying so.

'I am all for that,' I say. 'But keeping them alive is usually first on my list.'

'And delaying their surgery will not help that, will it?' Kierney says.

He has a point. I turn to Meera. 'What do we have coming in next week?'

Her fingers click on the keys of her desktop. Kearney shakes his head. 'That won't be necessary.'

'There's at least one cancer patient I can think of,' I say.

Kearney shakes his head again. Slower, bigger movements. 'The decision has been made. We're cancelling your lists. Your colleague, Mr Eastman, will vet the admissions and make sure that urgent patients are treated appropriately.'

Rob Eastman is a good surgeon. But he's going to welcome this extra workload like a hole in the head.

'I ought to speak to him.'

'By all means. But as of now, we suggest you have no more clinical contact with patients until further notice.'

I laugh. It sounds like a rattle in my throat. 'Are you suspending me?'

'We're offering you extended leave on full pay. I suggest you take it until this situation resolves itself.'

'And when will that be?'

Kierney shrugs. 'When we find Katy Leith.'

'This is insane,' I say.

He doesn't argue. 'Perhaps. God knows we can hardly afford to have a surgeon on gardening leave. But having you here and seeing patients will, I suspect, be counterproductive for you and all of your team.'

Meera looks horrified. I can see it in her eyes; the realisation that I might not be best placed emotionally to receive this extra blow to my psyche. But she's wrong. The pain of Sarah's betrayal was freshest in the weeks after I saw her and S.H. (I mentally add the i and the t) walking in to his flat in Kensington. Since then, that pain has turned into something else. Something hard and cold.

'What if I say no?'

Kierney shrugs. 'You've done nothing wrong. There are no grounds for disciplinary action. But we think it would be best for the hospital, you and your patients.'

I can see he's right, but it's a bitter pill. I could stamp my feet. I could refuse. But Kierney is appealing to one of the basic tenets of being a doctor. First, do no harm. And it sounds like me being at work could, indirectly, do exactly the opposite.

'Obviously, we'd be happy for you to continue with any admin you have to do. But we suggest you do that from home. Keep a low profile.'

I look from Kierney to Bilton. I'm searching for a smirk. I'm disappointed not to find one.

'Okay,' I say. 'But some work I'll have to do here. In the office.'

Meera looks surprised at my capitulation. So, if truth be told, am I.

Kierney stands up. 'Thanks, Jake. I appreciate your help. This will all blow over, I'm sure.' He offers a hand. I shake it. Bilton is already out of the door. Job done.

When they're gone, I sit back down and look at Meera. She's dabbing her eyes.

'Bastards,' she says.

'No, for once they're right. If me being here prevents even one patient from getting treated, that would not be something I could live with.'

Meera sniffs and dabs some more. 'Can I get you something? You said you were hungry.'

I shake my head. 'Funny thing, that. I've completely lost my appetite.'

24

I don't go home. Instead, I head for Paws for Claws.

It's run by a couple, Bonnie and Mick Renton. Mick is a gangly Canadian whose joints are slowly crumbling and who seems a little more stooped every time I see him. Bonnie is a feisty no-nonsense ex-hippy who divides people up into those she thinks she can trust with her dogs and those she can't. It's a red line. Any potential owner with whom she fosters or rehouses a dog gets two home visits from her and an interview the CIA would be proud of.

I drop into reception. Two teenagers in PFC logo'd polo shirts greet me with wide smiles and I'm directed to the kennels. Bonnie, in wellies and a muddy waxed jacket, is unloading a van full of blankets and dog beds. It's drizzling and her hair is a mound of grey spaghetti under her hood.

'Hi,' I call out. 'Need a hand?'

'Always,' she says but does not stop unloading. She has a clipped accent. I can imagine her reading Radio 4 news.

'Laundry run?'

'Exactly.' Bonnie hands me a bundle of blankets and I carry them through to a revamped steel container that may have once transported motorcycles from Japan, or salt from Timbuktu, on a ship as big as four football fields.

'So you've come to say you finally want to adopt Sid?' Bonnie puts her hands on her hips. Her face is ruddy from the outdoor life she leads; the radiating lines around her eyes are more pelican than crow's feet.

I smile and drop my head. This is a question Bonnie asks me at least once a month. 'No. But I will take him out, if it's okay?'

'It's always okay, you know that.'

'Even unscheduled?'

'They're the best times. Sid loves surprises.'

I toy with asking her how she knows. But Bonnie is a dog person. That would be rude. She turns back, pulls out a bundle of towels, and hands them to me.

'But you're not here to ask my permission to take Sid out, are you?'

'No,' I say over the top of the towels. They smell of something floral.

'Please don't tell me you're giving up on him.' Anger sparks behind those piercing blue eyes.

'No,' I shake my head. 'I wanted to warn you. I wanted to explain about–'

'All that gibberish on social media?'

'You've seen it?'

'The average age of volunteers here is nineteen, in case you hadn't noticed. They've been quite animated to read your name and see your photograph splashed everywhere. They even showed me. They won't do that again.'

'Then you don't mind?'

'Did you abduct that poor girl?'

'No.'

'Then there's nothing to discuss, is there. You'll not hear a word about it from my staff. I may sound reactionary, but before the days of online, we used to live in a country that believed in a presumption of innocence. Now we have a mob mentality where anyone can have their lives put through the ringer by the furious ignorant who like nothing more than to see someone suffer.' She pulls out a huge folded dog bed that wants to spring open. I take it from her.

'Thanks,' I say.

'Take Sid out,' Bonnie says, blowing a stray strand of hair away with a corner-of-the-mouth hiss. 'Make that dog's day.'

I do just that. He's overjoyed to see me. The feeling is mutual. We walk for a couple of hours, try a different direction to a patch of waste ground that he loves, but which, after finding some abandoned syringes, I decide would be best avoided as future destinations. When I get back, I get an even wider smile from the receptionists. At least I know Bonnie is on my side.

I cycle back to Headington. It's almost lunchtime by the time I arrive. I reverse engineer Sarah's exit route and creep in by the rear. The garden gate is actually a door in a narrow lane and, so far, the press have not found it. But they know where the front door is.

I sneak in, not making a lot of noise. The curtains are still drawn. Upstairs, I sneak a look through the spare room's window and recognise a black Ford Galaxy parked about fifty yards away. So the press are here, but don't know that I am. Yet.

Back downstairs, I smash some avocado on to a slice of toast and make some tea. It's as I'm rinsing my plate in the sink that I hear my phone buzz.

The WhatsApp logo appears, and a message follows. Sarah's photo is in the message's left window and two letters: SB. Sarah Barstow. But it's not a photo I've seen before. I wonder if she's changed it. The message reads:

. . .

SB – PHOTO FOR YOU.

An image appears on the screen. At first, I don't know what it is. But then, as I stare, my insides swoop. The lighting in the photograph isn't great, but good enough to show what's going on. Good enough to make my scalp crawl. A room with dull plastic sheeting hanging wall to ceiling behind a person sitting – no, strapped – to a chair. The floor is concrete. The subject is a woman. Young, silver tape over her eyes and her mouth, smudges on her cheeks from where she's been crying. Someone wearing surgical gloves is holding a knife to her throat. From the angle, it looks like it's the same person who's taking the photo. The woman is wearing a dress. The same dress she wore the last time I saw her in the Duke of Wellington pub. Katy Leith's dress.

The phone beeps again. Another message.

SB – You've realised that this is not Sarah Barstow's WhatsApp account. Be aware all messages will disappear ten seconds after you read them.

I go back to the image, but it has gone. So has the first message. The phone buzzes again.

SB – Three things you need to know.
      The knife I'm holding to her throat is yours. It's from your

garden shed. It has your DNA all over it. You left it on the path. Very handy. If you discuss this with anyone, especially the police, Katy will die. If you attempt to take a screenshot, I will know and Katy will die.

Another beep.

SB – Do not reply to these messages. This is the one and only time I will contact you on this phone. Cycle the Old Road, right on Blenheim. Find an abandoned van in the woods after 400 yards. There will be a phone under the seat. Check it. Enjoy the publicity. Know how it feels to have your life ruined. Do exactly what I tell you to or Katy Leith will die.

I scan this last message, desperately trying to grasp it all. I grab a pen and some paper and write "Blenheim" and "400 yards" on a scrap of paper. By the time I go back to the app, all the messages have gone. I sit down, trying to assimilate what's just happened. I check the phone, but though the new number is in my call log, there are no messages.

Is this a hoax? Is this some stupid trick being played by some sicko?

I recall the look of terror on Katy's face. Obvious despite the tape. This is no joke. She is still alive, but I'm the only other person on the planet that knows it.

Why? What reason would anyone have for implicating me in all of this?

The obvious thing to do is phone Oaks. Tell him what has happened. But then, what proof do I have? Can they do something to my phone to find the messages?

But if I do that, SB, or whoever it really is, says Katy will die, her throat slit by my knife...

My knife.

I rush outside and into the garden after retrieving a key from behind the back door. I fumble the key in the padlock securing the shed door and drop it. Fumble again and unlock the shed, smell oil and earth and paint, and find my toolbox. I throw out a mish-mash of tools, saws, screwdrivers... this is where it would be. Handy for sharpening stakes and cutting the odd piece of string. Sharp enough for a throat.

I squeeze the thought from my mind and look again for the knife. I haven't used the damned thing in months. But this is where it would have been.

It isn't.

I go back inside and stare at what else I've written on the paper. *Old Road, Blenheim Road, abandoned van.*

There's only one thing I can do. I grab my cycle helmet and, once more, sneak out of the back door.

25

My bike is a hybrid designed for comfortable city commuting but with features that allow it to go off road without falling apart. It has flat handlebars and fenders to keep off the worst of the rain on slick tarmac, but wide tyres for barrelling over tracks and eighteen gears to help with the work. I know some of my fellow cyclists like to punish themselves with single-speed workhorses, but I prefer to run or swim for my aerobic fix, not turn up to work dripping with sweat. But I'm not averse to taking the bike out for a fun spin on a dry day. As a result, I know the roads out of Headington pretty well.

I take back lanes to avoid the oglers but end up on the one road over the bypass that ends in the car park that Ella and I, for want of a better word, use. The "road" continues out of the back end of the car park as a dirt track. It's quiet this morning. Blenheim Road, off Old Road, leads to the village of Horsepath. Though we're only three or so miles from the centre of Oxford, there are no houses along this stretch of country lane.

Just before the outskirts of the village, the old barn appears through the trees on my right. The curved sides of galvanised tin still have a bit of grey colour, but the roof has rusted to a flaky brown. Behind and slightly to the right is the metallic hulk of an old van. There are no tyres on the wheels and most of the blue paint that gave it its colour has flaked away in the rain and wind. There's no glass in the windows and the engine block has long since gone. I get off the bike and push it towards the van along a faint path through the trees that flanks the lane.

Hard to believe that there's a phone of any description in this decrepit vehicle. But I squat down on the driver's side (there is no door) and look under the seat. Scraps of foam and plastic material still cling to the metal frame, but underneath sits a new black plastic pouch. I pull it out. Inside is a phone. It's not a make I'm familiar with, but when I touch the screen, it comes to life, revealing a WhatsApp message. This one does not have Sarah's photograph, nor her initials.

This is the phone I will use from now on. Do not reply to these messages. Do not take photographs of them. Put the phone back under the seat in the pouch and leave it. Come back and read your messages at 6pm every day.

There are only four other apps on the screen. A moment later, the message disappears. When I reopen the messenger app, it's empty.

The phone buzzes. There is no audible signal, but a new message appears.

I need proof that you will co-operate. I want you to go to the nearest ATM, remove 200 pounds, and put it with the phone back under the seat.

. . .

I wait for the next message. I have a feeling there will be one.

Why? Because I want to see you suffer and pay for the privilege :))

£200 is not a great deal of money. But it's clear that the caller wants to test me. I want to text back, but when I try, the keyboard doesn't work.

Instead, another message buzzes through:

Get the money. Leave it with the phone. Tell no one. If you do, someone will get hurt. Perhaps Katy, perhaps your wife, or perhaps your girlfriend. Come back tomorrow PM.

I wait, but no more messages appear. Fifteen seconds later, the thread vanishes once more.

I push the bike back out onto the lane. The nearest ATM is in the Co-op at Wood Farm a mile or two away. I head down through Horsepath and back across the bypass.

Twenty minutes later, I'm back at the derelict van, putting money in the plastic pouch. When I've done that, I get back on the bike and head the way I originally came. I still have no idea what any of this is about. But someone has taken the trouble of stealing my knife from the garden. At least, I think that's what's happened. That same someone has taken the trouble of getting my number so they can message me and set up this clandestine arrangement.

And that same someone, I'm certain, has Katy Leith.

I should ring the police. But it's not Oaks's number I dial. It's someone else's.

26

There are four cars in the car park at Shotover. One is a two-tone Renault Captur with a Batmobile sticker on the back bumper. I pull up behind, get off the bike, and remove my helmet. It's a grey late May afternoon by now. Lulu recognises me through a side window and this puts her tail into wag maximum. Ella is in the driving seat. She leans over to open the passenger side door and I slide in.

She sits, half turned towards me, those blue-grey eyes as startling as ever.

'Thanks for coming', I say, but get no further as I'm pulled into a tight embrace. Her hair is soft and clean and she smells of sandalwood.

'Poor you,' she whispers.

Sympathy. Ella, warm and tactile, has it in spades. Not like Sarah.

So not like Sarah.

We pull back and I look into Ella's big moist eyes.

'Hey,' I say. 'I'm a big boy. Don't worry about me.'

'But I do, Jake. I've seen what they've been saying about you. It's horrible.'

'Not easy reading, is it?'

'Disgusting.' Ella makes a face. Even then she's a ten.

I nod. 'I didn't ask you here to cry on your shoulder, Ella.'

'It's here if you want to.'

I put my hand on her shoulder. She bends her head so that her cheek touches my fingers and raises her own hand up to grasp mine. I wish the circumstances were different, that we were here for recreational purposes, but that isn't why I've asked her to meet me. Too much has happened for me to ignore involving Ella. I owe it to her. I only hope she'll understand.

'Two things,' I say. 'First of all, I confronted Sarah about Simon.'

Ella sucks in a sharp breath and her head snaps up.

'Took her by surprise but after the initial anger – that I'd dared to find her out – she didn't deny it.'

'How could she?' Ella asks.

I nod. 'She's gone back up to London.'

'To him?'

'Probably.'

Ella blinks those amazing eyes. She knows all about Sarah's affair. She knows all about the separate rooms. And about the manufactured illness to avoid intimacy. Ella's been patient. More than I had any right to expect. But now, despite my troubles, I see a sparkle in her eyes.

'What did she say?' she asks.

'What could she say? We talked for a while. She wanted to know how I found out. She thought I'd forgotten all about that misdirected text she'd sent.'

Ella shakes her head. 'I can't say I'm not glad. You couldn't go on the way things were. But to leave you now, with all of this going on...'

I shrug. 'She's better off out of it.'

'What about you?'

'I'm officially on gardening leave. Patients have been cancelling admissions. No one wants to see me, and management thinks I'm staining the hospital's unimpeachable character.'

'That's terrible.'

I don't deny it. I want to tell her about the messages. About the phone in the van, but I daren't. The threats are too fresh in my mind. I would never forgive myself if anything happened to her because of me.

Tell no one. If you do, someone will get hurt. Perhaps Katy, perhaps your wife, or perhaps your girlfriend. Come back tomorrow PM.

I try a brave smile.

Ella adds, 'I went for coffee with some girlfriends this morning and I spoke to Fiona Ormerod. Her husband is a sergeant in Thames Valley Serious Crimes. No one really knows what's going on, but he says they've had a tip-off that Katy's disappearance may have something to do with a trafficking gang.'

Now it's my turn to blink. 'Trafficking?'

'There's been a gang operating in Slough for some time. Shipping girls in from Romania, apparently.'

I stare at her, not knowing what to say. Slough of all places.

'But sometimes, so Fee says, they'll abduct a girl to order. A British girl. There's market for all of this on the dark web, so she says.'

I don't speak. I can't take in what Ella is saying. It's monstrous, but how does that all tie in with the messages on the phone in the burned-out van? She reads my silence as astonishment.

'I know. Sickening. Hard to believe something like that could happen here in Oxford, isn't it?'

'It's...' I don't know what to say.

'Try despicable, but if it's true then the police can't tie you to any of it, can they?'

'No, but then I haven't been completely truthful, have I. That's the other thing I wanted to speak to you about. I want to tell Oaks and Ridley that we met the night of Sister Morris's party. I want them to know you're my alibi. It's silly of me not to have told them before, but I didn't want to... I don't know, embroil you in it.'

'It's the truth, isn't it?' Ella smiles. It's a wonderful smile.

'So you're okay with me telling them we were here?'

She nods. 'Embroil away.'

This time I'm the one who pulls her close. I don't even remember why I was being so cagey before with the police. Healthy scepticism? To keep Ella off their radar? Or was I worried about Sarah finding out? Whatever the truth of it, it's a messy and dangerous game to play.

'I'd ask you back to mine, but I think someone will be watching,' I say.

'Who?'

'Reporters. I'm their top sleazy story.'

'I don't care about them,' Ella says fiercely. It makes something swell in my chest.

I nod. 'But I would never forgive myself if you got dragged in to this. I'll make Oaks promise to keep you out of it, though I expect they'll want to talk to you.'

Ella shrugs. I kiss her again. It's thrilling. Good and exciting. Two things that have been missing in my life for too long.

I leave Ella in her car and cycle back to Sedgewood. This time, someone spots me, but I ignore the shouts and the camera and head in through the front door with a great deal more bravado than I feel. I will ring Oaks, but first, I make some tea and fire up the laptop. I type "human trafficking in the UK" into Google and get sixty-seven million hits. I try to narrow it down.

"Human Trafficking to order."

From there I find newspaper reports of narrow escapes by women, usually walking home alone after a night out. Tragically more than one. Most involve gangs of men and cars or vans. I quickly realise that I'm reading only about those women who got away. Nothing about those who, by the law of statistics, did not.

I sip my tea and read on. The blogs and articles make for difficult, repugnant, reading. The last time I looked, slavery'd been abolished, and yet what I learn is that it still exists. Young girls recruited with false promises of jobs or glamour shoots, only to find a very different, sordid, reality. Most trafficking involves the underprivileged, those seeking a way out of their impoverished circumstances, or trapped by addiction. But some get entrapped by sheer naivety.

It's a xenophobic cliché, but Eastern Europeans seem to have a predilection for this type of crime. Gangs arrange for transport so that women can be exploited. And the crimes seem to be concentrated in the big urban centres; London, Manchester, and, incredibly, Thames Valley.

And then there are UK residents who go missing. The majority are female and under eighteen. Some are found, sometimes years later when they tried to reconcile whatever they ran from in the first place. But others are never found. No one knows how many end up being sold on to satisfy some maniacs' cravings.

I wish it was an urban legend. It clearly is not.

I peruse what's available for hours. The tea turns into a glass of wine, then another. I know how dangerous surfing can be. Even when I'm not researching something definite, it's easy to let the compulsive desire to seek the unpredictable distract. A

Pavlovian response. Who knows what gems might lurk under the next click of the mouse? I know the theory; that almost eighty per cent of people get a physiological response when they open their emails or click a link. We're hard-wired to expect surprises and the tiny micro spurts of triggered adrenaline makes the doing addictive.

Hours go by and my eyes feel scratchy. At around nine thirty, I stop. I'm hungry so I scramble some eggs and throw in some smoked salmon. While I eat, I sift through what I do know. What I've learned is that trafficking is real. Abductions are real. Being sold as a sex slave is real.

Those are facts.

But what's missing is any clue as to what any of it has to do with me.

By ten thirty, I've drunk too much wine to ring Oaks. That little nugget of delayed gratification must wait until the morning.

27

Comme de slaphead @libbyrational 11May2019
#JThorn Questioned by cops and released #findkaty What's he
hiding? If he wasn't screwing Katy he wanted to. Hate pervert
doctors. #isthishim

Rupe the Exterminator @extmntralpha 11May2019
Surgeons are all psychos #JThorn he must enjoy cutting people open
and getting his hands bloody. Doesn't anyone vet for psychos in
training? #isthishim He's probably got #findkaty in plastic bags in the
freezer.

Denise Lockhart @Denisethenurse 11May2019
Just heard that #JThorn has been let off work. Leave they're calling it
#findkaty Patients are complaining #isthishim

Slicer sindicate456 @SSdicate456 11May2019
What we need is an address for #JThorn Someone ought to pay the
shit a visit #isthishim Volunteers?

28

On Saturday, I get up early, shower and change and once more escape the cottage via the rear gate on the bike. It's spitting rain when I leave before dawn. I find a café open early and grab a coffee and, because I'm ravenous, some porridge. I usually pick Sid up at around eight thirty. At eight, I ring the number on Oaks's card. He answers after three rings.

'Any chance we could have a chat, today?' I ask.

'Sure. This morning?'

'It'll have to be late. Say eleven thirty?'

He agrees. He suggests the station; I suggest the café; an independent called Mariachi out on the Iffley Road. It's also next to a pub, just in case either of us feels thirsty.

Saturday walks with Sid are longer. We have a good couple of hours, so we head for the Thames pathway and go south. This is where I met Ella. Serendipity.

It's a different kind of walk, mainly on the lead. Lots of dogs, lots of smells, great for socialising thirty-five kilos of muscle and inquisitive fun.

Walkers and dogs come in all shapes and sizes. Because we're on a public path, the lead is a must. Not because Sid would do anything untoward, but he's very enthusiastic. And big enough to frighten small children into leaping into the canal. So we're on the lookout for toddlers, yappy dogs – usually small breeds – and humans who simply don't like canines. With my help, Sid is developing strategies to deal with them all.

Trouble is, somehow Sid can sniff a worried human a mile off and usually chooses them to be his new BFF, turning to sniff at them or wag his tail madly. A move that's guaranteed to make the nervous cynophobe think he's sizing them up for lunch.

People. Clueless most of them. And dogs do read expressions. They can misconstrue panic for an invitation to frolic. Or sometimes they simply want to prove anxious humans wrong. There's no hidden agenda.

I think I'd like to come back as a dog.

A mile along the path, we veer off into a patch of common land. A copse with a secret and one of Sid's favourite places; Frogger's Pond. We scramble up a bank and then down the other side. Not many people come to it from the river; it's more accessible from a road some half a mile away. But here, I can let Sid off. He needs no invitation. Though he stops to investigate the odd smell, his direction of travel is most definitely water driven. I hear the splash of his entry before I see it as by now, he's two hundred yards in front. I jog up and see him paddling away, happy as Larry. I have a ball and throw it out into the middle. Sid responds with a turn and retrieve. He brings it back and from then on, it's shake, rinse and repeat.

I'm on my fifth throw when I hear a dog bark behind me. I turn and see the third of my most frequent co-dog-walkers trying to hold back a golden retriever named Winston. She bends, unclips the lead and unleashes a shaggy-haired yellow ballistic missile who takes off from the bank and joins Sid in the pond with a tremendous splash. No marks at all for style, but ten out of ten for enthusiasm.

I watch as Galina follows along the path.

She's dressed in a thick shapeless coat and a beanie hat, dark glasses over her eyes and a scarf over the lower part of her face. It's not the weather for any of that, now that the rain has blown off. But then she doesn't wear these things as protection from the cold. She wears them to hide herself.

The fact that we meet here is not a contrivance. It's more a question of timing and convenience. Whatever her routine is, it meshes with mine of a Saturday and has for nigh on three months. Much the same as with the taciturn Rob and his Maisie, Sid and Winston get on famously. And that is really all that matters.

'Morning,' I say as Galina joins me at the edge of the pond.

'Good morning.' The salutation is tinged with an accent. I know what it is because she told me when I asked. I guessed it was Eastern European, but I'd never heard anyone from Moldova speak before. Intrigued, I asked. Her voice is low and deliberate with an occasional softening of consonants. And muffled, as always, through the scarf she never takes off.

There's another splash as I send the ball in over Sid's head and he follows with Winston right behind.

'Wow, they seem up for it today, don't they?'

'They do.' Galina smiles. I least I think it's a smile. I can't see through the scarf, but it makes the livid forked scar on her right cheek ride up. Over the weeks, I've learned to read that as a sign. 'Winston has been very keen to come today.'

I nod.

Galina watches the dogs. After a while, she says, 'I have seen your photograph on the Internet.'

I swivel towards her in surprise. It's not a comment I was

expecting. But then, half the world has probably seen me through #isthishim.

'Does that... Do I make you feel uncomfortable?'

Galina shakes her head. 'No. The Internet is a swamp. I do not think that you would do this thing.'

'But you hardly know me.'

She shrugs. 'I know you like dogs. I know you more than I know other people.'

It's an enigmatic answer, but I'll take it. I know little about Galina, except that she never takes off the glasses or her scarf. And I presume the reason for that has to do with the scarring that's visible between the two. I can postulate that the scar progresses downwards towards her mouth and lower face and that she's naturally self-conscious about that.

Because I can't think of anything else, I say, 'Thank you.'

'Did you know the girl?'

'She works at the same hospital as me. I know her because we sometimes come across each other on the wards. I've spoken to her a few times, work-related things. I know who she is but I don't know her. Not really.'

'Twitter and Facebook, they are for cowards.'

She's right.

'Sticks and stones,' I say, but it sounds pathetic. Unconvincing. 'Even though I don't know her, just like everyone else, I am worried about her. What might have happened to her. In fact, I heard that the police are investigating the possibility that this may be a case of human trafficking.'

Galina rounds on me. As she does, I hear a noise behind the scarf. A throaty gasp of shock. I can't judge her expression behind her glasses, but she stares.

'What?' I ask.

Sid has bought his ball back and dropped it. Winston is

barking, demanding attention. I pick the ball up and throw it. Both dogs scramble back into the water after it.

'What did the police say?' Galina asks. To my horror, she's trembling.

'I haven't spoken to them myself. But I heard they had a tip-off that gangs were operating in the Thames Valley area. The suggestion is that Katy might have been abducted to be... sold on.' I wince at what I've just said, the hideousness of it all.

Galina turns away. Something I've said has shaken her, I can see that.

'Are you okay?' I ask.

Without looking at me she says, 'At home, young girls go missing all the time.'

It's a blunt, shocking, statement. 'Really?'

She nods. 'I have dual citizenship. Moldova and Romania. I know what people think, that we are gypsies. That Moldova is full of crime. It is not. But in the cities, there are gangs and where I am from, in the country, it is very poor. Young people, boys and girls, will always find a better way to live. And the criminals offer new jobs in Ireland or Finland, sometimes even here in England. But they are not jobs. There is prostitution instead. The young girls and boys go, but only to find it is not what has been promised.'

It's my turn to stare. The dogs have found something interesting on the opposite bank. I dread to think what it is, but it's keeping them occupied. Galina's glasses are very dark, and I can't see anything in her eyes. She's looking across the pond when she says, 'I was in Holland. I went there to be a model, that was what they told me.'

Though Galina's shape is formless behind the layers she wears, I know she isn't tall enough to be on a catwalk. But then who needs reality to poison their dreams.

She shrugs. 'It was glamour work. I was very young. Too

young. The boy who promised me this was young too. I thought he liked me, but he was... a recruiter?'

I nod.

'Once we got to Holland, he went back to Moldova. Then I was alone. That was when I knew I had been tricked.'

'Oh God, Galina, I had no idea.'

Still she looks out at the pond and the dogs. When she turns back, her hand is on her glasses. She lifts them up, the other hand half covering her right eye, as if warding off the light. The scarf still covers her nose and mouth, but I peer in shock at the few inches of flesh in a once-pretty face that is now a ravaged mass of rawness. The exposed area; the soft flesh around her eye and cheek, looks like someone has poured melted wax over it and allowed it to dry. The lids are thickened and swollen by keloid scars. But it is her left eye that I can't stop staring at. The cornea is no longer a clear window covering a dark pupil. This is a blue-grey distorted mess, the surrounding sclera a road map of thick red vessels. Though it's a terrible sight, I don't react. My training prevents that. Sudden realisation and understanding come flooding in. But before I can find any inadequate words of sympathy, Galina adds the harrowing narrative.

'I gave evidence against the men who were hiding me and others. The Dutch police said they would protect me, but one of them gave me away. The gang got to me. Made an example of me. This is what a syringe full of acid does.'

She slides her glasses back down. 'They could not save my eye. Three grafts have failed. Now, perhaps, I will ask for it to be removed. For the pain.'

I'm dumbstruck. But my misplaced euphoria at wanting the tip-off regarding Katy to be true evaporates. I'd felt relieved that it took the spotlight off me. But Galina's revelation has soured all that. Anyone with a jot of humanity couldn't sanction being anywhere near the kind of people who could do something like that to another human being.

'I'm so sorry,' I mumble.

Galina shrugs. 'Why should you be sorry?' She replaces the scarf and the glasses.

I shake my head. There are no words.

It's Galina who relieves me of my awkwardness.

'My real name is not Galina. No one knows about this.' She waves her hand over her face. 'Only my doctors and my case worker. And now you. I came here from Holland to get away. Hearing you say that there are gangs here, that there may be others...' She shakes her head. 'If she is with them, then that is the worst thing that could happen to anyone.'

She's right. 'I'm sorry if I've upset you.'

Galina shrugs again. 'You say sorry too much.'

I laugh. 'Perhaps I do.'

Winston comes back with the ball this time. Galina reaches down and throws it into the water. The dogs follow, barking excitedly. I realise that the bond between the dogs has grown into a mutual trust between Galina and I. Strong enough to allow her to confide her secret in me. I feel an urge to do the same.

'I'd like to ask you something,' I say. 'Or tell you something and then ask you what you think.'

Galina inclines her head.

'I think I've been contacted by whoever has Katy Leith.'

29

I tell Galina about the WhatsApp messages and about the van and the money.

She listens without speaking.

'All that happened before I learned that the police had a tip-off about the trafficking gangs. It doesn't make sense.'

'Sense? What is sense?' She snorts. 'These men have no feelings. They are not human. If they think they can blackmail you, they will.'

'But I don't know Katy.'

'The world thinks you do. And they will know that. Perhaps the reason they took Katy is gone. Perhaps the police are making it too difficult for them to carry it out. I don't know. But they have seen what is happening to you and they see a chance to use that. Now they have two fish on the hook.'

'Two fish?'

'Katy and you.'

'But what is it they want? They made me give them money to prove that I can do what I'm told. And they have my knife. Why me?'

'These people do not need a reason.'

I frown. It's not what I want to hear. Is it really possible that they've seen an opportunity to manipulate me? Galina reads my mind.

'You are a doctor. You have money. Perhaps you have access to drugs.'

I let out a cynical laugh that sounds more like a cough.

Galina shakes her head. 'It is the way they think. They see someone in a trap and they squeeze until the blood runs.'

'You have a wonderful turn of phrase; do you know that?'

Galina drops her head.

'Sorry,' I say. 'I shouldn't have involved you. I ought to go to the police with this.'

Galina looks at me.

'What?' I ask.

'If they have threatened harm, they will do what they say if you cross them. It is a matter of honour to them. All threats must be carried out or they will be seen to be weak.'

'Oh Christ. So what should I do?'

'Give them what they want. It will keep Katy alive.'

I throw up my hands. 'I honestly don't know what that is.'

'Not yet perhaps. But they will tell you. You have a phone?' she asks. 'I will give you my number. You must promise me not to give it to anyone else.'

I nod and fish out my iPhone, watch as she punches a number into my contacts under the initials GV. 'Text me if you want to talk and we will meet. Tell no one. And no one must follow you here.'

'I'm really grateful,' I say.

She nods. 'Please, I am safe here in Oxford. I do not want to move again.'

She's still trembling and there's a great deal left unsaid in her words. But I understand enough. 'Of course. I won't tell anybody.'

I stay for another fifteen minutes, but our talk shifts back to the dogs. It's safer ground.

After Galina leaves, I trot back down to the river path and take Sid back to Paws for Claws before heading off to meet Oaks.

30

He's there already, sitting at a table for two with a coffee and flapjack, laptop open, earbuds in. He's dressed in jeans and a jacket, and looks like every other early thirties urbanite in Mariachis. And there are a lot of them, surfing and eating. I, meanwhile, am windswept in my waterproof jacket and trousers. I order a flat white and a bottle of water and join Oaks.

'You look... energetic,' he says.

'I like to be active.' I sit and sip my coffee.

Oaks shuts the lid of his laptop and takes a bite of his flapjack. 'So,' he says, 'you wanted to talk?'

'Yes. It's about the night Katy Leith went missing.'

He sits back, all ears. It's stuffy in Mariachis after riding the bike. I take off my jacket and drape it over the chair.

'I wasn't entirely truthful when I said I went directly home.'

'Go on.'

The coffee is nutty and smooth and lubricates my throat. 'I did go to Headington immediately after leaving the pub, but I did not go home. Not straight away.'

'Where in Headington exactly?'

'To the car park in Shotover Park. I met someone there. We stayed for about an hour. Then I went home.'

'That might explain why our ANPR picked up your vehicle leaving Headington at ten forty-five and coming back at just before midnight. Is that where you took Katy Leith? To the car park?'

I stare at him. 'You knew I wasn't telling the truth?'

'I wanted to bring you in, but the boss said to give you some space. See what happens.'

'Why?'

Oaks sniffs. 'She thinks if we arrest you, the press would explode. She's not a big fan of the MSM.'

I frown.

Oaks sees it and explains. 'The mainstream media. Thinks they muddy the waters when it comes to trials.'

I nod. I don't like the word trial, but it confirms my impression of Ridley. It's the process of law she's worried about, not me. I notice two couples at an adjacent table, late teenagers, huddling together, whispering and looking my way. They could be students, but they could equally be four of the 160,000 residents that live in this city when the 30,000 students go home. The girls are heavily made-up and unseasonably tinted. The men are thin and bony in dark clothing. They look like pallbearers. Up to now they've been the loud epicentre of the café, laughing and chatting in that boorish way some young people adopt to draw attention to themselves.

I turn back to Oaks and sigh. 'I didn't take Katy Leith anywhere. I know I should've told you before but it's... complicated. The person I met that night...we're seeing each other.'

'And you didn't want your partner to know.' Oaks lets a rare wry smile appear.

'No, that isn't it. I didn't want to involve that other person, that's all. But now I see the folly of that, given what's happened.'

'What do you mean?'

'I mean the video and the press and all that crap.'

Oaks contemplates this and takes another sip of coffee before asking, 'You have a name?'

I hand over a written note with Ella's name and number on it. Oaks looks at it. 'She's your alibi?'

'She's someone I care a lot about.'

'You know that lying to the police is an offence.'

I nod. 'But I was not under caution when we spoke at the hospital. Nor at the station, or so I understand.'

Oaks exhales, looks away and then back at me. 'No, you were not under caution. But that might change.'

'I'm telling you the truth now.'

'Glad to hear it.'

'You could have insisted I came to the station today,' I say.

'And that might still happen.'

'But not yet. Is that because you're looking elsewhere?'

Oaks's eyes narrow but he doesn't respond.

'There are rumours that there's a trafficking ring.'

His face hardens. He leans forward and sips more coffee, trying to hide his surprise. 'Who told you that?'

'I read it online. Is it true?'

His eyes swivel up from the coffee cup, heavy-lidded with suspicion, but we both know that just about anything and everything is on the web. It's a very believable lie.

There's a loud scraping of chairs and the two youths from the corner table get up and walk towards us. I see the girls' faces register shock and excitement. One of them giggles.

'You're him, aren't you,' one boy says. It's a statement not a question. He's wearing a black baseball cap with Givenchy written on it. He glares at me. I look back.

'Have we met?'

'My mum's a nurse. She says she'd like to cut your balls off.'

'Charming. Do I get a say in the matter?' I'm staying calm, but inside adrenaline is churning.

'You know where she is, you bastard.' This time it's his slightly shorter mate who pipes up. He's broader, wearing a tight shiny jacket and dark grey tracksuit bottoms with a tick on the thigh. He's high on bravado. Behind him, the girls are filming on their phones.

I don't get up because Oaks beats me to it. He has a warrant card in his hand. He steps into the boys' space. 'Go back to your seats. This has nothing to do with you.'

The boys' eyes open wide. They look from me to Oaks.

'You questioning him?'

'Go back to your seats.'

'Cool. Lock the perv up.'

Baseball cap turns away, grinning. But his friend, the more belligerent one, reaches over and tips over my takeaway coffee. Amazingly, the cap stays on, but a thin stream of brown liquid jets out onto the table and I jerk back reflexively. I right the cup and look up into a sniggering face.

'Lucky,' says shiny jacket. 'That won't fucking last.'

Oaks grabs his arm and steers him away. 'Sit down.'

Puffer jacket goes back to his table. Oaks pulls his chair around, so his back is to the filming phones. Most of the people in the café are staring too. My heart is pumping, pulse racing. I know that if Oaks had not been there, things could have turned very ugly in a matter of seconds.

'I'm not at liberty to discuss the case with you, Mr Thorn.' Oaks picks up where our conversation left off.

I hold up my hands. But we both know that his lapse into formality has answered my question about trafficking.

'Is there anything else you want to tell me?' Oaks asks.

Later, I'll think about this moment, about the two thugs with their Givenchy caps and violent threats and the anger and humiliation I felt at being accosted in a public place. I'll remember the hostile glares coming from every corner of the café. I'll remember feeling gratitude towards Oaks. Having him on my side for that unseemly moment is sobering.

So, despite the warnings, despite Galina's advice, I decide to come clean.

'There is,' I say. 'But not here. I'm on my bike. Meet me at the car park in Shotover Park in twenty minutes.'

Oaks looks surprised.

'It may, or may not have anything to do with Katy,' I say.

He frowns, but he's intrigued.

We walk out together. The two youths and their girlfriends send me off with a couple of charming goodbyes.

'Piss off, perv,' says baseball cap.

Thigh tick adds, 'Yeah, we'll be looking out for you, bellend.'

The girls laugh.

I'm glad when Oaks and I get out into the fresh air.

31

A s expected, Oaks is already in the car park at Shotover when I arrive. I tell him to follow me along the lanes towards Blenheim Road and Horsepath. I pull up opposite the barn and Oaks parks his Ford Focus on the verge. He gets out and looks at me warily.

'What's this about, Mr Thorn?'

'It's easier if I show you.' I wheel the bike through the trees towards the abandoned van. When I look back, Oaks hasn't moved from the side of his car.

'Over here,' I say.

'What's over here?' Oaks's wariness hasn't altered, but his lips tighten, and he begins to look angry.

I wheel the bike back, suddenly aware of how odd all this must seem. I'm not thinking straight. I guess the episode in the coffee shop has upset me more than I'd care to admit.

'Okay,' I say. 'I got a text message. A WhatsApp message and an image of Katy Leith with a knife at her throat.'

'What?' Oaks bounces away from his car towards me. 'Do you still have it?'

'No. It disappeared after ten seconds. So did the other

messages. But they told me to come here. That there'd be a phone under the seat of that van.' I point through the trees. 'Other messages on this phone said that if I told anyone, Katy would be killed. They said that the knife at her throat is mine. It's an old woodsman's knife I kept in my shed. I checked. It's not there anymore.'

'Jesus,' Oaks says.

'So I came. They made me take out two hundred quid to prove I was co-operating. They said they'd hurt Katy or someone close to me if I told you.'

Oaks blinks. 'Why didn't you?'

'This only happened yesterday. But then I heard about this thing with the traffickers and... I don't know. Now it seems more sensible that I do tell you.'

'And the phone is under the seat of this van?'

I nod.

'Show me,' Oaks says.

I put the bike down and push through. Behind me, Oaks is already pulling on some neoprene gloves. I approach the van, but he tells me to stand back. Oaks kneels, puts his hand under the seat and feels around. I watch with growing trepidation as fifteen and then thirty seconds go by.

'You say it's under here?'

'In a plastic pouch,' I say.

After another minute, Oaks stands up. He goes back to his car and comes back with a slim torch, gets back down on his knees and looks again.

'There's nothing here.'

'There must be. I put two hundred quid in that pouch. I have a bloody receipt.' I fumble in my pocket for the bit of paper the ATM spat out. I find it and hand it over. Oaks looks at it and then at me.

'All this proves is that you took out some money yesterday.'

'Yes and put it in the pouch under this seat.'

Oaks sighs. 'Well, it isn't there now. Neither is the phone.'

'You don't believe me, do you?'

'I believe you took money out. I can even believe that you put money under this seat. But do I believe that this has anything to do with Katy Leith?' Oaks shakes his head.

'What about the image? Is it possible there might still be a copy of it on my phone?'

'Oh, if it's there, I'm sure we could find it. But you can bet it'll be from an untraceable account. And what did it show exactly?'

'Katy Leith. Wearing the same dress she wore the other night.'

'And you're sure it was her?'

'There was tape over her eyes and mouth but...'

'So you can't be certain.'

His statement gives me pause. 'I can't be one hundred per cent certain.'

Oaks nods.

'You think it's a scam?'

'Either that or you're making the whole thing up.'

'Why would I do that?'

Oaks shrugs. 'Why would someone abduct a young woman?'

'Look, the phone was there. So was the pouch.'

'Okay.'

I sound desperate. 'You can have my phone. Let your tech people look at it.'

'Good idea. Come into the station this afternoon. I'll get one of the tech guys along. See what they can do.'

'But you're not hopeful?'

'We'll probably find something. But how useful it'll be, I don't know. If it's true, then you'd have been better off telling us right at the start. Not after you'd paid money.'

'That was just a test.'

'Was it though? Or was it someone making a quick two hundred quid? This sort of thing brings all the weirdos out from under their stones.'

Oaks starts to move away from the van.

'Aren't you going to get a forensic team out here?' I ask.

He looks back at me over his shoulder but doesn't stop walking. 'Let's take a peek at what your phone throws up first, shall we?'

I stand at the side of the road as his car pulls away, feeling foolish and powerless. When he's gone, I peer around at the empty countryside and the trees. Branches waft in the stiff breeze. A group of vocal crows in a nearby sycamore object noisily to my presence. They know I'm here. Anyone could be watching me. Anyone could be watching and laughing at how bloody naïve and stupid I've been.

32

I get to the station at around 2pm. Oaks takes me up to the same familiar interview room. Before I go in, I unlock my phone by pressing my thumb on the button. Oaks does something to make sure it doesn't switch off. He's left me with some paper and a pen. I write out a statement. I include everything I can remember that's relevant. I explain about meeting Ella after the leaving party and about the messages on my phone and the van. The only thing I leave out is what's happened between Sarah and me, and, of course, Galina. Sarah because it's none of their business, and Galina because I promised her I wouldn't involve her and I'm sticking to that.

Half an hour after I get to the station, Oaks picks up my statement, reads it in silence and then says, 'And you're sure there's nothing else you want to tell us?'

I shake my head.

'You're happy to sign this?'

I nod and sign. Oaks leaves the room. Ten minutes later he comes back with Ridley. She has a photocopy of my statement in her hands as she sits opposite me across the table. She doesn't bother with the formalities of a greeting and launches straight into dressing me down.

'First of all, you do realise that not telling us everything is almost as bad as lying?'

'I've explained why. That I didn't want to involve Ella.'

Ridley shakes her head. 'What you want or don't want isn't an option.'

I lock eyes with her. 'I'm sorry.' It seems inadequate, but it's all I have.

'We've spoken to Mrs Danes. She is willing to provide a written statement too.'

I nod.

'As for this business with the money and the phone under the seat of the derelict van,' Ridley shakes her head.

'You think it's a scam?'

'If it's true, then yes, I think it's a scam.'

'Of course it's true.'

Oaks nods. 'Then the next text would have asked you for a thousand or five or ten.'

'Why would anyone do that?' I ask.

Ridley's smile is almost pitying. 'There's nothing some people like better than to see the mighty fallen. You're an easy target for anyone savvy enough to get a friend to pose as Katy and set up a photo. The glitter tube dress she wore is not a Versace exclusive. It's a Forever 21 staple. Anyone can buy it and find an old garage and some duct tape.'

'But they have my phone number.'

'Normally not that easy. But there are database services who can and will find that out.' Oaks is leaning against a wall with his arms folded. 'You will have used your phone number online. On social media, or maybe to receive parcel tracking information. Something, somewhere. People can get hold of that for a price.'

'What about the knife? It looked like mine. Plus mine is missing.'

Oaks answers. 'Someone could have purloined that when the video broke. Before the press hoo-ha.'

'The shed lock wasn't broken.'

'Then maybe you really did leave it lying about the garden.'

I squeeze my eyes shut. I know I've been taken for a ride and it's a difficult pill to swallow. There's a knock on the door and a uniformed officer enters with a plastic bag. Oaks nods and hands it to me. In it are my phone with a sim card taped to the back.'

'Is this mine?' I ask, surprised.

Oaks nods. 'We've cloned it. Since you've given us permission, we'll go through everything over the next few days. We'll find the messages. We'll trace the phone it came from. But chances are it'll be a burner... Oh, and I've put my own number in your contacts. In case you ever need it.'

I nod, suddenly anxious. I have a lot of information stored: some passwords, contacts. bookmarks. Oaks reads my expression.

'Anything you're concerned about?'

I shake my head. I can't think of anything, but it is nevertheless unnerving to hand so much of your personal life and data over like this.

'We'll be discreet,' Oaks says.

I nod in gratitude.

Ridley changes tack. 'DS Oaks tells me there was an altercation this morning.'

'In the coffee shop?' I shrug. 'They were just kids looking to make trouble.'

She holds my gaze. 'The press is one thing. Social media and its power is something else altogether. Don't underestimate the great unwashed, Mr Thorn. To them, you are already a monster.

McCarthyism is alive and well and hiding in the web. I would stay away from public places if I were you. Anywhere you can get isolated. Be aware. Avoid situations like you found yourself in this morning.'

'Until?'

'Until we find out what's happened to Katy Leith.'

I lock eyes with Ridley. It's an unpleasant warning but I'm oddly relieved. She seems to be implying that I'm no longer a person of interest. But any idea I have that they're on my side is quickly dispelled by Oaks.

'And you're one hundred per cent certain you don't know what that is, Mr Thorn?'

I shift my glare towards him but there is no point getting angry. 'No, I do not.'

'If anyone else contacts you, let us know immediately.' Ridley lays heavy emphasis on "immediately".

'And if you leave Oxford for any reason, be sure to let us know,' Oaks adds.

'Surely you'll be tracking my phone.' I throw it out as a flippant suggestion, hoping for a smile if not a laugh.

Neither of them finds it amusing in the slightest. But neither of them denies it.

33

O aks watched Ridley write some notes; a status report on their interview with Thorn for the SIO. They were in their office and he'd come back from seeing Thorn out. Though it was a Saturday, half the team was in working on the Katy Leith case. Oaks waited for Ridley to finish. It was never wise to interrupt her when she was writing up, in his experience. More often than not he'd simply get a hand held up signalling him to go away and come back later.

Oaks amused himself while he waited by scanning threads about Thorn on social media. There were a lot of them. Mostly dripping with vitriol. Finally, Ridley finished and sat back.

'Well?' Oaks asked.

Ridley sighed. 'I don't know. Could be genuine. Then again, it could be a load of complete kaka. Mysterious callers. Blackmail.' She shook her head. 'Your friend Thorn is a trouble magnet.'

'He's not my friend. And if he's lying, we'll find out soon enough from his phone. It's if he isn't lying that intrigues me.'

Ridley wrinkled her nose. 'You said it. Someone with a

grudge or a chancer out for a quick smash and grab. Or he gets someone else he knows to text him.'

'Why?' Oaks pulled up the other chair.

'Classic distraction technique. Give us something else to worry about. Make him look like a victim.'

'He is a victim. Of the press and the even-handed right-thinking world of social media.'

Ridley nodded. 'The press know how to throw someone to the wolves all right. But we shouldn't get sidetracked by this. Our priority remains Katy Leith.'

They'd taken the tip-off about the trafficking gang seriously. Oaks had been seconded to chat with the Organised Crimes Task Force both in Thames Valley and adjacent forces to see what names they had. He hadn't learned much as yet. But there were potential scenarios. None of them pleasant.

In truth, it remained a possibility that Katy's abduction might have been opportunistic – of sorts. If a gang team had been out checking on their stock of prostitutes, those already deployed by them, and Katy had somehow wandered onto their radar, it might have been seen as too good an opportunity to miss. There were "buyers" out there. It was a terrifying and sordid idea, but one Ridley took seriously. And there were active gangs, linked to other European criminal fraternities in the Netherlands especially, already operating in adjacent areas and well versed in all aspects of kidnapping. But the lack of any contact or ransom demand, according to the Anti-Kidnap and Extortion Unit officer Oaks had spoken to on the phone, made the latter a less likely scenario. Far more likely, if a gang were involved, would be abduction and subsequent shipment to a different country.

Oaks sat back in his chair and grunted out a stretch. Saturdays were always slow. Getting Thorn in had been a bit of a bonus. 'Think he's told us everything?' Oaks mused.

Ridley sent her plucked eyebrows skywards. 'No chance. He's a deep one is our Mr Thorn. Knows more than he's letting on.'

'Maybe he wants to keep things from his partner.'

'Fair enough. But that's not our problem. And once you start filtering, trying to sort out what you think might be okay to hold back, it all gets very, very messy.'

'You really don't like him, do you.' A statement, not a question.

'What is it with you and this "like" business?'

Oaks shrugged. 'Just intrigued. You know, regarding the indefinable. Whether your emotional response to someone changes your approach to them in an investigation.'

'You've been reading those psychology articles again, haven't you?'

'I've been asking around. He is well liked by consultant colleagues. Nursing staff find him a bit daunting. But those who've worked with him are very loyal.'

'It's the power thing again, isn't it?'

'But that's not his fault.'

'No? People in that position need to work at making themselves accessible. Or perhaps he's too busy trying to get on with his career and boost his pension with private work to care. Maybe that's why Katy Leith became an encumbrance.'

Oaks blinked. 'So you still like him for the abduction?'

'She left that pub without calling a cab or an Uber. She's twenty-five. She knows the score. Knows not to wander about the street dressed the way she was. My informed opinion is that she was on the way to meet someone. So until we find her, all bets are off, Ryan. You know that.'

34

Outside, the afternoon is sliding away. A little late sunshine tries to splash colour on the drab day, tries to make me believe that spring is really here. But above me the clouds are flying by in a brisk wind. I shiver. It's getting cool quickly. I put the sim back into my phone. I fumble it twice. It's tricky. Or is it that my fingers are trembling a little? Once the sim's loaded, I slip the phone into my pocket and zip up.

As I head off and join the traffic, I ponder Ridley's words. It's clear they think me a gullible ingénue. Am I really a target for any thug looking to stir up trouble? If so, how am I meant to deal with that? I realise I haven't really looked that hard at what the media, MSM and social, are saying about me. I stop off at a garage on my way home for some water and two newspapers. I leave my cycling helmet and dark glasses on as I queue. They make me virtually unrecognisable.

I head back to the house and don't try to hide my presence. I count three cameramen and a TV crew. All of them fire off questions as I wheel the bike through the front gate.

'What did the police want you for, Jake?'

'Has your partner left you, Mr Thorn?'

'Will you be going to work next week, Jake? What do your patients think about you being a murder suspect?'

It's the first time someone has used the word "murder". It makes me pause momentarily, as the questioner knew it would. But if they'd found anything, Ridley and Oaks would not have been so... congenial. I catch myself and give a little shake of my head in lieu of a smile. I'd hate to meet Ridley when she was being deliberately frosty. Even so, it's obvious the reporters are baiting me.

I don't answer. But I sense I'm going to be hounded whenever I come and go so I put the bike away and get my car keys. I don't hang around inside. I stay just long enough to shed my cycling jacket and get a warmer coat.

They press cameras up against the windshield and the side windows as I reverse the car out.

'Are you going to Katy?' someone shouts.

'Is there a spade in the boot, Jake?'

I drive away. I see at least four people run to their cars to follow. The chase is on. Like every good drama. But I know these streets well and I'm already out and heading for the eastern bypass. I circle the Headington roundabout and double back, take a left at the engineering factory and park the car on Kiln Road.

Within four minutes of leaving, I'm walking back, winding my way through the smaller lanes; Trinity Road and Masons Alley, rejoining Trinity Road again until I can cross Quarry Road two hundred yards from the cottage. Once again, I get back in through the rear. But now, at least, I can access the car without them knowing I'm leaving. It's a game. An unpleasant, inconvenient one, but definitely me against them.

It's only when I get back in and hit the shower that the questions they were firing at me sink in.

#isthishim

I let the water pummel me. It's soothing. The press know I've been to the police. That I am not surprised by. They may have someone permanently watching the station. They may have a convenient source inside who gives them information in return for a few quid for a pint on the weekend. But they also know Sarah is not around. Again, hardly surprising as she's not shown her face. Still, it's disconcerting to have these strangers probing into my personal details. Knowing so much.

When I'm showered and changed, I make myself an omelette and switch on the lights. They'll see I'm home. Or that someone is home. But that's their problem, not mine.

It's then that I wonder about what all of this means. Somewhere inside, I suspect this is not a good idea, but I need to find out what I'm up against. I haven't heard from anyone since I gave the police my phone. In fact, no one has phoned me since I left work yesterday. But when I check, I see it's on silent with no vibrate. Force of habit when I'm operating. When I check my calls, I've had two from Ashish. There's a voice message.

'Jake, it's Ash. This is all so out of order. I wanted you to know that if you want to talk, I'm here. If you want to come over to ours, that's totally fine. You know where we are. Just don't be alone in this, okay?'

I toy with phoning him back, but I don't. I can't involve him. The last thing Ashish and his family needs is some journalist hassling him for details about me. I realise I'm being naïve in this. They probably already have. Instead, I turn to the newspapers, absently forking in mouthfuls of omelette. It doesn't take long for me to realise why Ridley gave me that stark warning. Katy Leith is still headline news. So, apparently, am I.

POLICE CONTINUE THEIR HUNT FOR MISSING NURSE KATY LEITH

Oxford hospital staff quizzed for a fifth day running. One senior doctor is advised to take leave while suspicion grows over abduction.

Detectives investigating the disappearance of nurse, Katy Leith, continue to probe her work colleagues at the hospital where Katy was a nurse. The 25-year-old has been missing for 7 days since leaving a party held for a retiring colleague.

The police are believed to be considering the theory that Katy was either kidnapped by someone lying in wait, or that her abductor may have followed her from the Duke of Wellington pub where she'd been celebrating at a colleague's leaving party. Thames Valley detectives have confirmed that they are gravely worried for her safety. Though refusing to comment directly on rumours that Katy may have been the victim of a trafficking gang, a spokesman said: 'Our investigations are ongoing and every line of enquiry will be followed up.'

In a new twist, and following the release of a video showing Miss Leith apparently arguing with a senior male colleague, sources at the Oxford Infirmary revealed yesterday that this same colleague, identified by fellow workers as surgeon Mr Jacob Thorn, has since been advised to take leave from his £100,000 a year job at the hospital. Police confirm that they have questioned the surgeon, who was also at the pub the night that Miss Leith went missing.

I stare at an image of myself culled from the hospital website. I'm in an open-neck shirt, smiling, clean-shaven. It's supposed to ooze "trust me, I'm a doctor". Now it just makes me look smug. Under the image is the text – suspended surgeon Jacob Thorn. Below that the article continues:

Thorn is unmarried and has worked as a consultant for Oxford University Hospitals for almost 5 years. Colleagues describe him as driven and work-obsessed but something of a loner. However, since the appearance of the video which shows a clearly upset Miss Leith in animated conversation with Thorn, several female colleagues have turned to Twitter and posted under the hashtag #isthishim. Some posts have been openly critical, with more than one suggesting that Thorn's approach to colleagues is less than exemplary.

@nurse677
    #isthishim JT is an arrogant, privileged patriarch. There are only two female general surgeons in that hospital.

@Lilly&stuff
    #isthishim I've seen him eyeing up his juniors. Lech of the first order.

@Suffragina
    #isthishim He's a Christmas party groper. Not surprised his partner left him. Run and hide, girl.

Since Leveson, newspapers are supposed to self-regulate and up their standards. And I also know that the story doesn't actually accuse me of anything. But anyone reading it could not fail to leap to the insinuated conclusion that I am somehow implicated. They've generously over-egged my salary. And played the inevitable gender card to buff up my toxic masculinity and doubled down by implying that the Twitter quotes are from nursing colleagues known to me, without naming sources. Even when they've tried to balance the narrative, it somehow comes across as collusion. With a sinking heart, I read on and see Ashish's name in the next paragraph.

However, Dr Ashish Hegde, who works closely with Thorn, said of the surgeon: 'The fact that anyone is even talking about Jake in regard to this is absurd. He's a straight shooter, intelligent and is in a stable relationship. There is no way he would be involved in anything like this.'

Dr Ashish, who lives in Oxford with his family, is an anaesthetist at the same hospital as Thorn and the pair work closely together.

A neighbour, who asked not to be identified, said, 'Jake is always out on his bike. Spends a lot of time on his own while his partner, Sarah, is away at work.'

Mr Thorn, a fellow of the Royal College of Surgeons, frequently lectures to nurses at the Oxford Infirmary. A source there, said: 'He's always dressed nicely. He's friendly and always willing to help if you don't get anything. He's willing to stay on after the lectures to go through things with you.'

Others, however, describe him as a 'bit creepy'.

A hospital source has confirmed that Thorn is currently on leave and not seeing patients or engaging in any clinical activity.

I feel a sudden rush of gratitude towards Ash. He didn't have to speak to the press; it was a brave thing to do. I won't forget that. But I'm also aware that the press is digging for dirt. It's a horrible sensation. Not that I have anything to hide, but all of a sudden it's very personal.

But it's all innuendo. Designed to whip up the great scandal-hungry public.

My laptop's on the table. All brushed silver with a tantalising white fruit logo that's suddenly as tempting as it was in the Garden of Eden. The urge to switch it on and take a look is strong, but something tells me that what I've read in the news-paper is but the tip of a very large and pungent iceberg. I wonder how wise a move that would be.

It's almost 7pm and I'm still contemplating the computer when my phone's ringtone jars me out of the reverie. I don't recognise the number, but answer it anyway.

'Jake?' The voice is familiar, but I can't immediately trace it.

'Who's this?'

'It's Simon. Simon Harding.'

I don't answer because I don't want to talk to the man who has taken my partner from me. But petulant is not my style. 'Look, whatever this is about, now is not a good time–'

'Jake, listen.' His voice is urgent and full of some emotion I can't pinpoint. 'Sarah's in hospital.'

'What?' My insides roil.

'She's okay. She was out shopping. On the way back to the flat someone accosted her. A mugging, we think.'

'A mugging?' I slump back into the chair, glad of its solidity.

'At knifepoint.'

'Oh Jesus.' A thousand thoughts cascade through my head. All of them dark. Most of them surrounding the victims of violent crime I've had to repair and stitch up over the years. Stabbings and assaults. Luckily, Simon realises he has to qualify what he's said.

'She's unharmed but pretty shaken up. She asked me to call you. She says she wants to see you.'

'Where is she?'

'At the Chelsea and Westminster.'

'I'm on my way.'

I pick up the car keys and lock up without another thought, slip out of the back door and into the lane behind and the church-yard beyond. The wall is rough under my hands. I feel the skin break on my soft flesh. That's the trouble with being a surgeon. But I'm not a surgeon now. I'm an escapee scaling a wall, running from the Stasi with their puffer jackets and big cameras.

Seven minutes later, I'm at the car on Kiln Road. No one has followed me. I wouldn't care if they had.

Fulham Road is busy. It's an arterial road, aka the A308. Given its SW10 location, it's an eclectic mix of shops and houses with the Chelsea and Westminster Hospital smack in the middle of it. The entrance is opposite a Tesco Express and there's even a Subway next door in case you're ravenous after your appendicectomy. The Hollywood Arms is just down the road. I've been there a few times when I've visited colleagues and friends in London. But this evening, I'm not thinking about beer and conversation.

The good, or some might say the bad, thing about London is that it is huge. That means the chances of anyone recognising me here are far less than if I were to walk along a street in Oxford. At least, that's my rationale as I find a parking space on a street close to the hospital – which means a quarter of a mile away – and hurry in.

No bike helmet and dark glasses this time.

It's almost 8.45pm by the time I reach a reception desk and ask for the Acute Assessment Unit. I take a lift to the fourth floor and I share it with some nursing staff in pale blue uniforms who murmur about getting off on time and what plans they have for the weekend.

Neither looks at me. I'm absurdly grateful for that.

Simon is in the corridor when I get out.

He's tall and lean and reminds me a bit of Jurgen Klopp but with a lot less hair. What there is is sculpted, with a touch of the Tintin about it, rising up in the front in a little mound. It strikes me he's one of those people who have decided on a hair-style and is sticking to it no matter what, and despite the passage of time. A passage that you'd think might require a radical rethink in style given the paucity of material he has to work with. Obviously, Sarah doesn't mind. Or, maybe, they're still at a point in their relationship where she has yet to mould him.

It'll come.

'Where is she?' I ask.

'In here,' Simon leads me to a two-bedded unit. There is only one occupant, Sarah, lying on the bed looking wan and unhappy. She looks unwell, I realise, because she has no make-up on. Sarah's a never-leave-the-house-without-some-slap sort of girl. I've long ago accepted that as a fact of life, though it's added hours on to planned trips. It's also meant a few missed trains and once a flight. Still, seeing her au natural is a shock. I don't tell her that.

'Jesus. Sarah,' I say. She immediately starts to cry.

I go to her and hug her. It doesn't matter what's transpired between us; this seems the right, the human, thing to do. She squeezes me tight and for a few seconds it feels as if she will never let me go. But finally, she pulls away and lies back on her pillows. She's crying, wetly.

'Sorry about all this,' she says.

'Don't be. Are you hurt?'

She shakes her head. 'No. More shaken than anything. But nothing broken.'

A bruise is blossoming to the side of her right eye. It'll get worse before getting better. 'What have they said?'

'I've had an X-ray, and that's fine. They're waiting for someone to see me and sign me out.'

'You're sure?'

She nods. Though she smiles, the corners of her mouth are sagging, and I wonder if she's on the verge of tears again.

'Do you want something?' Sarah asks. 'Cup of tea?'

'No, I'm–'

But Sarah looks up over my shoulder. 'Simon, be an angel. I could do with one.'

'Sure.' Simon pushes horn-rimmed glasses up his nose. I resist the urge to ask him what Liverpool's chances are in the Champion's league. He looks out of his depth here, as most people do in hospital. It's disempowering.

'Jake, sugar and milk?'

For a moment, I don't answer. It's all so bloody civilised I almost want to scream. But then I catch Sarah's eyes, pleading with me. Something clicks and I say, 'Yeah, great. Milk, one sugar.'

Simon exits and Sarah says, 'I need to talk to you alone.'

'Sarah, what's happened has happened. Like I said, it's probably best you're not anywhere near Oxford–'

'Not about us,' she cuts across me.

Her dismissal stings. But now is not the time to take umbrage. She realises how blunt it sounds and lets her shoulders sag. 'Sorry, I don't mean to be harsh, but I don't want to speak about us. I need to tell you what happened to me.'

I'm puzzled. 'Simon said someone mugged you, is that right?'

'Yes... no, I don't know exactly.'

I quell the little moth of anxiety that flutters around the

ember of fear glowing in my innards. Funny word, innards. One of my old bosses used it a lot. I stare at Sarah. 'What do you mean?'

'It happened so quickly. But now, the more I think about it...'

'Tell me. Exactly.'

The room is white with lilac-toned easy-wipe Respatex panels on the walls, white sinks and chrome taps. There are no windows. The people who end up in this bed are not here for the view. Sarah is in her own clothes but has a thin blanket over her. She looks diminished lying there, as if she's somehow shrunk, like Alice about to go down a rabbit hole.

'It was a little after six. I'd been food shopping in M&S. I crossed the road and cut through Kensington Church Walk. You can get through to Gordon Place that way behind St Mary Abbot's gardens. You know Simon's flat is on Campden Grove. You've been there. I've taken that shortcut a hundred times.'

I can't help raising my eyebrows. Sarah sees it and says, 'Sorry.'

I shake my head, dismissing her apology. I can envisage where she's talking about because I had been to the flat with Sarah to dinner when Simon was with Ginny. It seems an age ago. I concentrate. Yes, I recall a damp flagstone lane lined by faded brick walls and wrought iron fencing with gates opening onto gardens and a churchyard with medieval gravestones.

'As I said,' Sarah continues, 'it all happened so fast. I was crossing the garden when he came out of nowhere towards me. He was just someone with a hoodie, hurrying along. There were a few people around but not many. He bumped into me, pushed me over. I had shopping in both hands, so I went sprawling. Then I felt him tugging on my handbag. I tried to resist, but he was there, above me, with a knife. I let the bag go and then...' She catches herself, eyes narrowing as she remembers, 'He stabbed my bag. Stabbed it three times right the way through.

And he said something. I couldn't hear properly because of the balaclava over his face, but he held up the bag with the knife right through it, pointed at me and said, "Next time – you".'

Sarah's mouth is quivering. She puts a hand up to quickly cover it.

'Didn't anyone come to help?'

'Yes, someone did. But the mugger dropped the bag and ran. Back towards Ken High Street. No one chased him and it was all over within seconds. Someone called an ambulance and the police and here I am. But I've been lying here, looking at my phone, seeing what they're doing to you on social media and I can't help wondering if somehow it's connected.'

I sit back. A million thoughts come crashing over me in a wave. Could it be? Could it possibly be?

'You probably think I'm mad,' Sarah says.

I don't, but what I say is something very different. A blandishment. 'What a terrible ordeal. Must have been traumatising.'

'It all happened so fast. It took me by surprise but I keep asking myself why didn't he take my purse? Why stab my bag like that?'

'You're asking for a logical explanation for something we can't possibly explain. Who knows what goes through these people's minds.'

These people. The words echo through my head.

Sarah sighs. 'Oh God, I'm probably being paranoid. I haven't said anything about this to Simon. But the things they're saying about you online. It's so awful, Jake. I don't know how you can stand it. It's so wrong. And then I thought someone might have known that you and I were partners and that they'd somehow targeted me.'

It's a fair point. But I don't want her worrying. So I say, 'That's a hell of a stretch, Sarah.'

She nods. But inside I'm remembering the warning

messages I'd received on the phone and Galina telling me not to underestimate these people, whoever the hell these people are.

There's a long awkward moment of loaded silence while we both work out what to say next. I could tell her. I could explain about the message on the phone I found under the van seat and the warnings I'd had after talking to the police. But then what good would it do other than to make her feel even worse and ten times as anxious.

It's a huge relief when Simon comes back with the tea. We sit and sip it, go over what the police have said; that it's rare, an attack like this in broad daylight. Probably someone looking for a quick few quid to feed a habit. Or someone too high already to realise what they were doing. Standard stuff. Their way of saying that there's a snowball's chance in hell of them finding the culprit.

What they haven't said is what's bouncing around off the padded walls inside my head. The other unthinkable alternative. That Sarah is absolutely right. That this was someone sending me a message. Carrying out a threat.

I drink the tea too quickly, almost scalding my mouth. We chat about the knife crime epidemic, Sarah's attack our point of focus. Any animosity I have towards Simon is put on hold. I can see in his face he's grateful for that. I can see too how lost he is here in this scenario, whereas I'm not. Hospitals hold no fear for me because I know what goes on behind the green curtain.

When I go to leave fifteen minutes later, I hug Sarah again. She tells me to look after myself. I promise I will. Simon walks me out to the corridor.

'Jake, I haven't said I'm sorry.'

'For what? Stealing Sarah?'

Roses appear on his pale cheeks. 'That's not something I'm

going to apologise for. She's her own woman. Not yours to steal from.'

He's probably right. And Sarah and I were well aware that something had died in our relationship a while ago, but we were both too stubborn or scared to bury it.

'No,' Simon says. 'I'm sorry for what's happening to you. This business about the nurse. The press and social media. It's appalling. The thing is I know people who might help. Media experts...'

He lets the offer fade away. I shake my head. 'It's okay. I'll survive. They'll find this poor girl one way or the other. Then the truth will come out.'

He nods and holds out a hand. I don't take it. 'Look after her,' I say.

'I will. But it'll be much easier if you stay away.'

For a moment, I consider sniping. I want to say something to hurt him. To hurt them. But then I remember Sarah's bruised face. I think I've done enough damage. And there's no warning in Simon's request. Just truth.

In the lift, all I can think about is what Sarah has said. About the mugger's words to her.

Next time – you.

Just words? Or another warning?

I recall the expression on Simon's face when he offered his hand. Gratitude and sympathy. I'm sure he'll look after Sarah. But the feeling that I'm responsible for what's happened to her won't go away.

By the time I'm back in the car and heading home, I'm wracked with guilt. I toy with calling Oaks and telling him, but he's a policeman. He deals in facts. And all I have is empty supposition and that burning fear deep in my gut.

36

I t's well after 11.30pm by the time I park up at Kiln Road and walk back towards Headington. No one disturbs me as I hurry along Quarry Lane to the house. It's Saturday night and the photographers must be in the pub or gone home for the night.

Suits me.

The laptop and newspapers and congealing omelette are as I left them. I throw the egg in the bin. I know I should eat something but first I pour a glass of wine and grab a handful of nuts from a jar and switch on the TV. I avoid the news and find something to distract me and settle on *Game of Thrones*. I'm late to the party because Sarah's not a fan.

'If it has a witch or a dragon in it, it's definitely not for me.'

That was her reasoning, taking the unimaginative snob's high ground and dismissing fantasy as something irrelevant and childish. Never mind the staggering CGI, the amazing production values, and the historical parallels belying the fantasy elements; The War of the Roses, Hadrian's Wall, the Mongol hordes, Vikings. It's all there if you look under the surface. But Sarah was much more into *Strictly*. As if making celebrities dress up in sequins and cavort about to a tribute band is any more believable.

But I'm playing catch-up with the series and so watch a scheming queen detonate the holy sept. It's an episode full of intrigue and jealousy and violence. A bit like my life as it is. But it's a great distraction. I drink two glasses of wine and fall asleep with the TV still on.

At three, I get up, switch off the TV, respond to my bladder's wake-up call, and finally find my way to bed.

37

Rupe the Exterminator @extmntralpha 12May2019
#JThorn rides a bike. Is there a brave enough white van man out
there to do the necessary? #isthishim Put us out of our misery
#findkaty

Moon Soolantro @meanteen556 12May2019
#JThorn should be struck off. Wouldn't want his hands on me
#isthishim Uugh #findkaty

Lakin about @Feldfan77 12May2019
Looks so f***ng guilty #JThorn why are cops waiting. Waterboard the
c*** #findkaty #isthishim

Wizardsock @Wizsock619 12May2019
Reading all this bile is sickening #JThorn Don't know the guy but has
#isthishim actually done anything? #findkaty

38

I'm up with the dawn again. I text Sarah and ask if she's feeling better. I'm surprised to get an instant reply. She tells me she's home but unable to sleep. I tell her again to get better soon.

I shower and toast two slices of bread. I scramble eggs for one and stuff marmite and cheese into a sandwich of the other. I blitz some frozen berries and Greek yoghurt in a juicer, though Sarah would tell me that by doing so I alter the sugar structure of the berries and it's not good for me. Least of my worries. I punch in instructions for a strong espresso into a bean-to-cup coffee machine and get a double shot of the fresh stuff while I froth up some oat milk in an Aeroccino.

We have all the toys.

But then I can't help wondering who'll get what. The coffee machine was one of my indulgences, but the juicer was all Sarah. I suspect it will get messy. Unless I walk away from it all, give her the house and move into a flat somewhere. The good news is, Simon isn't exactly a pauper. And even though I've contributed more to the mortgage, Sarah and I shared the deposit. I have no problem with divvying up the spoils of the sale of Sedgewood, which, I now realise, will be inevitable. I don't really want to live here on my own.

Neither would I want anyone else living here in Sarah's place. To many memories. Too many ghosts. A chapter of my life that needs to close.

If circumstances ever let me.

I feel a bit better after the food. I'm up for it after the coffee. Outside, the day is shaping up nicely with the sun already bright. I text Ella and ask if she'd like to go for a walk. I'm delighted when she says yes. I dress and head for Kiln Road and my car.

I pick up Sid from Paws for Claws and head back up to Shotover Park.

Ella arrives at ten, and Ben and Lulu burst out of her Renault.

Lulu makes a beeline for Sid, Ben trots after her after waving to me.

'Hi, Ben.'

'Hi, Jake,' Ben calls out. He still has Lulu on her lead and he's being dragged along.

'Careful,' Ella says.

We watch as boy and both dogs hare down the forest track, leaving us alone to catch up. I take the opportunity to snatch a quick kiss. She returns it with interest. But I read real concern in Ella's expression when we separate. She faces me, hands on my elbows so I can't turn away.

'Are you okay, Jake? Really?'

I shrug. 'The NHS have decided to pay me not to operate, the press is outside my door, the police want me to tell them if I leave town. Otherwise, everything is hunky-dory.'

'They rang me. A Sergeant Oaks. Asked me about us. If I was with you when Katy Leith went missing.'

I nod. 'Were they difficult?'

She shrugs. 'No. Not at all. Besides, it's the truth isn't it?'

'It is. But I'm still sorry to drag you into my mess.'

'It's not your mess. You can't blame yourself for any of this. It's just wicked nonsense.'

She loops her arm into mine and we walk after Ben and the dogs.

'Have you read any of the online stuff?'

'I started to and then decided not to.'

I nod. 'Probably for the best.'

'I texted Fiona Ormerod too.'

'Your friend with the husband in Serious Crimes?'

She nods. 'They're still keen on this trafficking idea.'

I nod. I haven't told her about the van or the threats. That's something I'm determined to keep from her. I'd toyed with explaining, especially after Ridley and Oaks had suggested it was a hoax. I'm all for confessing my failings with this woman because I know I can. But Sarah's mugging and the mugger's strange words have thrown up a whole new set of nagging doubts. For now, I'm keeping my powder dry. Selfishly, I want nothing more than to enjoy an hour or two in Ella's company with nothing else to think about.

Instead, we talk about the Lannisters' machinations – Ella's a huge GOT fan and the person who encouraged me to abandon my scepticism and let the Martin universe envelop me. The final season is about to begin and I'm going to watch that anyway, even without the whole of the other seasons under my belt. Maybe I'll even watch some of it with Ella.

The walk is great. We let the dogs off the leash and the three of us find sticks which become a sword in my hands and a spear in Ben's. It stays a stick in Ella's because there needs to be an adult in the group. Ben's a little young for GOT but, as with all things that get to be a cultural phenomenon, he knows enough.

Pretty soon, we're chasing White Walkers through the trees, Lulu and Sid at our sides.

Ella's doing a great job with Ben. He's whip-smart and, she tells me, already getting good at football.

Maybe we should introduce him to Simon 'Klopp'.

We get back to the car park at a little after 11.20am. I'm putting Sid in the back of my car when I hear Ella's urgent cry. 'Jake, can you come here?'

I wheel round. Ella's car is three down from mine. She's kneeling next to a back tyre, Ben next to her with Lulu still on a leash and not yet in the vehicle. I walk over and see the tyre is flat. But it's the reason it's flat that sends a shiver through me. Jutting out from the wall is a white-handled knife.

'Someone's slashed my tyre,' Ella says.

She's right. Not only is the knife there, but there are five more thin puncture marks above and below it.

'What the hell's wrong with people?' she asks, her pretty face distraught.

'God knows,' I mumble. But I keep staring at the knife. I recognise it. It's the one missing from my tool shed. Though, on closer inspection, this one looks too new to be mine. But it's identical.

'Should we call the police?' Ella asks.

'We could. Probably should, but who knows when, or even if, they'd come out for this.'

Ella nods.

I get up. 'You have a spare?'

'One of those temporary things.'

'Let's get it changed. Ben, why don't you take Lulu and Sid back to the edge of the car park. Stay where we can see you. I'm sure I saw some rabbit holes there.'

Ben goes off to entertain the dogs while I go around to open the boot. My hand is on the release button when I see what's scrawled in the dust on the rear door. The Renault has black paintwork badly in need of a wash. Even so, it's obvious someone has smeared mud over it. Within that mud I read the word VAN.

'I wonder if anyone else's has been done?' Ella asks.

She stands and walks along the line of parked cars. If she's noticed the writing, she says nothing. I reach into my pocket and take out a tissue and quickly wipe the rear door. Most of the mud has dried, and it comes away as dust. But I can't erase what I've seen. The word VAN is seared on my retinas.

Ella joins me and we get the spare out and jack up the car. I'm glad of the physicality; it's a welcome distraction from the whirlpool of thoughts swirling in my head.

'You're quiet,' Ella says after several minutes of me not speaking.

'I'm annoyed,' I say.

She nods. 'Bloody vandals. But I don't see anyone else with a flat tyre.'

'Maybe they were disturbed, whoever it was. Might explain why they left the knife in there.'

'Yes. I hadn't thought of that. Should we keep it? For the police?'

I shrug. 'You could. But in all honesty, I think they're unlikely to be interested.'

Ella nods. Quick movements.

I tighten the locking nut and let down the jack.

'Right, you're good to go,' I say.

She kisses me again. More cinnamon gum. 'What would I do without you?'

A lot better, I'm thinking.

I wave them off, then I put Sid in the back of the car. I have to lean in to move a mat that's slipped, and he gives me a sneaky lick on the cheek as if to say, 'Thanks again for the walk.' So much affection in one morning. My lucky day. But why is it I don't feel I deserve any of it? All I seem to do at the moment is put people I care about in danger and what's worse is that I don't know why or what to do about it.

But as I drive Sid back to the kennels, I realise that I do know exactly what to do about it. It's obvious. That's why, at ten minutes after six that evening, I'm back in Shotover on my bike, heading once again out of the back of the car park, towards Blenheim Road on the way to Horsepath, and the derelict van.

There are more people about on a Sunday afternoon. That means a handful of walkers and the odd cyclist on the back lanes. Three lycra-clad road racers are coming towards me as I approach the tin barn. They're older than I am. Not built for tight-fitting clothes but with scant regard for aesthetics, MAMILS to a tee. I don't count myself amongst them yet because I only have the one bike, it's not the most expensive in the shop and when I'm out, I don't stop for a coffee and a scone. I know I'm bucking the trend by wearing merino wool and Road Rags shorts, but that's the way I roll. Maybe that sums me up.

I cycle past and double back once they're out of sight. I stop, make sure no one can see me and push the bike through the trees, just like I'd done with Oaks.

I park the bike so it's hidden from the lane and walk to the rusting hulk of the van. Trees rustle in the breeze. Somewhere from across the fields comes tinny music from a radio. Kids out sneaking a cider, I expect.

I kneel and reach with my hand, vaguely acknowledging that this is incredibly stupid. There could be anything under this seat: an adders' nest, a rat, even a mousetrap, so it's with a mixed sense of relief and horror that my fingers meet the textured surface of a plastic pouch. Once again, I retrieve it, unzip it, and remove the phone from inside. I power it up and check the app on the home screen. There's a red circle indicating a message.

A series of images appear.

The first is of me from two days ago standing behind Oaks as he kneels down, reaching for the pouch.

The second is of Sarah, shopping bags in both hands, on a flagstone lane with a redbrick wall and iron fencing on either side.

The third is of a deflated tyre with a white knife protruding from it.

A long few seconds pass before I remember to breathe again. Into that space, as I stare at the phone, a message appears.

We know EVERYTHING. No more games. Unless you do as you are told, Katy Leith will die with your knife in her heart. When you are in prison, we will kill your ex-partner and then your new partner and her son and her dog. If you contact the police again, we will kill your new partner anyway.

I almost drop the phone. The fact that they've added "and her dog" to the message tells me they know exactly who Ella is. But how? How do they know these things? I stand up quickly and wheel around. There's no one in sight, but then I realise that they could have rigged a camera in the nearby trees. That would explain the image of Oaks. It suggests a level of sophistication hard to contemplate. And as for Ella... someone's been watching me. Watching us. Once again, I'm struck by fear and confusion in equal measure. Why me?

What is it they want from me?

It's as if they can read my thoughts as another message appears.

The world already thinks you're a monster, yet you act as if you are innocent. But you are not innocent. You are a murderer. Time for the world to be educated. Confess your sins and post it online.

Michael Carstairs. DOB 07/11/1970. RIP 21/04/2006

Who the hell is Michael Carstairs?

I stare at the words, my pulse thrumming in my ears. It's insane, all of it. I'm caught up in some madman's wild imaginings. A madman who thinks I killed a Michael Carstairs a dozen years ago. Yet someone is so sure they're prepared to kill the people I care about. Kill an innocent nurse who hasn't done anything to anyone. Just to make me confess to something I haven't done.

I look up at the sky. Grey and bruised. I listen, hear the hiss of rubber on tarmac as another three cyclists stream past screened from my sight by the trees. I suck in air. It ratchets in my throat.

I can't go back to the police, not after what the messenger did to Sarah and to Ella's car.

But I have to do something.

Trouble is, I don't know where to start.

I spend the rest of the evening at home on the laptop trying to find out who Michael Carstairs is. Was. A Google search with his name and what, I presume, is his date of death in 2006 comes back with 55,000 hits. I try variations including date of birth and date of death. Again, there are far too many hits. But none of them mean anything to me.

As the evening wears on, a thought grows. An awareness that I can't get into focus at first, but then, gradually, it gels and hardens until it finally crystallises.

I'm doing this all wrong.

What was it Hippocrates said? Do good, or (at the very least) do no harm.

It's something I live by daily. As a surgeon, you weigh up the risks versus the benefits. Sometimes doing nothing is the best option. But often intervention is the only correct thing to do, even if when you do intervene, things can go wrong. I haven't ever deliberately set out to kill anyone, but death is a complication I, as a surgeon, have to warn everyone I operate about. A risk I have to live with every day.

Could it be that Michael Carstairs is one of those patients I did harm to? If he is, he isn't one I can remember and that bothers me because I always do remember the bad outcomes. Never mind the hundreds, perhaps by now even the thousands, that I've helped, or cured, or fixed. It's the ones that don't do as well as expected that haunt you in the early wakeful hours or the dark watches of the night. They're the ones whose names you don't forget.

But no bell rings in my head for Michael Carstairs.

By midnight, I think I have a plan.

MONDAY 13TH MAY 2019

Too many metoo. @Metwootwenty55 13May2019
All those women he's examined must be feeling filthy. #isthishim Are
we still paying him? #Jthorn I bet he knows #findkaty

Muskrat Elon @ratskikorsakoff 13May2019
#JThorn Apparently rides a bike see photos. Https://clipsgen.88.
Makes a good target for anyone with a lorry #needstobeputdown

Steve Bute @sbuteoo7 13May2019
Watching people tear into #JThorn. He has not been charged for
#findkaty Anyone here heard of evidence? #isthishim

Sammy Samunwise @samunwise. 13May2019
Fair shout @sbuteoo7 But when he's in the dock for #findkaty you
may regret defending the slime ball #isthishim You two screwing?

I 'm at my desk in my office at the hospital by 8.30am. I want to catch Meera before she settles in. She beams when she sees me.

'Can't keep away, I see.'

'Hiding isn't quite my style. Thought I'd wade through some of this stuff on the shelves. Have a clear-out.'

'Wonders never cease,' she says, and does it with a fixed, bright smile.

'Plus, I'm chasing up some patients. Queries I thought I'd dealt with. Any chance you can get the notes of a Michael Carstairs, date of birth 7/11/70?'

'I daresay.' She writes it down on a notepad. 'Tea?'

We settle into the morning. I busy myself with throwing old journals and papers into a black refuse bag, answering emails and trying not to hassle Meera too much. At nine twenty, she looks up from her screen and announces, 'There are no clinic records for a Michael Carstairs with that date of birth on the system, but there is a record of attendance at A&E from 2003.'

'Don't tell me, it's in an offsite archive.'

'No. Surprisingly. A&E ran the trials for electronic patient records for five years beginning in 2002. They are meant to have amalgamated it with our new all-singing, all-dancing EPR. Remember, we're on a "journey of change towards full implementation".' Meera delivers this quoted sentence in amazement speak with a heavy dollop of eyebrows-raised scepticism. It makes me smile.

Her fingers tap the keyboard at a speed that I can only admire. 'Yes, here we are. Michael Carstairs. Seen in A&E for a broken finger.'

I walk around the desk and read the page. He fractured his thumb after falling on the bank of the river on a family day out. I get Meera to print the sheet.

'He's not from Oxford,' she says.

I voice an enigmatic, 'Hmm,' and take the printout into an adjacent room. My pulse goes up a tick as I try to put two and two together and come up with only three and a half.

The address is in Chineham, a parish north of Basingstoke. I know it because I spent four years in Basingstoke at St Jude's hospital during my training. A hollow sinking sensation creeps over me. I was a trainee registrar at the hospital in 2006. The same year Carstairs died according to the phone message I'd read.

But as a junior doctor, albeit one just a step or two away from being a consultant, I certainly would have remembered anyone suffering at my hands. 2006 was also the year I went off to California for an eighteen-month fellowship at the UCLA medical centre. So it isn't one I forget very easily.

Confused, I ring St Jude's and ask to be put through to Linda Charles, my old boss's secretary. It's been a few years since I've spoken to her. I've no idea if she's still there. But when I ask the switchboard operator, there's no hesitation. Linda answers after five rings.

'Hello?'

'Linda, this is Jacob Thorn. Not sure if you remember—'

'Jake! Oh my God, how are you? We were just talking about you this morning.' Not quite a squeal, it's nevertheless loud enough for me to want to shut the door with one foot.

'I'm okay,' I say slowly, realising with dismay that I'm probably the topic for discussion at bus stops, offices and water coolers all over the country.

'It's disgusting, all this hearsay and conjecture. The press are just pigs.'

My mental image of Linda from a decade and a bit ago is of an energetic woman of thirty-something with chic glasses, a sweet tooth, a big smile and organisational skills that our boss, an old-school general surgeon called Roger Delany, could not function without. She organised his lists, his leave, his wife's birthday presents, servicing his car, hotels for conferences, and everything in between.

Bilton would have had a fit.

But Linda did so with an efficiency that made it all look easy. When she was away on holiday, the temps they brought in never stood a chance. Not that Delany was a bully or a fool; it was simply that he was a dinosaur. A good-naturedly chauvinistic, technophobe Luddite. Computers were an anathema. I doubt he'd washed a dish or emptied a washing machine in his life. He got away with it by wearing good suits, charm, and the odd funny handshake. At the time, I could only guess at what he earned from a thriving private practice. But "RD", as we called him, was hardly ever at home, which went some way to explain why he was also on his third marriage at the last count.

At home, as at work, RD relied on someone else to feed and clothe him. Hardly surprising then, that any sane woman with a spark of independence eventually woke up to the fact that what Roger wanted was a skivvy and told him to bugger off. Two of them already had.

At work, though Linda organised his professional life and most of his social, since she was getting paid for doing so, she never complained. But she was also a compassionate woman. For us juniors, she became a mother hen the minute one of us walked through the department door. I should not have been surprised to hear her concern for my well-being. Linda was fiercely loyal.

'Linda, I'm after a favour.' I explained my enforced leave, and that I was trying to catch up on correspondence and unfinished business, one of which was Michael Carstairs. Not the total truth, but not exactly a lie either. 'I'm after any notes you might have. Happy to come down there and look at them if there are any.'

'Of course.' I could hear a note of hesitation in her voice.

'Is that okay? If it's going to cause you grief–'

'No, not at all. It's just that the name rings a distant bell. Where are you now?'

'In my office.'

'At the infirmary?'

'Yes.'

'Give me fifteen minutes. I'll ring you back.'

I put the phone down and return to the shelves and the black refuse bags.

Linda rings twenty minutes later.

'Good news and bad news,' she says.

'Go on.'

'Notes have been destroyed because Mr Carstairs is deceased.'

'Ah, I should have told you that.'

'They only keep them for five years now. So Mr Carstairs's notes are gone. But when you said the name, it rang a vague bell. We had the notes here for weeks after the death. Something to do with CEPOD and social workers. But other people wanted them too, so I made a copy for Mr D and sent the actual notes back to file. Guess what, that copy's still here.'

'What?'

'On my "don't throw just in case" shelf.'

'You're amazing, Linda.'

'I never get tired of hearing that.'

'Will it be okay to come down and take a peek at them?'

'Mr Carstairs isn't going to mind, is he?' Linda says drily.

'Should I bring doughnuts?'

'Are you the devil? I'm on a diet.' I detect a little trill in her voice.

'But it's a no on the doughnuts then?'

'Now, I didn't say that.'

I huff out a laugh. 'Meet me in reception?'

'Will do. You'll be the one wearing a white tulip in your lapel?'

'No. I'll be the one skulking in the corner with doughnut sugar frosting around my mouth.'

'Mmm.'

It's nice to know things haven't changed in a dozen years.

42

It takes an hour and a half for me to drive the forty-three miles to St Jude's in Berkshire. The morning rush has gone, but the A34 is, as always, jam-packed with traffic, with Newbury an inevitable bottleneck.

Though it's years since I was there, once I'm in the car park at the hospital, memory kicks in. It's a good-sized district general with 450 beds and provides specialist services as a tertiary centre. From where I sit in my car, nothing much has changed. Huge grey concrete rectangles make up the main body, with a squat low-level reception and outpatient blocks.

I have to pay to park. When I get to reception, it's all pale blues and pastel pinks. The place has obviously had a facelift since I left. Linda is standing outside a WH Smith's clutching a big buff envelope, smiling as I stride towards her. She's as I remember her, though the years have made her broader in the beam and added the odd grey streak to her hair. But still there's a beguiling dimple in her smile.

Coming back is a little like going home to my parents' house, when they were alive, for university holidays. As soon as I walked through the door of their semi, in their eyes I was eighteen again; the boy setting out into the big wide world. And I may be the consultant surgical head of department in Oxford, but here, in this hospital, Linda remembers me as the mustard-keen junior, hell-bent on getting there.

She gives me a hug.

'You haven't changed a bit,' she says, giving me the once over, smiling.

'Neither have you,' I say.

She lets out a sardonic hiss. But then her expression shifts and hardens. 'No one here believes any of that rot in the press.'

'They are making a meal of things.' I nod.

'None of it is helping that poor girl or her parents. It must be so awful for them.'

I nod again. There's nothing I can add. But Linda's empathy puts my predicament into perspective. At least I'm walking around alive and free. The thought trips me up. Oaks's presumption that the image I'd seen of Katy was a staged photograph, seems now, considering what's happened to Sarah and to Ella's car, flawed. It's too risky for me to accept. I have to believe that the photo was Katy. And that she is still alive. Whoever is doing this wants me to believe it. And if there's anything I can do to keep things that way, I have to.

My eyes fall to the envelope.

'Yes, this is it. I haven't had time to copy it,' Linda apologises.

'No problem. I just want to borrow it. Give me an hour and I'll bring it back.'

Linda nods. 'Not that anyone else wants it. I mean no one even knows it exists. I'd forgotten about it myself. Such a tragic case.'

My mouth is parchment as I take the package. It's an inch thick.

'So,' Linda asks, 'how's Sarah?'

I lie and tell her all is well, that we're toying with buying a bigger house. The truth is too complicated and irrelevant. I ask Linda about her kids. Two are in university, the third doing A levels.

'And what about RD?' I ask.

'Mr Delany hasn't changed a bit. He's down to two days a week now. Plus a day and a half doing private work. He's talking about early retirement in six months.'

'Wow. He's not sixty yet, is he?'

'On the way. But he's supporting too many wives to stop work altogether. I think he'll carry on at The Three Counties.'

I nod. Roger Delany – it's he who used innards as one of his favourite words – had a booming private practice at the local clinic even when I was here. Could only have grown bigger with time. The Three Counties Hospital is owned by one of the largest private providers in the country and got swisher by the year from what I could remember. And a Wexford accent and a certain glint in the eye had done RD no harm when it came to charming the punters in that more intimate environment. Private patients pay for one on one. And in that arena, a sparkly smile goes a long way. We've kept in touch, bumped into each other at meetings, had a few beers in the evenings at conventions. Roger was a mentor who kick-started my career and, for all his quirks, I'm very fond of him.

I hand over payment to Linda in the form of four assorted Krispy Kreme doughnuts.

'Oh, you're evil, you know that?' Linda says, making eyes at me. 'I'll share these with the girls over coffee.'

'Give everyone my regards.' I check my watch. 11.15am. 'How about I meet you back here at half one?'

'Sure you don't want to keep it for longer?'

'No. I can make a copy if I need to.'

'Okay.' Linda smiles. 'See you later.'

She gives me a little wave and walks to the lifts.

The reception area is busy, but there's normally a quiet corner somewhere where I won't be disturbed. I scan the space, but it doesn't feel right. There's nothing normal about my presence here today. I need to concentrate with no distractions.

I grab a coffee, go back to the car and drive out to a business centre half a mile away; a mix of large red brick offices and prefabricated low steel-clad units. Half of them are empty. The economy is hardly booming here. Occasionally, as a junior, when the mess got too much, I'd bring my car here for valeting. Today, I find a shady spot in front of a deserted unit and find a mindless no-ads music channel on the radio as background while I sip my coffee and open Linda's envelope.

Inside is a plastic folder containing seventy or so loose-leaf pages held together in the top corner by a metal and green string file tag. I seem to remember Linda calling these treasury tags. I check the name and date of birth. The address in Chineham is the same as the one in the A&E notes from Oxford. My pulse gives a twitch. Confirmation that this is the correct Carstairs.

The first few pages are personal details, but it doesn't take me long to get to the dark heart of the horrible truth of what happened.

Michael Carstairs was thirty-four when he noticed some darkening of his stools a few months after his attendance at the A&E Oxford. No link to his broken finger, but Mr Carstairs knew not to ignore the signs. He was bright and worked as a teacher. His wife worked in local government. They had two children at the time he saw those telltale signs in the toilet bowl. A girl of ten and a son aged seven. He didn't tell his wife, but took himself off to his GP, who, like any sensible doctor, then referred him up to the hospital under the care of Roger Delany. In early 2005, Michael Carstairs underwent a series of tests, including a colonoscopy. The biopsy confirmed colorectal cancer. CT scans followed to establish staging and a treatment plan was set up by the multidisciplinary team. Preoperative radiotherapy commenced before Mr Carstairs underwent a J-pouch procedure.

The notes showed that Roger Delany had supervised one of his fellows – a senior trainee – in performing this procedure. Mr Carstairs's entire colon and rectum was removed, and a J-shaped reservoir of small bowel fashioned and joined to the anal canal. This meant no need for a separate exit, or ileostomy to capture stools in a bag.

The procedure and outcomes had been very good, and the patient had done well.

Until some thirteen months later when Mr Carstairs began experiencing symptoms of intermittent pain and vomiting. He initially thought that this might have been an infection, but his condition worsened, and he was admitted to hospital. Scans showed evidence of adhesions – tight bands of scar tissue – probably from the previous surgery and radiotherapy. Ominously, the CT scans showed likely ischaemia; the adhesions were not only blocking Mr Carstairs's bowel; they were cutting off the blood supply as well. Still, this was not an irredeemable situation.

And so, on Good Friday, the fourteenth of April 2006, Michael Carstairs went back to the operating theatre. The adhesions were divided, and an area of ischaemic dead bowel was removed before the two ends of healthy bowel rejoined.

Theoretically, there was nothing preventing Mr Carstairs from making a good recovery. Especially as no local sign of recurrence of the cancer was found. Once the new bowel anastomosis started to work, he should have been fine. But that isn't what happened.

I look up into the empty parking lot. Two crows are feeding

on something near a leaky skip. I'm glad I can't see what it is. I turn back to the notes.

Two days after surgery, Mr Carstairs reported feeling very ill, with nausea, bloating and sweats. It was a bank holiday weekend. The hospital was short-staffed. A series of junior doctors reviewed Mr Carstairs but reported nothing untoward. The senior doctor that weekend was a name I did not recognise. He signed himself "Locum registrar". On the Tuesday following the bank holiday, an entry in the notes indicated suspected leak from the anastomosis, confirmed on X-ray.

Mr Carstairs went back to theatre where the anastomosis was found to be leaking. It was repaired, but by that time sepsis had set in.

He died five days later of multiple organ failure, as a result of infection stemming from the surgery he'd undergone to treat his secondary bowel obstruction from adhesions.

I make notes as I read through the file. Someone had messed up here and messed up badly. Fear of a leak after surgery like this should have been at the forefront of any experienced surgeon's mind. But only junior inexperienced doctors seemed to have examined poor Carstairs in these crucial days post-surgery.

I turn again to the op note from the day Mr Carstairs had gone to theatre for division of adhesions on Friday, fourteenth April 2006. A bank holiday when staff would be thin on the ground. The notes had been typed up. No matter who did the surgery, Roger Delany insisted on this to ensure entries were legible. There was even a pro forma:

Surgical procedure

Type of anaesthesia

Details of Procedure.

And above all of these was a separate list of the medical personnel. Surgeon, assistant, scrub nurse and anaesthetist.

For some reason, I read this section last, only after scouring the operating notes which seem exemplary. It's only then that I see the name written next to the typed word "surgeon". Only then that my blood runs cold and my mind scrambles.

In black and white, staring right back at me, the typed-up name is Mr J Thorn.

I was the one who botched Mr Carstairs's operation that Good Friday.

I let the notes fall into my lap and let my eyes bore through the windscreen at a sign that says "Hallond Engineering", trying to make sense of this disaster. Despite the sun through the windscreen, I shiver. I don't know how long I keep staring, but what's left of my coffee is cold and undrinkable when I eventually snap out of it.

I scan the op note again. There's a signature at the bottom of the page. A loopy scrawl. Just the first letter of the first name, followed by a large first letter and then a tailing off snake that's the rest of the surname. It's messy, smudged by a curved ring that looks suspiciously like the bottom of a coffee-stained cup. I wonder how many sets of hospital notes are similarly tainted by spilled tea or coffee. Doesn't matter because I recognise the scrawl anyway. Looks as if it was written in a hurry. Like you might do when there are a dozen or more bits of correspondence to sign. But there is no doubt.

It's my signature.

My hands fly up to cover my face and block out the world.

But behind them, my mind fills with a single question that expands like a dark balloon to push every other thought away and occupy the space.

What the hell have I done?

43

I sit in the car, trying desperately to remember anything about this case. But I can't. Why can't I?

All kinds of disjointed thoughts flit in and out.

Have I forgotten? Unlikely.

Have I suppressed the memory as an inconvenient truth? Also unlikely... but how can I explain it otherwise?

My hands are on the steering wheel, thumb tracing a pattern etched into the faux leather, searching for a pattern where there is none. So how has this happened? How could something so awful have not even registered?

Something in what Linda told me when I contacted her rings an alarm bell. She'd said other people had wanted the notes.

I ring her number.

'Linda, it's me.'

'Jake, you're early.'

My voice sounds shrivelled. 'I'm not back yet. But it's about this case.'

'You okay? You sound a bit stressed.'

'No, I'm fine.' I swallow. It makes too loud a noise. 'You said that other people had wanted the notes after Carstairs died?'

'I remember that social workers were heavily involved.'

'Social workers?' Two words that add a little vinegar to the wound that is my lack of memory.

'Yes. It was Brenda Hudson. You remember her.'

'Is she still there?'

'Oh yes. One of the old guard. Positively ancient and crumbling. Like me.'

I visualise Linda's dimply smile in my head as she delivers this deprecating sentence. But my mind is too ragged with unanswered questions whipping around like the tendrils of frayed rope in a high wind to play.

'Linda, I need a favour. Can you ask Brenda Hudson about this case? There's a big piece of the jigsaw missing here and I need to make the picture whole.'

She could ask me why. Demand to know what it's all about. But to her credit, Linda does neither. Like I say, medical secretaries are worth their weight in platinum.

'I'll see if I can get hold of her. I'll let you know when you get back.'

I thank her and ring off. Outside, the sun is still shining. It beats in through the windscreen and it's hot on my face, but my hands feel cold and clammy as I clutch the steering wheel. I need to give Linda some time to do what she needs to do. I realise I haven't eaten any lunch, but I'm not hungry. I let go of the wheel and with trembling fingers, turn back to the set of notes on my lap and read through them again. What's striking is the fact that although I carried out the surgery, there's no entry from me after that date.

Difficult to believe no one read the signs of impending sepsis. It had been a bank holiday weekend and I might have been off the next day. But still, there's no excuse. Not really.

Anastomotic leak is one of the most feared complications of this kind of surgery.

Had I gone away after operating on Mr Carstairs, perhaps?

Even if I had, it makes no difference. I should have been more vigilant. I should have made sure someone...

I shake my head. It's almost 1.20pm.

I take out my phone and photograph twenty or so pages of the photocopied notes. The most relevant ones. The most damning. Then I put the notes back in the envelope, start the car and head back to the hospital to meet Linda.

I can't explain what I've read. But I know I'm going to have to. Not only for Katy Leith's sake, but for my own.

Linda's in reception, standing in front of WH Smith as before, still smiling. But it's a forced smile this time. And there's something in her eyes that tells me the news she has for me is not good. I'm half hoping it's because she hasn't been able to contact the social worker. But I'm wrong. Very wrong.

'I spoke to Brenda Hudson. She remembers the Carstairs case well.'

'Does she?'

Linda nods. Small vigorous movements. Her smile's slipping already. 'She said that the family dynamics were complicated to start with. Mrs Carstairs had been off work for months with depression. When Mr Carstairs died, it tipped her over. She started drinking heavily and four months later, she overdosed on sleeping pills and vodka.'

'Oh God,' I whisper.

'Brenda was heavily involved with her community colleagues because of the children.'

I swallow. My throat is a sawdust sump. Linda's words are like blows.

'They were ten and eight, I think, and there were no relatives. They went into care.'

I blow out air. It's like someone's sucker-punched me in the solar plexus.

'Jake, are you okay?'

I look up and say, 'Yes, I'm fine.'

Linda looks at me with bunched brows. 'You don't look fine.'

'Dodgy service station sandwich,' I offer, swatting her concern away.

'Oh dear. So yes, Brenda remembers Mr Carstairs. A genuinely tragic case.'

'Sounds like it.'

'Does any of this help?'

'Yes, it does.' Despite the horror that's trying to freeze my brain, I trot out an explanation. 'Someone's contacted me about a paper they're doing on post-op complications after adhesion induced ischaemia. Mr Carstairs fits the bill.' Another lie. I'm getting so, so good at it.

Soon they'll give me a diploma.

'Oh, then I'd better hang on to the notes and refile them under "you never know".' Linda attempts a proper smile.

'Good idea,' I say. 'By the way, where is RD today?'

Linda tilts her head. 'Where do you think?'

'Private hospital?'

Her lips curl up at the edges. It's all the answer I need. 'I'd like to catch up, but I won't bother him there.'

'Oh, please do. He finishes around four. I'm sure he'd love to see you. I'll ring him. Tell him you're on the way.'

'Okay,' I say.

Linda fixes me with a concerned look. 'Jake, I'm sorry to see you so troubled.'

Is it that obvious?

'I'm fine. All this will blow over.' Trite words. Who am I trying to kid?

'The sooner the better,' Linda says. 'And if there's anything I can do, just pick up the phone.'

'Thanks.'

Linda gives me another hug. I turn away, my stomach churning, as it has done ever since Linda told me about how my cock-up devastated the Carstairs family.

I'm shaking when I get back to the car. I sit in the seat and shiver. It's worse than I could ever have imagined. That poor man. That poor family. It's all I can think about. My thoughts are trapped in a whirlpool I can't break out of. It all fits in with the messages on the phone in the van and with poor Katy Leith. It fits, but I still have no idea how.

When I look at my watch, I realise I've been in a kind of fugue, sitting in the car for almost an hour and a half. My mouth is dry, and I'm sticky with sweat. I drive out, call in a garage for some water, and drink the whole bottle. At least my thirst has broken my paralysis. But I desperately need to talk to someone about this. Someone who understands.

44

I've never been inside The Three Counties Hospital. As a junior doctor, such places were taboo. The private sector was a different land on a different planet. You got to go there only after becoming a consultant and developing your skills and reputation. I have my own small private practice in a clinic in Banbury. It's run by one of the big providers and I dip my toe in once a fortnight. I've never been obsessed by it like some of my colleagues. Perhaps that will change. Perhaps if Sarah and I had bought the place in DOT, I would have needed the extra income. But somehow, in my current situation, I doubt that anyone with half a brain would pay to see me.

I haven't talked to the people at the clinic in Banbury. I need to do that. They need to cancel my appointments if they haven't done so already. Of course, there's nothing preventing me plying my trade there even now, but somehow, even more so than the NHS hospital, I suspect they're unlikely to want me around. It would send all the wrong messages.

Better to wait until my predicament is resolved.

Until Katy Leith is found.

Thoughts of Katy sends a new spasm of panic rippling through me, followed by a fresh wave of confusion and horror.

How? How could I have not known about Michael Carstairs?

Disasters happen. We're all human and things can, and do, go wrong. This has long been recognised. The Royal College of Surgeons and the General Medical Council recommend that all surgeons in practice attend M&M meetings. All part of the checks and balances. And despite the similarity of the acronym to candy-covered chocolates, there's nothing sweet about these meetings. The M&M here stands for morbidity and mortality. It's an opportunity to discuss adverse outcomes, identify failings, and help trainees. They are sometimes seen as a pain, an intrusion into busy schedules, but a once-monthly meeting is accepted as not being too onerous.

There's no point discussing normal, good outcomes at these meetings; they're not set up to allow people to preen or pose or gloat, though sometimes, the prima donna syndrome is all too clear in the more egotistical of my colleagues. We, the consultants in the surgical team, usually rotate as chairs. As gatherings, they're meant to be open and non-judgemental, patient-centred and not didactic. The whole aim is to provide an environment for trust. To allow people to admit mistakes and weaknesses, tap into others' skills and expertise. Usually, cases are presented by a neutral, someone not directly responsible for their care, and patients identified only by hospital number.

The end result is that cases are graded in terms of their acceptability to the team. If the care provided is considered less that satisfactory, we report the case as an incident or an adverse event. Sometimes, outcomes will require the sharing of information with a clinical governance lead, or a director of services, especially if the case represents signs of a wider problem. If deficiencies in care are found, they should be reported to the relatives either in writing or through face-to-face meetings.

Checks and balances.

So why was Carstairs not discussed at an M&M meeting?

And then with a death so soon after a surgical procedure, the coroner would have been informed. It would be up to him to decide if it needed an inquest into the death. I was not called to attend any inquest.

I need to find some answers.

The Three Counties clinic is out on the eastern fringe of the town. On the other side of the ring road. It's two storeys of red brick with modern coated aluminium windows in a leafy, manicured setting. I park and head for the reception, explain to the uniformed receptionist behind a long pale wooden counter that I'm here to see Mr Delany. She asks me for my credit card. I tell her I'm not a patient but that he's expecting me. Throughout the whole of this dialogue her pleasant cheerful smile never slips.

It's what you pay for.

I'm ushered through some doors into a different waiting area with upholstered armchairs and glossy magazines on a low coffee table. I'm toying with the idea of picking up a *GQ* to stop myself from fidgeting when a door opens and out walks Roger Delany in a pin-striped suit, pale blue shirt and a sober tie. He's a tall man with a loping stride and head of wiry hair that's now shot through with silver. He's slim and fit and his tan is not artificial. I remember something about a bolthole on an island in the West Indies. He's smiling, and when he speaks his tone is hushed and earnest.

'Jake. It's good to see you. Come in.' He offers a hand. I shake it. He looks up at a nurse sitting at a workstation. 'Could we muster up a cappuccino for Mr Thorn, Kirsty?'

The nurse nods and smiles. It doesn't look like the task will cause much hardship.

I follow Roger into his consulting room. Blue carpet on the floor matching blue drapes that can be pulled around a trolley bed in one corner. The chairs, one for the patient and one behind the desk, are of exactly the same shade. There's a sink with soap and alcohol hand scrub dispensers. Perched on the desk is a PC.

'Thanks for seeing me, Roger.'

'Any time, Jake, you know that. You're having a rough time, you poor chap.' He indicates a chair and I sit. There's a pile of half a dozen notes on the floor next to the desk. RD's clinic, I guess.

I nod. 'It's a bloody weird time, I know that.'

There's a knock on the door and Kirsty comes in with two coffees.

'You're an angel,' Roger says.

Kirsty beams. We wait until the door shuts and then he says, 'I've been reading about all this baloney with the nurse. It can't be easy.'

'It's not. I truly don't understand what's going on.'

'The press are like wolves, are they not?'

I nod. 'They've scented blood.'

'Well, I want you to know that none of us here in this neck of the woods believes a word of their lies.'

'Thanks, Roger. That means a lot.'

'What brings you down here? Needed a friendly face?' He stirs his coffee.

'Sort of. The police think Katy Leith's disappearance may be linked to a trafficking gang. But they have no proof and no idea where she is. In the meantime, I'm firmly in the press's sights. And also that swirling cesspit known as social media. And now, believe it or not, someone has accused me of killing a patient.'

'What?' Roger's tanned face creases.

'It's years ago. As I say, this sort of thing does bring out the crazies. The patient is from my time here in Hampshire. Does the name Michael Carstairs ring a bell with you?'

Roger frowns and shakes his head slowly. 'Educate me.'

So I do. I tell him about what I've found out. I even show him the photos of the notes I have on my phone.

'This is over a dozen years ago,' he says.

'I know. But it seems Carstairs's death was made all the worse by his wife committing suicide, leaving two kids with no parents. And I, for the life of me, can't remember anything about–'

A light seems to go on in Roger's eyes. 'Wait a minute. 2006 you say? Wasn't that the year you left us to go abroad?'

'Yes. I went to LA on an eighteen-month fellowship.' I take a sip of the coffee. It's good. No crusted granulated rubbish here.

He nods. 'Then I do remember this case.'

I frown. 'But I don't recall any of this being discussed at an M&M meeting. Surely I would remember–'

An odd look forms on Roger's face. 'You wouldn't remember because you weren't here for any of that.'

'What do you mean?'

He's shaking his head. 'I didn't think this would ever come back and bite you. I genuinely didn't'.

My heart slows. 'What are you talking about?'

'Not here. They'll be expecting me to vacate. There's an orthopaedic clinic at five. They need the room. But there's a nice little pub half a mile from here. Let's talk there.'

45

I follow Roger to the Maidenhead Arms a couple of miles away and we find a quiet corner table. He orders half a pint of beer for both of us. He holds up the glass of amber liquid. 'They call this "Old Sailor". It's good stuff. From a local brewery.'

I take a sip, but I can barely taste it.

Roger sees that I'm distracted. He puts down his beer. 'If Carstairs is the chap I'm thinking about, it all happened over a bank holiday. You were about to go away. We were going to miss you. I still say you have one of the best pairs of hands I've ever seen, next to mine.' He smiles, telling me it's meant as a joke. We both know deep down it isn't. Roger doesn't do self-deprecation. 'But you'd booked leave because you and Sarah were going to take a holiday before you left for California. How is the delightful Sarah, by the way?'

'She's fine.'

'Beautiful girl. Really.'

I nod. Roger continues.

'The managers had fixed up a locum. Someone not of these shores, but who came with glowing references. Beware of any locum with glowing references, by the way. Usually means the last lot to have him are only too glad to get rid of him and so will sell you a pup. And so it was with this chap. Carstairs, if I remember rightly, was obstructed and needed to go back to theatre. The locum who was meant to be vastly experienced, admitted that he was unhappy to take on the case. You volunteered, even though you were pushed for time. You'd done several resections like this on your own and I was happy to let you get on with it, which you did. I was there at the end of the phone if needed. You rang to say all had gone well. But then you left that night and the on-call team, unfortunately, did not spot the signs early enough. Did not put Carstairs on a sepsis pathway.' Roger follows with a thin-lipped smile.

I squeeze my eyes shut. This is not what I'd wanted to hear. 'I'd left the department when all of this went south?'

Roger nods. 'And as with all things that go wrong, from then on it's a chapter of accidents. No one really took responsibility. The locum was a waste of space. By the time I picked up the pieces four days later after the holidays, Carstairs's script had already been written.'

I stare at Roger in horror. 'But he had a leaky anastomosis. That was all down to me. Why didn't you tell me this?'

Roger takes a sip of beer and looks me in the eye. 'There was no M&M. Sherry Breedon did the post-mortem and said that one end of the bowel did not look as healthy as it could have been, and the stapling had given way.'

It was a classic fail. Not taking enough dead bowel away so that the end-to-end join could be between good healthy tissue on both sides.

'It was discussed. Some of our colleagues felt we ought to pass it on up the line as an adverse event, but I didn't see any point. Sherry found evidence of liver metastasis too. Carstairs would not have survived another year, eighteen months at the most. I argued that making this a mountain from a molehill and throwing you to the lions would not help anyone.'

'What about the coroner?'

He cocks his head. 'I knew the coroner's officers very well. I explained the situation to them. They saw no need for an inquest.'

'You covered all this up?'

Roger's brows gather. 'Those are strong and emotive words, Jake. We both know how this works. Juniors make mistakes. Up to that point, you'd been a first-class trainee. I saw no need in letting this blot your copybook.'

I squeeze my eyes shut and shake my head. Roger's words are like the stabbing of a knife. 'But Carstairs might have lived another five years. You never know.'

'No, you never do. But as I say, the mets were extensive. The end was inevitable.'

'But he could have had more time with his family if I'd have done my job properly.'

'Jake, I can see you're upset, but we both know that this sort of thinking gets us nowhere.'

I'm breathing heavily.

Roger picks up his glass and takes a couple of gulps. 'Finish your beer.'

But I can't. I want answers. 'What about the relatives? Did you speak to them?'

Roger nods. He is calmness personified. 'I did. I explained that this was a rare and unfortunate complication. At first, the wife was very angry. Understandably. There was talk amidst the tears of possible litigation. I suspect she was after compensation. But nothing came of it.'

Suddenly, Linda's memory of people requesting the notes made sense. It might have been a solicitor acting for Mrs Carstairs. But she had not survived her grief long enough for it to come to anything. Somehow, that made things even worse. I realise I've gone quiet, staring into my beer.

'I'm sorry if this has come as a shock to you, Jake. Sorry that someone is stirring up trouble unnecessarily.'

I look up into Roger's face. I'm angry and confused, but what I see looking back at me is a benevolent expression. Roger Delany is a renowned liver surgeon. Someone with an international reputation who could be a bit of a tyrant in the operating theatre and didn't suffer fools gladly. We trainees used to enjoy being on call with Roger because he'd let us do almost all the emergency surgery: the inflamed appendices, trauma, abscesses, resections.

The less generous amongst us hinted at the fact that he probably wasn't any good at anything much other than chopping liver, given the extent of his specialisation. But as a junior hungry for, and glad of, any opportunity to get my hands bloody, I had never objected. And, over the years, he's become a trusted colleague to whom I've referred more than one patient.

But sitting here in this pub, all I feel is resentment towards him for not telling me that my actions have probably killed someone. What's worse is that I know I have no right to do that. In fact, I should be eternally grateful. But then Roger knows nothing about the van and the phone under the seat or Sarah's "mugging". Nor the demand that I confess to something I didn't even know I'd done until a few hours ago.

'Shit,' I say.

Roger sighs, deeply. 'This is hard to hear, I know. But it was within my gift as your trainer, and as head of department. And you are not the first trainee we had who succumbed to lack of experience. It's part and parcel of the job, you know that.'

He thinks my reaction is nothing more than bruised pride.

He waits a beat and then continues, 'If someone is digging

up the dirt like this, accusing you, the questions we should be asking ourselves are who and why?'

'Could it be someone else on the firm?' I ask.

'Possibly. But you know what these things are like. There but for the grace of God and all that. If someone in the job was trying to drag you through the manure, they'd need a reason. Do you have many enemies, Jake?'

It's a good question. I didn't think I had any. 'Not that I can think of.'

Roger nods. 'How are things in Oxford?'

I know I'm tense. I let my shoulders sag. 'They've suggested some gardening leave. And my house is under siege from the press.'

'Oh dear. That can't be easy.' Roger's gaze is appraising and direct. Suddenly he smiles. 'Tell you what, we have a little place up near Burford. It's forty minutes from Oxford. You're welcome to use it until all this blows over.'

I shake my head. 'That's very generous of you–'

'It's empty this time of year. The children sometimes go up there over school holidays – I'm a grandfather you'll be delighted to know.' He adds the last sentence as if the thought of it is incredulous. 'But for now the place is empty.'

'I couldn't.'

'Are you sure? There's an agent up there who keeps the keys. I'd be happy to give him a call.'

He's insistent. Magnanimous. Typical Roger. And the thought of being able to stay somewhere incognito is suddenly very, very attractive. I know I'd benefit from somewhere quiet to gather my thoughts.

'Okay,' I say. 'I'd appreciate that very much.'

46

I say goodbye to Roger and punch the address he's given me into the satnav. I don't want to go back to Oxford. Not immediately. I need some time to think and driving to the Cotswolds seems as good a distraction as any. I try desperately to recall anything about that bank holiday weekend in 2006. Of course, I remember the trip to California. Sarah was in a flat share in London at the time, and we'd put off getting anywhere to live together because of my impending fellowship. It was Easter and I remember vaguely a discussion about either trying to grab some late skiing in a high-altitude resort or do the opposite and find some sun. But the details are a blur.

Maybe we'd decided against it to save a little money.

It's a dozen years ago and try as I might, I can't remember much. I had one eye on the States and Sarah and I were effectively splitting up, so it was a weird time emotionally. We survived that separation – though not the later separation of two nights a week away in London, ironically – sod you, Simon – but at the time it felt like a big deal that hung over our every moment together.

So I was preoccupied.

Too preoccupied to think about Michael Carstairs, obviously.

Roger's words ooze back into my brain. What he did for me in my absence probably saved my career. What might have happened if there'd been an inquest and I'd been found criminally negligent or at best incompetent? Would I have had to cancel my fellowship in LA? Would I ever have been offered a job as a consultant at Oxford? It doesn't bear thinking about.

But there's no escaping what's written in black and white in Carstairs's notes. Everyone makes mistakes. We all, as surgeons and physicians, have our own horror stories to tell. Our secret drawer where we keep things buried. And any medic who tells you differently is a liar. If it doesn't happen to you, it's happened to someone you know. In an attempt at developing an open and transparent system, parallels are often drawn between the airline industry and medicine. If an airplane crashes, there's an immediate inquiry. Sometimes, aircraft of the same design are even grounded until the reason for the disaster can be identified, so that the same disaster won't happen again. But unlike pilots, young doctors are expected to carry passengers before they're taught how to fly the plane. And we know it's true.

Recent banner headlines in the redtops suggested that 70,000 people a year in the UK die because of doctors' mistakes.

When I was in my first post, a gruelling job as a houseman on a senselessly busy medical ward, my mentor and Senior House Officer – senior being relative in that she'd qualified all of twelve months before me – missed seeing some air under the diaphragm of an elderly patient's chest X-ray; one of a dozen sick patients we'd admitted over a winter's night that January.

The patient had lots of things wrong with her: heart failure, polymyalgia, a history of urinary tract infections. All good reasons for her sickness. All good reasons for her deterioration into infection. We'd X-rayed to exclude pneumonia. The image showed no sign of that. But what it had shown, and that the SHO had missed, was that shadow, the telltale indicator that signalled a perforated bowel. That was the cause of the patient's horrible infection. What she eventually died from.

There was no inquest. My colleague confessed her error to the consultant in charge. She was not sacked. She was not reported. His approach was to tell her that we all made mistakes. That she was not alone. That the burden of responsibility required accepting that despite doing your best, you will sometimes make errors. Though he did not say so in as many words, he suggested she review the notes. She did, and with some help from a more experienced registrar, she judiciously buffed the entries to emphasise the helpful elements of her findings and bury, as well as she could, the negatives. The consultant talked to the relatives. They made no fuss.

The SHO told me all this much later over several drinks the evening before we were both due to move on to new jobs in different hospitals. And she did so with tears in her eyes.

Was I horrified? No. Because I'd swum in those shark-infested waters myself for six months by that time and had several close shaves of my own to haunt me. That was how this all worked. Theory is one thing, but becoming a doctor is more about the apprenticeship, the hands-on stuff, and the experience. The only way to become good at it was to recognise your own failings as well as others'.

Experience was something that no one could ever teach you.

Was it wrong? I didn't have the answer to that one. Some people felt compelled to blow the whistle on any shortcomings. But for most of those within the profession, such moralising tends to be looked down upon just as criticism from outside is never well tolerated. How on earth can anyone who is not a doctor appreciate what it's like to carry all of that responsibility?

We live in an era of blame culture and many doctors, Roger

Delany being one of them, are of the belief that covering up can always be justified in order to save careers, because doctors can be victims as much as patients.

It's an uncomfortable argument to wrestle with. One that has kept me awake well into the small hours when one of my trainees has made an error which I would not have. But then, how do you learn otherwise? Where do you draw the line?

If there is even a line. It's more like a smudgy grey area where there's always a risk of duplicitousness coming back with a vengeance to bite you.

Like Michael Carstairs has.

I'm still resentful towards Roger, though I know I have no right to be. I wonder if there are any similar skeletons in his cupboard. If anyone had ever done the same for him? For some reason, I find it hard to believe. Roger is old school. One of these surgeons who's never had to endure shifts. Whose approach to the trials and tribulations of the junior doctors' hours debacle is to shrug and say that it never did him any harm. It's outdated thinking and yet, with new consultants being appointed with perhaps 8,000 hours of training, whereas he, by the time of his appointment, probably had over 30,000 hours under his belt, it's not impossible to see where he's coming from.

That he's a narcissistic dinosaur, there is no doubt. He's nurtured and cultivated his reputation through being on all the right committees – locally, nationally and internationally – surgical societies – royal and European – volunteering to become the secretary of this one, the chairman of another. Some people thrive on that sort of sycophantic nepotism and it's always appreciated by those within the clique. He'd pioneered a much-needed service in the region; there was no doubt about that. But he also dined out on it and let no one forget. I'd also seen him shake hands with people with his thumb on the space between the second and third knuckle of the other chap's hand on countless occasions.

Roger is the sort of man who'd disarm an audience by dismissing the idea he would talk about himself and then do exactly that with little anecdotes about how his dyslexia had initially held him back. Of how he'd surprised everyone by winning the odd academic prize. Or how he'd captained the school team and received the plaudits of pundits and just missed out on international honours because of sacrificing himself to medicine. It can be cringe-inducing, but he seemed never to see it for what it was; self-aggrandisement. He drops names unashamedly with fellow professionals, celebrities in particular. He's pompous, he's self-important, never shy to let patients know how good he really is. Love him or hate him, and there are two camps, he's powerful and successful. But he's also generous and definitely someone you want on your side.

When I was his junior, he was the consultant I wanted to be so I have no right to hold a grudge.

But no matter how altruistic Roger's actions may have been at the time, now it's clear that someone knows the truth. And that someone wants me to suffer for my sins.

47

I head north as far as Abingdon and then cut west through Kingston Bagpuize and up on towards Witney to hit the A40 well away from Oxford. I park on the hill in Burford and I pick up the key from a smiling young man in an estate agent's office situated opposite the Cotswold Arms. He's stayed on late as a favour to Roger and directs me down the hill and across the river, north and then west towards a village called Taynton. I thank him and walk outside to stand on Burford's main street.

It's early evening. The rain has stayed away, the sun, when it emerges from behind the clouds, still warm. I survey the street. There are lots of pubs, a Caffé Nero, bakeries and clothes shops that pull in visitors by the thousands. The town retains a medieval vibe, with stone tiled roofs and weathered stone walls. More so in the narrow alleys than the garish High Street that more than tips its hat to the tourists that flock there on weekends. Not so many today on a Monday in spring. But beyond the town and traffic, the Cotswold countryside looks inviting. Rolling hills and patchwork fields spread out like a landscape painter's dream. I walk back to the car through streets mellow and weatherworn and quintessentially English.

It would be a town worth wandering through on a day when you had nothing on your mind.

Today is not that day.

I go back to the car and drive with the estate agent's typed instruction open on my knees. Across the bridge over the River Windrush, left at the roundabout on to the A424. Left again at a bend where the warning black and white chevrons indicate a difficult junction to negotiate on the way back. One and a quarter miles to Taynton. After a mile, the road narrows to a single-track lane with pull-ins for passing. When I reach Taynton itself, the instructions send me left to somewhere called Coombe Brook. It can't be more than a hundred yards from the accumulation of buildings that make up Taynton, but it has its own identity, clearly.

Some part of my brain remembers being taught that people never used to stray far from where they grew up in days when travel was difficult and dangerous. Probably a cliché, but place names were more important then. Especially when it came to water, which people needed to be near to survive. I drive over another bridge, see the brook and understand. Roger's "cottage" turns out to be a three-bedroomed detached property called Apple Drop Barn with an entrance through a gate in the stone walls that flank a narrow lane. It looks quiet and welcoming in the late afternoon light. A nice little hideaway on an acre of grounds. Beyond, across the fields, I see a line of trees, a gap, and then another line, suggesting water in between.

The River Windrush on its winding course again.

The cottage looks like it might well have once been a barn of some sort – hence the name. Part of the farm that's visible through the fields two hundred yards to the right, maybe. But the renovations it's undergone have added a wisteria-covered carport and an orchard that hides it from the road. It looks like an ideal spot.

I let myself in and realise that I haven't got any provisions. But there are several bottles of wine in the racks in a cool pantry, as well as opened packets of cereal and some crisps.

They'll have to do. I don't want to go back out again. I need to sit down and corral the scattered flock that are my thoughts.

There's a pen and torn-up sheets of paper for messages in a basket to the side of the fridge. I grab these and open some wine. It's a Malbec. I pour a glass and sit down at the kitchen table, open my phone, and look at the pages from Carstairs's notes.

Try as I might, I can't remember him. There's a great big empty canvas where there should be memory.

I look at the operating notes again. I was not the only one in theatre that day.

Anaesthetist: I Harrison

Scrub: SN J Thompson

Assistant: I Kourakis

There may be wifi in the house, but I don't have the password. I find the router. Underneath is a sticker with the word Delany1066 written in ink. Did he have a distant relative at the Battle of Hastings? His Irish heritage argues against that, but you never know.

I open my laptop and punch in the code. It meshes. A little wheel spins and opens the door to the Internet.

I start with Izzy Harrison. She was a senior registrar in the anaesthetic department at the time of Carstairs's surgery. I worked with her on call several times. I find her through an image search engine. She was an intense dark-haired girl who is now a consultant in Manchester. She looks different; hair longer, face a little more lined. Like mine, I suspect.

Jane Thompson is more difficult to find. Typing in search words like staff nurse Jane Thompson gets a ridiculous twenty-three million hits. But I have time. She was in her late forties in

2006; she'd now be late fifties. I eventually find someone who looks a little like her by cross-referencing names and photos. But she's no longer a scrub nurse. She's a practice nurse at a busy GP unit on the outskirts of Reading. Jane is blonde with a big smile. She's put on a few pounds, but I recognise her. The snippets of bio I can find tell me that she's married with two children.

Kourakis is much more of a challenge. I don't remember him at all. But it's an unusual name for these shores and my search fails to reveal anyone of that name practising locally. I realise that there's a distinct possibility that he may have gone back to Greece of course. It was not unheard of for European doctors to come over for the bucket loads of experience a spell in the NHS would get them. Some of them revelled in it. Others found it a tough gig.

From what Roger told me about Kourakis, he fell in to the latter group. I finish my glass of wine and pour myself another. I punch in Michael Carstairs's name to Google and get 800,000 results. I type in Michael Carstairs RIP 2006 and get a thousand. I start trawling, but quickly realise I have no idea what I'm looking for. Would I find an obituary a dozen years after his death? In 2006 Twitter was in its infancy and Facebook wasn't the monster it is today. I don't bother looking up Michael Carstairs there. I've already tried.

It doesn't take long to realise that I have to face the fact that I know nothing about this man that I'd helped kill.

I hear the sentence in my head and feel a bitter smile touch my lips. I'm diluting the blame already with the word "helping". If I'd messed up the surgery, I hadn't been helping. I'd been the cause.

The second glass of wine slips down with a smack of plums, sweet leather and tobacco on my tongue.

It's good stuff. So I top up my glass and try to think why any of the staff in that theatre might harbour a grudge deep enough to make them punish me now. Could it be that guilt of knowledge has weighed them down for all these years? And suddenly, seeing me exposed by social media as the predator I'm supposed to be has tipped the balance, perhaps. It seems unlikely. But not impossible. Yet, even if I manage to find a phone number or an email address, they're hardly likely to welcome contact from me at this moment. Here I am, the UK's supposedly worst doctor, an accused kidnapper, ringing them out of the blue to pester them about a case we were all involved in a dozen years before. And at some point in that conversation I will ask them if they felt that I had, in any way, been incompetent and if it had bothered them.

I shake my head and sigh. Contacting them sounds like flawed logic.

If one of them is my blackmailer, they're hardly likely to admit to it either.

But if not one of them, then who?

I take another mouthful of the excellent Malbec. It races over my tongue and does a taste salsa down my throat.

I have no idea what knowing these facts about the surgery is doing to help me. But who I can turn to for help? Or if not for help, then at least for understanding. Because whoever's sending me the messages and manipulating me knows me and knows about Carstairs. So if not the staff, then who? Did Carstairs have any other family? Is there a brother or a sister somewhere who has bided his or her time until now? What about the children? Are they out for revenge?

It's almost eight at night when I dig out the card from my briefcase and phone Oaks.

'Mr Thorn,' he says when he answers. It's a neutral tone with a hint of suspicion.

'Sergeant Oaks, apologies for ringing you this late, but I wanted to pick your brains.'

'You been drinking?'

'Is it that obvious?'

'Professional expertise,' Oaks says.

'I've had a couple of glasses of wine.' It's actually three by now. Big ones. I glance at the bottle for confirmation. It's less than a quarter full. Okay, four big ones.

'What can I do for you?' Wary now.

'It's these messages. The phone messages I've been getting.' I have to remember he knows far less than I do. He doesn't know there's been further contact. I need to be very careful. 'I have a theory, but I need your help. It's to do with a patient I operated on in 2006. A patient who died. I think this business with the van and the money have something to do with him.'

'Okay,' Oaks says the word slowly, emphasising each syllable, waiting for more.

'I know you don't think it has anything to do with Katy Leith's disappearance, and I'm not sure it does either, but this chap's name has come up.'

'What chap?'

'Michael Carstairs.' I give Oaks the details: Carstairs's address at the time, date of birth, date of death.

'What's the connection?'

'I've been wracking my brain about anyone who might be an enemy, as you suggested. Carstairs died as a result, possibly, of my surgery. I know you think this business of my extortion is all an elaborate hoax, but I have a lot of time on my hands, sergeant. So this is what I've come up with.' Again, the truth, but not the whole truth.

'What is it you want me to do?'

'Can you find out if he has, or had, any relatives? He had children, I know that. What about siblings? Anyone who might want their pound of flesh.'

'What do you mean by that?' I can hear Oaks's voice harden.

'This was early in my career. Sometimes patients have bad outcomes. Carstairs had cancer. He died from complications of surgery. But someone might be less than convinced and this may all have been festering away inside. Since, as you and Inspector Ridley have pointed out on more than one occasion, I am one of the most reviled people in the country for having supposedly abducted Katy Leith–'

'Did you abduct her?'

The question stops me in mid-sentence. But it also makes me angry. 'Oh, for God's sake, man.'

Several seconds of silence follow. Eventually Oaks says, 'I'll see what I can find out. Where are you?'

I'm glad he hasn't asked me to explain any more. He obviously gets the gist. I tell him about the cottage in Coombe Brook. That I'm not in Oxford. Oaks doesn't comment on the wisdom of me being there either way. He says he'll come back to me if he finds anything of note.

I end the call and walk out into the garden. There aren't any streetlights in the lane and I can look up into a moonless sky full of stars. It's giddying, though some of that might be the wine. I have my fourth glass in my hand and I can feel the alcohol well and truly kicking in. I stay out until it's too cold and then meander a little unsteadily back inside and find something to watch on TV. More GOT. Seeing a dragon immolate a battalion or two feels exactly like what I need.

Five stabbings, a thousand burnings and a sacking or two later, I've finished the bottle of Malbec. I make a mental note to myself to replace it but wonder if Roger, being Roger, imports it from somewhere. I think it's highly likely because it doesn't taste like anything you'd get in a supermarket.

I'm on a settee in the living room, the TV on, when I drift off to sleep thinking of massacres and mayhem. They both lull my aching brain. A small part of me realises that it's come to something when warfare is a better lullaby than the constant self-loathing fuelled by incompetence and possible manslaughter that preoccupies my waking hours.

I manage, just, to place the empty wine glass on a side table before slumping back and letting unconsciousness take me.

48

Rupe the Extreminator @extmntralpha 14May2019
Doctors are all psychos. #JThorn must enjoy cutting people open
and getting his hands bloody. Doesn't anyone vet for psychos in
training? #isthishim He's probably got #findkaty in plastic bags in the
freezer.

Joachim Peeve @Jopeevenot 14May2019
@extmntralpha Her head anyway #isthishim Maybe some other bits
#Needstobeputdown Bellfield, West and Thorn. Has a ring to it.

Steve Bute @sbuteoo7 14May2019
Evidence #findkaty Remember that? #isthishim

Ayvedaloco @ayvedalco33 14May2019
Where is the GMC letting assholes like him cut us open? #findkaty
He probably spits inside. #isthishim Or worse #shipman

49

A buzzing noise wakes me at four in the morning. I come awake, disoriented and hot. I'm on the settee. I haven't even taken my trousers off under the throw I'd climbed under and they cling like a sticky second skin. I sit up and open my eyes into the full glare of a strangers' sitting room lights and fumble for the phone. My brain feels like it's sloshing around in a tank full of jelly and thumping up against a wall of pain that someone has built behind my eyes.

I remember, with relief, that I'm still in Coombe Brooke and not in Headington. The buzzing indicates a WhatsApp message, and I see I've had a dozen I mustn't have heard during an anaesthetised sleep.

'What now?' I croak.

I don't recognise the number. But I open the messages anyway. Images blur as a download icon whirls. And then I'm looking at a photograph of Sarah. She's flat on her back on a flagstone floor flanked by red brick walls and wrought iron fencing. Her face contorted by fear and surprise. In the foreground is an image of her Mulberry handbag with a knife pushed through it. Her bag. My knife.

Beneath all of this is a message.

Do not go to the police again. Next time it won't be handbags and tyres. There is a website set up for you to post your confession. Bookmark it. You have twenty-four hours to admit your guilt over the murder of Michael Carstairs. If you do not, at midnight on the 15th, Katy dies with your knife in her throat.

Another buzz and another image. It's Katy Leith again. Still with tape over her eyes and mouth. This time there's a newspaper held up next to her head. It has my grainy photo on it and today's date. I've already seen the sub-heading online.

#ISTHISHIM: in big white letters on a black banner.

I drag my eyes back to the message. There's a login and a password. I open the site. The background is black with lurid splashes of red blood all over it and a red-eyed rat centre stage looking back at me. Above it is the words; The Killer Hiding in Plain Sight.

The rest of the text is an instruction of how to open the content manager of the blog site and post an article or a message... or a confession. I bookmark it on the search engine as instructed. When I revisit the messages and the images on WhatsApp, they're all gone. I lie back on the settee and close my eyes and realise I don't need the wiped off images from the phone. I can see them behind my closed lids well enough. If I had any doubts at all that Sarah's "mugging" is linked to me and whoever is trying to coerce me into admitting my mistakes, the constant pounding of my head is telling me otherwise.

I'm not sure how long I lie there, but any prospect of more sleep is fading fast. At five, I get up, find a kettle and make some tea. There's no milk so I drink it black. It takes two cups to lubricate my throat. I sit in the kitchen and watch the rear garden take shape in the slow dawn. Black gradually gives way to indigo and then a dull green, but there is no blue at the end, just a high dull white.

It's peaceful. But my mind is far from that. I don't know what to do. There's no point contacting Oaks. He won't have any news for me yet. And I'm becoming paranoid at the thought anyway. Whoever is sending me these images knows what I'm doing. What if they've bugged my phone?

I know that's unlikely given that the police cloned it – they would have found something like that, surely? But the truth is I don't know what to think. Try as I might, I can't put any of this together. It's clear that Oaks considers my ideas groundless, but also – from the repeated way he asks me if I did abduct Katy – that he still hasn't quite eliminated me from his list of possibles. And then I wonder if somehow the two theories are joined at the hip. Could someone who knew of Michael Carstairs also be a part of a trafficking ring? Have they seen a golden opportunity for payback? A way of killing two birds with one terrifying stone?

It sounds far-fetched. Ludicrous.

At 6am, I take some paracetamol, shower, and change. The shower helps more than the headache pills. I stand with my back to the jets, letting them pummel my skin, letting the water sluice in and out of my mouth, scrubbing the clammy sweat from my legs with an expensive shower gel that leaves me smelling of pomegranate.

Afterwards, I make toast from some sliced sourdough bread I find in the freezer. The food of champions – or a confused guilt-ridden hostage to his own past. Because that's what I've become.

I'll have to make do with yesterday's clothes, but that's the least of my worries. I find my phone and text the one person who might listen to my theories. That has some insight into a world I know bugger all about.

She comes back to me within five minutes; she's an early bird, like me. So now I have a plan and I feel better because it involves the one other living creature that won't judge me.

Time I left. It's an hour back to Paws for Claws, where I can pick up Sid.

By eight thirty, Sid and I are almost at Frogger's Pond. By eight thirty-two, Sid is in it. Five minutes later he's joined by the golden water-seeking fur bomb that is Winston. I watch as the dogs play-fight over a stick. It's not something we encourage. Sticks can splinter and God alone knows how many dogs die every year from ruptured oesophagi from shards of wood. You never see that warning up on the adverts for dog food when a poster-dog spaniel hares after a branch.

Like I say. People, advertising gurus included, can be clueless.

I call the dogs and they forget the stick. I wait and, as expected, Galina appears on the approach to where I stand at the edge of the pond. It's a dry morning, but there's an easterly wind keeping the temperature below double figures. So it's no surprise she's dressed in her usual coat and dark glasses, a scarf covering the lower half of her face. Today, the intemperate weather adds a degree of practicality to her camouflage.

'Hi,' I greet her.

'Good morning. It is cold for spring.' Muffled words through the scarf. She takes out the ball she always brings for Winston and holds it up. It's all the invitation he needs. He barks and Galina lobs the ball into the water. Two big canine-induced splashes follow.

'You look... tired,' Galina says. I can't read her eyes behind the glasses. But she's right. I'm dehydrated and I haven't eaten a proper meal in days.

'Difficulty sleeping,' I say. 'Thanks for coming.'

She nods.

'A lot's happened since we last met.'

She waits. Once again, I find myself opening up to this stranger. I tell her about talking to the police. I tell her it was a mistake because of what's happened to Sarah in Kensington and to Ella's car. And then I tell her about Michael Carstairs. About how someone harbouring a deep resentment has found out that I was instrumental in the botched surgery that caused his death. When I go to explain that until I got hold of the notes, I had no idea I was involved, she shakes her head.

'But how can that be? How can you not have known?'

'Because of the way the system works. I was young. Doctors move around a lot during their training. An awful lot. This all happened at a point when I moved hospitals. In fact, moved countries for a while. The place where it happened, there were some good people there. They wanted to protect me. They covered for me. Maybe it was misplaced kindness, but they kept it from me. They saw no reason to drag me back from California. It was a nice thing to do.'

Galina's eyebrows go up. 'Nice for you perhaps. But what about Michael Castor?'

'Carstairs,' I correct her.

'What about him?'

I nod. 'I know. And I feel terrible about it. I'm horrified at the thought that I'm responsible. And I'm sorry for you having to listen to all this, but it's driving me mad. I have no idea what's going on here, or what the hell I should do.'

The dogs emerge from the pond. For a moment, they're distracted by a flock of ducks swooping low over the water. They watch the aerobatics with keen hunters' eyes.

I keep talking. 'The police are still investigating the tip-off that Katy's abduction has something to do with trafficking. I haven't told them about Sarah's mugging or the slashed tyres. But last night I get another message, this time with more images of Sarah's mugging and mutilated handbag. Whoever sent those knows I've been to the police. So now I'm torn between telling the police everything and risking what that might do to Sarah, or Ella, or even Katy, if they really do have her. What am I supposed to do, ignore all of this? Wait until something else awful happens? I mean, what the hell has Michael Carstairs got to do with a trafficking gang?'

'I cannot say. But I do not think you can take a chance.'

'What do you mean?'

'Perhaps they are connected, perhaps not. But whoever is doing this thinks you are responsible for this Michael Carso... Carstairs's death, yes?'

'Obviously.'

'They want to see you suffer like he did.'

I shake my head. 'They're doing a bloody good job if that's the case.'

'But they have given you a way out, yes?'

I laugh. It's a hollow sound. 'Yeah. I must confess to what I've done very publicly.'

Galina cuts to the chase. 'Do you think they will carry out their threats if you do not confess?'

I nod. 'I saw what they were capable of with Sarah. They could have easily slashed her instead of the handbag.'

'Then you do not have a choice.'

I massage my forehead. Galina's right.

'What will you do about the police?' she asks.

'I've said nothing to them about these new photos. When I told them about the messages at the start, they thought it was all a setup. Someone who's seen me in the press and now sees an opportunity to blackmail me. But these people don't want money. They want my public disgrace.'

I turn to watch the dogs come back out of the water. I reach down and throw the ball again. 'Ridley, the inspector, she's a cold fish. Part of me thinks she believes I've made all of this up as some kind of deflection strategy.'

'And you have not?'

'Of course not. What would I have to gain?'

'Are you guilty over Carstairs's death?'

Again, Galina's question is blunt and to the point. Am I guilty? 'I didn't even know I'd had anything to do with his death until yesterday,' I snap. My voice is shrill. 'Sorry.'

Galina nods. 'I cannot explain all of this, but I know about trafficking. It is part of organised crime. They work in gangs. The way they make people, ordinary people, become part of their network is through fear and blackmail. If they do have Katy, perhaps they have found out about you too. And somehow it is now personal.'

'That's what I was thinking. Possibly Carstairs had a brother, or someone else who is a part of all of this.'

Galina nods. 'But does that change anything?'

It's a sobering question. When I don't answer, she provides one. 'They have given you ultimatum. Do you think they will do what they say they will?'

The images of Sarah on her back in Kensington Church Walk flashes into my mind and alternates with the terrified look on Katy Leith's face under the tapes.

'Yes, I do.'

Galina looks up as a couple of geese fly past overhead, honking their presence. Frogger's Pond has become an ornithologist's paradise. It's a haunting noise; a signal of change. When she turns back, she looks at me directly through her sunglasses.

'Then my advice would be to do as they ask, though it will be painful for you.'

'It might end my career.'

'Then I suppose it is your career or another death.'

I look away. More geese honk.

She's right. I don't have a choice. Not really. I nod. 'Thanks for coming, Galina. This has helped.'

I hardly know this girl, but somehow, we have a lot in common, Galina and I. We're both damaged goods. I hold out my hand. Galina looks at it and, after a few seconds, shakes it. Her hands are warm. Mine are cold. Just like the dread feeling in my heart.

50

I walk Sid back along the path slowly, mulling over everything that Galina has said. It still doesn't add up. She knows first-hand what organised crime and traffickers can do. How vicious they can be. She has the scars to prove it. I'd hoped that she might help me understand what's happening, but she can't explain it either and I realise how futile that hope was. Still, talking with her has done one thing at least. It's clear I have to do what's being asked of me. If I don't and someone else comes to harm, I won't be able to forgive myself. Sarah, Ella, Katy, they're all at risk here.

The price is steep. Humiliation and ruin are staring me in the face. But that's something I'll just have to deal with.

A cyclist appears on the path and I pull Sid close to my side, reach down and pat his still-wet head. Whoever is doing this knows all about me. I wonder with a shiver if they know about Sid. I feel my fingers run through his warm fur and tell him he's a good lad.

When I hand him back to the smiling twenty-something volunteer at Paws for Claws, I lean down and hold Sid's big head in both my hands. He tries to lick my face and I pull back. I rarely do this, but today, I need the contact, one last handful of fur. His muscular tail thumps against the door of reception as I give him a treat. Somehow, this feels like a goodbye and I hurry away before emotion overcomes me.

Back in the car, I sit and ponder. It's ten thirty. I have less than fourteen hours in which to do as the message asks. There will be consequences if I do and consequences if I don't.

Dire consequences either way.

I can't imagine what life will be like for me if I post my "confession". Perhaps someone might spin it as a way of saving Katy Leith. Or, and I think this is much more likely, the press will crucify me as the killer surgeon. It'll be like throwing petrol on a bonfire. I remember Simon said something about knowing someone in PR. Someone who might help with damage limitation. I examine that idea for a few moments, wondering if there's any scope for salvaging this... but then I realise how selfish that is. It's not me I'm scared for. It's those around me.

I toy with the idea of going back to the house in Headington. But there's nothing there for me. I'm still sitting in the car when the phone rings. It's Linda.

'Jake, how are you?'

'Oh, you know.'

'I heard you met up with RD.'

'Yes. We had an interesting chat.'

'He said you were a bit down.'

Yeah. Like the Titanic is a bit sunk. I crush the self-pity. I'm not sure how much Linda knows, what Roger might have told her. But Linda is a force of nature.

She says, 'I've already told you; no one here believes any of the rubbish about you and Katy Leith.'

'You may be the exception.'

She picks up on my despondency. 'RD says you have nothing to worry about.'

'Is that what he said?'

'Yes, he thinks the world of you. You were always one of his favourites.'

Hoo-bloody-ray. Roger's paternalistic massaging of the facts in the Carstairs's case was protectionism gone mad. I can't help but feel a smidgen of bitterness. 'I didn't know he had favourites.'

'Oh God, yes. He'll never admit it, but it's me who types up all the references, remember. I know who's been naughty and nice, in RD's eyes anyway.'

'You've run his life, haven't you?'

Linda laughs. 'I've done my fair share of wiping up the spilled milk.'

'It helps that you have such a great memory.'

'An elephant in more ways than one, me.'

'I'd never say that.'

Linda laughs. 'Despite his failings, RD has helped a lot of people over the years. Helped himself too, of course. I don't deal with his private practice anymore, but he's done well out of medicine. You know what he's like, always looking for the bigger car, the younger wife, the most acclaim.'

'How does he do it?'

'Ruthless charm. That's what I call it. He can turn it on like a tap. And he's not scared to make decisions about the big stuff. Not so good with the finer details though.'

A thought strikes me about Linda's elephantine memory. 'You don't happen to remember a locum by the name of Kourakis, do you?'

'Oh, Ioannes, of course I do. He only lasted a couple of weeks. Nice boy, but a bit out of his depth.'

I can't help grunting out a laugh.

'Oh, yes. Good-looking boy,' Linda adds. 'Wowed the younger

secretaries, did Ioannes.'

I'm surprised she can remember his first name, but it's suppressed by a little tingle of anticipation. 'What happened to him?'

'After he left here? I don't know exactly. But I dare say I could find out. Is he a part of your research?'

'He could be. He was involved with the patient's care.' It's a half-truth and I don't really know what or why I'm asking. But it could do no harm to find out.

'I'll see what I can do.' There's a pause before she adds, 'Jake, look after yourself and don't let the sods get you down. This will all go away, I'm certain it will.'

Linda's confidence buoys me a little. I start up the car and set off. I've already decided to go back to Coombe Brook. Roger's bound to have some old clothes I could borrow.

I'm in Newbury when the phone rings again. This time it's Oaks.

'Mr Thorn. You're driving.'

'Yes.'

'Are you in Oxford?'

'No, but I can be.'

'Can you call in at the station? I have some news.'

My pulse nicks up a notch or two. Why is it that talking to the police does that?

'What about?'

'I can't discuss this over the phone.'

'Okay. Half an hour?'

'I'll meet you in reception.'

Oaks ends the call, leaving me wondering. But it was a request rather than a demand. I take some small comfort from that. Yet the unpleasant sensation in my innards persists all the way back to Oxford, especially as I've been warned not to contact the police again.

51

We meet in the station reception. Oaks insists we go inside and so I find myself once more in the familiar featureless interview room. Ridley joins us. It's she who does all the talking.

'I hear you've moved out of Oxford.'

'Anything I can do to thwart the press,' I reply.

'You have an address?'

I write it down on a piece of paper already on the desk in front of me.

'In case we need to get hold of you quickly,' Oaks says.

I don't like the sound of that. We both know I have a mobile, but it's not just that. Not just them checking to see where I'll be. It's them wanting to let me know that suspicion still hangs over me and everything I do.

'And you're alone there?' Ridley asks.

I nod. 'That's the general idea.' I hand over the sheet of paper.

'Why did you want to know about Michael Carstairs?'

'He's a ghost from the past. An uncomfortable reminder of

my fallibility. One I wasn't aware of until my name and face was splashed all over the Internet.'

Ridley looks at me in that scary way she has with her laser eyes. Somewhere in my head, Shirley Bassey sings the theme tune to *Goldfinger*. What I've told Ridley is the truth. Maybe not the whole truth, but still the truth. Yet it doesn't satisfy her, and she waits for me to expand.

I shrug. 'I was involved in treating him before I went abroad on a fellowship. Think of it as dotting an "I".'

Still Ridley waits. She's an expert in expectant silences. But I stay quiet. Eventually she drops her gaze and glances at Oaks.

He sits forward. 'Then you'll know that Michael Carstairs died of a hospital-related infection thirteen years ago?'

I nod. 'Yes. I know. The infection was linked to the surgery I carried out.'

Oaks picks up a file. 'Carstairs's wife was threatening legal action. Unfortunately, she died before anything came of it.'

I nod. 'But there were children, weren't there.'

Oaks turns a page of the file and nods. 'A boy and a girl.'

'Do we know what happened to them?'

Oaks nods. 'A little. There were no grandparents. No aunts or uncles they could be looked after by, so they ended up in care. The boy flitted between foster homes and institutions. He did not do well. Darren Carstairs died aged nineteen from a drug overdose. He was a heroin addict.'

I squeeze my eyes shut. 'And the girl?'

'She was older. Adopted aged eleven. As far as we know she's still alive.'

'As far as you know?'

'Adoption agencies are very cagey about what information they reveal to anyone, us included, unless it's warranted. Adoption is a legal process. The Carstairs girl may remember little about what happened. It must have been traumatic to lose both parents like that. So anyone stirring the pot – such as asking for information – only gets access on a strictly need-to-know basis.'

I nod. But it's enough for me to know she survived, unlike her brother. 'Thanks,' I say.

'Is that all the information you wanted?' Oaks asks.

'Yes. That's that "I" dotted. Thank you.'

Ridley's looking at me again. 'Anything you'd like to share?'

I look back at her. Linda had hinted that there was fallout following Carstairs's death. I had no idea it had been this bad. My lousy technique has resulted in the family imploding. And now I hear that there is only one survivor. No wonder someone, somewhere is angry.

I know I should tell them about Sarah being attacked and about Ella's slashed tyres. It's the sensible thing to do. Maybe they could offer protection. But they can't protect Katy Leith from whoever has her and who is threatening to kill her unless I come clean. I strongly suspect that both Ridley and Oaks, were I to say anything, would reassure me that I could not be held responsible for the kidnapper's action. But if she dies, I would know that my action – or rather my cowardly lack of action – would be the trigger here. I've made my mind up. So I sit tight and say nothing.

'Have you been monitoring social media?' Oaks asks when my silence becomes embarrassing.

'I googled myself the other day. That was enough. I haven't looked lately.'

'Do you use Twitter?'

I shake my head.

'Just as well,' mutters Ridley.

'We're keeping tabs on some of the more... lurid and extreme users. Things that might be construed as inciting.'

Inciting. Now that's an interesting word. 'You mean people threatening violence?'

Ridley nods. 'Does anyone else know you're up at Coombe Brook?'

'Only the owner of the cottage. He's a trusted colleague.'

'Best you keep it that way for now.'

It signals the end of the chat. Ridley stands.

'Isn't this where you usually ask me if I know where Katy Leith is?' I try to keep it light but my words come out strained and high, and make both police officers look at me.

'You have my number,' Ridley says and turns to the door.

I follow Oaks out. He pauses at the station entrance. 'You okay, Mr Thorn?'

'As well as can be expected.'

'As bad as that.' Oaks's smile is wry. 'Take care.'

'I will.'

He nods. 'You know where we are if anything else springs to mind.'

52

Ridley waited for Oaks to return from once again escorting Thorn from the building. She kept thinking back to her first meeting with the surgeon. She remembered Oaks explaining away the cockiness she'd found so irritating in Thorn as nothing more that professional confidence. The certainty of a man who was sure he'd done no wrong. She'd been wary of it, and him, even then. And that wariness had been justified. This would make it three times he'd been to the station.

Oaks breezed back into the office. 'What do you make of all that?'

Ridley shook her head. 'To be honest, Ryan, I can't make head nor tail of Mr Thorn. I'm still convinced there's something he's not telling us.'

'And the Carstairs thing?'

'I think it's possible that someone has pounced on the chance to put Mr Thorn well and truly in his place. Seen an opportunity to make him dance the panicky quick-step.' Ridley was an avid *Strictly* fan. She couldn't help peppering her phrases, and her thoughts, with dance metaphors.

'He seemed genuinely bothered though, don't you think?'

'Yes, he does.' She had to agree that much of the cockiness had gone.

'Definitely seemed a bit distracted. See his face when I told him that the Carstairs boy had died of an overdose.'

'Probably feels responsible.'

'Funny that though. You'd have thought, being a surgeon, that he'd lost patients along the way.'

'I expect even the hardest nut never becomes acclimatised to that. But it does make you wonder if he might have "lost" one or two deliberately.'

Oaks made a face. 'Oh, come on. He's not bloody Shipman.'

'People thought Shipman was a wonderful doctor.'

'Yes, well, I'm a bit worried about old Mr Thorn.'

Ridley sneered. 'Why don't you ask him over to yours? You two could go out for a curry. Get to know each other a bit. I see a bromance brewing.'

Oaks shook his head and sent Ridley a withering glance. 'All I'm saying is it looks like it's getting to him. Twitter has gone bananas. It's unrelenting.'

'There is that,' conceded Ridley. 'He does strike me as a man who likes to be in control. And now all he sees is chaos.'

'That still doesn't make him a criminal.'

'No, but chaotic situations lead to chaotic responses.'

'You mean violence?'

'People do weird things when the red mist comes down. As you well know.' Ridley let her thoughts marinate. Eventually she said, 'Maybe we should have impounded his car and let the techs take it apart.'

Oaks snorted. 'On what basis? We'd never get a warrant.'

'It would be one way to make absolutely certain.'

'Yeah. And then we could do the same for every other male at the pub that night. Forensics would start posting doggy doo-doos through your letterbox.'

Ridley shrugged.

Oaks continued. 'We found stuff on his phone, as you know. WhatsApp messages.'

'I thought WhatsApp was encrypted.'

'It is, but the tech told me they have some keyword algorithm they can use on the internal memory of phones these days. Anyway, Thorn was telling us the truth about those messages.'

'Did we trace them?'

Oaks nodded. 'A burner, as expected.'

'Then he could have sent them to himself.'

'Ye-es.' Oaks responded with exaggerated slowness. 'But I ask again, why would he do that?'

'Deflection? Because he wants us to feel sorry for him?' Ridley threw both suggestions out airily, dangling them. Daring Oaks to respond.

He said nothing.

Ridley pushed away from her desk. 'Anyway, I can't spend any more time worrying about Thorn. There's a press conference in an hour. Something I'm not looking forward to.'

'Do you have to be there?'

Ridley nodded. 'Orders from above. Katy Leith's mother is being briefed as we speak. Appeals to the public are always so much fun. I can't wait.'

53

On the way back to Burford, I stop at a big Texaco garage, the kind with a decent-sized grocery that sells hot food as well as car air fresheners and soft drinks. I buy pizza slices and some bottled water, a bag of relatively healthy breakfast cereal and some milk. I'm in need of comfort.

'Any fuel?' asks the man behind the counter.

I shake my head and he tots up the purchases without comment. I dare say he's seen a worse shopping basket. I pay and exit. Outside is a stand with all the day's newspapers under plastic weatherproof lids. Katy Leith is still on three front pages, but she's no longer the headline on any of the others. That dubious honour goes to a royal who is about to produce another heir to the throne on *The Express*, and to a soap star's nightclub adventures on one of the red tops. But *The Telegraph* has a banner headline:

Police intensify search for missing nurse, Katy Leith

'I know she's still alive,' says desperate mother.

Further down, there's a subheadline.

Police refuse to speculate on the guilt of a suspended doctor who worked with Katy

There's a blurred photograph of someone crossing a road. A man. I stare harder. I recognise the face. It's mine.

I turn away and head for the car. I take off the baseball cap and dark glasses I now wear whenever I need to interact with the public, throw them on the passenger seat and drive on. They hadn't mentioned my name on the front page, but I have a sinking feeling that it's somewhere inside. I wonder if it's what's triggered one of my patients to react against me? I ponder this as I drive. I have to touch people all the time; it's intrinsic to the job. Palpating abdomens, running my hands around people's necks to feel for lymph nodes, breasts, testicles, sometimes inspecting parts of their body they might never properly get to see.

Often people find it embarrassing. But when does embarrassment turn into being offended? I always have a chaperone and I'm careful to always explain what I will do and why. It's a contract of sorts. No one has ever complained.

Until now.

I get to Coombe Brook and park outside Apple Drop Barn. Everything is calm and quiet, and I feel a huge sense of relief when I open the door and find the place just as I'd left it that morning. The first thing I do is open another bottle of Roger's good Malbec. I doubt the winemaker had pizza in mind, but it tastes wonderful with the food.

I sit on the sofa, careful to eat off the coffee table, switch on the TV, and scroll to a news channel. It's as depressing as always. Brexit dominates the debate. Pontifications on how long Theresa May can last. On how many times and in how many ways, the European Union mandarins can say no, and the politicians can bugger everything up.

But after interminable conjecture and opinions from correspondents outside Westminster, in Brussels and in the studio, the announcer shuffles her papers and drops her voice. All clues that the next item is something more serious.

'In the continued search for missing nurse, Katy Leith, police today held a press conference to appeal for any information regarding her disappearance. Katy's mother, Rona Leith, also made an emotional request for people to come forward.'

The slice of pizza halfway to my mouth freezes as the scene shifts to a large pressroom and a panel of police officers. In the centre, a middle-aged woman, her face ragged, eyes raw and dark-rimmed, speaks into a microphone.

'If anyone has any information, please, please tell us what you know. Katy is such a lovely girl. All she ever does is help people. She's never done anyone any harm. Her sister and I... we miss her so much. Someone must know something. And not knowing is the worst thing of all. We can't sleep or eat or do anything. Please, please ring the police.'

. . .

She sucks in a ragged breath.

I gulp down more wine.

Next to her, a female police officer puts a comforting arm around Mrs Leith's shoulders. And then the camera angle shifts, and I see Ridley sitting at the end of the row. She's dressed in her non-uniform of white blouse and black jacket, those eyes staring back at the camera. As if she's staring right at me. Willing me to say something.

I consider Mrs Leith's words. 'Her sister and I...'

No mention of a father, I notice. On screen, the scene shifts back to the studio.

'We can now get the latest from our reporter, Rory Green, who is outside the hospital in Oxford where Katy Leith works.'

Green is a man in a coat outside the infirmary. I listen for a minute, but he has nothing new to say. He reiterates everything I, and most of the people watching, already know. Just in case a licence payer has been on Mars for the last week. I turn the volume down and attack the rest of the pizza. But my appetite is shot. I gulp down more wine and refill the glass.

So many victims.

So, so many victims because of my mistake.

My phone rings. I check the number. It's not one I'm familiar with but I answer it anyway. It's Roger.

'Jake, are you up at the barn?'

'Yes. And I have to apologise for drinking a bottle or two of your good Malbec.'

Roger laughs. 'I get it from a buyer in London. Good, isn't it?'

'I dread to think how much it costs.'

'Don't worry about that. Have as much as you like. How are you?'

'I've been better.'

'The press are like dogs with a bone, aren't they?'

'You've read the papers then?'

'I have.'

'It's ten times worse on the Net, so I hear.'

'I'm not a big fan of all that,' Roger says though obviously he has a mobile phone. But when you have people to do things for you, neither the need nor the skills to be computer savvy develop. 'And if you want my advice, you'd be better off not letting the buggers get you down.'

'Not so easy,' I say before I can stop myself.

'Would you like some company? I'm only in Reading. I could be there in an hour and a quarter.'

'No need, Roger. Kind of you to offer.'

'I'm worried about you, Jake.'

'You need not. As you say, all this will end soon.'

Roger is persistent. 'It would be no trouble. I've been thinking about this business of the bad outcome... Carstairs, wasn't it? You mustn't let it get to you. I was surprised to hear you rattling that old skeleton. If you're worried about litigation, don't be. There's a time limit for this sort of thing. Little risk of anything happening now.'

'I'm not worried about litigation. More the shock of knowing that I'm responsible, that's all. I'm fine, honestly.' A lie. My specialist subject of late.

'You mustn't worry. They'll find this nurse, I'm sure they will. If the Malbec helps, drink as much as you like. Stay as long as you like too. Make yourself at home. I'm here at the end of the phone if you need me.'

'That's very generous of you.'

'I mean it. Ring me on this number at any time.'

'Thanks, Roger.' I end the call. I look at my phone and open the photo app, stare at the pages from Carstairs's notes I've photographed. The incontrovertible truth.

I finish what's in my glass and reach for the bottle again. Funny how things become so much clearer with a bit of alcohol on board.

It was me who killed Carstairs.

It's about time I told the truth.

I take out my laptop, power up and punch in the password. Then I find the website I'd bookmarked on my phone and the instructions on how to publish a post. The dashboard looks daunting, but it's bigger on the laptop and I realise it's a standard WordPress site. I've used these before. On the left is a menu. I find "Post" and press "new". Up comes a page that asks for a heading. I type in "Michael Carstairs".

Beneath this is a box for text.

I start typing.

My name is Jacob Thorn. I am a consultant surgeon at Oxford Infirmary. In 2006, I was a registrar surgeon at the St Jude's Hospital in Hampshire. In April of that year, I was involved in the care of Mr Michael Carstairs who was admitted with acute abdominal pain because of secondary adhesions following previous surgery for cancer of the bowel. These complications resulted in Mr Carstairs requiring a resection of a part of his bowel that had become ischaemic. The anastomosis – or joining – of the cut bowel ends unfortunately broke down, resulting in leakage of faecal matter into his abdomen. This leakage set up an infection which led to sepsis and, sadly, death, from multiple organ failure.

It was not until a few days ago that I was made aware of the fact that it was I who carried out the emergency surgery which ultimately led to Mr Carstairs's death. This is because I left the country shortly after performing the procedure. I am deeply sorry that my actions may have contributed to the tragic series of events that led to an untimely death. I would like to offer my belated condolences to his relatives. I am grateful to my colleagues at St Jude's who did all they could to redeem the situation, but who ultimately could not save Mr Carstairs. I have never apollogised to Mr Carstairs's family, but I would like to do so now.

I have examined the notes pertaining to Mr Carstairs's care. Occasionally, wounds break down. However, it is clear from the post-mortem examination that the surgery, for which I was responsible, was of sub-standard quality. I also realise that there is nothing I, nor anyone else, can do to alter the facts of the case. I am deeply sorry for the disstress that I may have caused Mr Carstairs and, subsequently, his family.

I'm not sure as to style, so I try to keep it formal. As I would in reply to any query from a solicitor or a patient's relative. I stick to the facts. I have no idea if this makes me culpable for anything. This is sticky legal ground. There is a duty of candour to be open about errors, but apologies in open disclosure amount to an admission of fault and liability in the eyes of the law. They can, and are, used in court as evidence.

I feel like Yossarian in *Catch 22*.

I'm also certain, given the press I've had so far, that anyone reading this will devour it with "I told you so" relish. I know the public's fascination with anything medical. I've seen the reality shows; programmes that highlight people's medical problems, or delight in showing the downside of surgical procedures – the bad outcomes and unscrupulous surgeons. So it isn't hard to imagine what publishing this confession is likely to lead to. I'm already burdened with being a privileged white male under suspicion of abduction or worse. At least in the eyes of the great Internet-using public I am.

Catchy headlines pop in to my imagination with little or no effort.

Botcher butcher admits mistake.

Doctor death holds his hands up.

Thorn – the angel of death.

I sit back, the laptop still open on the table in front of me. I pour out what's left of the wine and take a gulp. I finish it in two swallows. I see I need another bottle. Check that. Not need, but certainly want.

When I stand up, I have to put my hand out to steady myself. Now that I'm up, I use the toilet. Make a little more room for Roger's good Malbec.

The bathroom is all bleached wood and white tiles. The noise of urine hitting the water in the pan is loud and gratifying. It's a male trait; hitting a target and making a noise. Despite my predicament, I giggle. I wash my hands in the basin and notice the cupboard next to the mirror. I open it and stare at the neat arrangement of cosmetics, shaving paraphernalia, and two labelled plastic pill canisters. The name on the label is Mrs Andrea Delany. One reads temazepam, the other sertraline. Mrs Delany is on the happy pills.

I pick up the canisters and shake them. I'd put both at about a third full.

On the way back through to the kitchen, I find another bottle of Malbec and pop the cork and turn off the living room lights. It's just the laptop now that illuminates the room, though the kitchen lights are still on. Shadows lean in from the corners, as if they're trying to read what I've written. Through the French windows, I can see stars in the black sky beyond.

Back on the sofa, I pour more wine, spill a little on the table, thankfully missing the laptop, and reread what I've typed, looking for errors. There's a spell checker in Word. It finds a few gaffs. Distress and apologised need adjustments. But even after it's grammatically acceptable to the computer's algorithm, it gets more damning with each pass of my eyes. I'm not sure if it's enough, but there is only one way to find out. I've drunk a full bottle of wine and am now halfway through a second and I can feel it in my head. A balm for my troubles. It's making the unpleasant inevitability of my situation more tolerable. A lot more tolerable. I sit back and a big wave of exhaustion hits me. It must have been hiding in the bathroom and followed me in.

The bathroom.

Where the temazepam and the sertraline sit invitingly in the bathroom cupboard. Roger asked me if I'd had trouble sleeping. With all that alcohol already on board, a temazepam would probably knock me out.

Two or three might put me in a coma.

Half a dozen of each might depress my respiratory system enough to stop me breathing altogether. I snort out a laugh.

It must be the drink that gives me this weird sense of euphoria as I finally realise what's been bugging me. Posting this confession is like signing my professional death warrant. I can't see any way back. So why should I try?

It would be so easy.

A fresh idea puts up a hand to be heard.

Perhaps that's what the blackmailer wants, Jacob. Has always wanted.

'So what?' I say to no one in particular. 'So fucking what. Who's going to miss me?'

I stomp on that little idea. That would just be giving in. I'm still giving myself that pep talk as I get up and go back to the bathroom. To the cupboard where I take out both canisters. As I return to the living room, I'm answering the question I've already asked myself. If I tried to end it all, who exactly would miss me?

Ella, definitely. And Sid. Good old Sid would definitely miss me. Thinking of him ruins the moment and I suddenly need to be reminded of him. I pick up my phone and tap on the photo app. I type his name and twenty images appear. Of Sid running, diving, swimming, sitting in the car, tongue lolling. I know I'd miss him too.

I fight back tears.

Time passes, slowly, inexorably. Minutes. An hour. I sip wine.

Then I find Ella. Pretty, warm, lovely Ella. I have several pictures of her in jeans, lots in a summer dress, laughing at Lulu, holding hands with Ben. I consider sending her a message, but if I do, if I say what I ought to say, tell her what's going through my mind, she'd be confused. She'd ring me. And speaking to her is not what I want to do at this moment. Far too complicated.

And then there's Sarah. Thinking of her wipes the smile from my face. Funny that. I owe her an apology for what's happened. A great big one. I rue dragging her into all of this. But what would I say? Talking to her is not easy anymore. Far better to have my thoughts already written down than trying to wing it when the excrement hits the fan.

Once the confession is out there in the world.

I drag my eyes back to what I've written and the weird blog site with the blood and rats. I move the cursor so it sits over the save button. It takes three attempts to get it on the right spot. I swig some more wine.

All I have to do is hit return.

My heart's on a sprint. It surges and then settles. I'm tired, but I know I won't sleep. So I don't hit return. Not yet. I need to explain, in writing, to Ella and Sarah first. If I take a couple of chill pills now, by the time I've written to Ella and Sarah, they should kick in and I can sleep.

Sounds like a plan.

I open the box labelled temazepam. Take out two and knock them back with a swallow of Malbec. They will help me sleep. They'll calm the wild wind that's blowing through my brain. I look at the box of sertraline on the table in front of me. Why did I bring those out? Then I close my eyes and think about what it is I should write for Ella and for Sarah. Sarah first.

What will it be? An apology? An explanation? Another confession?

I'm still holding my phone. My fingers on the photo app scroll idly through the albums Sarah's put on the cloud and which effortlessly appear on my screen. I'd forgotten that we shared photos. I thumb through the hundreds of images. Sarah had been an avid snapper for the whole time we were together. Archiving our holidays, photographing hotel rooms, snapping at random scenes and buildings I was sure we'd never look at again.

And what am I doing now? I giggle. More of a guffaw. I almost spill the wine. I put it down for safekeeping. My Precioussss.

On the app, the library starts at 2004 and I open random

thumbnails to look at the photos.

There's a wedding we went to that year. I blink. My suit looks hopelessly dated. What deranged design aesthetic made me put on such a big carnation on lapels that were like passenger jet wings is anyone's guess. It's funny. I laugh out loud this time. Sarah is in a sky-blue dress with a navy fascinator on her head. It looks like a hummingbird is feeding on her hair.

Another giggle.

2005: a baroque hotel somewhere in Italy. I can't remember where, but it was late in the season, and we were the only guests. It was like an Agatha Christie novel. Us eating alone in the evenings with the sun setting on a terrace overlooking the Med. When we went for a post-prandial stroll, we joked about finding a body on the beach.

'Marjorie, is that a leg behind that rock?'

'Oh, Gerald, it's Lady Altringham's leg! I recognise her blue stockings!'

And later that same year, darker images, leafless trees, both of us dressed in layers of clothes. I zero in on one snap. The date stamp reads December 31st and the layered glowering city of mottled sandstone is recognisable instantly as Edinburgh. We'd gone up for Hogmanay. We're both in the image. Both of us laughing. We must have asked someone else to take the photo. Sarah's speciality. Behind us is the castle high on its hill, lit up for a pagan rite of passage.

2006: I thumb through. Stop in May as the block of images lighten and I realise they are mostly of me in a different landscape. Bleached earth, blue sky. I'm in California. The fellowship at UCLA. I frown and scroll back until I find the last images of Sarah and me from that year. They're darker, reflecting the slow transition of the British climate from winter to spring. Some are indoors. The last one of the two of us has us sitting at a table in a dimly lit restaurant. Probably taken by the waiter.

Sarah was always coercing waiters into photographing us. I'd joke that we'd look at them in years to come and never remember where the hell we were. But I remember this place because we'd been there a couple of times since. It's The Boar hotel in Painswick.

There are Easter eggs littered over the table behind us. Lined up in front of a family sitting like shadowy figures in a vampire movie. Strangers captured by our waiter. A big family party from the looks of it. I remember that this was the last day we spent together before I flew off to the States for my fellowship year. I can even read the specials board. Wild boar and pheasant and Herefordshire steak. Sarah is smiling. But I look strained. Wondering, I suppose, if we'd make it through a year away from each other.

2008: The evidence that we'd survived the separation is plain to see. We're on a skiing holiday in Austria. Pristine white vistas, sitting on a terrace in a lodge up on the mountain. Sarah barely recognisable in her skiing gear, winter tanned, goggles pushed up over her head, her hair hidden under a woolly cap.

2010: Another wedding. My suit is much better. Sarah's dress chicer. But still she wears a fascinator. What is it with weddings and hats? I can even remember whose wedding it is this time. One of Sarah's uni friends who'd decided to have their children before tying the knot. Which meant the reception was awash with overtired toddlers and screaming babies. But we look happy.

Better times.

The wine glass drifts towards my mouth again. I slurp. It tastes so good. But seeing the photos brings on a sudden surge of melancholy. Maybe coming here alone wasn't such a brilliant idea. Because I am alone with my thoughts and nothing but static images on my phone to remind me of old times. And Sarah's done a great job of that.

Before I can stop myself, I've scrolled to my contacts page and I'm pressing a button.

Sarah answers after the third ring.

'Hey,' I say.

'Jake, are you okay?'

'Yeah, fine.'

'You sound odd.'

'I'm, yeah... fine.'

'Are you drinking?'

'I've had a little wine.'

'More than a little I'd say.'

I sigh. 'Don't want to fight, Sarah.'

There's a pause before she says, more softly, 'Okay.'

I realise I haven't spoken to her since Saturday when I'd visited her in hospital. 'How're you holding up?'

'I'm not back at work yet. The police have been useless.' There's bitterness in her voice. Then she remembers me. 'But what about you? Are you doing okay?'

'Yes,' I lie. 'In fact, I'm sitting here with a good bottle of wine, just going through some old photos.'

'Which ones?'

'Of us in Painswick years ago.'

Another pause. 'Jake, is this about us? About what's happened?'

I realise then that Sarah thinks I'm ringing to discuss our situation. That maybe I'm being maudlin and that I'm about to ask her to reconsider.

'I was sitting here thinking about when I went away to the States. 2006. I just sent you some photos on WhatsApp.'

Faint rustling. 'Whoa. That's a long time–'

'Do you remember me telling you about a case I was involved with?'

'What do you mean?'

'Something came up about an old patient. An old complaint.'
I ease into the lie remarkably smoothly. Partly because it's plausible. Partly because I'm reckless from the Malbec.

'From a dozen years ago? You were in Hampshire then, weren't you?'

'Exactly. But now that I'm a persona non... thingummy, things creep out from the stones they've been hiding in... From under the stones... where they've been hiding under... you know what I mean.'

Pause. 'How much wine have you had, Jake?'

'Just enough,' I reply. 'And not too much.'

Sarah sighs. 'No. I can't remember anything. There was a lot going on.'

There was. I say nothing.

'Jake, are you all right?'

'Yep. I'm not in Headington. I'm in Roger Delany's place up near Burford. Very nice little gaff. His expensive retreat in the Cosswolds... the Cotswolds. How the other half live, you know.'

'Is Roger there?' I can hear the tiny edge in her voice. Sarah wasn't a Delany fan, though Roger made no bones about his admiration for her. Quite good at hiding his salaciousness as banter was Roger. Always made sure he kissed the girls on the mouth when he could. 'A proper kiss,' he would call it. 'None of this French malarkey.'

'No,' I say.

Quiet.

Me again. 'Roger's been very gener–'

Sarah interrupts me. 'I don't think it's a good idea for you to be sitting there alone, drinking.'

'Ah, but old Rog has a great cellar.' The word great somehow comes out twice as loud and twice as long as I'd intended.

'Exactly. I'm worried about you, Jake.'

I frown. Not because of what Sarah is saying, but because

this was exactly why I'd told myself not to phone her. And because the temazepam is now definitely kicking in, since it's made me forget that initial caveat. When I look up, everything moves on a three-second delay. There are suddenly two clocks on the dresser across the room.

'No need,' I say.

'You're slurring.'

'Iss a gift.'

'Promise me you won't drink any more.'

'Oh, now that's–'

'Please?'

'Okay, okay.' Not too difficult to agree. I think I've had enough. I frown at a pile of spilled capsules on the table. When did that happen? Another giggle.

'Go to bed, Jake,' Sarah says. Orders.

'Fine,' I say. I don't want to say more because it's hard to find the words suddenly. 'It's just that... I wanted to say sorry for the...' I stop myself. Just in time.

'Go to bed.'

'Yeah. Bed.'

We say goodnight or rather Sarah does. I can only manage a blunt 'night', before I end the call. I let the phone drop on the floor. When I reach for it, the room swims. Easier I just flop back on the sofa. When I close my eyes, everything feels better. Mainly because the room stops moving once the five seconds of stepping off an elevator feeling passes. I blow out air and open my eyes. The world looks fuzzy. It even feels fuzzy.

Temazepam and Malbec. Great idea, Jake.

Great idea.

But something is bothering me. Stopping me from yielding to the drugs even in this intoxicated befuddled state. Something I've seen or heard or said.

Something to do with Sarah...

It's important, but it's like a feather in the wind. I try to think, but it dances away. Drifting way above solid thought, faintly visible but beyond reach.

And then I remember why I phoned Sarah. The confession. I sit up, drag my eyes back to the laptop. It's in slumber mode. I wake it up by jiggling the mouse. I take even longer to get the cursor in the right place this time. But then it is. And I hit return.

I squeeze my eyes shut. But the sensation that floods through me is predominantly one of relief. It's done. Now I should take some temazepam to help me sleep. Not think about anything for a short while. That's a great idea, Jake.

I fumble for some pills, swallow two with the last of the wine – I haven't taken any already, have I? Course not – and sink deeper into the sofa. Maybe I'll be able to snatch that feather out of the air in the morning. The world buzzes around me. There are a million bees in my head. I giggle at how ridiculous everything is. I'm still giggling when I remember that I've written nothing to Ella. But it's too late. By now the buzzing is growing louder and insistent and all-encompassing. I say to myself that I'll do it first thing in the morning as the buzzing world finally engulfs me.

Sometime later, I think I wake up and I'm convinced there's someone else there, calling my name. Goading me. I groan out an objection.

'Sarah? Ella?'

I feel a cup on my lips. But it isn't wine. Nor water. Too salty for water. I cough and wave it away.

It's probably a dream. I hope it is because I don't want to wake up. Not yet. Maybe never.

I flop back on the sofa face down.

56

It was the last thing Ryan Oaks needed to be doing at that moment. Traipsing off to the middle of nowhere when there was a ton of work to be done. It wasn't every day that a misper turned up days after disappearing. In fact, it was unprecedented. But they had taken Katy Leith straight to hospital. And from what DI Ridley had told him, Katy was significantly the worse for wear. Dehydrated, dirty and, from the initial reports, drugged.

But very much alive.

And then the duty officer from central had contacted them because of a call they'd taken from a woman who said she'd received some very odd and disturbing messages from a friend of hers, and that she was extremely worried about him because he was not answering his phone.

The woman's name was Sarah Barstow. And the friend was Jake Thorn.

Respect to the duty sergeant who put two and two together and contacted the SIO in charge of the Katy Leith investigation. Not because Thorn was on any watch list, but because the duty sergeant, like the rest of the world, had seen Thorn's face splashed all over the papers. Weird too, that the call had come through just an hour after a woman answering Katy Leith's description had flagged down a car on a woodland track near Coleford in Gloucestershire. Oaks was on the verge of dismissing the whole Thorn thing, or at least parking it until morning, when he got a text from Thorn himself.

Burford. Need help.

Oaks immediately rang the number and got no reply. Consequently, while Joanna Ridley had gone straight to the hospital where Katy Leith was being treated, Oaks shot off, reluctantly, to Coombe Brook to find out just what the hell Thorn was doing. If this was some kind of sick game he was playing...

The satnav took Oaks exactly the same way that it had Thorn. It was almost 2am when Oaks arrived outside Apple Drop Barn. Three minutes later, a patrol car from Woodstock arrived and Oaks introduced himself to a couple of uniforms; his backup.

There were lights on in the cottage. Oaks sent a constable around the back while he and another officer went to the front door and knocked.

There was no reply. Not even after three attempts.

That was when Oaks heard a shout from the rear.

'Sarge! Someone's in there. Looks like he's unconscious.'

Oaks rushed around and found the constable standing on an upturned bin in the garden looking in through the kitchen window. The lights weren't on in the living room, but enough was spilling in from the open kitchen door to show them what had triggered the uniform's yell. Someone lay sprawled on the sofa. A male who didn't respond to them pounding on the window.

The back door was locked, so they smashed a glass panel and let themselves in.

Oaks went directly to the figure on the sofa, taking in the laptop, the pills scattered over a coffee table, a tipped-over wine bottle, the cloying smell of vomit smeared over the furniture.

Oaks turned the figure over.

Jake Thorn. Deathly pale, the side of his mouth still slick with thrown-up wine and the remains of half-digested pills. Oaks put his ear to Thorn's face. Frighteningly shallow though it was, he heard breathing.

'Mr Thorn. Jake!'

It was no good. There was no response.

Oaks shifted him to the recovery position and yelled over his shoulder to the uniforms, 'Don't just stand there! Get a bloody ambulance.'

57

I open my eyes onto an unfamiliar room. There's a lot of white on the walls and in the sheets. The floor and the doors are pale blue. The ceiling consists of square panels with integrated lighting. I've been in a hundred rooms just like this one every day of my working life. But I'm not usually the one in the hospital bed.

There are other clues that the tables have turned. Like the drip in my arm. I move each limb in turn. They all work. I'm in no pain. Other than feeling thirsty and hungry, a quick self-assessment tells me that I'm okay.

So why am I here?

The door opens, and in comes a nurse. He's dressed in light blue scrubs and by the name badge, I see he's called Hamish.

'Good afternoon,' Hamish says. His smile is cheerful.

'Hi,' I croak. It's more difficult to speak than I thought it would be. It's like I've forgotten how. I clear my throat. It hurts when I try.

'How are you feeling?'

'Not bad,' I manage.

'Try drinking something. It'll help.' Hamish, obviously, has been here before.

'Have I had surgery?'

'No. But you were intubated.'

'Intubated?' I ask, disturbed.

Hamish nods. 'You needed a bit of help breathing while the drugs got out of your system.'

'Drugs?'

Hamish smiles and his eyebrows go up. He goes to a bedside cabinet to my right and pours out some water from a plastic jug into a plastic beaker and holds it out. I drink it all. It soothes my throat.

'You don't remember what happened?' Hamish asks.

'I don't remember getting here. I remember drinking a bottle of wine and taking a couple of temazepam.'

Hamish nods. 'Right. So you're halfway there.' He pours more water. 'Drink the whole jug if you can. We need to see if your kidney function is okay. Are you hungry?'

'Starving.'

'I'll see if I can rustle up some toast.'

'Can you tell me what happened?' I ask.

'I think you ought to talk to one of the doctors. Or one of the policemen who have been hovering outside. It's above my pay grade.'

'Can you at least tell me where I am?'

'Gloucester Royal.' With that he leaves.

Someone else comes back with the toast. Someone wearing a different uniform that I recognise as not a nurse's. Probably hotel services. I thank her but don't ask her anything.

It's a two-bedded room. Much like Sarah had. Different hospital, obviously, but just like her room, the bed to my right is unoccupied. The toast is sliced white bread, the butter unsalted, but it tastes wonderful. I finish the jug of water but I'm still thirsty. There's a clock on the wall. I watch the minute hand crawl by.

When the door next opens, I am not entirely surprised to see who comes through it. Ridley and Oaks, for once, are all smiles.

'Mr Thorn,' Ridley says. 'It's good to see you.'

'Is it?' I slit my eyes.

'Yes,' Oaks says. 'The last time we met you weren't looking so good.'

I frown.

'Don't you remember?'

I strive to do just that. 'I remember being in Roger Delany's house in Coombe Brook. I remember drinking a bit too much. But that's about it.'

Oaks and Ridley exchange glances.

'So you don't remember taking the pills?' Ridley asks.

'I took a couple of temazepam to help me sleep.' I look at the drip in my arm. 'That was probably not one of my best decisions.'

Oaks nods. 'You took more than a couple. And what about the other stuff?'

'What other stuff?' My mind is scrabbling around, trying to find a foothold. It's like climbing up a mound of scree. I'm slipping and sliding as things fall into place. The photograph of Sarah and me in Painswick. The confession.

'It's called sertraline,' Ridley says, peering at a little notebook Oaks has fished out.

'I didn't take any sertraline,' I say.

'That's not what the toxicology results say. Luckily you threw up.'

A feel another frown coming on.

'I say luckily because of course you could have choked on

your own vomit.' Ridley sounds oddly like a teacher scolding an unruly child caught bunking off.

'I don't remember taking anything but a couple of temazepam.'

Oaks nods. 'You weren't trying to do anything... stupid, then?'

My frown deepens. Of course, it had crossed my mind as I'd stared at my written confession and the looming destruction of my life that would inevitably follow.

Who would miss me?

But that was before... what? Once again, I'm niggled by a tantalising thought that I already know the answer to this question. That I could not have done what I'm supposed to have done to Michael Carstairs. That something has changed between me writing my "confession" and lying here talking to these police officers. But I'm damned if I know what that something is.

A feather dancing in the wind.

I'm wondering exactly how much I should say to these two when Ridley breaks into my thoughts.

'Because that would have been an unnecessary act, given that Katy Leith is now at home with her mother, alive and well.'

As bombshells go, this one has a nuclear warhead. I can feel the blood drain from my face as my pulse surges and I jerk forward. 'What did you say?' I whisper.

'You didn't know?'

'No one's said anything.'

'That's because you've been out of it.'

'How long?'

'Today's Thursday.'

Oaks moves around to the side of my bed. It's he who gives me the details. 'Katy Leith was found on a farm track near the entrance to a woodland in Coleford in the early hours of Wednesday morning. We think she was kept somewhere in the forest there.' He pauses for dramatic effect before adding, 'This all happened while you were in Coombe Brook.'

I stare at him. 'Is she okay?'

'She's unharmed. Shaken up, recovering from the fentanyl they gave her to keep her subdued. But otherwise unscathed. No signs of any sexual assault. My guess is that they were keeping her unsullied. Maybe for a buyer.'

There's so much harrowing information in that last sentence, it will take me an hour to unravel it. Weirdly, I also wonder if Oaks is also a GOT fan. The word "unsullied" seems a little out of character for him otherwise.

'But what...?'

'At the Duke of Wellington, the night of the party you attended, Katy went outside for a cigarette. She'd run out so went across the road to a Spar to get some. On her way she was grabbed by two men and bundled into a car and driven to an unknown location. Some kind of old factory or garage.'

'We're rechecking our CCTV footage. But the camera coverage in the streets near the Duke is patchy to say the least,' Ridley says.

Oaks fills in the rest. 'There were old tools and bits of heavy machinery at the place they kept Katy, according to her. We are yet to find the location. We're still looking. The kidnappers were foreign, European accents. She didn't recognise the language.'

Ridley again. 'One of them injected her. There are tracks on her arms to confirm all of this. They kept her locked in a room with minimal contact except for meals and the drugs.'

'On Tuesday, she heard loud voices in an adjacent room. She thinks there may have been a fight of some kind. Either way, there was no contact for hours. Eventually, she jimmied the lock with a metal bar. There was no one in the outer room so she ran, blindly, looking for lights. She was found just after midnight and taken to hospital.'

I wait, absorbing it all. Katy Leith is free. 'So I'm no longer a person if interest in any of this?'

Oaks shakes his head.

'If I tell you that on Tuesday night, I posted a confession of my involvement in a surgical cock-up that lead to the death of Michael Carstairs, a patient I looked after in 2006, you would not be interested?'

Ridley shakes her head. But her eyes are slits. 'Is that what prompted all of this?' She's looking at the drip in my arm.

I follow her eyes down. 'No. It isn't like that... Look, I drank a bit too much, that's all. And I took some pills to help me sleep. And yes, I'm a doctor and I should have known better and I got pissed and probably miscalculated.'

'And you don't remember texting me?' Oaks asks.

'No.' I frown. 'Ask her. Ask Katy if whoever abducted her took photographs and sent them to me. I posted that confession. It's probably why she was released.'

Ridley's expression is priceless.

Oaks says, 'Inspector Ridley did ask. No one took photographs. Katy only knows you from work.'

I stare at him.

He shrugs. 'I know someone's been yanking your chain, but it has nothing to do with Katy Leith.'

I exhale loudly and lie back on the bed. He's wrong. So wrong. There's much I want to say, but I don't, despite the voice in my head shrieking to be heard. They have to be wrong. Katy was released because of what I admitted to... wasn't she?

'What about the press?' I ask, to shut up the voice. But it's with some trepidation that I wait to hear.

'They've dropped you like a snotty rag,' Ridley says.

I look away and stare at my fingers. The nails are dirty. I need a shower. But that awareness is fleeting. What I'm really thinking about is the press. There is no "Botcher Butcher Admits

Mistake". No "Doctor Death Holds His Hands Up". No "Thorn – The Angel Of Death". It's not what I was expecting. But I don't tell Ridley that.

I flick my head back up. They're both still there. Waiting.

'So I can get out of here?'

Ridley shrugs. 'Once the doctors give you the okay, yes.'

I nod. I'm a suspected suicide. No doubt the trick cyclists will want to speak to me.

Ridley adds, 'Take your time. Try to put your life back together.' She holds out her hand. I shake it. And then I shake Oaks's.

They leave.

Fifteen minutes later, Ella arrives. She takes one look at me and falls onto the bed with her arms around me, in floods of tears. She smells wonderfully of cinnamon gum.

58

FRIDAY 17TH MAY

Queeny Lovett @tinselqhrt 17May2019
#Findkaty heard that #JThorn survived attempted suicide. Now papers are reigning back. Have they been too harsh? No lessons from Leveson #Cantbehim Trolls in hiding.

Edward Dandelion @edandelion 17May2019
Katy free! WTF #JThorn But people only try to commit suicide when they're GUILTY #Thisishim

Steve Bute @sbuteoo7 17May2019
Or when they're hounded by press and social media and their lives become unbearable #JThorn #Cantbehim Remember accusing him of being Lecter in disguise? @dandelion

59

I stay in hospital for another twenty-four hours.

Physically, I pass all the tests. In fact, my blood work is A1. Mentally, I score a low B. I have a long mandatory "chat" with a consultant psychiatrist called Nia Yeldman. I suspect she doesn't get called often to do the frontline assessments, but it's a professional courtesy; consultant to consultant.

It's a long interview. She wants to know about my history, what's been happening to me, background, work, relationships. I have nothing to hide. But it's when we come to a discussion of suicide attempts and self-harming that we falter. I suspect Nia sees my refusal to accept that I have deliberately tried to end my life by "swallowing a handful"– her words – of pills on top of a bottle and a half of wine as some kind of pathological denial. A symptom of something else.

But I stick to my guns.

I concede that it's entirely possible that the benzodi-azepine/wine cocktail had made me confused enough to take more drugs without realising just how disorientating their effect would be. But I am adamant that I did not want to end things. I may have thought about it. But thinking isn't doing.

Yes, all the evidence points to it being me who messed up Michael Carstairs's surgery and his life. And if I'm in denial about anything, it's about that. But I don't tell the good Dr Yeldman any of that. It sounds way too paranoid.

However, the outcome of our interview is that Nia thinks I have good coping skills. That I've been under enormous stress in relation to my work but that I can tolerate well this psychological pain. I do not need intervention, nor treatment. I'm not mad and I am not a suicide risk.

I could have told her all that in five minutes. But it takes almost two hours. By the time Ella comes to pick me up, it's Friday afternoon. She drives me back to Taynton to pick up my car. She comes with me to Apple Drop Barn. Someone has cleaned up. I find my laptop neatly closed on the kitchen table and the broken window boarded. The living room smells of chemical flowers. It doesn't mask the vomit. The sofa has red wine stains all over it and I feel terrible for having thrown up in there. I pick up the computer and once I'm back in my own car, and following Ella out, phone Roger.

I get his messaging service.

'Roger, it's Jake. First of all, apologies for the mess in the barn. I expect the police have spoken to you. I am so sorry. I'll pay for any costs associated with the cleaning up and repairing the window. I'm going back to Oxford, so if you get a chance, give me a ring. I'd like to speak to you about this Carstairs case.'

I end the call.

On the way back, with Ella long gone to pick up Ben, I stop at a garage and pick up some newspapers. The headlines, naturally, are full of Katy Leith and her escape from her abductors. My hands are trembling as I flick through the pages, looking for my name and the story about my misdemeanours. I sit in the garage for twenty minutes, scouring the print. But there isn't anything.

My name is not mentioned once. Oaks and Ridley are right. The press are ignoring my confession.

I'm a snotty rag.

60

There are no cameras or puffer jackets outside the cottage when I get back to Headington. Suits me. Ella is waiting. She's deposited Ben with his grandmother so is here as support. Bizarrely, I realise it's the first time she and I have been alone together in the home I used to share with Sarah. I make Ella a cup of tea and we sit in the kitchen.

'I owe you an apology,' I say.

'No, you don't.'

'Yes, I do.'

She looks worried.

'First of all, I am not suicidal. Never have been. I made a mistake. At least I think that's what happened.'

'Oh, Jake. No one deserves what's happened to you.'

'Perhaps. I know how it looks. Like I've been hounded by the press and put under strain, but that's only the half of it. It's important that I tell you all of it.'

Ella frowns, but she says nothing. God, she's so pretty. So I tell her. Everything. About the van, Carstairs, Sarah's mugging, the slashed tyres, the confession, the wine and the temazepam. I see her face grow pale with the telling, her eyes getting bigger, her hands trembling over her cheeks when she realises the enormity of it.

'Jake... I...'

'I know. Sounds as if I'm completely mad, doesn't it? Sounds like a bizarre dream. The kind of thing a crazy person would make up.'

'But the police... don't they–?'

'They don't think it has anything to do with Katy Leith. And judging by what's happened, they're probably right.' The words bounce around in my head like a golf ball on concrete.

Ella shakes her head. 'And you've carried all this by yourself.'

'I didn't want to scare you away.'

I stop, not knowing what else to say. This is the point I've avoided like root canal surgery. Ella has a child. The sensible thing for her to do would be to walk away, distance herself from me. Stay safe.

I'm a world expert at underestimating people. Ella included.

She looks at me, her eyes dragging down at the edges. She's not talking and so I decide to help her out.

'I'd understand if you wanted no part of this.'

'Shut up,' she says. And then she's holding me, and I've never been more grateful for human contact. She kisses me. Hard. She stands up but doesn't let go of my hand.

'Which is your bed? The one you sleep in alone?'

I lead her to it, and it doesn't take a genius to understand why. She doesn't want us to use the bed I shared with Sarah. Neither do I. I'm suddenly grateful for the twenty minutes I spent scrubbing myself clean in the ward showers at Gloucester Royal.

It's been a while and we're hungry for each other. But it's not our first ride on the waltzers and I hope to God it's not our last. Yet, there's an urgency in our lovemaking. A need for affirmation. And Ella's way more adventurous than Sarah. It thrills me.

. . .

Afterwards, we lie together, her hair soft against my chest.

'I've never stopped believing in you, Jake.'

'You might be the only one,' I mutter.

She shakes her head. 'I've been monitoring social media. Apologies have been coming in thick and fast. The newspapers and the trolls are the ones getting a beating now.'

I caress Ella's smooth brown skin. Nothing like sex to reinforce the human spirit. I realise how lucky an escape I've had. Slowly, a determination to rebuild things grows within me. But it deflates with the realisation that nothing has changed in regard to Michael Carstairs. When I think of him and his family, a dark emptiness opens up in my gut. I can't just ignore it. Whoever it is that's been goading and threatening hasn't gone away simply because Katy Leith walked out of the Forest of Dean. Much as I do not want to confront it, it's a blight that needs addressing. One of many. I tilt Ella's face up.

'Thank you.'

Her big eyes are inches from mine. They crinkle in amusement. 'I hope you don't think we're here because I feel sorry for you.'

'Certainly not.' I shift my weight. 'I've kept the sympathy card for the second round.' I reach for her ribs and she squeals beneath me.

She wriggles out and grabs my hands. 'You're pushing your luck.'

'No harm in trying.' I roll off.

Ella pins my arms and sits on my chest. She's above me, looking down into my face. 'But I do feel a tad sorry for you.'

'How sorry?'

'Lie back, Mr Thorn. You're about to find out.'

. . .

Ella stays for supper. I make some pasta and we dine wine free. It's easy with her. She laughs a lot at my unfunny jokes. What a wonderful trait in a partner. I tell her I'm going to adopt Sid.

She beams. 'Ben and Lulu adore Sid.'

I nod. 'We should all go up to the lakes for a long walk on Sunday. We could stop for lunch on the way back. Somewhere dog friendly.'

'I'd like that. Very much.'

Later, I kiss her and watch her leave. I tidy the cottage and text Sarah to let her know I'm out of hospital and well. I thank her for phoning the police too. She tells me to think nothing of it and not to drink so much. An easy promise to make and keep. I try Roger's phone again and once more get the answering service. I leave another message.

Only then do I take out my laptop, shut since I picked it up from Apple Drop Barn earlier on. I plug in the charger and power up. The Killer in Plain Site blog is still open on the dashboard; the editing page, not the red-eyed rat, thankfully. I scroll to posts, open the page.

And there it is. My confession. As typed on Tuesday night, formal, dry, factual. And then I see the button up to the right. Brighter than all the other buttons. One that says PUBLISH.

I open a new incognito window. Type in the web address for The Killer in Plain Site. Now I'm on the site itself, not the admin pages, looking at it like any other web surfer might. The rat stares back. I press the button marked recent posts.

Blank.

I sit back.

My confession isn't there.

I blow out air, look back at the other open window, The Killer in Plain Site dashboard that I'm logged on to, realisation making all the hairs on my arms stand to attention. Like most sites, this has a failsafe. My confession is there, as typed. But it's in draft format. To get it out there, to let the rest of the world see it, I would need to press the PUBLISH button.

But I didn't. I haven't.

It's invisible to everyone but me. But then another thought sideswipes me. That isn't strictly true. The administrator of The Killer in Plain Site blog could have seen that draft post too as I wrote it. I've assumed my blackmailer and the website administrator are one and the same person, or if more than one person, certainly in cahoots. They wanted to expose me as a botcher. And yet I'm not headline news.

So why didn't *they* publish it for all the world to see? All it would have taken was a few keystrokes.

It doesn't make sense.

The irony is that I probably would be on every front page had I not been too drunk to press that publish button myself to send it into the ether. I edit the page, remove the text, save the draft so it's gone, 'trash' the post then 'delete permanently'.

You total idiot, Thorn.

I catch myself. What am I thinking? Confusion comes crashing down with a wallop. If it's not my public confession that's led to Katy's release, then what...

The insubstantial feather wafts in and out of my consciousness yet again. Something I did, or said, or saw, or heard on Tuesday night in my drug-addled stupor wants to give me an answer. But it's still too ephemeral. Still nothing more than a vague sensation.

I get up, invigorated suddenly by a sudden sense of euphoria steamrollering over my confusion. No one but the website administrator knows about me and Michael Carstairs.

Not yet.

I think about having a drink, then remember all that Malbec I'd drunk at Roger's and decide against it.

Instead, I make myself a cup of tea, this time with milk, letting the tumbling thoughts in my head find a level before eventually making for my own bed. It still smells of Ella.

But it's not that which prevents sleep from coming. I'm plagued with trying to explain all that's happened. With Katy Leith free and knowing that traffickers had abducted her, I have to accept what Oaks and Ridley have told me as true. I've been taken for a ride by someone who wanted to expose me as incompetent. Since I posted no confession, my admission could not have been instrumental in Katy getting away either. The images the "kidnapper" sent me of Katy were all made up nonsense. Elaborate, frighteningly real, but a confabulation undoubtedly. The facts speak for themselves.

But that still leaves me with knowing I was "guilty" of incompetence regarding Michael Carstairs. And someone out there knows it. They used Katy's abduction and my supposed involvement, as so energetically expressed by my fans in the MSM, as Ridley called the mainstream media, and the Internet, as leverage.

And now with Katy no longer a captive, that leverage has evaporated. My tormentors seem to have gone back into hibernation.

But it doesn't change the fact that I now know. And there's always the possibility of whoever it was that threatened me before doing it again.

Eventually, my whirling thoughts calm down. For the first time in weeks, I sleep well. Not exactly the sleep of the innocent, but at least neither alcohol nor drug induced.

61

Sweet pea gardener @Sweepea 18May2019
Have to admit, convinced Jake Thorn was guilty when saw video
#katyisfree Just goes to show #innocentuntilproved

62

On Saturday, I'm at Paws for Claws early. I want to speak to Bonnie and Mick. They greet me like I've just won the lottery. Which, in a way, I have. When I ask them if it's okay to take Sid home for the weekend, they grin like idiots. But Bonnie's face registers concern.

'What about your partner? I thought she didn't like dogs.'

'She doesn't. But that's no longer an obstacle.'

'Sorry to hear that,' Mick says.

But Bonnie shakes her head. 'It was never going to work between you two. The dogs always win. I've told Mick, if it ever comes to a choice between him and a dog, it'll be no contest.'

Mick nods. 'Fair enough.'

We both know she means it. I say, 'I'll bring him back first thing Monday. But after that, if you can get the paperwork sorted out, and if you think I'm capable enough, I'd like to offer Sid a permanent home.'

Mick makes a fist. Bonnie just hugs me. 'I knew you would, I knew it,' she whispers.

Dog people.

Sid and I take our usual route along the towpath and up to

Frogger's Pond. I'm early, but even so, when Galina doesn't turn up by nine thirty, I wonder if she's coming.

Five minutes later, I hear a dog bark and Winston comes bounding up to us. Before I can even scratch his head, he and Sid are off into the murky waters of the pond. I'm confined to being a bystander in the canine game the dogs play.

It's only five days since I last spoke to Galina, but it seems like a month has passed.

'You've seen the news?'

Galina nods. 'Congratulations. You must be relieved.'

'I am. No one has actually apologised to me, but at least they aren't calling for my head on a platter.'

She snorts. But it's a reigned-in noise and she doesn't look at me.

'Are you okay?'

She shrugs. 'I have to move away. The people who are helping me, they think it would be for the best. They have found me a new place. A job. A new start.'

'That's good.'

She shoots me a look.

'Isn't it?' I say. I want to ask more, but it would be unfair. Break our unwritten rule. I've had a lot of time to consider her predicament. If Galina has been housed in a shelter, some kind of halfway house while whoever is protecting her sorts out a permanent answer, then the less I know the better. The less she tells me the better.

She nods. 'Yes. It is. It is what I want. But starting again is not so easy.'

I nod. 'I haven't thanked you for what you did. For helping me.'

Again, she frowns. It's her default response. A kind of

Eastern European cynicism borne out of a past where she's learned not to accept anything at face value. 'But I did nothing.'

'Yes, you did. You made me confront the bogeyman.'

'Bogeyman?'

'Carstairs and my guilt. My confession never got out into the world. I wrote it but didn't post it, deleted it. And I don't regret that. I simply can't recall anything about the case and somehow that makes me think I'm not responsible. It's cowardly, I know. Arrogant too, I suppose.'

'I don't understand.'

'Neither do I. Everything points to it being me except that I don't believe it. Sounds mad, doesn't it?' I pause before continuing because I know how it will sound, but it's the truth. 'And even though I didn't confess, somehow I still think that the Carstairs case is linked to Katy Leith. That whoever held her concluded that crucifying me was the wrong thing to do.'

Galina shakes her head. 'The police say she escaped.'

'I know.' I don't say anything else even though I'm plagued by a nagging lack of conviction. All I have is feelings and unanswered questions, all tissue thin. Nothing substantial.

Galina considers this. It's a lot to digest. 'But you are no longer being hassled by press?'

'No, I'm not. And that's great. And I'm delighted that Katy is alive and well. But something isn't right here.'

Galina turns away and launches the ball Winston had retrieved into the water.

'Perhaps it would be better not to poke a stick into the nest of ants.'

I smile. She's absolutely right. Of course she is. But I'm acutely aware too, that I'm already sharpening that stick.

'I'll be sorry to see you go, Galina,' I say.

She nods. 'Winston will miss Sid also. I know that.'

'I really hope you get a chance to feel free.'

'I too, I hope. One day.'

I hug her. This close up, the livid skin in the gap between the
scarf over her mouth and her dark glasses is thick and red. She
breaks away and we play with the dogs for ten minutes until it's
time for her to go.

'I hope you find your answers, Jake,' she says as she walks
away.

I'm surprised by how much I think I'll miss her.

Sid and I go back to Headington with a borrowed dog bed in the
back of my car. He's confused to start with, follows me around
the house, spends an age sniffing out and marking his territory
in the garden. Remarkably, he settles down and dozes in his dog
bed, sleeps all night and is there, wagging his tail, when I get up
in the morning.

On Sunday, I pick Ella, Ben and Lulu up and we drive to the
Chilterns.

It's a nice day. A good day spent doing healthy, normal
things. That's something that's been sadly lacking from my life
of late. I tell Ella that and she kisses me on the cheek. We stop
for ice cream on the way home and I drop them off at eight and
go home and sort myself out for my return to work the following
day.

It's not something I'm looking forward to because somewhere in the back of my mind I can't shake off the feeling of
unfinished business. I don't have to ponder too much to know it
has everything to do with Michael Carstairs. His name hangs
over me like a dangling sword that might drop at any moment.
But I realise I'm not going to get anywhere just sitting at home
and mithering. Best I keep occupied.

So back to work it is.

63

Muskrat Elon @ratskikorsakoff 20May2019
Could still be him #isthishim Police have said nothing re #katyisfree

Steve Bute @sbuteoo7 20May2019
@ratskikorsakoff Christ, what does a bloke have to do? #katyisfree
Commit suicide obviously. He was in hospital when Katy found. Duh
#cantbehim

64

I take Sid back to Paws for Claws early Monday morning. The plan is to get everything in place by next weekend so I can formally adopt. Something Sarah said when I spoke to her on the phone rings true. That it isn't a good idea for me to be alone. Sid can fix that. Ella can too.

I chat again with Bonnie because I'm worried about leaving Sid alone while I'm at work. She eases my concerns by telling me there's a great day-care service I can drop him off at, just two miles from Headington. She knows of other adoptees who use them. They'll exercise and feed him. Sid, I'm sure, will not complain.

At around eight thirty, I park in my usual space at the hospital. I'm nervous, unsure of what sort of reception I'll receive. I'm hailed immediately by two colleagues on my way in. Both congratulate me and tell me how good it is to see me back.

Funny thing is I never really felt like I'd been away.

When I get to my office, Meera is already there and waiting with a fresh cup of tea.

'I heard on the jungle drums that you were back.'

I believe her.

'It wasn't you then,' she says, her eyes twinkling.

'No. It wasn't me.'

'Lots of people in this building are not looking forward to a lunch of hot crow.' The twinkle twinkles a tiny bit more.

'I've read it's best with lots of vinegar.'

Meera grins. 'It's good to have you back, Mr Thorn.'

'Good to be back.' I glance at her desk. 'Anything urgent?'

'Only this.' She hands me a sheet of paper. 'Fresh from the Stasi.'

I smile. Meera is wicked. I unfold the sheet and read.

Re. Return to work of Mr Jacob Thorn from paid leave.

Following discussions with the clinical director, Mr Thorn will need to complete mandatory interviews with both Occupational Health and Human Resources. Once these have been completed and following advice from the Royal College of Surgeons' regional advisor, a phased return to work is suggested. Beginning with two days a week for three weeks, building to a full return by week six. HR interview will be in Room 621.

Sincerely,

F Kierney
    Director of Change

I look at Meera and make a face. 'I've only ever been to Occy Health for a flu jab. Who's the medical officer these days?'

'Still Dr Steyn.'

I recall a silver-haired grey-bearded man of well over sixty whom I occasionally see in the corridors. But not for some months. I realise that I may have passed him without noticing. Occupational Health doctors are an unusual breed having opted out of mainstream medicine to look after the workforce. This includes those with physical ailments who will need treatment and time off work. But mainly it's dealing with those struggling with the mental strain that affects their ability to stand on the front line of the NHS and take a constant battering.

Occupational Health doctors have to make difficult decisions. They have to face people overwhelmed by the stress of the job they do. Dealing with sickness and desperation can grind you down. It meant Steyn had to be a bit of everything: psychologist and physician, father, confessor and mentor. It had never been a job that appealed to me.

While I sip my tea, Meera continues to chat. I tell her more about Sarah leaving. Meera tells me about her daughters – she has three – and the tribulations and the horrors that early teenhood is bringing. I enquire about her husband, Sashin's, hernia. He's due in in four weeks' time. Not on my list, thankfully.

The interview with Steyn takes ten minutes and is a formality. He asks me two key questions: am I depressed, to which I answer no. Am I on any medication, again I answer, no. He's not a big one for eye contact is Steyn. But I'm hoping that today is one of his decisive days. I answer all his questions with brief, short answers. It looks like he appreciates that. He shakes my hand at the end.

'I've been following the story, what they've tried to do to you in the press and social media. I'd say you have good grounds for defamation.'

I thank him. He seems more upset about it than I am, and I wonder about that. Is it relief on my part that seems to have compartmentalised all the venom? Is it the relief of hoping (not knowing, not yet) that I might now walk into Mariachi's and not be spat at? Or is it that I'm still so confused about what the hell is actually going on that I haven't given it that much thought?

If Steyn's interview is straightforward, the meeting in Room 621 is the exact opposite. There are three people in the room already. Not one of them is on my Christmas card list. Kierney and Bilton, I can understand being there. They were the two who put me on gardening leave in the first place. But Janet Catterick's presence confuses me for a moment until I remember that she is a Human Resources advisor. Must be my lucky day. It's Catterick who runs the meeting. All three are po-faced, and the greetings we exchange are cursory.

Kierney says, 'Good to see you feel well enough to return to work, Jake.'

'My pleasure,' I say. 'But I was never unwell. It was your suggestion that I take leave, remember?'

Kierney nods his podgy head.

There are boxes to tick. They need, so they explain, to ensure that there is no risk to my emotional well-being, nor to the clients. By that they mean the patients, and I grit my teeth on hearing the word. It's so woke, I want to scream.

But I don't. I listen patiently, nod at the appropriate moments, and say nothing.

Kierney says, 'We've put a plan in place after discussions with the medical director who has spoken with the Royal College's regional advisor. They both think a gradual easing in is a good idea.'

Bilton weighs in with, 'We're suggesting a phased return. Two and a half days a week for a month, fifty per cent clinical contact during that period. See how you get on.' She shows me a lot of teeth and I nod graciously.

Kierney ends the interview. 'Obviously, if there are any issues, if you feel at any time that it's too much, my door is always open.'

I smile and nod, amazed by my calmness. A part of me, the one who has to face the patients daily, who knows that my absence will only make their wait for surgery or to be assessed even longer, wants to bellow out obscenities. But I know there's no point in me arguing.

Besides, I have other fish to fry.

I go back to the office and wade through my admin.

At one thirty, I surprise Patrick and Sonia by rocking up to the clinic and helping them get through it. It means we finish early and take a rare tea break at around four thirty. Both of them seem delighted to see me. Hardly surprising because they've been on a rudderless ship. I explain about the phased return. That I have no say in it. It takes the shine off things a bit. But I tell them they can ignore the availability nonsense. I'm always there at the end of a phone. Even if, officially, I'll only be in the hospital on Mondays and Thursdays.

The upside is that there will be time for me to lay some ghosts.

I begin that evening.

65

Roger Delany rings me as I pull in to Sedgewood at around six on Monday evening. It's a video call. He's walking as he talks, and it looks like he's in a building; there are people behind him moving in the same general direction towards an exit, I presume. My phone is in a cradle on the dash. I can see myself in a small window to the bottom right of the screen. I need a haircut.

'Jake, my God, are you okay?' Concern adds an urgency to his voice.

'Roger. Yes, I'm fine.'

'I've been away for the weekend and I only learned the details this afternoon.'

'I'm sorry for the mess in the barn,' I say. I had texted, but the mess demanded a face-to-face apology.

Roger shakes his head. 'I got your text. But I had no idea you'd been hospitalised. We have someone who cleans for us. It was Bridget who told me that the police came and that they sent for an ambulance.'

'I threw up all over your nice sofa, Roger. I'll pay for a replacement. Red wine isn't easy to get out.'

My brain brings up a nose-wrinkling olfactory memory of stale vomit and Febreze.

'Forget about it.' There's a pause before he says, 'Andrea feels awful about having left those sleeping tablets in the bathroom.'

I wonder what rumours Roger has heard. 'I'd been tanking it on your good Malbec,' I say. 'I thought two sleeping pills would sort out my insomnia.'

My memory of events, after talking to Sarah, is hazy to say the least. I remember bringing the pills from the bathroom. I also remember thinking what it might be like to end it all. But that wasn't what truly happened, and I need for Roger to know that. 'It was a cock-up. Too much wine mixed with a couple of temazepams. I may even have got confused and taken an extra couple. It wasn't anything more sinister than that.'

Another pause, Roger's expression is full of remorse and pity. 'God, Jake.'

'I know what it sounds like, but it isn't like that. Wasn't like that. I didn't try to top myself.'

Roger slows down but there's a lot of extraneous noise. 'Let me move out of this lobby.'

I wait while he walks through foot traffic, the image on the phone veering giddily between floor, walls, Roger's navy coat. Eventually, it stops, and Roger's face reappears.

I continue. 'Admittedly. Katy Leith and the Carstairs case have been weighing heavy on my mind.'

'Most certainly they have.' Roger is standing still, but his breath sounds ragged after his effort. 'Understandably so. All that vilification in the media must have been a dreadful burden.'

'I'm back at work. But so help me, this Carstairs business is driving me mad. I can't believe I could have forgotten everything about him so completely.'

There's a long pause before Roger answers. 'It's a long time ago, Jake.'

'I know. And I was almost prepared to confess to killing him. That's why I'd drunk so much the other night. But how can I admit to something I don't even remember doing?'

'But it's your name and signature on the op note, isn't it?'

'It looks like mine.'

'Looks like...' Roger starts walking again.

'I know, I know, but what if someone had forged it?'

He's been holding the phone in his hand as he walks. He stops. The image changes once more as he drops the phone to his side momentarily. I hear footsteps and then a different angle. A steadier one. It's a torso shot. He's put the camera down somewhere and is sitting. 'What are you trying to say, Jake? That someone has tried to implicate you?' His voice is a harsh whisper.

'I suppose it is.'

Roger shifts his gaze, rubs his forehead with two fingers and hisses out air. 'You realise what you're saying? That someone has falsified the record.'

'Exactly.'

'But why?'

'To cover themselves. Deflect the blame.'

'Who on earth would do something like that?'

I bite the bullet. 'Wasn't there a locum there at the time? A Kourakis?'

Roger blinks but says nothing.

I press on. 'What if he did the surgery and when things went south, he put my name on the op note?'

Silence.

'Linda has offered to find him for me.'

Roger shakes his head. He looks stricken.

'What?' I ask.

'Kourakis was...' Roger drops his voice. 'He and Linda had a bit of a thing. He was useless anyway. That's why I got rid of him, but even in the few short days he was with us something happened between them. Something that went on long after he left.'

'They had an affair?' My words are whispers of incredulity, encircling my brain like the gallery at St Paul's Cathedral.

A sigh from Roger. 'I am very uncomfortable talking to you about this on the phone.'

Cogs were meshing in my head. Grinding down my thoughts into an unpleasant dark mush of fearful possibilities. Linda, amazing, efficient Linda. The one person who'd have unlimited access to patients' notes. The one person who had seen my signature written on dictated letters a thousand and more times. Who knew it like the back of her hand. I try to recall the Linda of 2006. A slimmer, more-vibrant Linda than the one who'd teased me about the doughnuts. She'd been attractive, but older than I was, and our relationship had been platonic; she the foil between the big boss and us, the apprentices. She'd mothered us. And yes, she'd looked after herself. Always smart, heels to work, often dresses. I'd never thought of her in any sexual way, but that's not to say other people might not have. And that bubbly, open personality enveloped you. If you were so inclined, it would be easy to interpret her tactile openness – Linda was a toucher – as an invitation.

Kourakis might have done just that.

'Linda and Kourakis?' I let the question hover; the implication too incredible for me to articulate fully.

'That was the rumour,' Roger says. He looks suddenly every minute of his sixty-odd years. 'She's been my right arm. Still is. I don't want to confront her without...' He chokes off the sentence.

'Should I speak to her?'

'No... No... Don't do that. I need to process this. The ramifications are... I need to think.' And then the old Roger is back. The surgeon, decision maker, the composed chair of a dozen influential committees. 'But I am glad to see you're well. We'll sort this out.' More noises as hurrying people appear in the background. I can see that most of them are wearing lanyards. Roger stands up, his image wobbling in the frame. 'I'll be in touch. In the meantime, do nothing about Linda. Promise me that.'

'I won't. And thanks for ringing, Roger.'

'Look after yourself, Jake.'

I end the call and sit in the car. My thoughts dart off in a hundred directions like sparks from a Catherine wheel. There's a lot to think about. Linda had not come back to me about Kourakis. I hadn't thought too much about that until now. Perhaps it's still a wound. One she doesn't want to reopen. But Roger's revelation might also explain why Linda still had a copy of Carstairs's notes with my signature on them on her do-not-destroy pile.

Her explanation had been plausible; good secretaries have a sixth sense about these things. But perhaps there's another reason. Perhaps it's an insurance policy. When emotion enters the fray, all bets are off. I've seen it a hundred times. The strongest man in the world can become a wreck when you tell him it's his son or daughter who has the illness he's been dreading. The quivering mess of neurosis that plagues your inbox with inconsequential emails suddenly finds strength to battle through major surgery like a trooper. There's no logic to it. It's raw and always a surprise.

At work, Linda was – probably still is – the master of her own universe. But outside, who knows? People have been more than willing to believe that I, the careful surgeon, was capable of heinous crimes. Perhaps it's about time I allowed myself to believe others capable of equally vile transgressions.

Perhaps, too, holding on to Carstairs's notes might be Linda's way of ensuring she still had a hold on Kourakis, wherever he was.

If there is a flaw in this twisted logic, it's that she showed me the notes in the first place. Why would you do that if you were involved in some kind of misdeed? I recall her gushing enthusiasm on seeing me again and squeeze my eyes shut. If all this is true, then Linda is one hell of a good actress. But isn't that what they say about all psychopaths?

It's then that an even darker thought crawls out from the shadows. What if she and Kourakis are still an illicit couple? Could it be that seeing me embroiled in the Katy Leith case gave them the opportunity to rid themselves of the festering sore that the Carstairs case was, once and for all? Perhaps they hoped that getting me to confess might also tip me over the edge, as it so nearly did. Then there'd be no possibility of the truth being found out about Carstairs. They'd both be in the clear.

There are gaps in my reasoning. Big gaps. It doesn't explain my twisted conviction that the Carstairs case is linked to Katy Leith's abduction more directly, for a start. Nor does it explain why Linda and Kourakis – they're my prime suspects now – had not simply let sleeping dogs lie.

It's a lot to contemplate. But that's what I do for most of the evening. Until I'm too tired for more contemplation and I go to bed.

Sweet pea gardener @Sweepea 21May2019
Jacob Thorn, wrongfully pilloried on social media and the press for
abducting Katy Leith, back at work. #cantbehim I think someone
should apologise. Bloke deserves better.

Ayvedaloco @ayvedalco33 21May2019
@Sweepea Apologise to a highly paid twat like him? #JThorn You
must be kidding.

Sweet pea gardener @Sweepea 21May2019
@Ayvedalco33 You wouldn't be saying that if you'd burst your
appendix and needed help from a skilled surgeon #lovethenhs
Grow up.

Comme de slaphead @libbyrational 21May2019
Katy Leith describes abduction by gang #terrifying My bad #JThorn
#cantbehim Opposition call for more policing. Why don't we use
drones? #bringbackbigbrother

67

On Tuesday morning, I still have too many unanswered questions. Kourakis is the key. I no longer expect Linda to tell me anything and will not be asking. I make coffee, fire up the laptop once more, and open the GMC site. If he's practising in the UK, he'll be registered with the General Medical Council. If he's gone back to Greece, then things will be a lot more difficult. I punch in the name and get a hit.

There's only one Kourakis, and he is registered to practice. He's also on the specialist register. The assumption therefore is that he's working as a surgeon. But there's no address. However, Linda isn't the only administrative help I can call on. I know an Olympic finalist when it comes to finding out things like this. And the best thing of all is that she actually works for me.

It's a little after seven thirty. Too early to ring anyone, so I open my email and type in Meera's address. I ask her if she can find out about a Mr Ioannes Kourakis. Where he works, etc. She's used to this sort of thing. She has a network. I tell her he's on the GMC register, that I need to know if he once worked as a locum in Hampshire in 2006. I have no idea how she does this sort of stuff, but she has her methods. Secretarial networks are like MI6.

However she does it, it works.

Then I'm back to my search engine. I get myself another coffee and google "how to find out where someone is buried". I spend fifteen minutes on a variety of threads and finally decide that the easiest thing would be to ring the local council for Carstairs's last known address. I still have the few pages of notes I photographed on my phone. It's a Chineham address. The local council is Basingstoke and Deane. At 9am, I telephone and speak to a very helpful woman there who confirms that Michael Carstairs was cremated on 29th April 2006. But the ashes were buried in Worting Road cemetery.

I'm showered and changed by eight thirty, on the ring road by eight forty-five. I've already put Worting Road into the satnav. It takes an hour and twelve minutes to get there. The cemetery is on a corner plot with busy roads on two sides and a residential development cradling the other two. It's a bright day, but there are clouds in the west; a dark threat that promises rain by evening. I drive in through iron gates along a tree-lined avenue. Beyond are mowed areas as big as football fields, all dotted with gravestones. I find somewhere to park and walk to the memorial office.

I ask about cremation plots and I'm shown a map indicating a large green area adjacent to the chapel. I thank the receptionist and go back out to walk up and down the lines of headstones. They are closer together than the graves for obvious reasons; urns take up much less space than bodies.

It takes another twenty minutes to find the Carstairs plot, marked by an oval headstone in red marble with gold letters. At first, I think I'm mistaken, but then I realise it has three names instead of one. My stomach churns.

Michael Carstairs, Tina Carstairs and Darren Carstairs. The

family, or most of it, buried together. I shake my head. All this because of my surgical ineptitude?

I look up. There are workmen busy on the site. It's probably a full-time job maintaining an operation this big. I've already learned from the memorial office that the cemetery is no longer council owned. It's wholly privately run. The workmen have a small vehicle, green, with an open pickup section for tools. There are two men. One is picking up flowers and placing them in the back of the pickup; the other is strimming a section of grass where the plot becomes hedge. He's wearing ear defenders and goggles. Both wear a high-vis jacket with Pilgrim Funeral Services written on the back. I walk over to the flower gatherer.

'Hi,' I say.

'Mornin'.' The workman is around fifty, ruddy complexion from outdoor work and a beer gut from spending what he earns in the pub. But he's friendly enough.

'I see you've got your work cut out here keeping this place tidy.'

'Yup.'

Conversation is not his strong point. But I try. 'I expect you see lots of people coming and going.'

'We do.'

The strimmer has stopped, and its operator is looking over at us.

'I've just found a plot. Someone I knew from old. It must be a dozen years since the father was buried. Now there are three of them.'

'Oh, which one's that?'

I walk him over and show him the Carstairs plot. He nods.

'I was wondering if you ever see anyone visiting on a regular basis.'

My new friend tilts his head and sends his eyes skywards. Clearly, thinking takes some effort. He calls over to his co-worker who has closed the gap between us. 'Nathan, remember seeing anyone visiting here?'

Nathan takes off his kit. He's younger and brawnier. His movements are athletic and energetic. My money is on him being a gym rat or maybe a rugby player. He ambles over to stand next to us. Beer-gut points to the red marble headstone. 'This one?'

'Yes,' I say.

Nathan says, 'Well, yeah. There is. Young girl comes once every couple of weeks. Brings a posy usually. Don't mind them 'cos they don't need much clean up. We just leave them on the grass. Weather takes care of 'em.'

'She been coming for a long time?' I ask.

'I've been 'ere twelve months. Seen her a few times. Usually a Friday. Always afternoons. Pretty girl. You notice them, don't you?'

'You do,' says the older man.

Nathan raises his eyebrows.

Beer-gut smiles. 'Just sayin'.' He looks at me curiously, face clouding when he realises he might have offended. 'You know 'er?'

I shake my head. 'No. She must be family though.'

'Yeah. Shame to see them all in there. The boy was a young 'un.'

I glance at the stone. Darren Carstairs. 02/03/1998 – 10/03/2017. Nineteen almost to the day.

I thank them both and turn away to walk back to the car. I am already planning to come back on Friday. I feel I owe this steadfast visitor an explanation.

68

Wednesday, I spend sorting out things for Sid. I buy a new bed, food, and talk to the day-care people. They seem on the ball and very enthusiastic about having him. In the afternoon, I take a train to London. Sarah is still off work. Still recovering from her ordeal. I offer to take her out to lunch and she almost bites my arm off.

I decide on the way up not to say anything about my suspicions. That her "mugging" was not a mugging, but a thinly veiled warning to me to do as I was told. We go to the Wigmore on Regent Street. It's at the quiet end of that manic thoroughfare and is a part of the Langham Hotel. But it's self-contained and their masala spiced scotch eggs are to die for. I go for that; Sarah has hummus and cheese. She's still looking a bit pale and I tell her so.

'I hurt my back when I fell. The doctors say it'll take a couple of weeks. It wakes me up when I turn over at night.'

'That can't be fun.'

'No. It isn't.' She arches her back and winces. 'But Simon's secretary knows this amazing healer, and she's given me some black cohosh tea which is really good for inflammation. And cramp bark as an antispasmodic.'

I nod and just about resist the urge to ask if she's tried leeches yet. I'm always amazed by people's willingness to accept any and all snake-oil tosh as a cure. Stuff unencumbered by even the slightest whiff of clinical evidence. But then there is the placebo effect which is not to be sniffed at. As opposed to the scent of an aromatherapy anti-stress balm that Sarah once used, which was meant to be sniffed at. Unfortunately, the balm reacted with her antimagnetic anklet to give her a nasty rash that only settled down with a GP-prescribed steroid. I had laughed at that. It doesn't seem like she's learned much of a lesson though.

'How are you?' Sarah asks as we dig into our food.

'I'm good,' I say through a mouthful of scotch egg. 'Much relieved now that Katy Leith is safe and sound.'

Sarah puts down her fork. 'Yes, have you heard any more about that? It's so weird.'

'No,' I say. 'It's ongoing, or so my police friends tell me.'

'Your police friends?'

'Oh yes. We're all the greatest of pals now.'

'I bet.' Sarah dips a gluten-free bread stick into her artichoke hummus. 'Thanks for sending me those photos by the way. God, did you see the clothes I was wearing? And you had that awful moustache in 2006.'

I'd forgotten about the photos. They were a part of my darkest hour. But Sarah has her phone out and I'm suddenly looking at us sitting at the table with the family behind and their great haul of Easter eggs.

'This must have been just before I left for the States.'

Sarah frowns mid-chew. 'Yes. Years ago. We walked up to Bull's Cross. The hotel sent us on the Laurie Lee trail. There'd been a gibbet there, remember? It was supposed to be haunted with ghostly stagecoaches rattling through on the moonless nights. So we tried to stay up there until it was dusk, but it got so cold we went back to the hotel. Then it rained on the Saturday and we had this huge lunch on Sunday. I was too full to eat my Easter egg.'

I nod. In truth, I don't remember much of the detail. But Sarah's reminiscences are always related to things emotional. It's a trait.

I elaborate on my explanation. 'As I say, my phone just threw up the photo and I couldn't remember it at all. I think I was a teeny bit preoccupied with my impending trip.'

'I remember because we had to get up at five on the Monday to drive back to the flat in Heathfield because your flight was at two that afternoon.' Sarah's tone is mildly critical. I won't miss that.

'Oh God, yes. I was on pins because the traffic was awful.'

I give her back the phone. Something has triggered a little itch in my head. The one that keeps being tickled by the nebulous feather. The one I've had since the night at Apple Drop Barn. But it's still too insubstantial for me to scratch. It dissipates like a drop of milk in a glass of water but momentarily disorientates me. I'm off guard when I say, 'You'll be glad to know I'm back at work on a phased return and I've been seeing someone.'

Sarah, for once, is speechless.

After ten long seconds, she manages an incredulous, 'What?'

'There's a woman I met walking the dog. We've been seeing one another for a month or so.'

Amazingly, Sarah blushes. She seems oddly flustered and angry. 'You? But...'

'I didn't think you'd mind, now that you've moved in with Simon.'

'But we were sharing a bed.' Incredulity.

'Yes, we were. Only very occasionally, if I remember rightly.'

'Are you telling me you were sleeping with someone while we–?'

'Just like you were with Simon, you mean?'

Sarah puts down her cutlery. Her breathing has changed. It's become uneven and short. 'How many times?' she asks.

'What?'

'How many times have you slept with her?'

'A few,' I reply, knowing it's enigmatic. But then I haven't been counting.

'In the bed we shared?' Her voice goes up.

'No. Never in the cottage. Not once while you were there. But what difference would that make?'

'It's a horrible thought, that's the difference. To think I was sleeping in the same bed as you and–'

'You weren't.'

'To think that you were sharing me with–' Horror-filled eyes stare back at me.

'Simon?' I say, rather cleverly, I think.

'It's not the same thing.'

I snort. 'Isn't it? I think it's exactly the same thing.'

Sarah gets up. Her plate clatters to the floor, ejaculating hummus over the planking. 'You're despicable,' she hisses.

'Now wait a minute.' I feel like I should have prefixed "minute" with "goldarned" but I settle for putting my own cutlery down emphatically, and say, 'I sense a pot calling the kettle black here.'

'It's not the same.'

Of course, to anyone else, it most definitely is. Exactly the same. But not to Sarah, who has her own Barstow frame of reference for this set of circumstances.

'How could you?' she says. The blush has gone, replaced by fury-induced white.

It's my turn to stare at her with my mouth open. 'I didn't come here to gloat.'

'I don't believe you.'

'Hang on a minute. What gives you the right to be so irate? You're the one who started this.'

'How do you know when I started this?'

People are staring. Though we're talking in whispers, the tone and the urgency of those whispers might as well be transmitting our words over the PA. Nothing like a bit of domestic altercation to get the punters going.

'Because I followed you once. Last March. When you were supposed to be cosying up to your BFF, Jess. I came up for a meeting and was going to surprise you. Instead you went in another direction. To Kensington. And you stayed there way after everyone's bedtime.'

'You followed me?' Sarah is glaring, lots of white showing around her flecked irises.

I know my story won't stand up to forensic dissection. I wasn't at a meeting for a start. And I won't tell her that her misdirected WhatsApp message gave the game away. These are small details in the overall picture. 'Yes. I followed you and caught you out. Long before you told me.'

I can see her eyes flashing, the anger pulsing behind them. We both know she has no leg to stand on. That it's me who's the injured party here. However, I've underestimated her again. Like I say, I'm a world expert.

'It was that sodding WhatsApp message, wasn't it?'

'Might have been.'

But logic has never impeded Sarah when it comes to arguments. Attack is always the best form of defence in her playbook.

'How dare you stalk me.'

I laugh then. She has a great skill of twisting things to her advantage. It's an enviable talent. But the laugh dies on my lips because another thought creeps in to my head. A really ugly one. Could there be another reason for her anger? I told her two things initially. That I was seeing someone, and that I was back at work. Suddenly, my imagination is conjuring something truly hideous.

Sarah knows more about me than any other living person. But she's been sharing a bed with someone else and I know how Sarah likes to unburden herself after work. That hasn't happened for some months with me, but it used to. In most intimate relationships, you share things you wouldn't dream of revealing to someone else. I begin to wonder if Sarah has told Simon about Michael Carstairs.

I almost laugh, but something stops me. The counterargument is compelling. Why would she even know? I didn't. I'd gone to America.

But she hadn't.

The thought pierces my brain.

It's ludicrous. It's far-fetched. But is it possible that somehow someone from work had contacted her about Carstairs at the time? Someone who'd forgotten I'd already left. Maybe a coroner's officer before RD had weighed in. Had someone perhaps left a message on our phone that Sarah had naturally followed up? She'd never mentioned it. But now my imagination stitches things together into a loathsome tapestry of deception. What if it wasn't clever traffickers, or an incompetent colleague and a flirtatious secretary who's seen the chance to blackmail me into confessing, but someone else? Someone with an axe to grind. Who might see my ruination as a way to get what she – or more likely, he – has always wanted?

I consider the possibility that Sarah and Simon are in it together. It's possible, of course, but still I don't want to believe it of her. Not after us being together for so long. But Simon, who'd coveted Sarah for a long while, might have seen a great opportunity. If I'd posted that confession, my career would be over. Coping with the press feeding frenzy over the rumours of my involvement with Katy Leith's abduction was one thing, but admitting that my botched surgery had led to a death and the eventual destruction of a family... No one would have blamed Sarah for sodding off then.

She's still standing, staring at me. I look back at her, the woman I'd been hoping to spend my life with, but who suddenly seems like a stranger I've just met.

'Don't worry,' I say, 'I'll pay for lunch.'

She picks up a glass from the table and launches the contents at me. She gets me square in the face and I taste white wine spritzer.

'Look after yourself, Sarah,' I say to her departing back as I wipe my face with a napkin. 'Give my regards to Simon.'

69

Thursday morning, I'm back in work. There's a theatre list and so I head up and change into scrubs. The list is small, no major cases because they've had no time to rearrange things since my phased return has only just been agreed. I plan on letting Patrick do the whole thing, but it's a chance for me to say hello to the team and Ashish, in particular. Let them know I'm still on the planet.

Patrick is halfway through a hernia when I arrive. He's a youngish patient, so Ashish is giving him a general.

There are smiles and hellos all around. Except from Ashish, who does smile, but in that way he has that heralds something caustic.

'Well, well. Nice of you to turn up now that you're not in prison.'

'Good to see you too,' I reply.

Ashish comes around from behind the anaesthetic machine and shakes my hand.

'Morning, Mr Thorn,' Sonia says from the operating table where she's assisting.

Patrick, who's concentrating on what he's doing, simply says, 'Hi.'

The rest of the staff give out shy hellos.

After ten minutes of banter with Ashish, it's as if I've never been away.

Later, in a quiet moment when we're alone in the anaesthetic room, I thank him for his support during the week when I was off. It's meant a lot to me.

'Hey, don't forget I've been your gasman for a good few years. I've seen you operate. I know you'd be bloody incapable of abducting that girl on your own. You'd need Meera to tell you where to go, Sonia to hold your hand while you did, and Patrick to stay in the background and look disapprovingly at your idiosyncratic technique.'

'Thanks.'

Ashish nods. 'But the bastards in the Twittersphere would have happily strung you up for it, wouldn't they?'

'Nothing like a bad doctor to whet the appetite for public humiliation.'

'But you're all clear now, right?'

'Phased return. Two days a week for a month.'

'You lucky bugger.'

Ash and his wife, Rita, have been over to Headington for supper half a dozen times, so I feel obliged to tell him about Sarah.

'Oh shit. I'm sorry to hear that.'

'Are you?'

Ashish narrows his eyes. 'Is this where I'm supposed to tell you that Rita never liked Sarah and that she thought she was a bit cold and more than a bit stuck-up?'

'Maybe.'

'I'll wait until six months have gone by and there's no chance of a reconciliation before I do.'

All I can do is shake my head at Ash's grin.

Another patient arrives, and Ash greets him with his usual ebullience. I duck out of the room while he does his voodoo. His head follows me around the door. 'Are you doing this one, Jake?' Ash whispers, the question out of the patient's earshot.

'No, I'm letting Patrick get his numbers up.'

'Shirker,' Ash says.

'I could make you a coffee?'

'Now that's a plan. One sugar and a biscuit.'

All in all, it's a pleasant morning. Though I'm itching to scrub, I'm test driving a new me. One that's trying to be a better delegator than in the past. There's a clinic in the afternoon, so I pop in to see Meera at lunchtime.

'I have news about your Mr Kourakis,' she says.

'Go on,' I say. 'I'm all ears.'

'Mr Ioannes Kourakis is a general surgeon up in Bradford. I have a friend who works in Leeds. Mr Kourakis did locums for a long time in the noughties, so there's a good chance it's the same chap.'

'How long has he been at Bradford?'

'About six years. He was there as a staff grade and got his consultancy through article fourteen, whatever that is.'

'It's not called that anymore,' I explain. 'But it's a route to entry on the specialist register for people who haven't had run through training, or an approved training programme.'

I'd known a few colleagues over the years who had succeeded. It was a slog, getting all the right boxes ticked. And it usually meant a much slower progress up the ladder. But it was the only other way – outside of the specialist training run through programme – to get a Certificate of Eligibility, the ticket to a consultant post. People who took this route ended up being appointed as consultants much later than the average.

I say, 'It sounds promising.'

'My Leeds contact has a mobile and a home number.'

'My God, Meera. Do MI5 know what they're missing?'

'I don't like London,' Meera says, as if she's considered the option.

I do the clinic and some teaching in the afternoon. I ring Kourakis's mobile number as I drive home that evening. The mobile goes straight to answerphone. I try the landline. That too goes straight to answerphone, but this time, I leave a message.

'Hi, my name is Jake Thorn. I think we worked together briefly in Hampshire in 2006. I wondered if you could ring me regarding a patient we may have looked after at that time.'

I leave my mobile number and head home, thinking about Sarah and Simon.

70

On Friday, I drive down to Basingstoke late morning. The cemetery gardeners told me the regular visitor to the Carstairs's grave went on Friday afternoons. But I'm not taking any chances. I arrive at eleven thirty and park up, armed with sandwiches and a bottle of water. I sit and wait and ponder.

At midday, I get a call from Roger.

'Jake, how are you?' There's concern in his voice.

'I'm fine, thanks.'

'Settling back in?'

'As much as they'll let me. Two days a week is hardly taxing.'

'Ah, it's all about a holistic approach these days. Listen, I've been mulling over our conversation of the other day. About Linda and our friend Kourakis, that is.'

'And?'

'As I said, it's complicated. I felt bad about getting rid of Kourakis the way we did, so I offered to help him. Come to think of it, Linda bent my ear a bit. Said he was a nice boy, keen, and bright too. That I shouldn't have been so hard on him. I remember giving him a leg up and a quiet word in someone's ear about a full-time job. This was all before I knew anything about him and Linda, of course. But if I'm right, he took his chance and ended up getting his article fourteen.'

'He's a consultant in Bradford now,' I say.

'You managed to track him down then?'

'I did. Thought I'd have a quiet word. Not managed it yet but I'll keep trying.'

'That may be the more diplomatic approach.' There's a pause before Roger says, 'I'm still unsure about how to broach this subject with Linda. To say it's a delicate situation would be an understatement.'

Roger's right. We don't know anything for certain.

'I won't lie to you,' Roger says. 'I'm losing sleep over this. Perhaps we ought to take a closer look at it all. I've been contemplating taking a day or two away from the family to get this sorted in my mind. I'm going up to the cottage in Coombe Brook tonight. I was wondering if you'd care to join me. Two heads will be better than one, I'm certain. There's a great little pub in Barrington. We could have a quick supper there and chew all this over. What do you say?'

'I think it's a great idea,' I say. 'In the meantime, I'll see if I can find Kourakis.'

'All right, you do that. But for now, leave Linda out of it, would you?'

'I will.'

I sign off, end the call, and turn back to my sandwiches and the radio. The news is on. More details of how they're making a pig's ear of Brexit. If I'm truthful, I'm fed up to the back teeth of even hearing the word.

I'm not alone in the car park. People come and go. Some get out and walk to a spot in the cemetery, others head to the admin office. Some have flowers, others do not. But the majority end up at a gravestone where they either stand or kneel. Most spend about fifteen minutes before getting back into their cars and driving off.

Remembrance.

At a few minutes after two thirty, a Mini pulls up. There's movement in the driver's seat. A young girl gets out. She's wearing a faux fur bobble hat, tight jeans and trainers. She zips up a padded jacket and strokes away grey-blonde hair from where it wafts about her head. I catch a glimpse of an attractive young face before sunglasses slide on to ward off the bright spring sunshine. She locks the car and walks away.

It could be her.

I'm suddenly filled with doubts. What the hell am I doing here? Opening old wounds, that's for certain. No one seems interested in my involvement with Carstairs anymore, except me. There have been no more demands for a confession. No one cares. No one wants to judge.

Except me.

I watch the girl for several minutes. When she stops to look at a headstone, I get out of my car and walk over.

There are other people in the cemetery and that makes me feel a little better about approaching this young woman. Fit looking, I put her somewhere in her twenties. If she objects, I'll walk away. Sarah has already called me a stalker once this week. This would be piling manure on the steaming midden that is already my reputation. I can see the headlines already.

I walk past one row behind. There's no doubt about it; she's standing in front of the Carstairs plot. I turn back and, from ten feet away, say, 'Excuse me.'

She turns. She's slim, looks after herself, curious but not

alarmed, her body language keen to help. I can't tell what her expression is behind the glasses.

'This is going to sound very weird,' I say, 'but bear with me. Are you a relation of Michael Carstairs?'

She frowns. I think I see recognition dawn, but she controls her response. I've seen it in many faces over the last few days. The vague awareness that they've seen me somewhere before, followed by #isthishim flashing up in people's consciousness. Not all of them twig why they're aware of me though.

If I were a minor celebrity, this recognition might elicit a little thrill. But for me, it's the unwelcome price of notoriety.

Slowly, the girl nods. 'No, but I knew Darren.' Her glasses are large, stylish, and thick rimmed. Her accent is not clipped. I'd guess the Wirral or the outskirts of Liverpool maybe.

I hold one hand up. 'I'm sorry to intrude. And to put you out of your misery, yes, I'm Jake Thorn, and you've probably seen my photograph in the news lately.'

'You're the doctor.' She states the fact.

'I am.'

I'm glad to see she doesn't flinch. 'The newspapers all say that the others got it wrong. That you've been made a victim.'

'I know. They're highly skilled at blaming each other while they conveniently refuse to look in a mirror.'

She glances to her right. There are people thirty yards away laying flowers. It seems to give her confidence, and she tilts her head. 'Why are you here?'

'Good question. This is where it gets a little strange. Can I ask your name?'

'Zoe. Zoe Seddon.'

I nod.

'Zoe, did Darren know about his father?'

She frowns. 'He knew he died when he, Darren that is, was very young.'

'Do you know Darren's sister?'

'Grace? No. I've never met her.'

I nod. Explain some more. 'I was a doctor at the hospital where Darren's father was treated. I know what happened to him and to the family.'

'Right.' Zoe waits.

'And obviously, if you're here, you know what happened to Darren and to his mother.'

'I know they all died way too young. When Darren was eighteen, he got his mum, Tina's, effects. He went to her solicitor. He got really upset because there were letters there. Letters that showed his mum was very unhappy with the treatment his dad had received.'

I nod. 'And she may have had grounds for those feelings. I'm here because I want to explain to Darren's sister.' I search for the words. 'Certain things have come to light about their father's treatment. Things that should be explained.'

'What sort of things?'

I pause. There's no easy way to say this. I still have doubts, but I also know that I have no choice. 'I suspect that there might have been some negligence surrounding Michael Carstairs's treatment,' I explain. 'To do with his surgery.'

Zoe frowns. 'Negligence? You mean someone messed up?'

Good question. I hesitate again. It's the first time someone has really asked me that – as opposed to assuming that I am to blame. I should put my hand up. Because still everything points to it being me. And yet, my stubborn refusal to accept what's staring me in the face is what's brought me to this point. To this cemetery. For me to say "Maybe" is suddenly not good enough. It sounds weak and desperate. Yet every fibre of my being wants it not to have been me. But what proof do I have?

None.

My silence is becoming awkward. What on earth was I

hoping to achieve by even coming here? I realise I can't tell this girl what I really think. That there's a conspiracy. Because I have absolutely no proof. All I have is supposition and rumour. The same cowardly MO the press used to hang me out to dry. And with Zoe staring at me, I realise, sourly, that it's exactly what I'm trying to do to perpetrators unknown. I have no proof that my signature has been forged. I have no proof that Kourakis was involved, or Linda, or Simon or Sarah. All I have is my own twisted belief that it could not have been me. That I would have remembered.

Realisation that my denial is built on a foundation of pure hubris makes me want to turn away and run to the car. Who am I trying to convince here? Zoe or myself?

'I...' That one faltering, hesitant pronoun is all I can manage. But then I find some words from somewhere. 'Truth is, I don't know.' An unfunny laugh follows, and I say, 'I wish I could go back to 2006 and find out.'

Zoe nods. 'You never know, one day we might be able to.'

I smile. She's a nice kid. Wondering, no doubt, what she's done to deserve being accosted in a cemetery by me. Forcing herself to humour this strange bloke and his talk of time travel... My brain stops there. Freezes. A flicker of electricity licks at my spine and the hair on the back of my neck stands to attention as realisation surges. Knowing is like plunging into a bath of cold water.

Time bloody travel.

I fumble for my phone, drop it – onto grass, thank God – retrieve it and start pressing icons. I look up to see Zoe staring at me.

'Sorry,' I mutter. 'You asked about blame. And it's a fair question. The truth is, I've been blaming myself but... It's confusing because I've had no way of being certain. I know that sounds odd, but I've just realised how I can find out.'

My fingers are trembling. I don't shake when I open someone's abdomen up, or peel back tissue around nerves and arteries. But now, this simple act of trying to press buttons on a phone brings on the jitters. It's as if I've got some awful palsy. But I get the photo app open, scroll to a year. 2006. The photograph of us in The Boar at Painswick. Sarah and me in front of the Adams family with their table laden with Easter eggs.

Easter eggs.

A hundred thoughts crowd into my head. I left for California on Easter Monday. I remember it because the airport was weirdly quiet, and I was full of mixed emotions, both excited and a little empty because I was leaving. We'd had a weekend away in the Cotswolds, Sarah and me. A final fling before I left. But the weather had been iffy. We spent the weekend at The Boar, went back to my flat early and took a train and then a taxi to the airport, leaving Sarah at the station. A tearful goodbye.

But the night before we'd been together. At The Boar. On Easter Sunday. And at the Wigmore a few days earlier, before we'd fallen out and Sarah had given me a spritzer facial, she said we'd gone for a walk on the only dry day of that weekend. But it had rained on the Saturday. I look again the Easter egg photo, the specials board, the shadowy family in the background. That's not what's important. I press an information icon and up pops a box with the date and time of when the photograph was taken. Seven thirty pm on sixteenth April 2006.

My hand quivers as I thumb through the photo roll. Find what I'm looking for five images back. A windswept spot; Bull's Head. Where superstition has it that ghostly carriages run on the darkest nights. Sarah dressed warmly with a scarf around her face. Another of the both of us in a crude selfie with the bare branches of the dark trees and the grey sky behind. We're standing under the "Bull's Head" sign, uber tourists, Sarah grabbing me for warmth. I press the information icon again.

My heart is pulsing in the back of my throat as I read, Friday fourteenth April 2006.

Which meant I couldn't have been in Hampshire operating on Michael Carstairs that day.

71

I stare at the image on the phone. Suddenly, it's a Picasso. Worth more than any amount of money. To me, at least. I punch the air and laugh out loud at how amazing technology is. My hands are still trembling as I press the keys to take a screenshot of what's now showing, with the image and the date stamp.

When I look up, Zoe is still staring at me.

'Are you okay?'

'Yes. Yes, I am. Because I've just found the absolute proof that I didn't carry out the surgery on Darren's father. I couldn't have because I was somewhere else at the time, though the notes say otherwise.'

Zoe regards me with raised eyebrows that ride above the rims of her glasses.

'Sorry, I must seem like a complete lunatic. It's just that I've been blamed–'

'How could you be blamed if you weren't there?'

Her question stops me in mid-apology. Another great question. 'Because it's my signature in the hospital notes.'

Zoe, my rabbit in the headlights, waits for me to finish.

'I guess someone altered those notes to make it look like it was me.'

But it's not a guess anymore. It's the truth.

'Why?' Another great question.

I reply quickly. Spitting out the thoughts as they occur to me. 'That's what I'm trying to find out. I know how all of this must sound. I'm here because I didn't know of any other way to reach out to the family. Look, if you know Grace Carstairs...' I let the sentence hang. It won't be her real name now after adoption, I realise that much. And I'm still not sure what good this is doing. There's an argument for saying nothing, of course. Letting it all slip back into the past again. But that doesn't change the fact that someone messed up. So I add, 'I can't help feeling she ought to know. She has a right to know.'

Zoe blinks and shrugs. 'There may be a way. When Darren died, I posted it on my timeline. There was someone who asked questions. How I knew him. Stuff like that. It could have been Grace. She seemed to know a lot about Darren and his parents. She hasn't been in contact since. I suppose I could post again. Try to find her that way.' Zoe half turns back towards the headstone. 'I didn't know them. None of them except Darren. They separated him from Grace when they were kids. But whoever adopted her didn't have room for him. He was really messed up. I tried to help him when we were both in care. But I was the only one at his funeral.' She turns back to me. The wind wafts wisps of hair over her face and she strokes it back once more. I can't see if she's crying behind her glasses. 'He'd been an addict for years, you know that, right?'

I nod.

Zoe sniffs. 'Thank you for telling me this. I'll try to find Grace, but I can't promise anything.'

I take some steps towards her. The ten yards between us

seems like too big a distance. I cut it to five but no closer. 'Thank you. At the moment, I don't even know what or who is to blame for any of this. But, if you like, once I find out, I could tell you.'

'Sure.' She pauses, uncertain, expressionless behind the glasses. 'You're not at all like I'd imagined you'd be. From the papers.'

'Is that a good thing?'

'Yes. They haven't painted a very flattering picture.'

No, they have not.

My phone rings. I look at the caller number. It's a landline and not one I'm familiar with. But then something about the dialling code rings a bell because I'd rung it myself yesterday. It's a Bradford number.

I turn to Zoe. 'Will you excuse me for one minute? I need to take this.'

I walk a few feet away and speak. 'Hello?'

'Hello. Is this Jake Thorn?' It's a woman's voice. A worried voice, tremulous and raw.

'Yes, it is.'

'I'm Laura Kourakis. You rang yesterday.'

'I did. I'm trying to get hold of your husband, Ioannes. Is he–'

My question is cut off by a sob on the line.

'Hello? Mrs Kourakis? Is everything okay?'

'No,' the reply is a sing-song wail of despair. 'No, it isn't. I don't know where he is. I thought you might be...'

I wait. Another sob, some sniffing, and then Laura Kourakis speaks again. This time her voice is more controlled. 'Io went to a meeting in Liverpool four days ago. He should have been back on Wednesday, but he hasn't come back. He hasn't rung. Now every time the phone rings–' Yet another sob.

It's very quiet in the cemetery. I can hear Laura Kourakis's pain loud in my ear. I look up at Zoe. She's watching me, hands held together in front of her like a small child would do. She has long fingers and well-kept nails painted a dark blue.

'I am so sorry to hear that,' I say into the phone.

'Do you know what's happened? Do you know where he is?'

'No. I'm sorry, I don't. I wanted to talk to him about a clinical matter. A mutual patient. I wasn't at the meeting in Liverpool.'

Another sob wracks the connection between us. When she next speaks, it's in a whisper. 'I don't know what to tell the children. If you find him, will you ring me? Please?'

'Of course I will. I'm sorry to disturb you.'

'Thank you.' Her voice has become a small frightened animal.

I end the call, put the phone away, and step back towards Zoe. 'Sorry about that. Bizarrely, that was the wife of one of the other doctors looking after Darren's dad.'

'I heard. Kourakis. An unusual name.'

She nods politely, her smile thin. Things are awkward again. I've outstayed my welcome. I try to put her at ease once more.

'Are you in university?'

She shakes her head. 'Finished last year.'

'What did you study?'

'Media and visual arts.'

I whistle. 'Tough industry.'

Zoe gives a little shake of the head and her deprecating smile is charming. 'I'm just starting out. I've done internships on one or two productions. And it is tough, but now that Netflix, HBO and Amazon are taking over, there's actually a big demand.'

'Do you specialise?'

She shakes her head again. 'Just trying things out. But film is what I like.'

'Special effects take your fancy?' I ask. 'I read it took something like five hours every day to make up a white walker. That would keep you in work.'

Zoe beams. 'You're a *Thrones* fan?'

I knew it would come in useful one day. 'Totally. Lots of special effects there.'

'I know. I've actually been to Winterfell.'

My mouth drops open.

'I was a runner on the last series night shoot. The big battle, remember?'

Who can forget? Some people say the whole thing should have ended with that. 'Wow,' I gush. 'I'm impressed.'

'Don't be. I spent most of my time making sure that the army of the dead didn't have any bits of chip left under their green screen masks after they'd had lunch.' Zoe wrinkles her nose. 'Continuity.'

'Sounds interesting,' I say.

She smiles. It tells me that not all of it is. I sense it's time to end this. 'So if I find anything else out, how can I get hold of you?'

Her smile falters, becomes tinged with wariness. I realise I've shot myself in the foot. She's never met me before and I've been cast as the nation's number one predator. Not smart to be asking for her contact details. But she lets me off easily. 'I know who you are. Why don't I contact you in say, a couple of weeks? Is that okay?'

I nod. 'It is.' I write a number on the back of the receipt from the shop where I'd bought my sandwiches. 'This is my secretary's number at the Oxford Infirmary.'

Zoe takes the receipt. I notice her hands again. She has an inky stain on the inner side of her middle finger. I catch a glimpse of a long thin streak. She pockets the receipt and I wonder if there's a leaky pen in there somewhere. Then she holds out a hand and I shake it. I turn away and go back to the car. I'm not sure why, but I feel a lot better for having talked to this girl.

She's still standing at the grave when I drive away. She waves. She seems like a nice kid and now I feel even more certain that I have to understand all of this. Not just for myself, but for Zoe and for Grace and for all the Carstairs dead.

72

I drive back from Basingstoke, brain buzzing. I find a playlist – one of mine, not Sarah's – and chair dance to some Motown as I sit at the endless traffic lights that guard the way in, and out, of the town. Things are, at last, looking up. I need to make sure that everything is okay for Sid's arrival the next day. I'm breaking with my routine and picking him up mid-morning. Then I'll meet Ella and Ben and Lulu in Shotover Park, and I'll bring them back to the cottage for lunch.

Sod Sarah.

But first I'm meeting Roger. I delay heading to Coombe Brook until after six to let the worst of the Friday afternoon traffic evaporate. It's a clear evening as the satnav steers me west of Burford to The Foxhound. The pub sits off a junction of minor roads next to the river, hidden down a labyrinth of lanes, straight out of a Tolkien novel. I spot Roger's Bentley in the car park. He never could say no to the biggest and best when it came to cars.

I've googled The Foxhound. It's a gastropub with rooms. I park and walk into a big space busy with a mix of locals and visitors. I spy lots of waxed jackets and wellies. The bar has beams and low ceilings, stone walls, and glass mugs hanging from hooks.

Roger's standing, chatting to the landlord. Roger calls me over and pumps my hand.

'Glad you could make it, Jake. Pint?'

I order an IPA and, after a few exchanges with the landlord, Roger takes me to an annexe with tables. It's quieter here. This is obviously where people eat, so we sit in a corner to study the menus.

I lift up my mug. "What the doctor ordered" is etched in elaborate lettering.

Roger shrugs and grins. 'They keep three for me here. I did a charity thing for them three years ago. An auction of sorts. they gave me these as a thank you. Alan, the landlord, always insists I use my own glass.'

The beer is malty and dry and we both finish within five minutes. I offer to go to the bar, but Roger insists that this is all on him. He gets up and lopes across to the other room. I hear his voice and his deep laugh as he engages with people he knows well. This is Delany territory.

'What about driving?' I ask when he gets back with two fresh pints.

'Two and a half's my maximum over a couple of hours. The back roads here are empty. I've only ever met the odd tractor on any journey. No need to worry, but you enjoy. You can leave your car here. Al will keep an eye out. You'll stay with me overnight, I hope?'

'I could, I suppose.' I hadn't planned on it, but the beer is very good. And, unlike Roger and his questionable drinking limit, I will not drive after more than a pint. I don't think it's worth the risk.

'Great. Now, I always go for the chicken and leek pie. It's homemade and an absolute winner. What do you fancy?'

I order the beer-battered fish and chunky chips. A rare treat given Sarah's long list of food taboos. A young waitress takes the order and Roger insists I try the Albarino. 'You have a glass and we'll take the bottle home with us. I'll help you polish it off there.'

While we wait, I tell him about the phone call with Kourakis's wife. Roger listens while we munch on some appetiser olives.

'That's odd,' he says. 'Think he's flown the nest?'

The olives are crunchy and salty. I'm halfway through my second pint by now and it's slipping down far too easily. 'I've been mulling that over,' I say between olives. 'And this is the part you'll not like. Today is Friday the twenty-fourth. I spoke to Linda first on Monday the thirteenth, that's eleven days ago. Kourakis has been missing for two days.'

'What are you saying, Jake?'

'I'm saying that Linda knew I was sniffing around Kourakis last week. She could have warned him.'

Roger shrugs. 'So your opinion is he's simply taken off? Skipped the country and headed south to Greece? What would that achieve?'

'Not sure. But I don't like coincidences. I don't think his absence can be a coincidence. Someone's behind all this.'

Roger looks uncomfortable. As anyone listening to someone paranoid enough to suggest he'd been set up, would. In Roger's eyes, I'm still a conspiracy theorist of the worst kind.

But this isn't a theory anymore.

I drop my voice. 'I also have definitive proof that I couldn't have operated on Carstairs.'

Roger sighs. 'Jake, I realise how hard this must be for you–'

'No, you don't understand. This isn't me being holier than thou. This is proof.' I show him the photo, the date and location.

He stares, blinking. 'I wasn't anywhere near Hampshire or St Jude's that evening,' I add to emphasise the obvious.

Roger sits back and shakes his head. 'My God. You're right. Someone did falsify those notes.'

I smile and heave a deep sigh of relief. Hearing Roger say those words is like having a ton weight taken off my shoulders.

The waitress comes with the wine. I finish my beer and use the loo.

When I come back, Roger has a half of beer in front of him and I have a full glass of white wine. The food comes. The chips are triple cooked to give them a wonderful crunchy texture. The batter is delicious. The wine is excellent. Despite everything, I relax.

'You must tell the police about that photo,' Roger says.

'I will. First thing in the morning. But I wanted to run things over with you. See what you think. The police already have me marked as slightly unhinged.'

Roger grins. He tells me more about Kourakis. About how Roger's made some calls and learned that Kourakis is well liked, but a nervous surgeon. His wife, the anxious woman I'd spoken to earlier that day, is his second. The first is still in Greece.

'So definitely possible he's panicked and buggered off to think things through,' I say.

'Possible, yes. Or maybe he and Linda are still in cahoots.' Roger tilts his head and sighs. 'I just can't get my head around Linda as the scarlet woman though.'

Scarlet woman. Roger really is from the eighteenth century. I fork some fish into my mouth and it slides off before reaching its target. I realise that I'm a little drunk. 'What percentage is that IPA?' I ask to cover my clumsiness.

'Around four and a half.'

'Has a kick,' I laugh.

'You're obviously not used to good Oxfordshire ales.'

'I do have another theory about Carstairs,' I say.

Roger lifts a glass. I note his half pint is untouched. It's water he's sipping now, conscious of his driving duties, possibly. But the glass stops mid-lift, and he says, 'I'm listening.'

I tell him about Sarah and her affair with Simon. About how all the mud-slinging in the press has undoubtedly contributed to the breakup. 'My theory,' I say, 'is that somehow Simon heard about Carstairs, possibly from Sarah, possibly from another source. He used that to get me to confess my sins. Perhaps he saw outing me as his best chance for Sarah to make the move.'

Roger inclines his head grudgingly. 'That's stretching things a bit far though, isn't it?'

I reach for the wine and take a sip. The glass clinks against my teeth and I end up spilling it over my trousers. I try again and this time the wine finds its mark. Roger is right, I'm reaching. But it's a theory worth considering. I dip a chip into some ketchup and munch on it. Some red stuff joins the wine on my trousers, and I brush the smudge away with the napkin.

'Okay,' I say. 'If not Simon or Linda, who?'

'Well, the unpalatable theory, the one you don't want to hear but which I will articulate because you've asked, is that all of this conjecture about someone trying to manipulate you is merely deflected guilt. Perhaps you did do that surgery and you're trying to weasel your way out by blaming someone else.'

I stare at him, suddenly livid. 'What? Why would you say that?'

Roger sits back, looking slightly alarmed. 'I don't believe it, but it may be what others believe. The police for example.'

'But the photo... thass proof...' I'm slurring. Again.

'But they haven't seen your proof, am I right?' Roger's words are soft, but they sound suddenly harsh and tinny in my ears. There's a familiar faint buzzing somewhere. I look round for a fly but see nothing. The sudden movement of my head makes the room follow on a half-second delay. I push myself back and up from the table, sending my knife and fork clattering to the floor.

'Roger, whadda a thing to say,' I narrow my eyes but my head is wobbly. 'What a shiddy thing to say, I...' And then I'm falling, and the world is spinning. My head meets the wooden floor with a hard and painful crack. I hear the room go suddenly quiet, and then there are voices. Roger's mainly but mixed with others. All of them concerned.

'...he all right?'

'...fainted?'

'...drunk a bit too much, too quickly.'

'...be okay. Get Alan. He can help me get him out to the car.'

Everything's a blur. But the odd thing is I don't feel ill. I'm weirdly calm and fighting a terrible urge to shut my eyes and go to sleep. Someone picks me up. I lift my head, but it lolls on my chest. Cold air hits my face and then I'm sitting in the car, and someone is strapping me in.

'Rojjer...' I mutter, 'wha...?' but it takes a huge effort. The car starts, rumbles off. I look across in slow motion. Everything seems bathed in a blurry shadow. Two Rogers sit in the driving seat. A part of me that's still the doctor knows that I have double vision and that binocular motor control is one of the first things affected by alcohol. Smart-ass. But I haven't drunk that much, surely?

The two Rogers look back at me.

'Five minutes and we'll get you home.'

All I can do is nod. It takes longer than five minutes. It doesn't matter because I can barely keep my eyes open.

The car finally comes to a stop and Roger helps me out and across to his nice warm cottage. My legs won't do what I tell them to and I stumble twice. But then I recognise the couch I passed out on just a few days ago.

I tap an armrest and mumble, 'There you are, old feller.' I have no idea where that came from. For some reason I find it highly amusing. I laugh. Hard.

'Let me get you some water,' I hear Roger say. But he sounds like he's in a tunnel in another county. Then he's holding a glass to my lips. I sip. Something smooth and round is being pushed into my mouth. A capsule.

'These will make you a lot better,' Roger says.

I swallow obediently. Five times.

'There,' Roger says. 'That should do the trick.'

I slump over. All I want to do is go to sleep.

Roger has other ideas. 'But you have a tendency to throw up when you've overdone it, don't you? My poor sofa can attest to that. Tell you what, why don't we try walking it off in the fresh air? You up for that?'

I nod. It takes an age for my head to travel up and down four times. Then Roger's hand is under my arm and the night air hits my face once more.

I open my eyes. We're at the back of the property, in Roger's garden. I'm propped up against a wall. Suddenly, all the lights go out except for one. It bobs up and down in front of me. I peer and giggle. Is it a headband torch? Roger's voice seems to come from a long way away.

'There we go. Out of the back gate and along the edge of the field. No light pollution here, Jake. On a moonless night and if the sky is clear, you can see all the constellations. I often come out here and walk down to the river and sit and listen and remember how bloody lucky I am.'

'Tired...' I mutter.

'Yes. Forty milligrams of temazepam in your beer will do that to you. It worried me you might taste them, but the old IPA is bitter enough to mask it, thank God. But don't worry, the sertraline will soon send you to sleep.'

I smell grass and something musky-sweet in the air. Hawthorn blossom. I remember because Ella told me. She also said that it reminded her of the aroma of semen. I didn't need to ask her how she knew. Not after what we'd been doing. I giggle. But thinking of Ella brings me up short. It's only then that I wonder what the hell's going on. I stop moving. Something is wrong.

Temazepam.

I've taken no temazepam... have I?

Roger yanks me forward. 'Now, now. Come on, Jacob. It's for your own good. Hear that silky whisper? That's the Windrush. A few more yards and we can sit on the bank and listen to it slide past.'

There's another gate and Roger's light illuminates a path and willow trees and a little further on the glittering reflection of water.

'Wonderful, isn't it? And hear the wind in the trees at this time of year? So seductive. Carrying its secrets on and on.'

I try to pull back, but I have no strength. I try to sit down but Roger is too strong. Or maybe I'm too weak. Either way, it doesn't matter.

'Still tired? Of course. I don't understand what all this nonsense is with Carstairs reaching out to you beyond his grave, but I can't let you meddle any more. I've dealt with Kourakis. They'll find his body in a ditch. Hit and run while out jogging in unfamiliar terrain while at the conference in Liverpool. Tragic for his family. And you? They'll have seen in the pub how drunk you were. And they'll have washed the glasses by morning so there'll be no trace of anything in the beer mugs or the wine glass. And I'll dispose of the bottle I brought with me. The story is, not that anyone will ask, that I put your drunk and incapable arse in the recovery position on the sofa, but I wasn't to know that you still had some of Andrea's drugs with you. That you'd taken them before meeting me. That the booze would react with the drugs to make you hallucinate and wander off out of the garden towards the river.'

I feel Roger's weight shift and again I pull back. His voice grunts with the effort of resisting me.

The river.

Roger mutters, 'Not very deep here. But deep enough for a meddling little shit like you.'

Roger yanks on my arm. I feel myself turning, swivelling around off balance. I step back, reaching out. I grab a branch but the leaves rip away like paper in my fingers. And then I'm falling backwards. Falling until I hit the water, gasping as it welcomes me under with a cold airless kiss.

73

The shock drives all the air out of my lungs. My knees clatter painfully with the river bottom and I scrabble for purchase. I slip and slide, but somehow push myself up to the surface and the sweet cold air as I suck in oxygen. I can't see, but I suddenly feel hands on my jacket. Feel it being pulled up over my head. The movement drags me down, back into the water, again face down. There's soft mud on my eyelids and I suck in air, but there isn't any, only water. It triggers a spasm in my larynx. I gag and cough and I'm fighting to move, to get up, to find air. But I can't. There is a weight on my back, pinning me down. I somehow close my throat and stop coughing, feel the coldness in my chest that is now a quarter full of water.

Adrenaline is pumping, but it has to fight against the drugs that have dulled my senses and weakened my limbs. I slide sideways and the pressure eases for a moment. I push up, out of the water and once again suck in air, cough out water, suck in air.

I see a blurry light to my left in the distance. A moving dot in the darkness.

Something strikes me just above my left ear and my arms

give way. I'm plunging back. This time, the pressure comes on my neck. Pinning me, face flat against the rocks on the river bed. My eyes are open, but all is blackness. I hold my breath, wriggle and push with my hands, but I can't shift the pressure on my neck. Suddenly, ridiculously, I know it's the sole of a shoe or a boot. But it's a millisecond of thought as panic once again grips me.

Through the water, I hear something. A noise. A dog barking. Is Sid here?

He isn't.

My struggles are futile. I'm screaming, but it comes out as nothing more than a rough gurgle. Worse is the fact that my screams are using up oxygen. And I know I will have to replace it. But I can't hold on any longer. I try shouting and the effort pushes out the residual air from my tortured lungs. The carbon dioxide sensors in my head take over. I reflexly inhale and suck in water.

For several more seconds I fight, I writhe and buck, but there isn't any oxygen going to my brain and suddenly, surprisingly, darkness comes quickly. It begins as a grey wave and flows over me. There's no more urge to breathe. I'm half conscious. Aware that I'm drowning, aware that it's too late, and that I can do nothing more.

Everything goes a dull yellow then colourless and then black. I have no more thoughts...

Until a vague but stark awareness impinges. Something hits my face. The pain, when it comes, is like hot lava, burning through my chest and stomach. I'm retching, coughing, water spewing out from my stomach and lungs. I gasp and splutter. It brings up more water. I can't see though my eyes are open. And then I know I can't see because it's dark.

There's someone above me pushing me over onto my side. There's a voice. Muffled. Indistinct. Sexless.

'Keep moving or you'll die.'

There's rustling. Someone hurries away quickly. I'm wet and cold, but somehow... somehow, I'm alive. And I want to stay alive.

Keep moving or you'll die.

The darkness is unremitting, but I get to my knees. Shuddering with adrenaline, shaking with cold. Foliage brushes my face. My limbs quiver under my weight and I'm on all fours. Beneath my hands, the ground is hard. Packed mud. A path. I can't stand. I daren't stand. Instead, I crawl. I stop only to vomit half a dozen times. The last two are dry retches. I can't see anything. Clouds cover the sky. I can hear the river on the one side. It's my guide. I crawl an inch at a time, until the noise gets louder. I'm getting nearer the river but I don't want to go in again.

I turn slowly, gingerly, on all fours. I crawl back the way I came.

Slowly, slowly, my brain kicks in. To remember. I should have known. Should have seen it coming. But I've been blindsided by a charming monster. Roger Delany has his reasons for wanting to kill me. He knows who falsified the notes to make it look like it was me who operated on Carstairs. He can't afford for the truth to come out.

I'm shivering violently, but I make myself crawl. They aren't steps I take. But they are movements. I don't want to die here. If I die, Roger will win. I can't let that happen. Someone wants the truth to come out. Wants justice. So do I.

And Roger has to be judged.

Eventually, despite the uncontrollable shivering, it becomes a rhythm. I count thirty forward juddering reaches first with an arm, then a knee, then the other arm, then the other knee, one after the other. When the river noise changes, I stop. Far enough, I say to myself. I turn around and crawl back. I do this again and again. Fifty, a hundred, two hundred times. Gradually, I get warm. There is very little wind and, low down, the grass either side of me acts as a barrier. I think of nothing except the last words I heard.

Keep moving or you'll die.

I could be on another world, in another universe. My system is still full of drugs, but I force myself to crawl.

After two hundred and seventy-five crawls, I'm no longer shivering. But I am tired. I have no idea how much time has passed since we left the pub. But now I lie down and close my eyes.

When I open them, there is light and sky and trees. Someone's standing over me and I can hear voices.

'Can you hear me?'

I shiver again. It's violent, tooth rattling and uncontrollable.

Another voice, further away. 'He's freezing. Looks like he might have fallen in.'

I focus in on the face above me. He's young, dressed in running gear. He turns his head towards the second voice. 'Call an ambulance.' He turns back to me. 'Can you hear me?'

I nod. It's a bigger movement than the shakes rattling my body. I hope he sees it.

He does. 'My name's Gavin. We'll get some help, okay?'

I nod again.

From behind, I hear the second voice. 'Yeah, we're on the river path at Coombe Brook out at Taynton. There's a bloke here. He's in a bad way, semi-conscious... Okay, right... Yeah, we'll stay.'

'What did they say?' Gavin asks, head turned.

'Not to move him, but to get some blankets if we can.'

'Right. You run back to the car. There's a space blanket in the first aid kit. I'll stay.' He turns back to me. 'What's your name, mate?'

'J-Ja-Jake.'

'All right, Jake. Ambulance is on the way. My mate's going to get a blanket. Anyone I can ring for you?'

I nod. 'O-Oxford police. A-ask for DS Oaks. Tell him it's J-Jake Thorn.'

The shivering returns with a vengeance and I can't speak again.

I don't until Gavin gets hold of Oaks.

Then I speak to Gavin again. The words come out in fits and starts. 'D-D-Delany's cottage. B-b-bring b-b-baton.'

74

Once again, I end up in Gloucester Royal. Same white walls and pale blue floor. A similar room but a different bed this time. I'm no longer hypothermic and the vomiting I did when I came out of the water rid my system of the undigested capsules.

That must have helped because I'm remarkably awake when, for the second time in a week, Oaks and Ridley come in.

It's almost midday by the wall clock. I've been in hospital for five hours.

'This is getting to be a bit of a habit,' Ridley says, but she does it without a smile.

'It's not one I want to cultivate,' I reply.

Oaks is behind her. He too is grim-faced. 'How are you feeling?'

'Warmer, but still badly hung over.'

'Too much temazepam?'

I study his face. He's trying to push my buttons. I don't bite. 'I don't know, you'd better ask Roger.'

No reply.

'Have you?'

'We'd like to hear your side of the story first,' Ridley says.

I look from one to the other. 'Only if you agree to tell me what Roger's said.'

Oaks and Ridley send each other a knowing look. Ridley inclines her head. Oaks says, 'Fair enough.'

I tell them exactly what happened from the moment I arrived at The Foxhound. I tell them I don't know how I got out of the water. That it felt like someone had pulled me out.

Oaks nods. 'And the last time you saw Roger Delany was when he threw you into the river?'

'Threw me in and held me down to drown.'

'So why didn't you?' Ridley asks.

It's a fair question. 'I can't be sure, obviously, but I thought I heard a noise. Someone shouting. A dog barking. Maybe he was disturbed.'

Again silence. My eyes swerve from one to the other.

'What? It's the truth. You surely don't think I'd do this to myself? For crying out–'

'We do,' says Oaks sharply.

'Believe you,' Ridley adds.

Her words stop me in full rant.

She explains. 'We believe Delany drugged you and tried to drown you to make it appear like a suicide.'

I let my head fall back to the pillow and blow out air. But then I narrow my eyes and stare at them. 'Why?'

'Because Roger Delany said he did.'

'You've got him?'

'No. We don't.'

'Then, how?'

Ridley pulls up a chair. Oaks stands at the bottom of the bed. 'When Ryan got your call, he rang me immediately. At first, I wasn't sure. I wondered if you'd finally lost it. That you were stringing us along.'

I shake my head.

Oaks says, 'Oh, you'd not believe the number of people who think wasting police time is a game well worth playing.'

Ridley continues. 'We were in Coombe Brook by eight forty-five. The door to the property was open. Roger Delany was sitting on his sofa; laptop open next to him. He'd posted something online.'

'What?'

'A suicide note in the form of a confession.'

For a moment, the world spins. I want to ask something, but I can't.

Ridley's still speaking, and her tone is even. I want to believe she's thawed towards me a little. 'Delany was dead when we arrived. Unpleasantly so. He'd taken the same cocktail you had. Temazepam, sertraline, this time washing it down with vodka. But to make sure, he'd also drunk a tumbler full of drain cleaner.'

'Jesus,' I whisper.

Oaks nods. 'I hardly need to tell you how unpleasant a death that can be. The pathologist hopes he was unconscious before the alkali burned through his stomach and into his lungs.'

I gulp. It's the loudest noise in the room for ten seconds. 'What did he say in his confession?'

Oaks retrieves some papers from his inside pocket and hands them to me. 'We've made copies, obviously.'

I take the sheet and open it. It crackles as it unfolds. Looking at it engenders a dreadful sense of recognition in me. There, but for the grace of God.

My name is Roger Delany. I am a consultant surgeon at St Jude's Hospital in Hampshire. In April 2006, I was the consultant in charge in the case of Mr Michael Carstairs, who was admitted with acute abdominal pain as a result of secondary adhesions following previous surgery for bowel cancer. These complications resulted in Mr Carstairs requiring a resection of a part of his bowel that had become ischaemic. The anastomosis – or joining – of the cut bowel ends unfortunately broke down, resulting in leakage of faecal matter into his abdomen. This leakage set up an infection which led to sepsis and, unfortunately, death from multiple organ failure.

I confirm it was I who carried out this surgery. I also confirm that I had attended a golf club lunch that afternoon, and that I had drunk a considerable amount of alcohol. At the time, I was not aware that the junior locum we had on duty was incapable of carrying out this surgery and that I would need to attend. I admit I was not in a fit state to have carried out this surgery, and it is likely that an excess of alcohol affected my performance.

I also confirm that following Mr Carstairs's death, I falsified the notes to make it appear a colleague of mine, Mr Jacob Thorn, carried out the surgery. I typed up a new operating sheet and added Jacob Thorn's signature. I used my influence to convince the coroner not to start an inquest because Mr Thorn was a promising surgeon and that this might be a career-halting event if it went ahead. Mr Carstairs had bowel cancer and liver metastases and a poor prognosis overall.

It was my intention to save a successful career. But it was mine, not Jake Thorn's that I saved.

When Katy Leith was abducted and Jacob Thorn accused, somehow, the Carstairs case came up again. Thorn became convinced that someone knew a mistake had been made and was trying to get him to admit it. Thorn found a copy of the notes. He realised that the locum who had assisted me in the case must have known for certain who had done the operation. I had dismissed Kourakis soon after the surgery. He was not aware of the potential negligence surrounding Carstairs's death. To ensure his loyalty, if anything arose, I helped engineer his career path. He has always been grateful to me for that.

Unfortunately, realising Kourakis was the key to the truth, Thorn attempted to contact him. I deflected things by suggesting Kourakis had had an affair with my secretary. Four days ago, at a meeting in Liverpool, I convinced Kourakis to go on a hike in the Peak District. There, I ran him over. I have left separate instructions where his body can be found.

That left Thorn. Having accidentally overdosed on alcohol and sleeping pills a few days ago, he appeared to all the world as a likely suicide. This evening, I tried to finish what he'd started. During the meal at The Foxhound, I laced his drink. The whole pub saw him fall over drunk. I brought him back here and took him down to the river where I drowned him. You will find his body at the end of the two-acre field in the Windrush.

But now that I have the blood of three people on my hands, I can no longer live with the guilt. I fear there might be more. I can only hope my wife and my children will find it in their hearts to forgive me.

Roger Delany.

75

Oaks crossed the hospital car park and unlocked the car. He opened the passenger door and dangled the keys as Ridley arrived. She shook her head.

'No, you're driving. I have texting to do.'

With a shrug, Oaks came around the front of the Focus, got in and set off for Oxford.

They drove for ten minutes without talking. Ridley texted and Oaks fiddled with the radio for something he hoped she might find acceptable. Eventually, he settled on an eighties rock channel on DAB. Toto started blessing the rains down in Africa and Oaks sent a wary glance across towards his boss. Ridley had a black and white relationship with music. It was either okay or total crap. Tuning in to a station was an eggshell walk for Oaks.

Ridley didn't react. He took it as a good sign and chanced his arm with a little conversation.

'Thorn's had a rough time.'

'Lucky to be alive,' Ridley replied.

'Luckier than Delany.'

Ridley nodded. Her eyes drifted up from her phone screen to peer out at the passing countryside.

'Come on, ma'am. What's going through that suspicious mind of yours?'

'Why didn't Thorn die?'

Oaks frowned. 'You heard him. Someone pulled him out of the water.'

'Really?'

'Why would he make that up? Delany was sure he'd drowned. He confessed to it.'

'Right. So we assume someone either heard or saw Delany pushing Thorn into the river. Maybe they shouted, and Delany took fright before he could fully finish the job. Which also means...'

'That someone might have followed Delany home.'

Ridley nodded. 'There was no sign of anyone else in that cottage.'

'Agreed, but Delany was sure he'd killed Thorn. So what, or who, made him suddenly reconsider and confess his sins.' Oaks paused before asking, 'You think someone might have helped him do that?'

'People will do the strangest things when they're staring down the barrel of a gun.'

Oaks snorted. 'Do you literally mean a gun?'

Ridley shook her head. 'Maybe, or the even worse mess that might come from someone convincing him they know everything, and that he was facing humiliation and ruin. Just like they'd supposedly threatened Thorn with.'

Oaks overtook a stationary delivery van. He toyed for a moment with challenging the "supposedly" in Ridley's sentence but said, instead, 'One thing's for certain, it couldn't have been Thorn.'

Ridley slid her gaze towards Oaks. 'Unless Mr Thorn "helped" Delany confess, then threw himself in the river.'

Oaks tried to laugh, but disbelief morphed into a spluttering cough. When he'd recovered, he croaked, 'Are you serious?'

'It's a thought.'

'The bloke had water in his lungs, for crying out loud. You can't fake that.'

Ridley sighed. 'Maybe not.'

Oaks's eyes narrowed. 'What? Do you still think Thorn knows something he isn't telling us?'

'As I say, he's either a disaster magnet or a very devious psychopath.'

Oaks searched for something to say and came up blank.

Ridley sat up. 'Right, stop at the next garage. I need some water and crisps.'

'Crisps?' Oaks's face crumpled. 'You've been watching *Master-Chef* again, haven't you?'

'Enough with the derision, sergeant. Crisps are sometimes a necessary indulgence, when–' Her sentence ended with the pinging of her phone. It took her far longer than was strictly necessary to read the message. Oaks surmised that it might be because of not wanting to believe what she was reading.

'What?' he asked.

'Derbyshire police have found a body.'

'Shit.'

Ridley nodded. 'Better make that two packets of prawn cock-tail and a KitKat, Ryan. Carbs are called for before I tell West Yorkshire they're going to have to ask Mrs Kourakis to ID a body. I think we can write off another Saturday.'

'Happy days,' muttered Oaks.

'Indeed,' Ridley said. 'Indeed.'

76

They keep me in hospital for two days. They call what happened to me a near-drowning. In other words, I drowned, but I didn't die. And I didn't die because someone pulled me out of the river. I know that because I'm one hundred per cent sure I was incapable of doing it myself.

They pump me with antibiotics, X-ray my chest, and tell me I'm lucky it was fresh water and not the chlorinated stuff from swimming pools. Chlorine is a lifesaver, but it's also a chemical that causes lung irritation and inflammation and oedema that can progress to acute respiratory distress. But there's no sign of that in me, nor of pneumonia.

So I was lucky it was river water. Not exactly potable, but not full of sewerage either. And having swallowed a significant amount and then thrown it up on the bank, the river had performed a gastric lavage to rid me of most of the extra tablets Roger had made me swallow.

I read his confession a dozen times. He thought he'd got away with it. Thought he'd survived a nasty glitch in his career. I contemplate what might make someone do such a thing, and I remember struggling under the water with Roger's boot on my neck. I'd fought. I'd wriggled and writhed.

Survival is a powerful instinct.

And, in Roger's case, greed is another. Carstairs's death might have derailed Roger's career badly. So instead he put the blame on someone else and bribed the only real witness with a job. The nurse and anaesthetist in that theatre would have been unaware of Carstairs's post-surgical demise. They were not part of the conspiratorial equation. And to be fair to Kourakis, he, like me, had already left the hospital by the time Carstairs died of complications. He probably knew nothing about it.

But he knew he'd assisted Roger that day. May even have smelled the booze on his breath. Roger could not afford to let him remember.

They tell me I'm very lucky. When Ella comes to visit, I know I am.

She takes one look at me and, this time, doesn't burst into tears. Instead, from out of her bag she pulls two uninflated water wings.

'Ben sends you his love and insisted I bring these.'

I laugh. So does she. And then she kisses me.

I leave hospital on the Monday and pick my car up from The Foxhound. Then I drive straight to Paws for Claws. Bonnie and Rich are, as always, laid back and understanding when I apologise and promise to never swim in a river again.

At least not in the dark and with a cocktail of alcohol and downers on board.

But I know that I can't avoid rivers altogether. They're one of Sid's all-time favourite things. He greets me with his usual unbridled enthusiasm. He doesn't care what I've been up to. All he cares about is the here and now with me. I'm all for that.

That afternoon, Ella takes Ben out of school early and we have our delayed walk and they come back to mine for tea. I buy ice cream and we let Lulu and Sid run each other – and Ben – ragged in the garden.

There's afternoon sun, and Ella and I sit and watch boy and dogs play. She holds my hand and asks, 'Is that it now? Is it over?'

'Yeah,' I say. 'I think it is. Almost.'

She puts her head on my shoulder.

I could get used to this.

77

I don't let my swim in the Windrush mess up my phased return. Three weeks later, after another rip-roaring interview with Steyn in Occupational Health ('You feeling okay? Good, good.'), I convince Kierney and Catterick that I am fit enough to return full-time. And though they're keen to stick to their schedules and PC HR rules, Kierney knows that the workload has not diminished. In fact, with me effectively on half time, it's got a lot worse.

Bilton does not make an appearance. Probably crushed with disappointment that I'm still here.

But that's unkind. I'm sure she believes in what she's doing one hundred per cent. It's just that another discussion on the apparent role of the oppressive patriarchy – given what we now know about Roger Delany and which I'd happily engage in – would be... misplaced. Delany was greedy for success and all the trappings, a manipulative functioning psychopath. I won't argue with anyone about that.

What needs to happen now is that I get back to full-time work, seeing men, women, and children in equal measure. Sickness is non-discriminatory.

After a brief discussion with my clinical director, in which he insists I immediately let him know if I can't cope ('You'll be the first to know, don't you worry'), they let me get on with it. I feel like I've somehow dodged a bullet.

Oaks calls me twice after I give them a formal statement to clarify a few points. He sounds genuine on the phone. Like he cares. Like he knows I've been through the mill. Ridley never phones; too busy working on her moguls, I expect. When I press Oaks for details of where they are with finding out who it was that abducted Katy Leith, he slips back into officialdom like a tortoise withdrawing into its shell. All he says is that their enquiries are still ongoing.

In other words, they have no idea. Katy, meanwhile, continues to make the headlines. Her pretty face beams out from the pages, first from a hospital bed, then from her home and now from various locations set up by the newspapers to reassure the public that she's almost "back to normal". There are dire warnings about being careful on the streets. Katy was a little drunk. Her story is a salutary lesson in being vigilant. On the night she was abducted, on her way to buy cigarettes, she saw someone collapsed on the floor near an entrance to an alley. Alcohol-fuelled, her nursing instinct overruled her natural wariness, and she turned to offer help. The entrance to the alley was dark, but the collapsed "victim" was half in and half out, face down on the pavement. He was also nothing more than a tethered goat. One minute she was crouched, asking if all was well, the next, two other men appeared and she was grabbed, muffled and within seconds, bundled into a van in the alley and driven to a location where she was drugged and, so the newspapers suggest, offered up to the highest bidder on the dark web.

No hard evidence is provided for this last bit of journalistic hyperbole, and when I ask Oaks directly about it, he can't answer. Still, the sheer repugnance of the idea is, I suspect, enough to sell thousands more copies.

But now she's a golden girl. The one that got away. Katy, "Our Angel". It's only a matter of time, I muse cynically, before she has her own line of make-up and clothing under that name. But that isn't fair. Katy may have almost been the cause of my demise, but she had nothing to do with that. I'm just being curmudgeonly.

Though the Carstairs episode is a dark stain on Roger Delany's copybook, no one mentions it at the funeral. It's a small affair, peppered with half a dozen of the great and the good. The president of this society, the chair of that. There is no eulogy – that would be in bad taste – yet there's disbelief aplenty. But I'm a believer. I read Roger's confession. So I don't include myself amongst the mourners. I sit in the car and watch from the car park. Radio on as a calming distraction. That way I can be more objective. But inside I'm seething.

I decide there and then never to pay my respects to people who try to kill me.

But I do attend Ioannes Kourakis's funeral and service. After introducing myself at the little wake, I talk to his widow, explain to her that he was as much a victim as Carstairs was. Roger had all the power to make or break a young locum desperately trying to kick-start a career. Laura Kourakis, all in black, her pale face drowning in despair and bewilderment, thanks me. But I can see in her eyes that she finds little comfort in my words.

After all, if I hadn't asked Linda about Carstairs, Kourakis would never have appeared in Roger Delany's crosshairs. But I don't burden her with my guilt. It's there for her to consider if and when. Laura Kourakis sees me out and I watch her usher her children back into the house. Watch them cling to their mother, not wanting to be at this sombre event with these unhappy people. Not yet understanding.

That will come over the years of emptiness ahead.

There's a great deal I'll never forgive Roger Delany for: his lies, his attempt at doing me harm, his greed. But seeing first-hand what he's done to this family tops all of that. He killed Kourakis to protect himself. If there is a hell, I hope they've kept a special spot for Roger.

78

S arah doesn't call. I'm genuinely amazed at how little that bothers me.

But something does. Another mental itch that I can't scratch. When I tell Oaks during one of his follow-up calls, the line goes silent for several seconds. I imagine his long-suffering expression at the end of the line.

'You're not still on about whoever was trying to fit you up for buggering up Carstairs's surgery, are you?'

'It irks me I don't know,' I say.

'Forget it. Delany admitted it was him. Isn't that enough for you?'

It should be, but it isn't. Someone knew about Carstairs. And that someone saw me being pilloried for Katy Leith's abduction and used it to get their oar in. At least, that's how I've rationalised it. Oaks likens them to Internet hyenas. Wait for the weakness in a member of the herd to show itself, follow and gang up for the kill. Patient predators biding their time.

But I don't see it that way. Something must link Katy Leith to me having my name forged on to Carstairs's operating note. It's maddening. It's unsubstantiated. And yet I spend an awfully long time trying to put those two things together. Every time I do, I keep coming up with nothing.

I know it's not Linda.

I know it's not Kourakis.

I'm coming around to the idea that it couldn't have been Simon too, though an ugly vengeful part of me believes that's still a remote possibility.

But if not them, who, and what and why?

I substitute Malbec – weekends only and then two glasses max – with some seminal albums. Things – "Let's have something more meaningful than this drivel, for God's sake" – that Sarah never allowed me to listen to.

As a result, I am depressingly familiar with the Avril Lavigne, Alanis Morissette, Tracy Chapman oeuvres. Nothing wrong with any of them. Just not at all my thing.

Now, I listen, with the volume right up, to Santana, Kings of Leon and The Foo Fighters. Yet, listening to any or all of them still doesn't free my mind enough to scratch the damned itch.

Finally, a light bulb moment arrives in the middle of *Oye Como Va* one afternoon. I realise I haven't spoken to the one other person in this equation who was as badly affected as me.

It's June and I'm well into my return to work when I act on it. Oaks tells me they think they've found the place that they held Katy. Some abandoned outbuildings near a disused mine in the Forest of Dean. They have no clues who her abductors were yet, and despite cracking down on the trafficking gang in Thames Valley and several "taken in for questioning"s, no one's admitting to anything. No one's arrested.

One Tuesday morning, I leave Patrick in the middle of a simple anal fistula repair and pop down in my scrubs to the ward where Katy Leith works. It's buzzing. I collar the senior

sister and ask if Katy's at work. She explains that she has not yet
returned. Is still off with stress and will be for a few weeks.
Someone has mentioned PTSD. She gives me a toothless smile
of understanding, but I read frustration too. Like everywhere,
the ward is understaffed, and they could do with Katy back.

But she suggests I talk to one of her pals, Fergus, a staff nurse
on the same ward.

I find him making his way back up to theatres to collect a
patient from recovery. Fergus is painfully thin with the remnants
of acne on high cheekbones and peeling lips from a weekend in
the sun with not enough factor thirty. If he's a staff nurse, then
he's likely to be in his early twenties, though he looks more like
late teens.

I call to him and he waits for me to catch up to him in the
corridor.

'Hi there. Fergus is it? Sister says you're good friends with
Katy. Katy Leith?'

He looks at my lanyard and then up into my face. 'I am. We
were in the same year.'

'How is she?'

'She's doing great,' says Fergus.

'Is she? Isn't she off with stress?'

Fergus's eyebrows go up an inch. 'Yeah, the stress of working
out who to sell her story to for megabucks.'

'Really?'

'Bound to happen, wasn't it? *The Express* is going to serialise
it. "My ordeal with the traffickers". I can see it now.'

'Wow,' I say. What I don't add is that I'm not at all surprised.

Puffer jacket girl and her cameraman turned up once at the
cottage a few weeks ago, wanting to do a story about me. About
how I was hounded on social media and the press. Trial by Twitter. I declined. I kept looking at her face for any signs of remorse,
or some acknowledgement of her breathtaking hypocrisy. I

couldn't see any. Needless to say, she went away empty-handed, but posted a card through my letterbox. I've stuck it on the back door of the toilet. Something to contemplate while I'm sitting there.

'By the way, it was awful, what happened to you. The press and Twitter and stuff.' Fergus is a mind reader.

'I survived.'

We get to the lift and wait. Fergus is quiet for a moment, but then makes his mind up to share something with me in a low whisper. 'Between you and me, she isn't coming back. New Zealand beckons.'

'Does it?'

He nods. 'Sister doesn't know. She's going to go ballistic when she finds out.'

I suck in air through my teeth in a show of solidarity.

'Lucky cow,' Fergus adds. 'I really, really want to go.'

'I've been. It's as good as they say it is. North Island especially.'

Fergus sighs.

'I suppose I could always visit her at home.' I dangle the suggestion, though I think it's probably a lousy idea.

'Fat chance. No one's supposed to know, but she's in Tenerife.'

The lift doors open, and we push through two other people to stand at the back. 'I see,' I say. 'Understandable. Bit of R and R.'

'Yeah. She needs to rest and recuperate from too many nights out.' Fergus tilts his chin down with sardonic emphasis. 'She sent me these last night.' He takes out his phone. His fingers are deft and soon I'm looking at blue skies and white plastic poolside recliners. But mainly the screen fills with an image of a girl in a bikini and a straw hat holding up a glass of something sickly yellow. It's a "cheers" selfie. The rim of the glass is frosted and there's a pink straw poking out from the surface. I recognise the girl as Katy Leith. Behind, fingers wrapped around an identical, held-up frosted glass, is another girl with a dazzling smile and huge sunglasses.

'See what I mean,' says Fergus, his words flat with envy.

He flicks through a carousel of images. By the look of things, Katy appears to have recovered from her ordeal very well. The second girl is in a quarter of all the photographs.

'Who's that with her? Her sister?' I ask.

'No, that's Donna, Katy's partner. Gorgeous, isn't she? Katy's a lucky sod. Survives abduction by traffickers and then has Donna to go on holiday with.'

We're on the last photograph. It's evening. No sunglasses, just two girls at a table laden with food, arms around each other, looking very much in love. Donna is in shadow. But her great smile lights up the background, as do her big blue eyes.

'I'm glad to see Katy's recovering,' I say.

'I'll tell her I bumped into you when I see her. If I ever see her,' Fergus sounds exasperated.

'Surely she'll be back at some point?'

'Only to repack her bags. Once she's put in her resignation, she and Donna are off for three months backpacking in Oz with jobs across the Tasman sea at the end.' Fergus lets out another big envious sigh.

The lift stops on the theatre floor. Fergus gets out. I go back down two floors and walk. I'm suddenly in need of a coffee because my brain is doing all kinds of gymnastics. The itch is almost unbearable, so much so that I feel like I want to rip off the top of my skull to scratch it.

Finally, as mad as it may seem, I think I know the truth.

79

In all the time I've been searching for a link between Katy Leith's abduction and my supposed involvement in Michael Carstairs's untimely death, nothing has made any sense. They're two separate incidents. I've blamed Linda. I've blamed Simon. But I realise now I was way off in both instances.

Because now I have the key.

At the Post Grad Centre, I stand in the queue at the counter and order a flat white. A double shot. Not to take away, but to sit and ponder. A part of me thinks I've been incredibly stupid. But another part of me suspects it's more that someone else has been very, very devious and clever.

Fergus is right. Katy's ordeal will make a great story serialised in the papers. Worth a good few thousand, I suspect. Maybe even a book deal – ghost written no doubt. Enough to get her and her partner off to a great start in New Zealand. And why on earth not? She's escaped a terrible, harrowing, horrible fate. She's a one-in-a-million statistic.

Unless, of course, she was never in any real danger.

The idea solidifies in my brain. Sends static crackles across my scalp.

What if there was no collapsed man at the mouth of an alley near the Duke of Wellington pub? What if there was no bundling into a van? No one witnessed any such thing. No shadowy grey scale figures on CCTV. But Katy's blood work showed that she'd definitely been drugged, Oaks confirmed that. But getting injected with fentanyl would be a great way of adding credence to her story. And fentanyl isn't street heroin. It's much safer if you know the right doses to give. Especially if you're trained. Like a nurse.

It's wild speculation, I know. And I can't be sure. How can I? But if I accept that Katy is a part of all this, everything falls chillingly into place. It's all there in that first photograph of the two girls in Tenerife. Two lovers lifting a glass to the world.

The barista smiles and hands me a flat white. I smell the coffee and return the smile. The aroma provides a perfect irony. I take it to a table and sit, finally able to organise my thoughts. I let it run over me just like the River Windrush did in Coombe Brook. Only this time, I'm not drowning. In fact, it feels like I'm waking up from a deep confused slumber.

Katy's partner, Donna, has auburn hair in the photograph I've just seen. But hair can be dyed.

Galina's hair was dark under her beanie hat.

At the cemetery, Zoe had grey blonde hair and her eyes were hidden under her glasses. They might have been brown; they could have been blue. But these days, contact lenses can make them whatever colour you fancy.

I think about Galina's damaged and burned left eye. It still makes me wince. But now not only from the pathology it was meant to suggest.

I know from bitter experience with Oaks and Ridley that the best way to lie is to not stray too far from the truth if you can. That's why I suspect Zoe didn't lie when I asked her what she did. Helping out with the army of the dead in Winterfell: make-up and prosthetics.

Maybe there was even a touch of devilment in that admission.

Because now I believe that Donna is really Zoe who is also Galina, who is probably Grace Carstairs, whose adopted name I have no clue about. All different. But really all the same. And when I think it through, it's obvious. Galina's damaged eye could have been a contact lens designed to look frightful. Her ravaged face, the small part of it she showed me, bears no relationship to Donna's smooth skin. But it too could have been nothing more than layers of silicone touched up by an expert in prosthetics and made to look like a nightmare.

I only caught one shocking glimpse. Closer inspection might have revealed the truth. I'm a surgeon, for God's sake. But I wasn't given that opportunity. I saw the damage from too far away and for only a few seconds.

Point is, you see what you want to see.

I'd glimpsed an ink stain on the inside of Zoe's middle finger. I'd assumed it had come from a leaky pen. But in the photograph of Katy's girlfriend, Donna, that same finger holding a glass was also stained. But not by accident, and not by a leaky pen. By a tattoo. Long and thin like an arrow, the pointed end linked to the feathered fletching by a handwritten word in lieu of a shaft. What I'd read etched into the skin was the word "brother". I'm willing to bet that Darren Carstairs had one on his middle finger too. Perhaps his had the word "sister". An indelible bond.

Galina, Donna, Grace and Zoe. Four girls. All the same age, same height, same general build. All with different hair admittedly. But with wigs and make-up these days, who can tell what's real? Especially with Galina, the one I'd spent most time with.

She'd hidden herself under all the layers; the dark glasses, the hood, the accent, and the gloves to hide the incriminating finger.

Then there's the message sent to Oaks from Delany's cottage that first time. When I was throwing up after ingesting temazepam and sertraline by mistake. In my altered state I thought I recalled drinking salty water that night. I wasn't capable of doing that; getting up, filling a glass, stirring in the salt. I didn't even know where the salt was kept. Someone must have given it to me. And that someone else had used my phone to send a cry for help to Oaks. All they'd have to do to unlock was use my thumbprint on the wake button. Not difficult with me out cold.

Once accessed, a simple search would have shown them my recent activity. The messages and images I'd sent to Sarah via the phone; the photo of us in Painswick on that Easter Sunday in 2006. Plus all the others in that month's album. Including the one of Sarah and me at Bull's Cross on Good Friday 2006.

It took me days to work that out.

It would have taken Grace Carstairs just minutes.

And once she'd seen that, even if she read my false confession on the Killer in Plain Site blog, once she knew it could not have been me, there'd be no more reason for the charade of having Katy still abducted and me in their sights.

It all adds up.

But Grace Carstairs would only be twenty-three. Too young, surely, to plot anything so elaborate. Could she really be my Villanelle? But I'm forgetting the years of anger and resentment. Forgetting that at eighteen, she could have accessed her birth mother's possessions. Or perhaps inherited them all when her brother Darren died. Seen the letters of complaint. The platitudes and excuses. Read a copy of the notes with my name on that operating sheet. She'd have seen her brother implode from drugs too. All thanks to some inexcusable ineptitude from a half-drunk surgeon.

I wonder if she's told Katy the truth. That she is Michael Carstairs's daughter. I shake my head. Of course she has. Otherwise, why on earth would Katy have gone through with it? Fooling the police and the whole country into believing someone had abducted her. With Donna, her partner, anonymously tipping the police off about traffickers. Pumping me for information as Galina. Who has now conveniently disappeared under supposed police protection...

Christ, I've been an idiot.

But what proof do I truly have?

None.

Yet the pieces all tumble into place. I realise that the person who shot the video of me and Katy supposedly arguing on the ward could easily have been Katy herself. She could have positioned her phone somewhere convenient once she saw me alone. I recall how steady those images were, as if the phone was set on a solid surface. But that's hard to prove too.

A few days of no food and some shots of fentanyl in a remote corner of the Forest of Dean would not be so difficult to arrange, either. Especially if you had a partner to do it with.

When Delany tried to drown me in the Windrush, it must have been Grace Carstairs who interrupted him. Had she followed us to The Foxhound and beyond? And the dog I heard? Could it have been Winston? I'll never know.

There are other things I'll never find out. Like knowing if Grace Carstairs, after dragging me out of the river, thumping me back to life and instructing me to "Keep moving or die", went back to Delany's cottage and surprised him there. Confronted him with knowing the proof of my not being anywhere near Carstairs when I was supposed to have operated on him. Roger thought I'd shown those photographs to no one. He was right. But he'd underestimated Grace Carstairs who'd already found them the night I'd phoned Sarah from that very same sofa.

For Roger, there would be only one way out. And, with a little bit of help no doubt, he took it.

I can't help thinking the drain cleaner was her real revenge. There can be few more painful and atrocious ways to end it all. Even if you're half anaesthetised by drugs.

But I don't feel any sympathy for Delany. Others had suffered. Like the three members of the Carstairs family interred at Worting Road cemetery. And Kourakis, who paid the ultimate price for making a deal with the devil and keeping his mouth shut.

But this is all supposition. I could call Oaks and Ridley and tell them. By rights, I should. I could expound my theory and wait for Oaks to laugh, watch Ridley listen in that cold and calculating way of hers. But they'd both want evidence.

Which I don't have.

We could go down the route of getting Donna to do a DNA test and exhume one of the Carstairs to get a match. But they're all cremated. Though Darren might have something on record, given his history.

But to what end?

I recall the last image on Fergus's phone. Donna and Katy look happy together. Genuinely happy. Weirdly, despite the fact that she was almost instrumental in destroying me, I also owe Donna my life.

I sip the coffee and am unable to quell a silent little laugh.

How ironic to think Grace Carstairs is my guardian angel and Katy almost my downfall. I know little about the scales of justice, but by my reckoning, as they stand, things seem just about even.

Yet, if I don't go to the police, then suspecting all of this makes me responsible for Katy. I'll keep a weather eye open through Fergus. I don't want to see her. I don't even want to talk to her directly. But I need to know that she'll be okay. Because now, knowing what I know, I can't turn my back and pretend it didn't happen.

But if I'm honest with myself, I feel safer knowing that New Zealand is 11,000 miles away.

New Zealand.

That's the one thing that casts real doubt as to how credible my theories are. Galina had a dog. If she really is Grace Carstairs aka Zoe, aka Donna, Katy's partner, about to go off on a back-packing tour and a new life, what would happen to Winston? It's a small thing, a tiny thing, and yet it bothers me because I'm a dog person. But I'll never know. And I'll not go looking.

I glance up at the Hippocrates quote again. It's as if I'm seeing it truly for the first time.

The physician must... have two special objects in view with regard to disease, namely, to do good or to do no harm.

Maybe not so old hat.

And then I'm thinking of the call I'd taken from my private patient asking about wanting to keep her nail varnish on. Is that what I've become? What the hell happened to Miseris Succerrere Disco – I learn to care for the unfortunate?

Good question.

When I get home, I send Linda a big box of doughnuts by way of an apology. She never had an affair with Kourakis, of that I'm pretty sure. Roger lied about her as he did about everything else. I regret believing him. Linda won't even know what I'm apologising for. But we'll keep it that way to assuage my conscience.

80

The Luton Town Gazette
June 8th 2019

Mystery of the Boomerang Dog

Sheila and Jack Williams woke up last Tuesday to the
sound of barking from their garden. It was a sound they'd
heard before, but not for eight months since their
beloved golden retriever Winston went missing. When
Sheila went to investigate, she was astonished to see that
same Winston, fit and well, wanting to be let in.
'I couldn't believe it. It was like he'd never been away,'
said the delighted fifty-four-year-old Sheila.
Her husband, Jack, a porter at the local hospital, said it
was like a miracle. They'd almost given up hope of ever
seeing Winston again.
'We'd taken him to the park,' explained Jack. 'We threw a
ball for him to chase and he saw some rabbits and went
tearing off after them like he always does. Through the
trees in a second. Just gone. The police told us some

criminals snatch dogs. Sometimes to be sold on. It's
disgusting. We thought we'd lost him for good. Still, it's
obvious someone has looked after him because he's
healthy.'

Victoria Ursell, a local vet, told *The Gazette* that dog theft
is not that uncommon, though it is unusual in such a
large breed. 'Winston's a lot to handle,' she said. 'But
someone took a shine to him.'

Sheila is considering renaming Winston "Boomer".

'That's the weirdest thing. He had his ball with him in
the garden last week. The same ball. Took him eight
months to retrieve it, but he has. He's the original
boomerang dog.'

Winston was not available for comment.

81

The following Thursday, I get up early and take Sid to Florence Park. Summer has retreated into its shell, and it's only a chilly thirteen degrees in an easterly breeze. People look bewildered by the grey "autumnal" weather. Some try to defy nature and wear shorts. But British knees shouldn't be exposed until at least mid-July in my book. In confirmation of my theory, the ones I see this morning are almost all blue with cold.

I've already discussed it with Ella, my big idea. She responded with a hug of approval and a kiss on the cheek when I told her what I'd like to do. I think I even saw a drop of moisture in her eyes. She's a keeper, as I said.

We're looking for houses. Not a DOT twee special. Something more substantial; a family home. Sid and Lulu need a proper garden. And we need somewhere to set up goalposts. I'm rediscovering an interest in football because Ben needs to practise taking penalties. He's got a great left foot. Guess who's the goalie?

Florence Park is way off our beaten track, but we're on a mission, Sid and I. I know if I go there, I'll probably bump into

Rob Eastman and Sid will find Maisie. We're halfway around when we spot them.

The dogs do their usual rude hello.

'It's good to see you, Jacob. And looking so fit.' Rob pins my gaze. It's a heartfelt sentiment.

I shrug. 'Thanks, Rob. I appreciate it.'

And that's it. All there is to it. All there needs to be. The rest is an unspoken understanding. I know Rob thinks I've been to hell and back, there's no need to say it. I can see it in his eyes, like I've seen in a lot of colleagues' eyes. Almost without exception. And where there has been the exception, it's in people who aren't worth my time anyway.

'Good to see young Sid so full of beans. You still pick him up early, I see.'

'Actually, not anymore. He's moved in with me.'

Rob's face lights up. 'And about bloody time, if you ask me. You wore down Sarah's resistance then?'

I grin. 'Removed it altogether.'

Rob nods sagely. 'So why here? Revisiting old haunts, is that it?'

'Not exactly. We came because I was hoping to bump into you.'

'Oh? What can I do for you?'

When I ask him for Médecins Sans Frontière's phone number, his smile becomes a grin.

When I broach the subject of me tagging along on his next trip abroad, the grin becomes a full-blown laugh. He leans down to pat a wriggling Sid.

Then Rob straightens and shakes my hand.

THE END

ACKNOWLEDGEMENTS

Oxford and Basingstoke exist, but the hospitals mentioned in this book are all fictitious, for obvious reasons. A big thank you to those NHS colleagues - too many to mention - who answered all my questions patiently. Keep fighting the good fight.

Enjoy the ride? Why not help spread the word?

Authors live and die by word of mouth. Honest reviews by genuine and loyal readers help bring the books to the attention of others.

Please feel free to jump right in and leave a review wherever you bought this book – it can be as short as you like on the book's Amazon/Goodreads page.

You can contact me and check out the website for forthcoming titles as well at:

https://www.dylanyoungauthor.com

I'm also delighted to hear from readers and will always endeavour to reply to questions or comments via:

Twitter: @dyoungwrites

Facebook: https://www.facebook.com/dyoungwrites/
Email: dylanyoungauthor@gmail.com